IRONSIDES' PERIL

A ZACH COLT ADVENTURE

By

Michael D. Urban

IRONSIDES' PERIL

WINNER – SUSPENSE/THRILLER
2013 Next Generation Indie Book Awards

HONORABLE MENTION – BEST THRILLER - TERRORIST
2013 Readers' Favorite International Book Awards Contest

Praise for *Ironsides' Peril*

"This is a fun read; it could easily be the premise for a feature film. The author clearly knows the style and pace of modern international thrillers coupled with a milieu he knows and has researched well.... [I]t's an adventure tale for nearly all ages."

— *Judge, Writer's Digest 21st Annual Self-Published Book Awards*

"When Old Ironsides turns 215, the 200th anniversary of the War of 1812 and the Fourth of July all happen to fall within the same time frame.... Boston is poised to celebrate.... That is until a series of terrorist attacks strike the day of the big event. The bombings and the firefight are only the beginning of what will turn out to be one of the most terrifying and harrowing days in American history.... There are not many authors who will take you inside the mind of a terrorist, but Urban takes us into the minds of three. Not only that, he provides captivating details about the history of Old Ironsides, the military and his main characters.... I really enjoyed this book and will definitely be interested in finding any more by this author."

— *Readers' Favorite (5-Star Review)*

Also by Michael D. Urban

Drake's Coffin is the rousing adventure tale of a search for lost treasure. Four hundred years ago the English adventurer Sir Francis Drake stole it from the Spanish and buried it in the jungle of Panama. Thirty years ago an unsuspecting group of teenage boys stumbled upon it in a night of violent death that would change their lives forever. Now, as adults, led by Zach Colt, they have come back for Drake's legendary lost treasure, in a race against time, old enemies, and modern foes.

FINALIST – ACTION/ADVENTURE
2012 Next Generation Indie Book Awards

NOMINATED – BEST THRILLER
2012 Global eBook Awards

FINALIST – BEST eBOOK COVER
2012 Global eBook Awards

PRAISE FOR *DRAKE'S COFFIN*

"Urban's debut novel [is] ... fast-paced ... real and intense .... A coming-of-age story and thrilling adventure rolled into one."
— *Kirkus Reviews*

"*Drake's Coffin* is a highly well-written ... adventure story that is packed with violence and high-paced action.... [t]his is one thrilling, readable story that readers will love. The plot proceeds with twists and turns, often unexpected, to the story's end. The characters ... are well-drawn and totally believable .... *Drake's Coffin* is a must read, to say the least!"
— *Readers' Favorite (5-Star Review)*

IGTBA is a trade name of Michael D. Urban

For information contact:
IGTBA Enterprises
P.O. Box 812618
Wellesley, MA 02482
or
mike@michaeldurban.com

Print ISBN: 978-0-9853599-2-8
Digital ISBN: 978-0-9853599-3-5

Second Edition

Cover by IGTBA Enterprises

Map of Boston Harbor courtesy of NASA

Dedication

For Liz, more on that later.

And for those men and women
who fight and die
in defense of liberty
on land, at sea, and in the air.

Also, *Ironsides' Peril* was first published February 21, 2013, almost two months before the Boston Marathon bombings. I dedicate this Second Edition to the men, women, and children injured in the attack, to the first responders who so ably protected the innocent, and to the people of the City of Boston who persevered and overcame the tragedy with grit, dignity and epic pugnacity.

Old Ironsides
By
Oliver Wendell Holmes

Ay, tear her tattered ensign down!
Long has it waved on high,
And many an eye has danced to see
That banner in the sky;
Beneath it rung the battle shout,
And burst the cannon's roar; —
The meteor of the ocean air
Shall sweep the clouds no more.

Her deck, once red with heroes' blood,
Where knelt the vanquished foe,
When winds were hurrying o'er the flood,
And waves were white below,
No more shall feel the victor's tread,
Or know the conquered knee; —
The harpies of the shore shall pluck
The eagle of the sea!

Oh, better that her shattered hulk
Should sink beneath the wave;
Her thunders shook the mighty deep,
And there should be her grave;
Nail to the mast her holy flag,
Set every threadbare sail,
And give her to the god of storms,
The lightning and the gale!

Excerpt from Lieut. Commandant S. Decatur's
Report to Commander Preble
On Board Ketch Intrepid, *at Sea*
17 February 1804

"Permit me also, sir, to speak of the brave fellows I have the honor to command, whose coolness and intrepidity was such as I trust will ever characterise the American tars."

Stephen Decatur
United States Navy

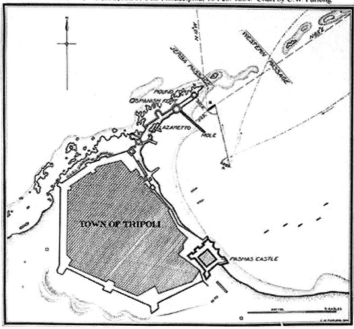

Boston Harbor

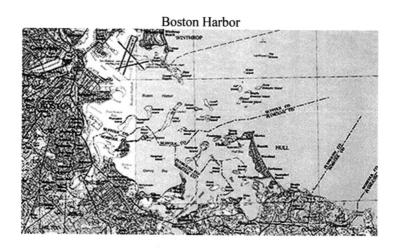

~ PROLOGUE ~

February 16, 1804

Tripoli Harbor, Barbary Coast, Africa

9:30 P.M.

"Closer, closer!" he hissed under his breath. The small rowboat towing his ketch *Intrepid* seemed barely to make any progress. The USS *Philadelphia*, newly rechristened *Allah's Gift* by her captors, remained anchored just spitting distance away in moonlit Tripoli Harbor. If he did not soon reach her, the enemy would discover his ruse, and all would be lost.

By God, if only we had a puff of wind! Just one damned breeze! Even a fart!

But there was no wind. There had not been any for the last twenty minutes, the most crucial time of the raid. The delicate time needed to deceive the enemy crew. The desperate time before an alarm was raised and the 18 massive guns on *Philadelphia*, aimed point-blank at them, erupted and blew *Intrepid* to perdition. The necessary time to strike and escape.

Two months earlier, Captain William Bainbridge lost *Philadelphia* to Barbary Pirates when he ran her aground on a submerged reef near Tripoli Harbor. Not only had Bainbridge allowed his ship to be taken, his

1

entire crew was captured and held hostage by the Bashar of Tripoli. The Barbary Pirates were emboldened. Commerce in the Mediterranean was at a standstill.

It was an inauspicious start to the first campaign of the fledgling United States Navy. President Jefferson and Congress were dismayed. The honor of the Republic was at stake. America's maritime prestige and political credibility hung in the balance.

It was young Lieutenant Stephen Decatur's mission to change all that.

Snippets of Commodore Preble's dispatch echoed in his head. *"You are hereby ordered to take command of the prize ketch, which I have named the* Intrepid, *and prepare her with all possible dispatch... proceed to Tripoli, in company with the* Syren, *... enter that harbor in the night, board the* Philadelphia, *burn her, and make good your retreat...."*

Indeed.

Aboard *Intrepid,* Decatur found himself ticking the seconds off in his head. Surely, the heathen bastards ahead in the boat towing *Intrepid* could pull faster. His hand ached from gripping the pommel of the cutlass concealed beneath the Maltese merchant disguise he wore. He could feel sweat trickle from his scalp and drip down the enormous muttonchops sideburns he affected, and which now, in the sweltering heat, were just an itchy annoyance.

At the rear, his crew of 72 volunteers crouched beneath *Intrepid's* rail, pressed themselves prone to the deck, or secreted their shadowy forms behind masts, barrels and coiled piles of rope. Armed with cutlasses, dirks, boarding axes, tomahawks, pikes, mallets, bayonets, marlinspikes and clubs, so as not to make noise during the assault, their tension was palpable in the cloying night air.

Now they were close enough to smell fried garlic from the *Philadelphia's* galley. He heard sailors on the captive frigate jabbering in their strange tongue. At first, the voices were calm, but suddenly one man leaned over the side, pointed directly at Decatur and shouted. Soon a handful of Tripolines crowded the starboard rail and hailed him. He made no reply. A rifle pointed downward and discharged, promptly followed by another. The feeble volley was too late.

Decatur rose and severed the towrope. He willed the creeping *Intrepid* to glide the last few feet. As the ship's prow was about to bump against *Philadelphia*, he leapt for *Philadelphia's* thick hemp anchor cable, caught it, and climbed hand-over-hand. He was on top of the cathead in seconds, danced across it and sprang onto the deck. Around and behind him his crew swarmed up the hull, scrambling, crawling, and clawing aloft, a fierce, silent pack of jackals eager for the kill.

As Decatur cleared the rail, another of Preble's admonitions raced through his mind.

"On boarding the frigate, it is probable you may meet with resistance – it will be well, in order to prevent alarm, to carry all by the sword."

A scimitar arced toward Decatur's head. He parried the blow, stepped into the man, and shouldered him to the deck before chopping at him with his cutlass. Whether his stroke killed the attacker or not, he did not know, for straightaway two others took his place. He feinted left, dropped to his right knee, and swung his cutlass low to the ground, slicing through a kneecap. As the man toppled, Decatur used the falling body as a shield while he lunged at the second man and gutted him with a short, upward stroke of his dripping sword.

Then it was a constant flourish of parry, stab, slice, as the American officer hacked his way through the onrushing Turks. To his right, he spied a handful of the enemy hop overboard, descend into a tethered skiff, and row furiously for the quay. Ahead, Midshipmen Ralph Izard and John Rowe battled back to back against a relentless knot of Turks armed with pikes and short swords. Nearly overwhelmed, they were rescued by four U.S. sailors. The raging tars fell on the Turks from behind, dicing them to bloody bits in seconds.

Decatur picked out a tall, bearded man in a flowing white shirt and loose red balloon pants. The giant stood planted near the wheel, fending off several attacking Americans. The gargantuan Turk, from his raffish bearing and accomplished swordsmanship, was obviously the Captain. Using his colossal strength and skilled swordplay, he pushed his assailants slowly back. One swab stumbled, took a vicious cut to his ribs, and fell with a scream. A second comrade faltered, and then another, and before long the American seamen were on the verge of retreat.

In that instant, Decatur charged forward and engaged the brute. Steel sparked against steel. Both men danced and slashed at one another, seeking the advantage, trying to force a mistake.

4

Decatur slid back, tripped over a line, and nearly fell. The wounded sailor, Boatswain Reuben James, pushed up from the deck and threw himself at the Turk officer. He was slapped back to the ground. Decatur regained his balance and reengaged the enemy. Shifting to a two-handed grip, the hulking Moor cut the air near Decatur's neck with his curved sword, missed, and buried the blade in the mainmast. With a short downward chop, Decatur severed the man's arm. Then he finished him with a thrust to the abdomen.

Carry all by the sword.

Indeed.

Decatur paused. By now, the fighting had slowed. He counted at least 20 dead Turks littering the deck. Miraculously, the only American casualty was James, injured by the Moorish Captain. Lt. Thorn had hold of one Turk sailor. The captured man was badly wounded. He was the lone enemy survivor of the attack.

"To me, lads, rally to me!" Decatur called. The men gathered round.

"Now we burn her, boys!"

A "Huzzah!" erupted from the crew.

"Look lively, now!" he ordered.

Posthaste, Decatur sorted out the two squads tasked with torching the ship. Combustibles were passed from *Intrepid* and packed into *Philadelphia's* gun deck, forward storerooms, cockpit, and berth deck. On Decatur's signal, the flammable materials were set alight.

Fire and smoke rapidly filled the lower decks and poured upward through the hatches. Two 18-pounders were unlimbered, shotted and hauled to the main hatch.

Their barrels were pointed downward and discharged, blowing gaping holes in *Philadelphia's* bottom.

As flames began to belch skyward and then run up the rigging, Decatur and his marauders slipped overboard and swarmed back onto the waiting *Intrepid*. The nine tars who stayed behind to man the ship had already hoisted sail. For a moment, the inferno sucked the *Intrepid* toward *Philadelphia*, threatening to burn her. The men put oars in the water and pulled for their lives. They broke free of the vacuum and the ketch made its way from the harbor under a freshening breeze.

As they passed beneath the walls of the Bashar of Tripoli's main fortress, dozens of enemy cannon let loose. A hail of small arms fire from the various ships at anchor near *Philadelphia* added to the chaos. Although several balls passed through her sails, *Intrepid* and her crew were otherwise untouched.

Decatur's eyes swept the scene. The roaring conflagration enveloping *Philadelphia* painted the entire inner harbor in dazzling streaks of red, yellow, and orange. Scores of Tripoline galleys, gunboats, and schooners were illuminated by the blazing vessel. They looked to Decatur like a swarm of fireflies dancing on the water. Once they reached the entrance to the harbor, a series of thunderous booms rolled toward them as each of *Philadelphia's* overheated guns discharged, hurling ball and shot about the moored vessels, against the castle and into the town. A second "Huzzah" escaped the crew.

Another portion of Preble's order flitted through Decatur's mind. *"The destruction of the* Philadelphia *is an object of great importance, and I rely with confidence on your intrepidity and enterprise to effect it . . . . May God prosper and succeed you in this enterprise."*

Indeed!

Decatur allowed himself to relax a little. He had done it. Now Bainbridge's unfortunate mistake had been rectified, at least in part. Honor was restored. More important, *Philadelphia's* powerful guns would never be used against American ships.

He permitted himself a brief flight of fancy.

By God, there ought to be a promotion in this! Dare I covet command of Constitution? A small smile curled the corners of his mouth.

Indeed . . . .

The sole prisoner lay on the deck near Decatur. The Surgeon, Lewis Hermann, attended his wounds. An occasional moan escaped the Turk's lips. Whether it was from the pain of his injuries or distress at his country's defeat was unclear.

History failed to record the prisoner's name or his fate. But, as he lay there in shame and agony, Mustafa Almari vowed on the blood of his children, and his children's children, and that of all his line, that one day he would have revenge on these Americans, these invaders, these infidels who had attacked his nation.

Insha'Allah.

One day . . . .

On April 27, 1805, the Bashar of Tripoli, Yusuf Karamanli, signed a peace treaty with the young United States of America.

The First Barbary War, America's earliest overseas military adventure, ended.

Its conflict with Islamic states had just begun.

Part I

Stalking Her

~ Chapter 1 ~

Tehran, Iran

October 2010

He would come down to the café near the bazaar early each morning to sip his coffee and watch the city awaken. It was his private ritual, a way to collect his thoughts. More important, it was a way to connect to others. A former senior member of the Iraqi military, now living in exile in Iran, his was a closeted life. He had a privileged job, resided on a special base in a restricted housing area, dealt only with high-ranking Iranian military or government officials, and seldom had any contact with regular people.

He was born a peasant and missed the connection with family, clan, and village. Now, because of his secret status, this normalcy was forever lost to him. His sweet cup of coffee and quiet contemplation of the merchants opening their stores, the mothers buying fresh bread, lighthearted children skipping by on their way to school, burly truckers unloading produce, the beggars setting up their territory for the day, briefly, if imperfectly, connected him to other human beings. This quiet time filled a hole in his soul that years of shadowy warfare and horrendous loss had made.

His name was Muhammad Al-Buyid. His family descended from early rulers of Iraq and Iran. He was born July 14, 1958, the day the Iraqi Revolution had begun. At 52 years old, he was six feet tall and solidly built. Years of exposure to sun, salt and wind had weathered his face. Glittering black eyes peered searchingly from deep olive skin, but his hair and scruffy beard had the uncharacteristic light brown tint of his mother's Iranian people, giving him an oddly Southern European look. After meeting him, one was left with a lingering sensation of uneasiness, of danger, of some hidden coiled force waiting to spring loose at any moment.

His village was south of Basra, on the small segment of the Iraqi Persian Gulf coast near the border with Iran. His father was a fisherman. Through hard work and cunning, he had built a small fleet of vessels into one of the premier fishing operations in the region.

Al-Buyid could sail by the age of six. At sixteen, he captained one of his father's trawlers. The old men in the village joked that he had saltwater in his veins and that his beautiful mother was a mermaid. His father, proud of his son's prowess on the water, agreed.

In the early 1980s, at the onset of the Iran-Iraq War, he joined the modest Iraqi Navy. The force consisted of a ragtag collection of missile boats, patrol boats and light corvettes, whatever had been scrounged and left over from Iraq's WWII colonial masters, plus odds and ends bought from other countries, notably the Soviet Union, with armaments to spare. Hit hard by Iran's sneak attack at the start of the war, this force valiantly battled the slightly larger and better-equipped Iranian Navy.

10

Neither side had any clear advantage. There were no grand sea battles. Fighting was marked by a relentless series of coastal sorties, cutting out expeditions, night raids on oil fields, missile attacks on freighters, and harbor blockades, as each side did its best to destroy oil refineries, mine harbors, take out docking facilities, and disrupt trade.

The young Al-Buyid quickly distinguished himself. His superiors noted his skill and courage, particularly in coastal raids, and he swiftly advanced through the ranks. In one particularly astonishing and bloody engagement which acted as a feint to a massive ground attack in the Maysan region in 1986, Al-Buyid's squadron, under his command, sank five enemy craft and captured two more. From then on, the Iranians called him "the Sea Snake." His own men soon took up the sobriquet.

When the Iran-Iraq conflict deflated in 1988, his masters in Baghdad, looking to the future, decided that his raw talents should be honed. Al-Buyid was sent to Moscow and received a formal education at the USSR's elite Naval College. After graduating, he returned to Iraq and played a prominent role in the buildup of Saddam Hussein's Navy. He oversaw a program of foreign acquisition that gradually gave Iraq a small and highly mobile fleet supported by helicopters, ground-based missile batteries, and extensive mining operations.

On August 2, 1990, the day Iraq invaded Kuwait, Al-Buyid was the second-ranked officer on active duty in the Iraqi Navy. He sailed into the harbor of Kuwait City on the bridge of an Osa guided missile fast-attack patrol boat.

Almost everything that Al-Buyid had built was annihilated in the first seventy-two hours following the U.S.-led attack on Iraq in February 1991. Cruise missiles, bombs, and artillery from the American and British fleets located and destroyed virtually every ship in the Iraqi Navy. Piers and dry docks were demolished; armament and munitions factories vanished; supply depots vaporized. Al-Buyid's life's work became smoking ruin and sunken rubble.

Inexplicably, the allies did not take Baghdad. On March 3, 1991, the war ended with Iraq's surrender. Saddam Hussein survived, and with him much of the Iraqi war machine. Although cut off from the world and crippled by the U.N. blockade, the Iraqis once more set to work. And with them went Al-Buyid, doing what he did so well: planning, building, buying, molding some semblance a workable navy from the bits and pieces left over from the war and what help he could find from the world's renegade states and outlaw arms merchants.

By 1994, there was some rebirth. Saddam was again flexing his muscles, quelling internal opposition and moving against the Kurds in the north. The country was approaching normalcy. Factories hummed, crops grew in the fields, and the nation's swagger, so deeply wounded, was rebounding. Defeat was not a complete loss. However, with the world allied against Saddam, despite Al-Buyid's best efforts, Iraq's naval capabilities never reached significant strength.

In March 2003, spurred by fears Iraq possessed weapons of mass destruction, the United States launched Operation Iraqi Freedom. The war was fierce but short. Baghdad fell in April. The fledgling Iraqi Navy was destroyed. Saddam was captured in December. Al-Buyid, like many military from Saddam's regime, was without a job or a future.

Worse, during combat, an errant missile struck the naval housing compound in Umm Qsar where Al-Buyid's wife and infant daughter lived. They died, and their deaths killed that one small part of Al-Buyid's soul that laughed and loved and hoped.

Afterwards, what had once been professional respect for his American foes turned to blood hatred. He became mad with grief, and the target of his madness was the United States and in particular, the American Navy.

A hunted man, albeit one with a unique skill set, Al-Buyid fled Iraq. He approached his former Iranian adversaries and brother Shia and asked to be of service. The Iranians could easily have killed him. Instead, they respected his credentials, his motivating hatred toward the U.S., and his naval skills, and so allowed him to live. He became a special consultant to the new Iranian Revolutionary Guard Corps Navy.

In effect, he became a terrorist. Soon, an accomplished one.

Escaping notice by the CIA, he played a small but significant role in 9/11. Other successful operations followed. America's suffering had been his greatest joy since the loss of his family.

This day, as was his habit, his mind sifted through the material he had reviewed the previous day. The IRGC-N's intelligence community, like those of most countries, gathered information from a wide variety of sources, including the world's newspapers.

Something had struck him yesterday about a story in *USA Today*. The piece concerned an ancient American frigate called USS *Constitution*.

The ship, apparently the oldest commissioned battleship in the U.S. Navy and the world's loveliest extant, intact 18th-century warship, had been completely overhauled in the late 1990s.

In March 1996, in preparation for her 200th anniversary of her launching in October 1997, the Navy had completed an extensive $15 million, four-year restoration designed to make *Constitution* last another two hundred years. As part of the overhaul, she was refitted with new sails and rigging and her crew was taught the art of how to sail her. On July 21, 1997, she was put under sail for the first time since 1881. Although the trip lasted only one hour and *Constitution* spread only six of her 36 sails, the magnificent spectacle of *Constitution* once more gracing the sea under her own power captured the imagination and spirit of the whole country.

In two years, America would celebrate the 200th anniversary of the War of 1812. The *Constitution* had played a major role in that war. In celebration of the bicentennial, *Constitution* was slated to sail on July 4 under full sail and lead a parade of tall ships from around the world in Boston Harbor. The goal was to reach her maximum speed of 17 knots, a little more than 19 mph (considered "warp speed" in her time). Boston would at the same time host Fleet Week, an event drawing Navy ships and sailors to the city, including a flyover by the Blue Angels. Thousands of tourists were expected.

Constitution's turnaround cruise would draw the participation of many celebrities, foreign dignitaries, and high-ranking U.S. officials. These included former President George H.W. Bush, the architect of the First Gulf War. His son, George W. Bush, was the man responsible for the death of Al-Buyid's family.

Al-Buyid swirled his coffee. An idea formed in his brain. His hand shook with excitement, sloshing a tiny amount of coffee over the rim of his cup. He ignored it, his mind elsewhere. The idea blossomed. A plan took shape. Both eyes narrowed, and then sprung open. For the first time in months, his face creased in a brief, harsh grin.

A pity the Iranian Revolutionary Guard Corps Navy was not invited to the party.

He finished his java and set the ceramic cup decisively back on the saucer. The harsh clink of crockery turned some heads. Eager to begin, he pushed back his chair and bolted from the café.

The Sea Snake would strike anew.

So many jihads.

So little time.

~ Chapter 2 ~

Boston, Massachusetts

July 2, 2012

1138 hrs.

Fucking global warming.

It wasn't the only thing on Detective Lt. Paul Murphy's mind as he trailed the Patrol Sergeant through the woods. Global warming and the suffocating heat suffered by Boston were not usually high on his agenda of worries. It was, however, the thing he most wanted to concentrate on. The trick he used to divert his thoughts from what was ahead.

Otherwise, he didn't think he could do it. Go to the place where the bodies were. The place he hadn't visited in 40 years.

If he could just take his mind away from where he was, maybe he'd feel better; maybe he could keep his heart from pounding so wildly. Maybe hold the bile down that burned at the back of his throat.

It wasn't working. The bad memories intruded. The closer to the old bear pit they came, the more he felt nauseated. So far, no one could tell. Even if they saw how green his face was and how crazy his eyes looked, they'd probably chalk it up to his horror at

16

viewing the two bodies. That was understandable. At least they wouldn't guess the truth.

After another 100 yards of meandering down the trail, tripping on stray roots and rocks, chasing the Patrol Sergeant's bobbing flashlight, Murphy entered the clearing. There wasn't much of a moon, too many clouds. Ahead he could hear voices murmuring.

He spied a cluster of men, some standing quietly, flashlights pointed at their feet, others wandering around aimlessly, scanning the scruffy grass with their own flashlights, looking for clues. A couple of officers walked the perimeter, shining their lights into the woods at the edge of the clearing, as if it were possible the perp might be conveniently found waiting in the underbrush. All they found were ground out cigarette butts and the spent syringes of junkies who hung out at the park.

They were all uniforms. He was the first detective to arrive. *With luck, the crime scene won't be too badly screwed up.* That tended to occur at night, in the middle of nowhere, especially when no one really wanted to look at what had happened.

By the time he reached the group of men, a few had heard his approach and turned around to examine the newcomer. He threw his arm up to shield his eyes from the bright flashlights.

"Fer chrissakes get the fuckin' light out of my eyes!"

At least one uniform recognized him. "Sorry Lieutenant." The beams were lowered.

He let his pupils readjust to the dark. The Patrol Sergeant walked over to him. "It's all yours now Detective. Tell me what you need."

What do I need? I need to get the fuck out of here, that's what I need. I need a shot and a cigarette, and maybe a hug from my dead mother.

Of course, he didn't say that. "Show me the bodies."

"Here, take this." One of the cops shoved a flashlight in his hand. The Patrol Sergeant gestured to him, "Over here."

Murphy was rooted to the ground. *Why did it have to be here? A million frigging back alleys, abandoned buildings, deserted parks and scummy nooks and crannies all over the city, and it had to be here.* He'd been avoiding coming back to this one place all his life.

He was eight at the time. His mother wanted to take him to the Franklin Park Zoo. It was a special occasion. She let him skip school. They packed a lunch and headed there by bus from Dorchester. It was a big adventure.

Just him and his Mom.

Happy. Laughing. Safe.

He got separated. Or rather, he separated himself. His Mom was too slow. He wanted to see everything. He was a big boy. He could handle being on his own.

He'd tramped along an overgrown path to this place, the old bear pit. The site had been abandoned long before he was born. A rusty spiked fence circled the top of a broken down stone wall. Inside was a sunken hollow. It felt like a miniature Roman Coliseum. He imagined that he was a gladiator. When he gazed at the pointed spikes, he conjured what it would be like to fight and kill in an arena with a howling mob egging you on. That was the moment when the man caught him from behind, put a hand over his mouth and dragged him towards the woods.

Kids from Dorchester don't give in easily. A stomp on the man's foot and an elbow in the crotch freed him. As fast as possible, he ran for the woods. Footsteps pounded after him. When he reached the tree line he leapt for the nearest large tree, an old oak, and shimmied up its trunk until he reached a branch. Then he began to climb. A hand grazed his ankle. He kicked at it and soon was out of reach. He didn't look back. Up he went until he was too winded to go further. In a crook, he wedged himself against the scratchy bark of the trunk as tightly as he could, trying to disappear.

Two hours later, he was still hiding in the branches, tucked tight in a ball like a lost bear cub, when he heard the police yelling his name. When he finally looked down, it was into the upturned faces of two sweaty cops.

"C'mon down, son. It's O.K."

His mother burst into tears when she saw his filthy clothing and the cuts and scratches on his hands, arms, and face made by the branches. He ran to her and threw his arms around her hips. "It's alright, Mom. Nothing bad happened. Really."

From then on, things were never quite the same. Not with his mother, not with himself. Everyone assumed he'd been molested. Neighbors, friends, even his teachers, they all looked at him with curiosity and pity. His little world treated him as if he were a wounded bird or a freak.

It didn't matter that he protested over and over again that nothing had happened. No one believed him. Their behavior made him feel ashamed and guilty, as if something terrible had actually occurred, and he was to blame.

As he swept the light along the walls of the pit, he tried to tamp down his emotions. This was a homicide scene. The wrongdoing attempted against him was over. *Done. Ancient history.* It was his job to solve this new crime.

His light illuminated the bodies. They were both women. They hung like broken dolls from the spikes. Naked, gory, skin impossibly white, heads hanging onto their chests as if embarrassed by the manner of their deaths.

Other flashlights joined his. More details were visible. Cuts on their breasts, stab wounds everywhere. Their groins hamburger. Blood oozed from the butchery and dripped onto the ground.

No one spoke. The only sound was crickets chirping, until Murphy bent over and retched.

The evil of it was overwhelming, palpable. He'd first experienced evil here as a child. It still saturated the small, confined space, choking him and the others, making their skin clammy, their breathing ragged.

He stared at his shoes, glad they were not soiled, taking a moment to regain his composure. He had to fight the evil. Like when he was a kid. If you didn't fight evil, it would win. That's why he had become a cop.

He stood up and wiped his mouth on his sleeve. The other cops tried not to notice what had happened, knowing it could just as easily have been one of them.

It was time to get himself under control. Now. There was a job to do.

IRONSIDES' PERIL

Shake it off.
Breathe in. Breathe out.
Fucking global warming.

~ Chapter 3 ~

July 3, 2012

1100 hrs.

Mustafa Almari entered the grounds of the Charlestown Navy Yard. Beneath his feet was the worn red stripe of the Freedom Trail, which ran throughout Boston from one historic site to another. He walked into the brick guardhouse, nodded politely to the private security guards on duty, easily passed through the electronic screening and pat down, and casually strolled outside onto the docks. The old granite Federalist-style barracks housing the Constitution Museum were to his left. One hundred yards ahead, the *Constitution* and her towering masts filled the sky, silhouetted against the backdrop of Boston's waterfront skyscrapers.

He was desert born and no great fan of the sea, yet never tired of the sight. The old warship sat at her berth, black and shiny, a glistening white band circling her hull. Menacing cannon poked from gun ports. Her sleek, no-nonsense shape hinted at great speed. Every inch of the ship suggested she was a special tool made for war.

Mustafa was part of Al-Buyid's advance team. He had infiltrated across the Mexican border seven months

22

earlier and traveled by bus and car from safe house to safe house, arriving in Boston in early March.

Boston was home to numerous colleges. It welcomed thousands of foreign students from all over the globe. He effortlessly posed as a wealthy Middle Eastern scholar. His East Boston landlord was glad to be paid cash, in advance, and asked no questions.

His true university days were spent in France and Germany. He liked Boston's European feel, enjoyed its eclectic architecture, its varied neighborhoods, and the graceful esplanade extending along the Charles River. He especially appreciated the women. He was not a Muslim fundamentalist. For him, there was no reason to delay the joys of the flesh until one entered heaven. A clean-cut, handsome, wiry 28-year-old, he was delighted when giggly American girls told him he looked like the movie star Robert Pattinson. The lucky resemblance paved the way for easy conquests.

Like the two women he'd lured to the bear pit last night.

He walked up the gangplank and stepped onto the deck. It was his final visit to *Constitution*. He had been coming once or twice a month since his arrival. Unnoticed, he joined a group of tourists for the tour. An active duty Navy officer was waiting to lead the group.

The officer smiled broadly and launched into his routine. "Welcome to the USS *Constitution*, America's oldest warship...." As the officer droned on, Mustafa closed his eyes, familiar with the spiel. He had walked the ship from stem to stern, prowled every inch of the spar deck, gun deck, berthing deck, and orlop. He had poked into its wardroom, all of its cabins, and its many storage areas. On occasion, he had slipped unnoticed into the bowels of the vessel to explore areas tourists were not permitted to visit. He'd photographed and filmed her from every angle, read all the books in the Constitution Museum's well-stocked gift shop, and studied the information available on its official website. Other team members had done the same thing. With more than half a million visitors a year, it was easy for Mustafa and his cohorts to be lost in the crowd.

He and his confederates had also studied the contingent of 140 naval personnel assigned to *Constitution*. By now, the entire team was as familiar with the ship and its crew as if they had once billeted on it.

His tour group moved toward the main hatch.

"Who knows when *Constitution* was built?" Silence. "OK, 1794. Who knows where?"

A hand shot up. "In the U.S.A." a teenage boy answered.

The sailor was poised to make a smart response but held his tongue. "Well, that's correct," he smiled. "She was actually one of the first six frigates authorized by the U.S. Congress to form the new United States Navy. She was designed by Joshua Humphreys and built in Hartt's Shipyard, over yonder." The sailor pointed behind at the Boston skyline.

Mustafa was confused. He had never heard the word "yonder" before. While he was trying to discern its meaning the group moved on. "At the time, she was state-of-the-art, the finest ship afloat. She first saw action against the Barbary Pirates in North Africa.

You remember Muammar Gaddafi in Libya? That's where *Constitution* first fought, only back then it was part of the Barbary States. Instead of terrorists, they were pirates disrupting shipping in the Mediterranean."

After another short history lesson near the cathead, they plunged down the steep fore staircase to the gun deck where they reassembled at the back of the ship. Cannon lined both sides of the deck. An oversized cook stove was near the bow.

"OK, here's a tough one. Who knows when the War of 1812 started?" the guide asked.

A moon-faced teenager in an Ohio State T-shirt pocketed his smartphone and raised his hand along with a serious-looking little girl in pigtails. The adults played along.

"OK, you answer, young fella."

"A long time ago!" the teen chirped. The girl gave him a sour look while the adults chuckled.

"Well, you're a little bit right. How about you, young lady?"

"1812. Obviously." Her voice dripped disdain.

"You are totally right, miss. Two hundred years ago. 1812 – that was *Constitution's* banner year. She fought two fierce battles. The first naval engagement of the war took place August 18, off the coast of North Carolina. *Constitution* was sailing for Bermuda. Lookouts spotted the 49-gun British frigate *Guerriere* on the horizon. As *Guerriere* approached for close action, *Constitution*, under the command of Captain Isaac Hull, steered directly for *Guerriere*. He held his fire and *Constitution* took lots of hits from *Guerriere's* stern chasers. *Constitution's* guns were loaded with double shot and grape shot. When *Constitution* was within a pistol-shot, she unleashed a full broadside. *Guerriere*'s masts were shot off. The ship was reduced to a floating wreck. *Constitution* took up a fresh position ahead of *Guerriere*, to rake her from bow to stern. *Guerriere* surrendered."

The sailor looked around to see what affect his story was having. He plainly never tired of reciting it. To his satisfaction, the audience was rapt.

"And who knows *Constitution's* nickname and how she got it?"

This time, no one raised a hand. The girl in pigtails frowned, annoyed she could not come up with the proper answer.

"Well, in the battle, an American seaman observed a cannonball bounce off *Constitution's* side. He exclaimed, "Good God, her sides are made of iron!" Thus was coined the nickname, *'Old Ironsides.'"

The officer than began to describe *Constitution's* second major victory against *H.M.S. Java.* The man loved his history. When done, he signaled everyone to go back up the ladder to the spar deck.

Mustafa hung back. When the last tourist went up the ladder, he headed down, to the orlop deck, closed to tourists. He wanted a last look to see if any changes had been made. There was no room for surprises tomorrow.

The orlop deck lacked natural light. In port, *Constitution* was electrified. Bare bulbs encased in metal cages hung along the ceiling. Mustafa crept along the deck, hunched at the shoulders due to the low overhead. He poked his head into the various small cabins, alert for any weapons, communication gear, or other items that might be used to thwart the plan.

As he backed out of a cabin, he heard a scrape behind him. He whirled. A foot away, the dour-faced little girl with pigtails contemplated him.

"You're not allowed here." Her high-pitched voice was prim and accusatory.

Mustafa had killed children, but seldom talked to one. For a second he was at a loss. He smiled at the girl.

"Then neither are you."

The child looked perplexed. She squinted at him. He could feel her brain working. *An ugly, inconvenient child. Her parents will not mourn much.*

"Maybe. But I'm a kid. You're a grown-up. You should know better." She pointed a boney finger at him. "I'm gonna tell on you!"

Mustafa's hand shot out and grabbed the girl's wrist. His other hand moved to his pocket where he stored his clasp knife. He stepped toward her. The girl's eyes widened with fear.

A voice boomed behind him. "What's going on here?"

Mustafa turned, holding the girl's wrist. A naval officer and a civilian had materialized from the bow of the ship. He recognized the Captain. The civilian, a tall, fit-looking man with a scar running down the right side of his face, was unfamiliar. The Captain looked merely quizzical. The scar-faced man looked angry and ready to fight.

"Thank God you are here! I saw this little girl come down here where she is not supposed to be. I followed her to rescue her. I imagine her mother is by now frantic."

When the girl opened her mouth to speak, Mustafa tightened the grip on her wrist. She remained silent.

The Captain reached out and took the girl's free hand. He stared searchingly into Mustafa's eyes. Mustafa felt the limited, narrow space inhabited by the three men and the child grow smaller. Finally, in an even voice, the Captain addressed him, "Thank you. I'll take over now."

The Captain glanced at his companion. "Zach, why don't we make sure this gentleman makes it topside."

"My pleasure, Raff," the scar-faced man answered. He smiled at Mustafa. There was no warmth conveyed. His voice contained a hint of menace. Mustafa felt his pulse quicken. But he was a professional, and ignored the unstated challenge.

"Thank you! Thank you so much!" Mustafa grinned slavishly and obediently trailed the Captain up the three ladders to the spar deck. As he ascended, he could feel the scar-faced man at his heels. It made him uncomfortable. *Someday, I will kill that man.*

Back in the sunlight, the girl's mother spotted them and ran over. She snatched the girl from the Captain. "Oh my God! Thank you! I was so worried."

"Everything's fine," the Captain answered.

As she was pulled away, the little girl looked back and pointed at Mustafa. "He's a bad man!" she shouted. "He was going to hurt me! He's a terrorist!"

Mustafa froze. The mother and girl halted. No one spoke. He looked around. White faces surrounded him. Blue eyes scrutinized him. He knew how to play this.

First, he looked hurt. Then profound disappointment swept his face. A tear glistened in the corner of his eye. He called softly to the girl. "Not all dark-skinned foreigners are terrorists, little one."

The Captain interceded. The last thing he wanted spoiling his career was an accusation of racial profiling.

"Whoa, whoa! Let's not get carried away here." He reached out and shook Mustafa's hand. "Sir, my name is Captain John Raffington. I'm sorry all this happened. Please, let my Lieutenant escort you off the ship." He signaled to a nearby junior officer to assist. Mustafa returned a dispirited handshake.

Captain Raffington rang the ship's bell twice and shouted, "Everyone, the tours are over for the day. Please, ladies and gentlemen, head back to the gangplank. My crew will help you disembark."

With a grave countenance, Mustafa thanked the Captain and rejoined the pack of tourists herded off the ship. He walked slowly, feigning sadness. When he reached the gate, he chanced a look back. The scar-faced man stood by the rail, looking at him. Mustafa nodded at the man. The man just stared back. Behind the stranger's bland mask, Mustafa sensed barely checked rage.

Mustafa's knowledge of the Koran was sketchy, at best, but some things he recalled.

Zach. Zechariah. Arabic for "God has remembered." According to the Koran, a prophet. A pious man.

We shall see. One thing I know, I will remember that name and face.

It was a pleasant summer day. Mustafa had escaped. This part of the mission was over. Really, it had been easy.

Mustafa ambled in the direction of the nearest bus stop. Strangely enough, his biggest fear upon arriving in the United States was the prospect of driving a car. He had grown up in the slums of Tripoli and had not driven much, even when he studied abroad. What little experience he had driving was mostly in Amman, Cairo and Damascus. When he first drove stateside, he worried about being pulled over by a Boston cop for some innocuous driving infraction.

He was extremely pleased to find that Bostonians drove like Egyptians on the streets of Cairo, like Syrians on the thoroughfares of Damascus. Complete anarchy prevailed. An apparent blithe unconcern for human life was the norm. Nothing short of deliberate vehicular homicide was likely to draw the attention of local police.

He reflected again on his day's work. There was no evidence that special armaments had been added to the ship or that extraordinary security precautions were implemented for the next day's sailing. This jibed with the intelligence other members of the team had gathered from various sailors and dockside personnel.

Constitution would carry favored guests, her crew, a small Marine re-enactor honor guard, and a group of caterers. Tall ships from around the world and an American naval escort would surround her. Smaller craft from various law enforcement agencies would be on the water.

However, Mustafa did not worry about these trifles. Muskets and destroyers could not stop him. Nor could the local Keystone Cops. Extensive surveillance convinced him *Constitution* was ripe for taking. It would be a Fourth of July Boston would never forget. His own 2012 overture.

Revenge, achieved after two centuries of shame.

The thoughts of impending death and destruction aroused him. To perform his best on the morrow, he required fresh release. Tonight, he would prowl.

*****

Zach Colt was back in his office. The earlier incident on *Constitution* was almost forgotten. He'd been sure the man had been up to no good. Zach had gotten his blood up, ready to fight. However, in deference to Captain Raffington, he'd stood down.

The remainder of his day was much less eventful, filled with meetings and telephone calls. Now, late in the afternoon, the pace had finally slowed. He had time on his hands.

Bored, he swiveled his chair around and stared out the plate glass window framing his desk. His building was located in Boston's Financial District. From his office on the 46th floor, he had a sweeping view.

In the foreground was the new ribbon of greenery where Interstate 93 once blighted the city. Farther on was the North End, Boston's Little Italy. It was crammed with fine restaurants, bakeries, street fairs, and historic monuments like the Old North Church, where American patriots had signaled to Paul Revere that the British were coming, triggering his historic ride.

And there was the ocean. His vista encompassed a wide swathe of the inner harbor. A ceaseless array of watercraft plied the water. Coast Guard cutters, ferries, tankers, cargo ships from around the globe, and the occasional fireboat practicing with its giant water cannon made for daily entertainment. He spotted an MBTA launch ferrying riders across the harbor from Constitution Wharf to the New England Aquarium. The ferry was, in his opinion, by far the most enjoyable ride in Boston's storied mass transit system.

He loved best the sailboats. They came in all configurations, sizes, and nationalities. Along the inner harbor's northwestern boundary were Charlestown and the Bunker Hill Memorial. Almost in the shadow of the monument was the Charlestown Navy Yard, home of his favorite sailing ship, the most beautiful vessel of them all, USS *Constitution*.

He sighed, content. Zach Colt was a rich man. Sir Francis Drake's lost treasure, wrested from the jungle of Panama a few years ago, had accomplished that. It was a close run thing, seizing the gold. Some of his friends had died accomplishing it.

Panama was where he had first killed. It was where he'd almost lost his life. And nearly forfeited his soul. The personal cost of the venture was still being tallied. Even as he enjoyed the fortune it had brought him.

After the Panama affair, in order to manage his wealth, and for diversion, Zach started his own foundation, SFD & Associates. These days, his toughest decisions in life were how much money to give away and where to bestow it. He enjoyed doing good. It assuaged his guilt and kept him out of trouble.

Two floors down was the law firm that handled his affairs. A former prosecutor, Zach liked to torture its lawyers with convoluted tax law questions and queries about the complexity of creating offshore investment accounts. They enjoyed tormenting him with exorbitant fees. So far, it was a tie.

A voice roused him from his reverie. "Morning, Zach. How 'ya doin'?"

Putt Forster, his most senior advisor, was always polite, invariably cheerful, and unbelievably demanding of himself and his subordinates. He pretty much ran the show, leaving Zach more time to play.

Zach swiveled in his chair to face the older man. "I'm well. How about you?"

"Good. No, grand!" Putt's bonhomie was at odds with his WASP upbringing and button-downed appearance. "I was passing your office. Got a glimpse of you staring at *Constitution* over there." He grinned at Zach's sheepish look. "It reminded me about tomorrow. You must be excited."

"I am. Eleni and I will be on board from start to finish."

"Eleni?" Is she the young lady you brought to the firm's Christmas party? The one in the slinky black strapless dress?"

"Yes, you old horndog. I'm flattered you remembered her," Zach replied, considering anew those rumors he had heard about Putt's bachelor days. "I bet you even know the designer."

Putt reddened. "Who could forget her? A real knockout."

The old man paused with a faraway look in his eyes. He cast a doleful look at his egg-splattered paisley tie and the bowling-ball-sized-gut straining his blue oxford-cloth shirt. "Alas, too young for me."

He shifted topics. "Say, aren't you worried? Women are supposed to be bad luck on ships."

Zach leaned back and clasped hands behind his head. "Putt, that's the ancient mariner in you talking. Nowadays there are many women on ships. In today's Navy, 15 percent of personnel are women. They do a fine job. You know me. I'm not trying to be politically correct. A good sailor is just a good sailor."

"Hell, maybe you're right." Putt had that slightly embarrassed look on his face that so many men of his era got when caught in a modern gender blunder.

"Anyway, it should be one hell of a time," Putt tossed back as he turned to leave.

"You know, Putt, I owe it to you," Zach called out. Putt was the one who got him involved with *Constitution*. The old man's Brahmin roots ran deep. Through some long-forgotten connection, decades ago Forster had been appointed to the Board of Directors for the USS Constitution Foundation, the civilian body that oversees the maintenance of *Constitution*. Its principal purpose was fundraising. Membership traditionally imposed no more strenuous duties than attending the occasional cocktail party and writing a sizable check.

A short while ago Forster had felt he was stretched a little thin at work. He asked Zach if he was interested in taking over his seat on the Board. The position provided high visibility, a great intro to

Boston's moneyed elite, and a painless avenue for major networking. Zach gladly accepted the offer.

"Damn right you do," Putt added with a wave of his hand. "Make sure you give me a detailed report when you return. And don't make it dull." His scratchy baritone voice trailed off as he made his way down the hall.

Now Zach was completely distracted. Tomorrow's cruise was something he had been looking forward to for a long time. His visit earlier in the day had whetted his appetite.

Screw it. He signed off his computer.

The *Boston Globe* lay unread on the corner of his desk. Under the fold was a headline that caught his eye. Zach picked up the paper and scanned the story.

Two dead women at the Franklin Park Zoo. The details were shocking. Revolted, he tossed the paper into the trashcan. More murders in the city. It was becoming worse than Chicago.

Something had to be done. Maybe his foundation could fund a pilot program aimed at community policing or some other useful law enforcement strategy. He picked up a pen and scribbled a quick note to call his friend Walt Fenway. Walt had been with him in Panama and was a member of SFD & Associates. Walt was born in Boston and raised in Roxbury, a tough neighborhood. He now lived in the gentrified South End. Walt might have some good ideas.

Zach examined his watch. It was close to six o'clock. He tossed the pen aside. *Damn, I'm late. That's it for the day.*

Zach turned and gazed out his window one last time at where *Constitution* docked. A beehive of activity enveloped the ship.

By this time tomorrow, I'll be feeling her deck roll under my feet and gazing up at an incredible spread of sail.

No little boy turned sailor could ask for more.

~ Chapter 4 ~

July 3, 2012

1650 hrs.

On *Constitution,* the crew was readying the ship for service. For months, they had labored to learn the intricacies of sailing the ancient ship. It was a daunting task. The Navy no longer had anyone on its rolls with experience handling an 18th-century warship. Efforts to train the crew were largely an exercise in naval archeology.

While the verities of wind and tide remained the same, the practical aspects of ballasting the ship, maintaining her rigging and sails, as well as the actual mechanics of sailing her had to be learned and then taught virtually from scratch. The Navy garnered this arcane knowledge from an exhaustive review of naval literature and from interviews with living sailors around the world who possessed practical experience handling large two- or three-masted vessels. These sources were few and had been carefully mined.

Constitution was nearly 175 feet long. She weighed 1,576 tons. She carried a foremast, mainmast, and mizzenmast, each of which could be supplemented by increasingly smaller topmasts, topgallant masts, royalmasts, and skysail poles, reaching up to spear the sky. There was a bowsprit and flying jib boom, as well as rear spankers. Each mast had its own yards and booms carrying a different sail.

Dozens of sails could be set in numerous combinations, depending on her sailing needs and the whims of her captain. Fully rigged, she could carry 42,000 square feet of canvas. A spider web of 27 miles of standard rigging and seven miles of running rigging supported the masts and sails.

Each sail and piece of rigging had a name and a purpose. Even more amazing, all the sails and rigging were operated by human strength and knowhow, not by computers and complex machinery.

Her sails were specially woven Dacron fiber, colored golden ivory to simulate old canvas. The cost of the sails and rigging alone was estimated to be half a million dollars. Funding for the sails came from America's schoolchildren, who collected pennies, as they had decades earlier when they first saved *Constitution* from being scrapped.

Chief Petty Officer Prospero Zajac was sure his sailors were ready. The practice drills had gone flawlessly. His crew stood at ease, exhausted but happy, awash in the strong July sun. They were mostly youngsters, ordinary Americans, men and women, black, white, Asian, and Hispanic. Some were teenagers. For many, this was their first deployment.

Zajac considered them his children. Like a good parent, he had kindly, yet firmly, acquainted them with their tasks. They were eager to learn and excited about the role they would play in the upcoming pageant. They worked hard, mastered the necessary skills quickly, and had jelled into a well-honed team of professionals.

Zajac was proud of his sailors. Hell, he was proud of himself. Anyone looking at him could see it. He was born in Pittsburgh. His mother was black and from the north side. His father was a big Polish steelworker from the south side who turned bright pink in the sun. They'd met tailgating side by side at a Steelers game. When the mills shut down his mother supported the family as a saleswoman at Kaufmann's.

Football ruled western Pennsylvania. It was Zajac's savior. Too poor to afford college, his gridiron skills lifted him from obscurity and earned him a scholarship to Penn State. He blew out his knee junior year in a game against West Virginia. With no chance at a professional career, a recruiter enticed him into joining the Navy. He never looked back. From these humble origins, he had risen to a place of importance on one of America's national treasures.

At 37 years old, he stood 6'4" tall and was all muscle. People on the streets of Boston often mistook him for a member of the New England Patriots. However, his sport was no longer football. While stationed in South Korea, he picked up Hop-Kido, a form of Korean karate. After 20 years, he had progressed to a Sixth Degree Dan. Although a big man and deadly when provoked, he had a sweet temper inherited from his North Carolinian grandmother. He had also inherited from his parents a slew of Pittsburghese, which often peppered his speech.

He called his crew together at amidships for a meeting.

"Listen up, yunz. Tomorra's the day. Ev'body ready?"

A chorus of "Yes, sir!", "You bet, Mr. Z!" and other affirmations of confidence greeted his question.

One spunky recruit shouted, "We could sail *Old Ironsides* to Hell and back!"

"Well, Seaman Stehlin," Zajac replied, "I don' think that's gonna be necessary. Jist show up wearin' the 1815 regulation uniforms, rested and ready to do your best. And no jagoffing! We're in good shape. Nothing needs fixed. The weather looks fine. I prophesize a short, sweet cruise. Any questions?" He surveyed their sunburned faces. "None? Dismissed!"

*****

Fewer than 100 yards from Constitution Pier, inside the squat red brick building that housed *Constitution's* shore-based headquarters, Captain John Raffington was about to give his final briefing to the assembled ship captains and other personnel who would participate in the next day's event. The small conference room used for the briefing was crammed. At one end, on a raised tripod, was a chart of Boston Harbor and Massachusetts Bay. Small cardboard triangles were pinned on it, representing the various participating ships. Overall, more than 30 vessels from 13 different nations had turned out to join America in commemorating the War of 1812.

Before Captain Raffington began, he paused, lost in thought about what had brought him to this moment. He had assumed command of *Constitution* a year earlier when the previous Executive Officer, Captain Winfield Scott Kraven, died in a skiing accident at Cannon Mountain in New Hampshire. Although

Raffington had made the command his own, he had never felt completely comfortable in taking over from Kraven. Kraven had been one of the young officers tasked with shepherding *Constitution* through her intensive rebuilding program begun in 1992 and had been made her Captain in 2010. Kraven deserved a lot of credit for bringing the ship to this moment, and Raffington, as well as most others under his command, knew this.

He recited a silent prayer of thanks to Kraven for his skill and dedication. He also thanked his old Navy Academy roommate, now Naval Chief of Staff. The Chief remembered Raffs had once written a term paper on *Constitution* while at Annapolis. When Kraven died, the Chief happened to recommend this "expert" for command. Raffington knew he was not one of the best sailors in the Navy, but he was certainly one of the luckiest.

No longer lost in thought, Captain Raffington raised his head and addressed the group. He was a short man, only 5'7", but well-proportioned for his height and muscular from regular use of the weight room. What he lacked in stature he made up for with a booming bass voice that carried like a foghorn, and which he seldom used at less than full volume. It was his most potent weapon as a commander. He used it now.

"Ladies and Gentlemen, tomorrow we step into the history books. As you know, *Constitution* will lead the Parade of Sail. Eighteen-twelve was her most glorious year. Let's make 2012 equally memorable. On behalf of the United States of America and the Navy, I thank you and your nations for providing an honor guard for this magnificent event – and for saluting America on the 200th anniversary of the War of 1812."

Captain Raffington paused, cleared his throat, and picked up a pointer. He then turned his attention to the map table. The tip of the pointer tapped Constitution Pier.

"At 1200 hours *Constitution* will leave her berth. The tugboats *Revere* and *Washington* will tow her into Boston Harbor. As she enters the inner harbor, each of you will take up your assigned position behind her. We will proceed at no more than 5 knots. As the convoy forms, USS *Muskie*, the newest destroyer in the U.S. fleet, will fall into place behind *Constitution*. The frigate USCGC *Eagle* will be behind *Muskie*."

"Here," he tapped the map, "the tugs will disengage and Constitution will raise its sails. The entire convoy will then move past downtown Boston and to the outer harbor."

The pointer shifted positions on the map. "At approximately 1330 hours *Constitution* will reach Castle Island. *Constitution* will hoist additional sail, proceed on a northeast course past Long Island into Presidents Roads and then into the North Channel as far as Green Island, where she will circle back into the South Channel and return via the same route."

Raffington carefully traced the route with his pointer.

"During this, *Eagle* will sail directly behind *Muskie* as an additional honor guard. While Constitution does her loop, all other tall ship escort vessels and *Muskie* will remain stationary near Fort Independence on Castle Island. *Constitution* will complete its circuit and head back to the inner harbor. She will proceed under shortened sail past downtown Boston. As she approaches the new federal courthouse on Fan Pier, she will fire a series of three ceremonial broadsides from both her starboard and port guns.

Raffington perused the room. Bright eyes looked back at him. *Everyone loves shooting off the guns.*

"*Muskie*, which will have followed *Constitution* into the inner harbor, will then fire a 21-gun salute. Various fireworks displays will launch both from shore and from stationary barges anchored near the piers. The Blue Angels will execute a flyover. The Leap Frogs will parachute onto Fan Pier.

"From the deck of *Constitution*, President Bush the Elder will speak. At Long Wharf, she will furl her sails, reengage the tugs and be towed back to her berth. The tall ships will follow in *Constitution's* wake and reassume their anchorages."

Raffington stopped speaking and took a sip of spring water from his cut crystal tumbler. He looked up and smiled.

"I will captain *Constitution*. Captain Theodore Smartwood, seated here to my left, will command USS *Muskie*. Captain William Newtowne, at the back of the room, skippers *Eagle*. Everyone in this room is an old hand. All of you who captain the tall ships have done similar types of escort duty in the past. This exercise may be bigger, but it is no different, and frankly, less complicated."

A chuckle rippled through the room.

"The eyes of the world will be on us. Please, let's give everybody a good show. Without any incidents." He looked around. "Comments or questions?" No one spoke.

"Very well, then, I shall see you all tomorrow. Good sailing and Godspeed."

The briefing room emptied, each captain eager to return to his vessel and complete last minute tasks. Captain Raffington remained at the head of the table. Captain Smartwood joined him.

Smartwood was born in Maine and grew up sailing the coast off Camden and Mt. Desert Island. He looked a little like Abraham Lincoln, minus the beard and some of the melancholy. He was in his late fifties and considered by many to be too old for command of *Muskie*. However, his brother-in-law donated several hundred thousand dollars to the Democrats in the last presidential campaign. This and his Maine connections landed him the plum assignment.

"Well, Raffs, I hope things go as smoothly as you anticipate," Smartwood began in his thick Maine accent.

Captain Raffington smiled and responded, "Ted, we've both been in this business long enough to know that things never go as planned. However, my crew is well trained and we are working with some of the finest sailors in the world."

"Ayuh, I know, I just get worried when so many politicians are involved. I'm glad you're transporting the big shots and not me. The last thing I want is the former President falling overboard or the SECNAV taking a tumble down an open stairway."

"I'm not worried about that," Raffington chuckled. "It's more likely some weak Nellie will get seasick and puke all over my newly polished decks. Having too many landlubbers on board, especially bigwigs, is never easy, even on a picnic cruise like this one." They both laughed.

Smartwood became serious. "What about a real problem? Has Naval Intelligence indicated any nasty surprises might be in store?"

"Ted, between our people, the FBI and the Secret Service, we've got this town sewed up tighter than a mummy's lips. I expect we'll have to police a couple of drunken partygoers. Not much beyond that. Hell, this is Boston. The last international incident this city saw was that German girl Pippig crapping her way to the finish line at the 100th Boston Marathon. If the ship doesn't break up around me, all should be well."

Captain Smartwood got to his feet, ready to go. He paused at Raffington's new tone of voice.

"Something odd happened this afternoon. We found a guy alone with a little girl on the orlop."

"You're kidding! A pedophile?"

"No, I don't think so. He claimed the girl got lost and he was rescuing her." Raffington scratched his chin. "I didn't like his looks – young guy, Middle Eastern-looking. I didn't have anything on him. It could have been a real shitstorm if I detained him. Everyone is so damn sensitive these days."

"I hear you. I'm sure you made the right decision. Don't worry about it. No one in their right mind would chance anything with all these ships around." He took a step toward the exit.

"Well, I've still got a few things to do, mostly paperwork. You've done a fine job planning this event. I hope it helps earn you another step up the ladder. Good night." Smartwood made a casual salute.

"See you at first light, Teddy." Raffington saluted back.

Smartwood left. Raffington was alone. He looked at the map with its brightly colored surface, dotted with the small cardboard ships. It looked like the aftermath of a child's game.

Toys. I'm just playing with big toys in a big bathtub. He packed his briefcase and moved briskly from the room.

*****

Zach cleared his desk and packed his briefcase. The swank pre-sail party at the Boston Harbor Hotel on Rowes Wharf started at 8:30. This barely left enough time to make it to his townhouse, take a run along the Charles, clean up, and then pick up his girlfriend, Eleni.

He briskly walked through his floor to the front exit, nodding good night to his colleagues along the way. In the elevator, he decided to swing by his lawyer's office to check on a transaction in the works. Although after six, the law firm hummed along as if it were noon. Most, if not all the lawyers still toiled in their offices, driven by overwork, ambition, fear, or a combination of all three, and stayed chained to their desks until nine or later each night. The late shift of secretaries had just checked in and taken up their stations.

"Let them put in their 'face time'," he thought. "Been there, done that." He knew that staying late was, for many big firm associates, a charade. For the unmarried ones, staying late was a relief from the crushing loneliness of being single in a big city. For many of the married ones, it was an excuse to avoid a harpy wife or domestic chaos. For others, it was all part of playing the partnership game. Bill as many hours as humanly possible. Stay longer than the next lawyer to prove your dedication.

At any rate, a lot of deception took place in the game. Some associates purposely stayed far into the night just to compose meaningless e-mail messages to senior partners after hours to document how late they were working. Others constantly kept their lights and computers on, paper strewn on their desks, and a half-empty cup of coffee visible to create the illusion they were working around the clock.

Zach had always preferred to work smart, not long, seeking to balance his work life with pleasure. He was glad to be free of that insanity. America wasted too many good minds on the law at the expense of science, medicine, and industry, areas where the country truly needed the best and the brightest.

He walked by the mahogany and brass reception area, his shoes smacking lightly on the polished granite floor. Phyllis, the night receptionist, looked up and smiled brightly at Zach. She liked him. Unlike the men she worked for, he was not a bullshit artist. To her, Zach was a straight shooter with a heart of gold.

"Hello, Mr. Colt, Can I help you?"

"Is Fred around?"

"No, he left early. Golf."

"Again? Slacker. Tell him I dropped by, will you, please."

"I will, Mr. Colt. Oh, say, you're going out on the ship tomorrow, aren't you? I'll be watching for you on the six o'clock news tomorrow night."

Zach grinned at her. "I can see the headline, 'Boston Lawyer Lost Overboard While *Constitution* Sails On.'"

Phyllis laughed with delight as Zach waved a hand and stepped back into the mahogany and brass elevator with its lead crystal chandelier and pressed the polished button marked "L."

He lived on Beacon Hill, a swank part of the city, full of multi-million dollar brick townhouses lining steep, leafy streets. Many of Boston's moneyed elite resided there. Zach liked it because it was convenient and quiet. His digs were near the TD Garden, the new structure which had replaced the beloved Boston Garden, where the Celtics and Bruins played. It was also close to the North End, theaters, his health club, and only a short walk to his office in the Financial District. The neighborhood was the perfect spot for a single urban professional.

As he walked home, he passed Faneuil Hall. The place was hopping, packed with visitors from all over the world in town for Fleet Week and the Fourth. He glimpsed uniforms from a dozen nations. Families and kids were everywhere, enjoying the warm July evening and the many diversions of the marketplace. The smell of fresh seafood permeated the air, along with more pungent smoke from fried Italian sausages. Jugglers, street musicians, and clowns performed for the amusement of the crowd. A man dressed as Ben Franklin circulated among the tourists.

In twenty-five minutes, he was at his doorstep. Ziggy, his Portuguese Water Dog, greeted Zach's entrance as if he'd been absent for 100 years. Zach fought off the frenzy of jumps and licks and changed for his run.

The evening was perfect. He jogged with Ziggy on a loose leash west along the Charles. The late sun warmed his face. As the miles slid by, he shed unresponsive attorneys, greedy undeserving callers begging for money, and the everyday stress of running his small foundation. Soon his mind was free. He felt only his body – heart pumping, lungs bellowing, and sweat soaking his T-shirt. Crossing Memorial Bridge to the northern bank of the Charles, he circled back toward his building. Part way across the Craigie Bridge, near the Museum of Science, he stopped running and walked the last mile. Now he was relaxed and ready for Eleni.

Forty minutes later, Ziggy was asleep on the sofa and he was in a cab on his way to Eleni's place in Back Bay. A bouquet of roses sat on the seat next to him.

They'd first met decades ago. Eleni was the most beautiful woman in his law school class. She was a tall blonde with perfect carriage, mysterious sea-green eyes, and a husky, breathless voice that teasingly hinted at the passion in her soul. Unlike most law school women, who usually wore blue jeans and ratty sweatshirts, she was impeccably dressed in tailored silk suits and blouses and always well made-up. She was a woman where all the others were just girls.

The first time he was attracted to her, she had on a brown-striped suit that stretched deliciously over her derrière. He was smitten and had been ever since. The fact that she was the smartest woman he had ever met was just icing on the cake.

After graduation, ambition took them on separate paths. She stayed in Boston and joined a top law firm. He moved to New Hampshire to clerk and later served in the U.S. Attorney's office. Over the years, they had both married and divorced others. Now he was back in Boston, filthy rich and president of his own nonprofit, and she was a partner at her firm. They met by chance at a cocktail fundraiser for Senator Scott Brown. The electricity was instantly renewed.

Zach paid the cabby and bounded up the granite steps of Eleni's brownstone. He rang her buzzer and the front door clicked open. In 30 seconds, he knocked on the door of her third floor flat. On his fourth rap, the door swung open. Eleni stood, naked, in the front hallway. The fading light streaming in through the windows behind her turned her hair to shimmering gold. Her body was all cherries and cream.

He growled low in his throat, stepped inside, and closed the door behind him. The roses hit the floor. Zach and Eleni avoided thorns as they did, as well.

*****

Several miles away, in a decrepit row house near the East Boston waterfront, Al-Buyid faced the first crisis of his operation. He stared coldly as Mustafa briefed him.

"Ibrahim is uncertain he can do it. He has doubts," Mustafa reported.

Al-Buyid turned his head slightly to the left and sighed. He removed his glasses and laid them on the tabletop. Its surface was crowded with maps, lists, and photographs, all neatly organized and labeled in his meticulous Arabic. He pushed his chair out, stood, and faced Mustafa.

"Take me to him."

Mustafa turned and exited the room with Al-Buyid at his heels. They descended the four flights of stairs leading from Al-Buyid's planning room to Ibrahim's basement hideaway. As they walked down the darkened stairs, the accumulated funk of stale tobacco smoke, cooked cabbage, and oil soap assaulted their nostrils, legacies of the house's generations of Irish tenants.

Al-Buyid at times wondered what these former owners would think of his mission. Would they sympathize with his fight against imperial power? After all, the Irish had been subjected to British domination for hundreds of years, and had fought sporadically and at times nobly, even if ineffectively, against the tyranny. Would they understand his struggle, all of the Arab world's struggle, against a similar enemy, a power even greater than the British, which routinely scorned his people and sought to destroy his religion and culture? Certainly, his contacts in the IRA had helped him in Boston. He suspected the group's sympathy was based on cash, not ideology.

They came to the basement. Mustafa knocked and slowly pushed open the door to Ibrahim's room. He leaned in and spoke.

"Ibrahim, the Sea Snake has come to you."

Mustafa backed away, and Al-Buyid entered the chamber. Ibrahim was kneeling on a prayer rug in the middle of the tiny space, head pressed against the floor, pointed east. The room was cell-like. There was an iron bed with a white sheet and old blue blanket. Beside the bed was a small wooden table with a desk lamp and straight-backed wooden chair. On the table was a copy of the Koran. Pasted above the bed was a picture of an elderly Arab couple, clothed in traditional dress, with a small boy standing between them, all three staring warily but proudly at the camera. The whitewashed walls glowed softly in the subdued light. Everything was spotlessly clean and smelled of disinfectant. The room could have been a hospital room, a monk's retreat . . . or a prison cell.

Al-Buyid knew it was the room of a condemned man, for Ibrahim was his suicide attacker and a crucial part of his plan. Ibrahim finished his prayers and looked up. He was short, plump, and soft looking. No one would take him for a fanatic. His eyes did not blaze with hatred. Instead, they had the unfocused glaze of a wounded animal. Of course, Al-Buyid knew better.

He had recruited Ibrahim for this mission with the help of Hamas. He knew Ibrahim was a Palestinian who had been raised a devout Muslim. His father, a village headman in a small hamlet north of Jerusalem, had made the mistake of questioning Israel's West Bank settlement policy. As a result, Ibrahim's parents had been dispossessed of their land and their house reduced to rubble. The once comfortable family was forced into a refugee camp in the Gaza Strip where his mother soon died of disease and his father of grief, leaving the small boy in the photograph over the bed an orphan. Al-Buyid knew that the lost youth who knelt before him had found solace in the Koran and the radicalism of Islamic extremism. He believed, at least until several minutes ago, that Ibrahim's faith in Allah, fueled by hatred for Israel and the West, made him capable of sacrificing his life. Ibrahim was 17 years old.

Mustafa closed the door and waited outside. Al-Buyid stood quietly in front of the boy. Ibrahim quickly scrambled to his feet and faced Al-Buyid, hands clasped in front of his stomach, fidgeting, plainly reluctant to look Al-Buyid in the eyes. A long silence endured. Al-Buyid let it stretch to near the breaking point before he reached out and took the boy's elbow, guiding him to the bed.

"Sit."

Ibrahim sat on the edge of the bed and Al-Buyid took the chair from the table, turned it toward Ibrahim, and leaned on it. He did not know the boy well enough to like or dislike him. Three days ago, Ibrahim was flown into a remote northern Maine airfield. After landing, he was ferried by car to Boston. Before that, he had been carefully prepared in Tehran for this mission. Since his arrival, he lived alone in his room, immersed in prayer and meditation. The members of the team knew his function, and out of respect, left him alone. Al-Buyid, who had been busy with other aspects of the mission, had also ignored him. Now he faced the curious task of coaching this young stranger to his death.

"Mustafa said you have doubts. What are these doubts, Ibrahim?"

Ibrahim raised his head and stared at Al-Buyid. He opened his mouth to speak. Before he could say a word, Al-Buyid interrupted.

"Tell me, what are these doubts, Ibrahim? Do you have doubts that the United States paid for the weapons and training for the Israeli soldiers who stole your home and exiled your parents? Do you have doubts that the United States supported the Israeli government in its campaign to seize Palestinian lands? Do you have doubts that the United States has been responsible for the deaths of hundreds of thousands of Arab people – and the abject misery of millions more? Do you have doubts that the blasphemous culture of this country seeks to destroy Islam and rejects Allah and all things holy?"

Al-Buyid moved around the chair and sat down, his face inches away from Ibrahim. His eyes bore steadily into those of the teenager before him.

"Tell me, Ibrahim," he continued, "when were these doubts formed? Were they formed as you sat at the bedside of your dying mother? When you watched your father wither away from grief? Were they formed as you lay awake at night in the camps listening to the children cry from hunger and the old men weep from frustration and shame? Were these doubts born when you dedicated your life to Allah's justice and accepted entry into paradise in exchange for one glorious act of courage against the scourge of your people and your faith?"

He stood and swatted aside the chair. He gazed down at the boy. "Tell me, Ibrahim, what are these doubts – and how will they affect the fate of the comrades who depend on your bravery tomorrow and the hope of little children who will revere you as a martyr in the years to come?"

Al-Buyid's voice had steadily risen throughout the tirade of questions. When he suddenly stopped, the silence was a shock. Ibrahim sat, tears streaming down his cheeks, rocking back and forth. Dropping to the floor, he threw his arms around Al-Buyid's feet and wailed.

"I have no doubts, father. I have no doubts!"

Al-Buyid rested a hand on the boy's shoulder. When the sobbing stopped, he gently lifted Ibrahim and reseated him on the bed. He then looked Ibrahim in the eyes, this time with a kinder gaze.

"It is only the strong, the true believers, the ones who sacrifice, who enter paradise and sit at the feet of the Prophet."

"I will be strong."

Satisfied, Al-Buyid turned and left the room. Outside the door, he rapidly bolted the stairs back to his room taking them two and three at a time. Mustafa cursed as he tagged behind, struggling to keep up. When they were alone in the study, Al-Buyid turned and addressed him,

"Tonight we will strengthen our lamb's will. Stoke his dinner with hashish. Bring the woman in to him in the early hours of the morning. Have him up at first light for prayers. More hashish with breakfast. Not too much, he must be able to drive the boat. Do you understand?"

"Yes, Sea Snake." He gave a harsh laugh. "You forget one small detail. I am assured he prefers boys to girls."

55

"Not like you, Mustafa," Al-Buyid's voice held a trace of disdain as he looked down sharply at the younger man.

"I'm glad you've done your homework. I don't give a damn what he likes. Bring a donkey if you must. Just keep him dumb and happy and committed until tomorrow."

Al-Buyid looked away, then back. "If you don't, I will chain you to the steering wheel of the speedboat and you can enter paradise courtesy of 500 pounds of C-4 jammed up your ass. Is that clear?"

The two men coolly took stock of each other until both unexpectedly grinned and laughed.

"A donkey? Really? A donkey? Where would I find such a beast in this city?"

"Anywhere and everywhere. They are all donkeys in America."

Refreshed by the black humor, Al-Buyid waved Mustafa out of the room, and then returned to the work on his desk.

He had seen many dead boys in his military career.

Tomorrow he would see at least one more.

~ Chapter 5 ~

July 3, 2012

2030 hrs.

The evening was intoxicating. It began with the delicious sex, an exercise both lovingly tender and ferociously raw, which ignited her senses and left every inch of her body hyper-alive. Even now, she could taste him. Her skin carried the faint scent of his Royall Lyme.

Now this glorious party. Stepping from their taxi, they entered a scene from another era, a time of opulence and indulgence, of men in ornate uniforms, and lovely, bejeweled women held rapt in their arms. Eleni felt transported into a Jane Austen novel where she was the heroine.

Rowes Wharf was one of Boston's premier waterfront locations. Rectangular brick buildings flanked a 10-story vaulted dome, open to the air front and back. The site housed the Boston Harbor Hotel, condominiums with private boat slips, restaurants, shops, and some of the city's most prestigious law firms. Outdoor terraces, walking paths, moorings for elegant watercraft, and a commanding view of Boston's inner harbor graced the waterside.

57

Tonight, the entire wharf blazed with light. Inside the dome hung the largest American flag Eleni had ever seen. It rippled softly in the ocean breeze, casting undulating shadows across the walls and floor. A military band located within a dockside cupola played a familiar waltz. Directly beneath the flag, on a grand circular dance floor, were dashing officers flirting and dancing with Boston society's loveliest and most eligible women. As Eleni looked more closely, she realized that some of those twirling officers were servicewomen held by handsome men.

The ribbons, medals, gold braid, and polished brass on the uniforms mixed with silver, gold and jewels to create a flashing whirl as entwined bodies moved gracefully to the music. Adding to this visual feast, off to the sides were tables mounded with plump pink shrimp, silky oysters, blood red lobsters in the shell, and racks of rare roast beef, surrounded by long-stemmed glasses brimming with chilled Dom Perignon as well as a selection of America's finest micro-brewed beers.

Constitution rocked gently on the ebbing tide, anchored near the wharf. The old girl held the place of honor at the party. Her rigging was ablaze with white lights as if she too had donned her best jewelry and party dress for the fete. Every mast carried a colorful pennant snapping in the breeze. Spotlights bathed her hull. Officers and enlisted men in period costumes trod her decks. Guests were ferried back and forth from the pier to her anchorage for privately guided tours.

Zach's hand tightened around Eleni's waist as he led her away from the curb into the dazzling soiree.

She did not resist. Tonight, she let him take control, luxuriating in the comfort and security of his competence and vigor. Almost immediately, she and Zach encountered Eldridge Horsley and his wife Margaret, who everyone called "Mags."

Eldridge served with Zach on the Constitution Board. He was Old Boston Money – Groton; Harvard; charge account at Brooks Brothers when he was thirteen; wood-shingled summer house with gazebo in Osterville on the Cape; lunch at Locke-Ober's and a wood paneled office in Daddy's downtown investment firm where no one was quite sure what he did to pass the time. When Eldridge Horsley spoke, there was not an inner "r" to be heard.

Although in his late fifties, he had that ridiculous, boyish chirpiness typical of a New England preppie grown to dubious manhood who never has to worry where his next Volvo station wagon payment comes from. His bride of 15 years, Mags, was similar in her own way – especially in the boyishness department. Ten years younger, tanned, fit, and rail-thin, she was painfully homely and quite mannish, a fact accentuated by her silver blonde pageboy held in place by a severe black velvet headband. She wore a plain, unadorned black dress by Newbury Street's finest designer, which she nevertheless seemed to make drab and frumpish. An antique engagement ring the size of Plymouth Rock emphasized her lack of ornamentation and makeup. She lived in a busy-busy brick pile on Cliff Road in Wellesley and was perpetually ferrying her children to hockey games, soccer practice, or dance lessons. Alternatively, she and Eldridge were in

Bermuda or Tuscany, leaving the children with one of an endless supply of revolving Euro-nannies.

He ostensibly ran a non-profit company, V-Oil, which provided free oil to needy citizens. However, both he and his wife managed to extract six-figure salaries for their alleged charitable activities. His old family name and healthy donations to Democratic candidates let him get away with the charade.

Privately, Eleni and Zach called Eldridge, Mags, and their ilk "DWs," short for "Desiccated WASPS." As well-educated, self-made children of the middle class, they both shared secret disdain toward those who earned their money through birth, not merit.

"Hello, Zach. Hello, Eleni. How do you two fare on this delightful evening?" Eldridge extended a hand to Zach, while surreptitiously giving Eleni the old up-and-down, which she noticed. Eleni and Mags air-kissed. As Zach gripped Eldridge's hand, Eleni suppressed a laugh while thinking that the older man would probably gag if he knew where those fingers had been twenty minutes ago. She then turned to Eldridge, and after first teasingly running her tongue over her lips, said to him in a throaty growl, "We fare . . . well," and without pausing, turned her back on him and sashayed away into the crowd. Zach muttered excuses and hurried after her.

"What is up with you?" he asked, catching her by the elbow. She turned and scowled.

"Did you see the look he gave me when we said hello? I'm not going to let that dried up old frat boy mentally undress me in public. It's too delightful a night to spend time talking to a man like that, especially when he just talks to my chest."

Zach sighed. "I understand. He's a jerk. Hell, I have to spend time with the guy on the Board. Please try to be a little more diplomatic. And," he nibbled her ear, "don't be too harsh on him. It is such a lovely chest."

Her annoyance evaporated. There was no point to spoiling the evening. Zach's crooked grin and outstretched hand awaited her. With a small curtsy, she stepped with him onto the dance floor.

"You're damn lucky to have me as your trophy girlfriend." She playfully stroked the scar on his cheek.

"Just behave."

"That's not what you said a little while ago, sugar," she whispered, in her best Mae West voice. Zach cocked his head back and hooted.

They danced five dances together before taking a break for champagne. The floor was packed. It took effort to make their way slowly to the buffet and bar. Zach steered them clear of further obstacles.

*****

Behind a table, decked-out in a white waiter's jacket, Mustafa Almari served drinks. As always, his eyes ranged over the crowd, here and there spotting an officer he had surveilled, or a dignitary whose face he paired with the next day's passenger list. He also noted the many beautiful women in the crowd.

Mustafa was stirred. He felt the surge of excitement that came from being so close to prey.

Fools. All of them. They do not know they are already dead.

Nearby, a male voice bellowed laughter, followed by a woman's infectious giggle. His head pivoted to search for the source and his eyes locked on Eleni and Zach, who embraced a short distance away on the dance floor.

Mustafa froze, a bottle halfway raised in his hand. He stared without appearing to stare. He felt his cheeks flush and his pulse pound. He cursed his bad luck. The man with the scar.

His apprehension quickly faded as he appraised Eleni.

What luck! The woman – I have never seen a more beautiful one. I must have her.

When the music stopped and Zach and Eleni moved toward the drink tables, Mustafa deftly seized a tray of full glasses and briskly moved in their direction. Approaching the couple, he smiled his most roguish smile, bowed his head, and extended the tray.

"May I offer you refreshment for your thirst?"

Zach reached for a glass. "Thanks. You are a life saver."

Mustafa replied, "In my country, we understand thirst."

"And what country would that be?" Eleni politely replied. There was something slightly sinister about the waiter that piqued her curiosity.

Emboldened by her attention, Mustafa played along and uncharacteristically told the truth.

"A small North African desert nation called Libya."

Perhaps it was the strange sound in his voice; perhaps it was the oddity of conversing with a suave foreigner from a sworn enemy of the U.S. in such a setting. Whatever it was, Eleni took a closer look at the man. He was fit, dark-complected, with handsome features. Most women would find him attractive. Not Eleni. She did not like the way he looked at her. Beneath his charming veneer, she sensed malevolence. His black eyes were dead and she was afraid. For the second time that night, she turned abruptly away from someone, this time with a shiver.

"Come on, Zach, let's dance some more. They're playing 'Beneath the Southern Cross' from 'Victory at Sea'." She took Zach's hand and moved away while Richard Rogers' music made the soft July night even more romantic. Zach put his now empty glass on Mustafa's tray.

"Thank you, my friend," Zach spoke over his shoulder as he let Eleni drag him into the crowd.

Of course, he'd recognized the man. It was odd to see him again so soon, especially here. The fellow was arrogant, even defiant, unlike the way he'd acted earlier. Zach was immediately on guard.

For a moment, he was tempted to probe past the server's smooth exterior, to see if he could make him sweat. He let it pass. It was not the time or place to make a scene. Later, perhaps, he'd corral the fellow and have a little chat. In the meantime, he memorized the name on the waiter's nametag, "Mustafa."

Left alone, Mustafa stared hungrily after them.

You are not my friend. Not you, not your woman, not all these rich fools, not your diseased country.

The quick brush-off stung. Mustafa felt once more like the homeless waif on the docks in the port of Tripoli, begging candy and spare change from rowdy sailors and fat European tourists from cruise ships.

Marveling at the foreigners' clean clothing and their stylish running shoes. Hating them because they could buy everything his land had to offer: fresh food, carpets, even women. Envying them for their ease, their wealth, and their casual power over so many things, his country included.

As a boy, he never possessed new clothing or owned shoes. He survived by theft. He grew to manhood a homeless, impoverished, powerless pariah. Although that life was long gone, tonight, surrounded by opulence and power, slavishly serving these comfortable Americans, he felt the overwhelming shame of his youthful impotence, insignificance, and poverty.

Tomorrow would change all that. Tomorrow he would create new and better memories.

Mustafa returned to work, once again playing the dutiful servant. He made sure to circulate throughout the crowd, paying particular attention to the officers and guests he knew would be on board the next day. He felt it was time wasted. The odds of him picking up any useful information so late in this setting were slim. Nevertheless, Al-Buyid was thorough. His boss wanted nothing left to chance. So Mustafa stayed, served drinks, and listened.

The crowd was excited about the morrow. The Navy men and women talked with pride about *Constitution* and the other ships, trying to impress their dates with their historical and nautical knowledge. The politicians circled methodically like sharks, plunging in here and there to shake a hand or grab a shoulder in a false gesture of appreciation or pretended delight at seeing one of their "good friends."

Mustafa tired of the scene. The only interest it held for him was the occasional stolen glance at Eleni. She never looked his way. As the evening progressed, even his secret knowledge of tomorrow's surprise was not enough to squelch the growing fever inside him. He knew the feeling well. He welcomed it.

After the fireworks and the "oohs" and "ahs" of the delighted crowd; after the pink shrimp lay flaccid on their serving plates and the last Sam Adams beer bottle was emptied; after the final stolen kiss took place in the shadows and the immense American flag hung limp in the early morning stillness; after the merriment gave way to the clinking of bussed crockery and rattle of silverware slopped into plastic tubs and the curses of tired busboys clearing away the expensive rubble of the feast; after all that . . . .

Mustafa went hunting.

*****

Many people are born evil. Mustafa chose to be evil. He took what he wanted. He did what he liked. More than anything, total control over the life of another human being gave him exquisite pleasure.

He remembered well the day he chose evil. In his early teens, Mustafa had been a petty thief. Evil was an abstraction. His criminality, although deliberate, was not exciting or spectacular; rather, it was merely a way to survive. That changed the night he was jailed for robbing a British tourist. After the routine beating and interrogation, he was cast into a squalid, unlit cell, given a pan of fetid water to drink, and left alone for the night. The routine continued for three days.

Well before dawn on the fourth day, a flashlight shined into his cell awakened him. A high-pitched voice directed, "That one." His door opened. Guards dragged him blindfolded down a corridor and through several doors to another ironbound door. When they stopped, they jerked him upright and ripped free the grimy rag covering his eyes.

The jailers shoved him through the door into a large, sand-colored room. There were a table and two metal chairs. A young woman, dressed in tattered prison garb, bound and gagged, sat in a chair. Her beautiful face was bloody. A clump of long, black hair dangled from the side of her head, exposing an oozing scalp. A man sat behind the table, wreathed in cigarette smoke. The air was hot and thick, so thick Mustafa could hardly breathe. His vile garments were soon soaked through with sweat. Plaintive Arab music filtered in from outside the prison walls, mixed with the occasional screams of tortured prisoners. On the table was a 9 mm Browning semi-automatic pistol.

At first, Mustafa could not clearly see the face of the man behind the table. The shadowed figure was dressed all in white. He was thin and had a square-jawed, slightly effeminate face topped by a coiffure of oiled and curly hair. The man waved the guards from the room and raised his head slightly to better look Mustafa in the eyes.

"Come here, insect."

Mustafa shambled forward. There was something familiar about the voice, and as he drew nearer, he recognized the man. To his horror, it was Muammar Gaddafi, leader of Libya. Mustafa began to tremble.

The stories of this sadistic man's pursuits were legendary.

Gaddafi smiled at him, and in a pleasant voice, asked, "Would you like to be free?"

"Yes, leader," Mustafa quickly answered, "I would like to leave this place at once. The food is bad. They beat me. I have no blanket for the night cold."

Gaddafi's sour look stopped his complaints. The Colonel crossed his legs at the knee. He tapped a forefinger on the thigh of his silk trousers. Mustafa noticed a heavy gold ring circled the finger. The ring was shaped into a skull.

"No, insect. I mean truly liberated. Do not think small thoughts. Do not think only of the body. I offer to make you free of your whole life, of who you were and what you are likely to become."

The tapping stopped. Gaddafi settled back into his chair. He rubbed his ring. "If you do my bidding, I will make you not just physically comfortable for life. I will give you a new spirit. You will roam the world with no wants, no needs, no rules, no master but me."

Mustafa was intrigued. He knew there would be a terrible price to pay if he said yes – or no. His fear emboldened him.

"How do I become free?"

Gaddafi pushed the pistol across the table toward the trembling boy.

"Kill her."

Mustafa advanced and picked up the weapon. He turned to the woman. Her pupils were wide with terror. Sweat beaded her forehead. Mustafa lifted the pistol higher. She twisted and bucked in her chair, animal growls escaping from her gag.

He hesitated. "Who is she?"

"An Israeli spy. A Jewish whore sent here by the thugs in Tel Aviv to kill me." He spat. "They send a woman to kill me!" Gaddafi trembled with rage. A speck of spittle clung to the left side of his mouth. Aware he had lost his decorum, he struggled to remain calm. "Only now you will execute her, and earn your freedom."

There was something hypnotic about Gaddafi's manic performance. Mustafa pointed the gun and moved closer to the prisoner. His left hand gathered a fistful of the hair hanging down to her shoulders and he delicately pulled it behind her neck so that he could see more of her face. The softness of her hair stirred him. He was aroused by the woman's beauty, despite her injuries. His penis stiffened.

Mustafa knew he would kill the woman. He wanted to kill her.

In a slow arc, he swung the pistol to her temple. Their eyes met – his afire with excitement, hers blank with despair. With a gentle pull on the trigger, he discharged a bullet into her brain.

The sound deafened him. The smell of cordite and burned powder choked the room. Mustafa found he was breathing heavily, excited in a manner he had never been before. He whipped the gun around, this time leveling it at Gaddafi. His hand did not shake.

Gaddafi stared at him, unflinching. "You know I am the heir to the legacy of the old man of the mountains. When the will of the Arab people fails, I will step from the shadows to avenge their wrongs." To Mustafa, the man seemed godlike.

He pointed at Mustafa. "You are now my assassin."

Mustafa lowered the gun onto the table, reluctant to let its power slip away. He knelt and bowed his head. "Yes, leader."

Gaddafi opened his arm wide. "Come, my son. Stand by my side. You have a unique heritage. Let me tell you about your family."

Mustafa thus joined the ranks of Libya's small, dedicated band of homicidal fanatics, a fellowship of killers pledged to serve Gaddafi's every whim. As his reward, he was well educated, amply fed, smartly clothed, and given a healthy allowance.

From time to time, some small service of blood was required of him by his master. This he did not mind. As Gaddafi had promised, he was finally free. Free at last from hunger, poverty, and obscurity.

Free to avenge his family's ancestral disgrace.

For, as Gaddafi had explained to him the night he was recruited, it was his ancestor disgraced during the torching of *Philadelphia* in 1804.

What Gaddafi and no one else ever suspected about the bombings and assassinations was how greatly Mustafa enjoyed them. In his heart, he knew he would have inevitably picked a dark path even without Gaddafi's invitation. Better a monster on the world stage than a back alley cutpurse.

By the time Gaddafi's regime started to crumble in 2011, Mustafa had cut his ties with his old boss and started to freelance. Decent jobs were scarce. Money grew tight. Boredom set in. He was rudderless. Until the call from Al-Buyid and the one-way ticket to Iran.

Intrigued, he accepted the invitation. Upon his arrival, the gruff Iraqi naval officer met with him and outlined the plan. The mission was suicidal but held strong personal appeal given his ancestor's unfortunate clash with America in the distant past. Al-Buyid appeared confident. Iran was the new bully on the block, one with muscle and panache. Its resources were vast. He decided to mull things over.

In the lobby of a seedy hotel in Qum, he had considered his options. The overhead fan clacked noisily. Grim-faced Russians and humorless North Koreans meandered in and out. The furniture was gray and dingy. The cloth covering his chair smelled of mold. The carpet was frayed and filthy, its once vibrant red, green, and blue faded. Unhappiness suffused everything. And fear.

He shook his head in disgust. *Stupifyingly dull and vile.* The same atmosphere he'd felt in Pyongyang and Khartoum.

He longed for a cold beer, a decent cigarette, a laughing girl. But this was Iran. Pleasure was forbidden.

Al-Buyid entered the lobby. The big man approached and sat opposite Mustafa. Salt and pepper stubble covered his jaw. An elaborate handlebar mustache graced his weathered face.

"You Iraqis love your mustaches. Don't you, Sea Snake."

Al-Buyid ignored the jibe. He leaned in Mustafa's direction and growled, "Have you considered your options?"

Mustafa's eyes swept the room. Al-Buyid noticed the younger man suck in his cheeks. "My options," Mustafa uttered in a bitter voice.

His mentor, Gaddafi, overthrown, murdered, mutilated, and defiled by his own people. Bin Laden taken out by American SEALs. Assad tottering on the brink of defeat. There was a vacuum of leadership in his chosen line of work. The mullahs in Tehran offered to fill the void. Given his family history, Mustafa found their proposed plan quite intriguing. Still . . . .

Al-Buyid enjoyed Mustafa's obvious discomfort. For him, men with options were useless. He sought out and courted the desperate, the abandoned, the ones without country, family, or friends. Men without hope. Lost souls who considered mayhem, murder, and their own violent death a viable career path.

Again, Mustafa spoke, this time to the ceiling, "My options."

The Chechnyans – a joke. Al-Qaeda in Yemen, compromised by turncoats and far too dangerous. The Uyghur, amateurs, and anyway, the Chinese are ruthless, even more so than the Israelis, at neutralizing the opposition. Jemaah Islamiya in Indonesia, too far away and unbearably tropical. The Mexican drug cartels, simply too violent and crazy, even for me. Afghanistan and the Taliban? A shithole run by primitives.

Screw it.

I have no options.

He sipped a tepid glass of tea. A woman glided by several feet away, encased head to foot in a shapeless black burkha. Their eyes briefly met. She looked quickly away. *Even the prostitutes are cowed and spiritless.* He finally settled his gaze on Al-Buyid. The man's placid countenance was unnerving.

"How do you do it, Sea Snake?" He gestured toward the retreating woman. "I could not live in a country where men and women are too afraid to fuck."

"I no longer fuck. I kill. It is messier, but equally satisfying." It was unclear whether the statement was a joke.

Mustafa began to laugh. He laughed until his stomach ached and tears ran down his cheeks. By then, all heads had turned to watch the lunatic and the self-contained, emotionless man sitting opposite him.

Mustafa made up his mind. *What difference does it make? Anything to get out of Iran.* He extended his hand to Al-Buyid, who took it, gave it a quick shake and let go, plainly displeased by the human contact.

"I am yours, Sea Snake."

Al-Buyid's upper lip twitched. Mustafa took it for a welcoming smile.

Meet the new master.

Same as the old master.

*****

The party had lasted longer than anticipated. It was nearly 2:00 A.M. Mustafa had changed from his white waiter's outfit into a pair of black jeans and a white cotton polo shirt. He wore black Nike sneakers and an aluminum diver's watch. There was no need for a gun. Instead, he armed himself with a razor-sharp clasp knife worn in a tooled leather pouch looped on his belt on his right hip. In his experience, wearing knives of this sort aroused no suspicion in the U.S.

He crossed Atlantic Avenue and walked quickly through the deserted streets at the edge of Boston's Financial District. Other men might have found the walk eerie. Not Mustafa. He feared no one. On Water Street, he found a white 750i xDrive BMW sedan parked under a broken street lamp. In seconds, he was in. A spare valet key was in the glove box. *Idiotic Americans.* He started the engine and headed toward Boston Common and the Public Garden in the heart of the city. As he drove down Beacon Street from the direction of the State House, he saw the Swan Boats, one of Boston's famous tourist attractions, glinting softly in the moonlight as if a group of giant prehistoric birds were huddled together asleep on the pond.

His goal was a discrete alley on the southern side of the Common near the Theater District, which housed several of the city's most exclusive dance clubs. Rich, foreign-born businessmen owned most such establishments. They catered to the city's wealthy foreign youth, some of whom were actually attempting to achieve the college degrees they were ostensibly in Boston to earn. American girls frequented these haunts for their glamour and mystery, not to mention the decadent display of wealth, drugs, and flesh. Parking by the front door, he exited the sleek car and tossed his key to a valet.

Mustafa entered License, an establishment he had read about in *The Improper Bostonian*. It was his first visit. A tsunami of pounding European techno-rock instantly engulfed him. The décor was all mirrors, chrome, and neon. The dance floor was jammed with bodies virtually vertically coupling under a pulsating laser show synchronized to the music. Men and women were packed three-deep along the large half-moon-shaped glass bar located to the right of the dance floor. All were young, tanned, and expensively dressed. The men favored Armani sport coats and silk shirts, the uniform of Euro playboys. The women proved that a simple short black sheath, on the right body, held no peer.

Mustafa snaked to the bar and ordered a beer. He drained the glass in four quick, greedy gulps and ordered another. As he drank, he noticed two blonde women to his left. They sat on bar stools, heads bent together, engaged in an intense argument. One of the women abruptly stood and walked away. Her marooned companion turned in her seat to call after her. Before she could say anything, her friend was lost in the sea of lean bodies milling around the dance floor. Mustafa sensed an opening.

"It seems you have lost your friend. Would you like to make a new one?"

He turned his best smile on as he bent toward her, lightly brushing her arm with his. She was in her early twenties, heavily made-up, with blue eyes set a little too closely together for true beauty. Good shoulders. Ample breasts. She looked at him boldly, a seasoned veteran of the pickup scene. He could feel her appraise everything from the price of the watch on his wrist to what type of designer underwear he most likely wore. Apparently liking what she saw, she gave him an encouraging smile.

"Sure. I am new to this country and I am always looking for interesting friends. My name is Svetlana. Who are you?" She spoke very good English with a heavy Russian accent. Unfortunately, she appeared far too sober for his designs.

"My name is Ari. Where are you from? Are you Russian or Ukrainian or what? How long are you here for?" He moved to sit next to her.

"You ask a lot of questions. I am not used to such directness. Do you not have any small talk? In a place like this, I expect clever lines to sweep me off my feet. Am I not worth a little more wit?"

She shook her head, flipping half of her blonde mane over her shoulder as she bent to sip the straw in her drink. Her eyes strayed upward over the brim of her glass to look him over once more, this time considering the value of what she could not see.

He laughed and moved closer to her. He touched shoulders with her.

"I have no small talk. Life is too brief to waste time on words when our bodies tell us all we need to know without speaking. All I can say is that you are beautiful and alone and I am handsome and lonely."

She allowed him a small, sly smile. He knew she was hooked.

"Then I will answer your questions," the girl purred. "I am a Muscovite. I am here to visit my brother who is studying at Harvard University. As to when I return to Russia – why, that is up to you. If you ask to marry me, I may never go back." She giggled at his raised eyebrow.

Soon they were arm in arm on the dance floor. On their third drink together, he tipped a small packet of white powder into her vodka while she was searching her purse for a lipstick. In less than a half hour, he was escorting her up the stairs to the dimly lit alley, one arm around her waist. She was relaxed and laughing, hanging on his neck, singing Russian rock songs and smothering him with kisses as his hand slowly slid up her ribcage and fondled one of her large, soft breasts. To the world, they appeared to be just another drunken couple bound for a night of true romance.

*****

Sergeant Frank Bernier was on a roll again. It was almost three in the morning and he was hungry. He glanced at his companion in the parked cruiser.

"So they close down the Combat Zone and what's left? Lotsa crappy Chinese restaurants that don't stay open late and don't serve any real food. I mean, where can I get a steak and egg sandwich? A mocha frappe? At least when all the hookers were around they had to eat, and there were a few decent places open at this time of night. Geez, now it's nothing but fucking shrimp balls and noodles. If I have to look at another G.D. eggroll, I'm gonna puke."

Bernier had been on the force nearly twenty years. To him, fighting crime was typically a brief interlude between culinary establishments visited on his nightly patrol. The man was a legend in the department for his knowledge of late-night eateries throughout the city. He even wrote a restaurant review linked to bpdnews.com. Unfortunately, while he had a ravenous appetite, his tastes were restricted to what some would call traditional American cooking, meaning anything involving red meat, potatoes, grease, and store-prepared condiments. For him, Italian food was exotic, and he limited himself to spaghetti, not "pasta," and, when adventurous, lasagna. That's what he had as a kid at Mrs. Roselli's house and so his tastes had ossified at an early age. He only had two other requirements for his restaurants of choice: the entrees had to be very large and very cheap, like something featured on *The Phantom Gourmet*. Bernier continued his lesson.

"You're too new, you don't know shit. Over near the old Naked I, which by the way had the greatest neon sign ever made, there was a terrific sandwich shop, open all night. Served grinders, any kinda sandwich, and breakfast 24 hours a day. Half the guys on the beat would meet there. It was full of hookers, snitches, thieves, every kind of lowlife you could imagine. Good food, good place to get information."

Bernier sighed. "It's all gone now. The whores have moved their business online so now you have to own a freak'n computer to get laid. There are no decent con men working anymore 'cause their brains are fried on drugs. Your typical smartass street kid has joined one of the gangs and never leaves his neighborhood to come downtown. And you know what suffers the most from this? The small businessman, especially the all-night, hole-in-the-wall diner. What the hell am I supposed to do now, drink cappa-fuckin'-chinos at Starbucks all night, for chrissakes?"

Bernier left his question hanging in the air and turned to face his young partner. Officer Johnny Quinn had heard it all before. He'd endured similar tirades every night since he started working mids with Sgt. Bernier three months ago. He couldn't understand how anyone could miss the old Combat Zone. When he was a kid, it was a cesspool of triple X-rated movie theaters, adult bookstores, street hookers, junkies, and dive bars. Small-scale riots, catfights between ladies of the night, knifings, shootings, and robberies were the norm. He and his friends would come in from Revere once a summer to cruise the Zone and watch the animals. Personally, he was all for anything that opened the neighborhood up to newer, more legitimate businesses and cleaned the garbage out. He loved Asian food and looked forward to working here every night just for the chance to stop by a new spot for dinner. Hell, you couldn't tell Bernier any of this; he wouldn't understand or care. Jamokes like him just lived to bitch.

Bernier and Quinn were parked a half-block up Boylston Street from License near the Public Garden. They had a straight view up the thoroughfare to where it intersected with Tremont Street. Tonight's crowd was heavy. With all the activity in town, the shops and bars were going 'round the clock. Quinn scanned the crowd periodically for suspicious behavior, hoping to God something would come in over the radio to break up Bernier's tiresome monologue. In the distance, he could see a valet drive up a white sedan and hand over the keys to a swarthy man who had a firm grip on a very loud and very intoxicated young woman.

"Hey, Sarge, what do you think? True love, or does she look like she needs a hand?"

Bernier, his rant on hold, looked up the street to where Quinn pointed. Ordinarily, he wouldn't get very excited about some drunken chick tumbling into the front seat of a Bimmer. Tonight was different. For one, he was mildly racist. He didn't like the idea of some third-world Romeo with nice wheels taking off with a good-looking blonde.

The other reason was more laudable. The precinct had been receiving increased reports of men in bars and frat parties using powerful animal tranquilizers to disorient women and later rape them. It was a problem that recurred every few years. Bernier wanted to catch one of the assholes in the worst way. A creep using that MO had assaulted his niece six months earlier at a college dorm party, so he knew firsthand the pain and humiliation felt by the victim and her family. The only way to stop those crimes was up front, in the open, before the poor woman was trapped behind closed doors and it was too late.

The blonde swayed on her feet a little and lurched against Mustafa. He reached out to steady her while slipping the valet a tip. She was starting to get sleepy and he had to move a little faster before she passed out. He poured her into the front passenger seat and then hurried around to the driver's side and slid in. The car was unfamiliar to him and it took a few seconds to find the ignition and light switch. He punched the engine button and then pulled slowly away from the curb, left turn signal light flashing, and eased into the stream of traffic.

"I want to pop the guy," Bernier stated.

Quinn was sitting up straight in his seat now, watching the white car as it merged into traffic.

"I don't know, Sarge. We don't have any PC for an arrest. We don't even really have any articulable suspicion for a vehicle stop."

"Look, kid, this was your idea. My gut tells me something's up. What you and the pussies on the SJC call an unconstitutional deprivation of civil rights is simply good police work in my book." Bernier pounded the wheel for emphasis.

Quinn tried to stand his ground. "I don't want any citizen's complaints in my file. The guy could sue us."

Bernier was done arguing. The kid had a point. His own jacket was full of beefs, mostly legitimate. No need for another one,

"OK, I don't want to offend your tender sensibilities. If it'll make you feel better, let's shadow the S.O.B. for a while, see what happens. It's a nice night for a ride. Maybe he'll head over to the North End and we can pick up a meatball sub."

The hefty cop settled back in his seat and slouched behind the wheel, leaning against the door, head barely poking over the top of the steering wheel. Quinn recognized this as Bernier's serious driving position, the one he assumed when actually engaged in police work as opposed to bellyaching about the world.

The patrol car slid into traffic a few car lengths behind the white sedan and tailed it. The BMW didn't do anything remarkable. It took a long, slow amble through Chinatown and turned north on Atlantic Avenue, driving in the slow lane until it hit the North End. Bernier, already tasting the grinder, muttered, "There is a God." However, instead of turning into the North End, the car bypassed Hanover Street and made for the bridge to Charlestown.

"I wouldn't have figured that guy for a Townie," Quinn opined. "He sure doesn't look like he belongs around here."

Townies were Charlestown residents. Mostly blue-collar whites. The neighborhood had the highest incidence of bank robbers in America. In most towns, kids grew up wanting to be doctors or lawyers or rock stars. In Charlestown, kids grew up wanting to knock over armored cars and rob banks.

"Hey, that's the beauty of integration these days. You don't know where anyone belongs. Maybe he'll turn back onto 93-North and head out of town. We'll tag along some more and see what the buttwipe's up to. If he hits the interstate, he's out of our jurisdiction."

Quinn marveled that Bernier knew a word as long as "jurisdiction," much less that he could use it correctly in a sentence.

Near the intersection of Constitution Road and the I-93 on ramps, Mustafa turned right toward the Navy Yard.

"This could get interesting," Bernier opined. "What the fuck's he doin' here? Hey, Quinn, whadya think? Is he some kind of history buff doing a night tour of the Freedom Trail?"

The BMW's movements were suspicious. There was nothing in the Navy Yard to attract anyone after sunset. There were no clubs, stores, or restaurants, just lots of long, shadowed alleys, old abandoned warehouses, and empty factories. Bernier slid the car over to the right, doused the lights and watched as the sedan suddenly hooked a hard right. Instead of going into the Navy Yard, it drove under the North End

Bridge and into the area surrounding the Metropolitan District Commission Locks.

This location had a small dam with moveable locks controlling access between Boston Harbor and the Charles River. The locks consisted of two chambers with a metal catwalk running along the top, open to foot traffic, which served as a pedestrian way connecting the Cambridge side of the Charles to the area around the TD Garden.

Because of the $22 billion "Big Dig," a massive late 20th century rebuilding of Boston's highway, tunnel and bridge system, the land surrounding the locks on the Cambridge side of the Charles, once used to store construction equipment, was transformed into Paul Revere Park, a tiny oasis of green abutting the river. At this time of night, it was a deserted and ominous landscape. Both Bernier and Quinn looked at one another.

"Are you thinking what I'm thinking, Sarge?" Quinn's voice was low-pitched and serious.

"Yeah, a perfect place to get laid. Or dump a body," Bernier replied, equally serious.

Both men could feel the adrenalin begin pumping into their systems. They were poised for the chase. When they lost sight of the BMW's red taillights, they quickly parked their patrol car and Bernier radioed in their location.

"Dispatch, Alpha-One-Alpha. Unit 5. Code 19. Out on foot patrol in the area of the M.D.C. Locks. Over."

"Roger Alpha-One-Alpha Unit 5. What do you have? Over," crackled the response.

"We have a suspicious male with a female on the grounds of Paul Revere Park. We're going to check it out. Over."

"Affirmative. Do you have a tag to run? Over."

Bernier turned to Quinn. "What's the plate number?"

Quinn felt his cheeks flush. "I didn't get the tag. I thought you had it."

"Shit!" Bernier was steamed. "We're doing some crackerjack police work tonight, ain't we rookie?"

The sarcasm stung Quinn, but Bernier was right. SOP was to memorize the license plate number, and he had forgotten to do so. He vowed to himself to make no more mistakes that night.

"That's negative for now, over," Bernier spat back into the handset.

He keyed off and slipped out of the car. In his left hand, he grasped a large, battered Kel-Lite. With his other hand, he unclipped the safety on his holster, prepared to pursue the suspect on foot.

"Should I take the shotgun?" Quinn softly called.

"Nah. It's just one bozo. We'll sneak up on them and make sure the party's not getting out of hand." Bernier slipped into the tunnel beneath the Charlestown Bridge that led to the park, Quinn close behind. Soon their ink-blue Boston Police Department uniforms merged with the shadows and they disappeared.

Mustafa maneuvered the BMW down a crushed gravel road, which ended at the riverbank. He parked and turned off the engine, leaving the key in the ignition. The orange dashboard lights faded to black. He sat quietly, enjoying the view. The engine fan cycled on and off with a soft whir. With a flick of a switch, he rolled down his window, letting in the night air and traffic sounds from the city.

The blonde woman lay snoring peacefully in the seat next to him. As his eyes adjusted to the subdued light, he could make out the outlines of her face and see the gold mist of her hair splayed against the car's tan leather seatback and headrest.

She smelled good. It was an expensive perfume that he could not identify. He reached out to stroke her hair. It reminded him of the girls he had known in Amsterdam so many years ago. It reminded him of the bitch who had angered him earlier that evening.

He slipped the clasp knife from his pocket and flicked it open. The stainless steel blade winked in the moonlight as he deftly cut open her dress and then sliced her lacey bra in two, exposing her breasts.

With perverse tenderness, he teased the knife along the skin of her neck. He traced tiny, bloody patterns with its tip over the top of her breasts and up over her jaws onto her cheeks.

The drug had done its job. She did not even twitch as he cut her. Quietly he began humming to himself a Tuareg folk song as the movements of his blade grew more intricate.

Quinn and Bernier walked soundlessly up the track toward the BMW. The white sedan was outlined against the backdrop of the nearby, spotlighted MDC dam and the towering façade of the Garden rising across the river.

About twenty feet away from the vehicle, they slowed their pace. Hunched over and hyper-alert, they crept slowly up beside the Bimmer. They had done this sort of thing many times before. Bernier delighted in surprising couples necking in cars. On a good night, he'd find one or two couples going at it, oftentimes buck-naked.

As usual, Quinn let Bernier take the lead. Besides, he couldn't figure out what was going on in the car. There was some kind of weird singing coming from inside. It was in a language he could not recognize. In any event, he was relieved that it did not sound like someone was in distress.

Bernier signaled Quinn to move up the passenger side while he sidled toward the driver. When Bernier reached the driver's door, he cautiously straightened up.

The curious singing coming from the car continued, the occupants unaware of the cops.

Bernier flipped on the powerful Kel-Lite and yelled, "Police!" The singing immediately stopped. In the moment the light flooded the interior, Bernier and Quinn saw a man hunched over the woman's inert body.

At first, Quinn thought they had been kissing. When the man swiftly reared back, Quinn saw exposed in the harsh light the entire top of the woman's torso. Thin, bleeding swirls of knife cuts tattooed her neck, face, and breasts.

The unknown man's left arm swung toward the open driver side window. There was a shout. Bernier's flashlight dropped to the ground. Quinn heard Bernier scream, together with dull thuds of something pounding repeatedly into the older police officer's chest. The muzzle of Bernier's .40 Glock pistol exploded, accompanied by a dazzling flash of light.

Quinn jumped away from the car, scared and disoriented. He cursed. His eyes could not adjust quickly to the gloom. He fumbled for his weapon and accidentally dropped his own flashlight.

His pistol free, he tried to focus on something or someone to shoot, to decipher the sounds, to figure out what the hell was happening on the other side of the car. He started to run around the front of the vehicle, determined to help his partner, to stop the screams.

As Quinn rounded the hood, the beam of light from Bernier's dropped flashlight showed a terrible tableau. Bernier was on his knees, his pistol in the dirt in front of him. His hands clutched his chest, which was pumping streams of red blood through his fingers, splattering the ground. He groaned in agony as he lifted his head toward Quinn, attempted to stand, and then toppled helplessly into the freshly seeded loam. His fall released a cloud of dust that swirled above and around his body before blowing away in the soft night air.

Quinn fought his panic. He sensed movement to his right. Crouching low in a combat stance, he pivoted and fired twice at the hole in the night where he thought the man should be.

His own gunshots scared him even more. Now fully panicked, he started to scramble toward the lighted locks. If he could make the catwalk that extended across the top of the lock gates, he could cross over them to safety on the other side of the river.

He ran frantically, gasping for air. The soft lawn of the park quickly transitioned to the concrete of the dam. Soon his footsteps clanged on the metal catwalk as he zigzagged across the top of the lock chambers. He could see the Garden ahead and even a few cars cruising up and down Causeway Street.

Halfway across the dam, he looked over his left shoulder and glimpsed a gray shape rapidly overtaking him. Then Quinn felt a stab of excruciating pain in his lower back. His legs stopped working and the momentum of his body propelled him another few feet before he collapsed on the iron catwalk.

Quinn's head faced the direction of Causeway Street. He wanted desperately to keep running toward the white lights and safe haven that beckoned ahead. The fingers of his outstretched right hand twitched and grasped the air.

He could not understand why he had stopped moving and why he suddenly felt so cold. With all his will, he tried to stir his unresponsive body. He failed. His vision dimmed. His brain shut down before he could frame a last prayer. Darkness, fear, and death swallowed him.

Above Quinn, his killer paused for a brief moment, sucking in oxygen.

The sight of Quinn's hand clawing feebly at the ground as death embraced him amused Mustafa. It was always the same, death. Unexpected. Unpleasant. Unwanted. He bent over, lifted Quinn's body, and rolled it over the rail into the Charles.

The corpse splashed into the water. Mustafa gazed for a moment at the ripples spreading prettily across the surface, shimmering in the light. The graceful outline of the Leonard Zakim Bridge looming one hundred yards away added to the view.

A loud noise came from behind him. Mustafa looked up at the tower where the lockmaster worked. The lockmaster pounded the window glass with his fists, shouting. Mustafa neither heard nor cared.

Time to go. The dam was close to the State Police Marine Unit. He risked capture. So far, it was surprising to him no one was in pursuit.

Mustafa calmly walked the remaining twenty yards across the locks and into the parking area behind the Garden. There was no attendant on duty at this hour of the morning and few cars in the lot.

He crossed the parking lot and down a side street. His destination was the Green Line MBTA station, where he intended to catch the T, connect with the Blue line, and ride back to East Boston.

The many bars in the area were still open and doing a lively business. A few drunken revelers reeled past him. A siren sounded in the distance. Soon there were more. Mustafa picked up his pace.

It was late.

For him, the evening's fun was over.

The sun would soon be up.

In a few hours, he had a ship to catch.

And a city to destroy.

~ Chapter 6 ~

July 4, 2012

0430 hrs.

Zach's eyes popped open. The bedroom was black. His jaw was clenched. The scar on his cheek throbbed. He reached up and touched the old wound. It burned.

It was the dream again. Panama. Jungle. Night. Screams in the distance. A gunshot. Butchered bodies scattered along a shadowy trail. An open pit. Thousands of gold doubloons. Drenched in blood. Glistening evilly in the moonlight. A grinning skull looking down at him.

His naked body was damp with sweat. Groaning, he rolled over and glanced at the time on his alarm clock. The green numbers glowed 4:30.

He flopped back onto the mattress. The dream happened at the same time, every time. Four-thirty ante meridiem. The hour of night he'd first encountered death. The minute his boyhood ended.

His shrink called his nightmares PTSD. The doc said they would eventually go away.

Zach called the dreams reality. He knew the ugliness seared into his brain would never stop. The haunting memories that tormented him were the price he'd paid for his stolen wealth. Some days, he'd gladly trade his money for peace.

It was an hour before the alarm would go off. From experience, he knew once he was awake, there was no chance he could fall back to sleep.

He swung a leg over the side of his bed and stepped on a hairy body. There was a yelp. "Sorry, buddy! Didn't see you!"

Ziggy didn't hold a grudge for long. A warm, fuzzy nose poked his thigh, only to be gently turned away. "Easy, boy. We'll go out in a second." He rubbed the dog's ears as he considered the day ahead.

He had to take Ziggy to the dog sitter and return in time to shave, shower, dress, and make it over to *Constitution* on time. That gave him about three hours to work with. His dog sitter, Skip Smythe, a retired firefighter and recovering alcoholic, lived in Charlestown with a disabled daughter. The man was a find. He cared about Ziggy, was reliable, and charged a reasonable fee.

Smythe's home was about two miles away. He decided to walk. The short jaunt was probably the only vigorous exercise he was likely to get all day. His mind made up, he used the bathroom and then slipped into a T-shirt, some shorts, and a pair of Adidas. He pocketed his wallet, grabbed a wad of cash from his dresser, and clipped a cell phone to his waistband. As he shut his front door, a cautious man, he tested the lock. With Ziggy straining on his leash, Zach took the stairs down to the ground floor and went outside.

The street lamps were still on, leaving small puddles of light dispersed along the sidewalk. Zach and Ziggy walked down the hill to Staniford Street and along it to Causeway Street. The city was virtually deserted. A few cleaning crews were out sweeping the streets. As he neared the Garden, Zach encountered a few boisterous drunks heading home after a long night partying. Instead of crossing the Charlestown Bridge, he opted to take Beverly Street and walk across the MDC Locks and through Paul Revere Park. It was a pleasant morning and it felt good to stretch his legs. Besides, Ziggy loved the park and it would be nice to let him run off leash before he was cooped up for most of the day.

On the northern side of the Charles, Zach noticed blue and red flashing lights. A lot of them. Then the wail of sirens started on his right as a convoy of police cars raced across the Charlestown Bridge to descend on the tip of Paul Revere Park. He hesitated. Something big was going on across the river. He decided to change course to avoid the mess, whatever it was.

Ziggy stopped and growled. Ahead, a man was making his way across the lot behind the Garden. The growls turned to barks. Ziggy pulled at the leash, trying to rush the advancing figure.

"Ziggy, heel!" He tugged harder on the leash. It did no good. The dog was in a positive frenzy. Normally, he was a good-natured and friendly beast. Something had set him off.

Must be the sirens.

The man glided past, head down, walking at a brisk pace. His hands were in his pockets. Ziggy made one last lunge and broke free. He charged toward the stranger. A few feet from the unknown man, the hound stopped, barked, and snarled.

The man turned toward the dog and kicked. Zach saw his face. It was the man from *Constitution,* the waiter from last night's party.

Mustafa! The Libyan. What the – !

"Hey, he's friendly!" Zach shouted. "There's no need for that!" Zach started to jog over. Something flashed in the man's hand. Ziggy let out a yelp of pain and scampered off, limping. Within a few paces, he slumped heavily to the ground and curled up. His whimpers were pitiful.

"You son of a bitch!" Zach yelled. Oblivious to the knife, he tried to tackle Mustafa. He missed and sprawled to the ground. The man took off running. Zach got up and went to check on Ziggy. There was a gash in his flank. Luckily, it was not deep. He would live. Zach tied the leash to a nearby signpost. Enraged, he bolted after the attacker.

Zach chased Mustafa east on Causeway. They ran along the opposite side of the street from the main entrance to the Garden, then past the saloons and sports bars on Portland before Mustafa turned south toward Government Center. The race was even. The Libyan had a good-sized head start and kept his lead. Zach settled into a steady lope, keeping pace, hoping the bastard would falter.

At the intersection of Market Street and Congress Street Mustafa paused, and then pelted south on Congress Street toward Faneuil Hall. A Hubway Station loomed ahead near Union Street. An early riser had just paid for one of the City-sponsored rental bikes and was about to mount it. Mustafa shoved him to the ground. He seized the bike, threw himself onto the seat, and took off.

Zach reached the Hubway Station. He helped up the dazed man.

Lightly shaking the hapless fellow by the shoulders, he screamed "Your pass, give me your pass!"

The man meekly held out his pass. Zach swiped it through a bike lock. Nothing happened. Cursing, he swiped again. The green light came on and the lock opened. Zach yanked the handlebars free and jumped on. He tossed the bike pass over his shoulder to the commuter as he sped away.

The three-speed, step-thru, Canadian-built cycle was no speed demon. Zach shifted into high gear, stood up on the pedals and gave it everything he had. He slowly began to close on Mustafa, who had failed to set the proper gear.

Mustafa blew through every red light as he zoomed down Congress Street past Faneuil Hall and through the Financial District towards South Station. After blocks of dodging the few early-morning pedestrians and some traffic, he reached Purchase Street and turned left. It was one-way, heading south. Traffic was heavier. Mustafa pedaled against the flow, careening around buses and cars. He glanced over his shoulder. Zach had gained. The American was less than 100 yards behind.

Near North Street, Mustafa skidded to a stop and looked back. The American was not giving up. Alarmed, the Libyan set off pedaling even faster. He needed a plan, an escape route. Fifty yards later, he banged a U-turn to his right and sped down a steep on-ramp leading into the Tip O'Neill Tunnel.

Close on his tail, Zach tore down the ramp after him. At the bottom of the slope, Mustafa braked hard, turned left and threw himself into the oncoming traffic, pedaling the wrong way north on I-93. Zach stuck with him, now only 40 feet behind.

The tunnel was four lanes wide. It was already starting to jam with traffic, although given the holiday, not as crowded as usual. The low ceiling and eerie yellow light made it claustrophobic. The air was thick with gasoline and diesel fumes. Potholes and seams scarred the road surface. Cars and trucks moved much faster than the posted speed limit.

Mustafa charged on, heedless of the danger, weaving through the onrushing vehicles, braking, pushing off vehicles, clinging desperately to the narrow breakdown lane to his left. At the Haymarket Street on-ramp, he swerved up the slope, heading for daylight. Zach veered after him. Halfway up the incline, a big produce truck barreled down the ramp, its driver oblivious to the unexpected cyclists charging his way. Mustafa narrowly escaped being crushed by twisting right.

Zach was not so lucky. The driver braked. The rear wheels locked and the back of the truck lurched violently in his direction as he tried to squeak by on the left. Almost free, the rear bumper clipped Zach's back wheel. He fell, skidded along the uneven road surface, and came to rest in the middle of the lane under the front bumper of a startled young woman driving a rusty Toyota Corolla. She had braked just in time to prevent squashing him. The woman was visible through the windshield, her hands clapped to her cheeks, her red painted lips opened in a wide "o" of astonishment.

Zach jumped up and dragged his bike free. It was trashed. He tossed it aside and sprinted up the last 50 paces to the on-ramp's entrance. At the top, he did a three-sixty, searching for Mustafa. The man had disappeared.

The mad bike chase had lasted only 20 minutes. They had raced in a tremendous circle. Zach was near the Garden, almost back where they had started.

His right leg ached. Road-rash painted his thigh. He limped back to Ziggy where he'd left him. When he reached his dog, he saw Ziggy's wound had scabbed over and was no longer bleeding. He called Smythe. While waiting for the old firefighter to arrive, he sat cross-legged on the pavement next to Ziggy and cradled the dog's head.

Within ten minutes, a pick-up truck careened into the lot and stopped next to them. The driver's side window rolled down and Smythe stuck his head out.

"Jesus Christ Zach! What happened?"

"Nothing much. Ziggy cut himself on a metal fence. I fell chasing him."

By now, Smythe was out of the truck and next to him. Zach waved him off. "Here's my credit card. Please take Ziggy to Angel Memorial and have him treated. I'm going home. I've got a previous engagement I can't miss."

"Right, your boat trip. Don't worry, Zach. I'll take care of Ziggy." The old man bent and lifted Ziggy, who licked his face. "You sure you're OK?"

Zach wasn't sure. He was rattled. More than anything, he wanted badly to catch the man who'd slashed his dog. There just wasn't time to handle it right now. Calling the police would tie him up for hours. There was no way he was going to miss the turnaround cruise. He decided it could wait.

"Yeah. I'll live."

I'll deal with this later. My way.

Zach jogged back to his place to keep his leg loose. Once inside, he stripped off his soiled clothing and walked naked into the bathroom. First, he brushed his teeth. Afterwards, he showered and shaved. He had a heavy, brown beard. The awkward scar running from the bottom right of his jaw up to the missing lobe of his ear made shaving a chore, more so when, as now, he was agitated.

Undressed, he padded barefoot to the front door. He peeked out the peephole to see if anyone was outside. Assured no one was about, he flung the door open and picked up the *Boston Globe* from the doormat. It was a little game he played every morning. He reasoned every unmarried man is entitled to a few eccentricities, and this one was his. Besides, given the shape he was in, he vainly believed few of the residents on his street would likely complain. Many were young, urban professional, single women.

After grabbing the *Globe*, he went to the kitchen and made coffee. While his *Intelligencia* brand java brewed, he microwaved a blueberry scone from Trader Joe's, his favorite supermarket chain, and poured some fresh-squeezed orange juice into a tumbler. He ate some mango Greek yogurt and then gulped down the juice along with a handful of vitamin pills. The cold from the juice spread through his chest and made him finally feel better.

He munched on the scone as he scanned the paper. As usual, the *Globe* could be read in minutes. It wasn't much of a paper, except for the sports page. The front-page story was about *Constitution.* He rapidly skimmed through the main article and several accompanying sidepieces that discussed the upcoming turnaround cruise and the previous day's festivities. On page seven of Section B, he saw a picture that made him reach for the phone and dial Eleni's number.

The photograph showed him standing with his arm around Eleni, both of them smiling at the camera, glasses raised in a toast, with *Constitution* twinkling in the background. He had almost turned the page when he noticed in the shadows the face of the man he had just chased. Mustafa was not looking at the camera and he was not smiling. Instead, he was staring at Eleni with such a disturbing look of intensity that it set Zach's teeth on edge.

That S.O.B. looks like he's ready to devour her. Who is he? What's his game?

A good shot ruined. Maybe he could get a copy of the photograph and Photoshop the waiter out. He set the paper aside. Eleni needed to be warned.

Her phone rang twelve times. Finally, the answering machine kicked in. Even now, after just being apart for two hours, the sound of her voice aroused him.

Jeez, I must be in love. I'm certainly in lust.

After the beep, he spoke, "Hello! Eleni! Rise and shine! It's your lover boy calling. Eleni?"

It was obvious that she was dead to the world. He decided to let her sleep and left a message.

"Honey, check out the photo on page seven of the *Globe's* Section B. I think you'll like it. Oh, don't forget to send a copy to your mother. It will remind her of what a handsome boyfriend her daughter has. By the way, the waiter in the background. The guy from last night. He's bad news. I'll explain later."

He ended the call and picked up the paper again to study the photo.

The waiter had a lot to explain and even more to answer for.

God help the asshole when I find him.

When he put down the paper, the flashback hit. Panama. He was in the ocean, fighting for air. A huge black man rose from the water. Muscled, arms reached for him. The man's face morphed into Mustafa. A gun discharged and the face disintegrated.

Zach sat trembling. His head throbbed. He'd never had an attack like this during daylight hours when he was awake. It worried him.

A hell of a way to start the day. Am I going insane?

*****

On board *Constitution,* Chief Petty Officer Zajac was busy supervising stowage of provisions and other supplies. *Constitution* was a commissioned ship, on active duty, heading off on a real sea voyage, however short the duration. The Navy had rules and regulations regarding the proper quantity of food and water for her crew and guests, emergency supplies, spare sails, rope and tackle, and numerous other items deemed necessary for her brief journey.

While most of these articles were already aboard, there were always a few last minute additions. In particular, with *Constitution*, proper stowage of the cargo was of concern because its weight distribution and location affected how much water she drew and her trim while under way. The Navy had left nothing to chance. Every piece of equipment had been allotted its own special place, all intricately fitted together to accommodate her antique design and comport with her sailing capabilities. The work was even more complicated because the heavier items had to be lowered through the main hatch and then transferred to the lower decks by hand. It was backbreaking, time-consuming duty.

The outside temperature was in the sixties. Below deck, with little ventilation, the air quickly became hot and stale, and the men and women doing the heavy labor sweated profusely as they worked. On the spar deck, Zajac carefully checked each delivery off his clipboard as his crew reported the task completed. He wanted everything in order by the time Captain Raffington called the watch forward for the morning report.

Raffington slept in the tiny starboard Captain's Stateroom. It was located on the gun deck in the stern of the ship. He had started staying there from time to time about a month before. He loved *Constitution*. Sleeping aboard her allowed him to soak up every detail of her being, giving him an organic feel for her moods, rhythms, and needs.

Not only did he believe living on her made him a better Captain, but he also unexpectedly found he loved the tranquility of resting on board at night. He roamed her decks, flashlight in hand, silently inspecting every nook and cranny, eager to understand the living thing that was his charge. He drifted off to sleep listening to the rhythmic slap of water on her hull, hearing every creak in her old superstructure as she rocked gently at her berth, smelling the unique aroma of salt water, fresh paint, and wood that made her a real ship in subtle ways no steel or fiberglass craft could ever match. Later, in his dreams, he refought her great battles and communed with the spirits of her long-dead captains.

This morning, the flurry of activity topside roused him early. Raffington sat up in his narrow bunk, swinging both feet out onto the deck. Like an old lion ruffling his mane, he shook his head a few times before standing up.

Contrary to popular belief, the two elegant windowed areas hanging off either side of the stern, known as quarter galleries, were not picture windows for the stern cabins. Instead, historically, they were outhouses reserved for the captain and his officers. Raffington did not fancy using *Constitution*'s original privy to relieve himself in full view of Boston Harbor and so ordered a small portable chemical toilet installed in the quarter gallery attached to his cabin

However, there was no running water on the ship and he had to content himself, as did sailors in the past, with washing his face and hands using a jug of water and an old-fashioned basin. A battery-operated lamp was the only other modern convenience. For showers, he had the luxury of returning to his quarters in the Navy Yard, only a short walk away.

Overall, his quarters were remarkably simple and similar to those of his forebears. He liked his monastic retreat. It made his nightly sojourns more authentic.

After washing, he dressed in a Type I MARPAT dark–patterned Navy Working Uniform and black leather combat boots. By the time he finished combing his hair, his steward was knocking at the door.

"Up and at 'em, Sir," called the steward, Greg Freyerhoff. He had been with Raffington for nearly ten years. The two men shared an easy familiarity.

"The officers are gathered on the quarterdeck and ready for the morning briefing. It looks like a fine day outside, Sir. Air temperature is 65 degrees and climbing. Water temperature 66 degrees. Wind is east at 8.7 knots. Sun should be up at 0604 hours. High tide will be at 0715. Skies are clear."

Freyerhoff had been giving the same greeting, with minor variations, for the entire time they had been together.

Raffington opened the cabin door. Freyerhoff handed him a steaming cup of black coffee. Raffington received it, put it to his lips, and drained it in five long gulps. The heat seared his mouth and tongue and the steam made his sinuses ache. He didn't care. The coffee also played hell with his kidneys and the fifteen cups a day he drank would likely give him stomach cancer, but by God, he needed it to get his heart pumping in the morning.

Raffington handed the empty cup back to his steward. "Freyerhoff, I do believe I'm ready for a fuck, a fistfight, or a fandango."

"Maybe all three, Sir," Freyerhoff cheerfully replied.

It was all part of their morning repartee. Raffington patted Freyerhoff on the shoulder as he eased past him.

"That would make for one heck of a party, now, wouldn't it?"

He clapped his utility cover onto his head as he passed through the Captain's Great Cabin, exited to the portion of the gun deck housing *Constitution's* 26 cannon, and sprinted up the aft ladder leading to the spar deck. At the top, he paused briefly to scan the expanse for passing foot traffic and allow his eyes to adjust to the bright morning light that was beginning to creep over the horizon. He pulled himself topside and walked toward the mainmast. His officers were gathered in a knot, speaking softly and telling the occasional joke. As he approached, the small talk ended and they turned, came to attention, and saluted. He was showered with a chorus of "Good morning, Sir."

Raffington snapped back a quick salute and returned their "good mornings" with one of his own, then took a clipboard from his Number 3 and began flipping through the pages, using a small highlighter extracted from his breast pocket to underline key points.

"The morning report, please?" he absentmindedly asked without looking up.

Lt. Commander Peter Germano, a skinny Italian-American from South Philadelphia, stepped forward. He was new to the crew and bursting with pride about the turnaround cruise and Parade of Sail. His whole family had travelled to Boston to watch.

"Sir, Commander Meyerson delivered a healthy, 7 lb. 4 oz. baby girl at 0100 hours yesterday. I received word she's being discharged from the hospital. She named the child Connie, after *Constitution*, Sir." The news caused Raffington to look up. Meyerson had been on extended leave due to the death of her husband, a Marine, in Afghanistan and a difficult pregnancy.

"What, you didn't tell me earlier?"

"She asked me to keep it quiet. She wanted to tell you personally, but I figured the news couldn't wait any longer."

"Well, good for her. I know she'll hate missing today. If this were 1812, I would issue the crew an extra half-ration of rum to celebrate. Hah! It's a little too early for that, and we have a long day ahead. Make a note to order ice cream for supper."

He paused to consider the ramifications of Meyerson's new situation. "Mr. Germano, you're doing a great job as my interim XO. Can you keep it up a while longer?"

Germano grinned broadly and answered smartly, "Yes, Sir."

"Outstanding. I expected you could."

He faced the other officers. "Well, the addition of little Connie to our crew is certainly an auspicious beginning to the day. Mr. Sanchez, see that my steward sends Commander Meyerson a big – and I mean big – bouquet of flowers from the wardroom and crew with special greetings from all and heartfelt congratulations. Any other news? No? Good. I don't expect any problems today. However, I want everyone on his toes and giving 110 percent. Now is the Chaplain here?"

The Chaplain, Lt. Sal Turro, stepped forward. Lt. Turro was not a morning person. His eyes were half shut. Yet every day he did his best to please his Captain. Looking at the group of assembled officers, he lifted his head skyward and prayed, "Lord, guide us this day as we do our duty to God and Country. Keep us safe from harm. Give us fair weather and gentle seas. Bestow upon us your grace and love. Help us this day, by our labors, to remind our nation of the virtues upon which this great Republic was founded. Make this ship, our *Constitution*, a living example, to this generation of Americans and the generations to come, of our freedom, our democracy, and our resistance to tyranny and oppression in every form. Bless us, our country, *Constitution* and the United States Navy."

"Amen," the officers responded.

"Good job, Chappy, now you can go back to sleep."

Raffington's remark elicited a few chuckles.

"All right, gentlemen, let's go to work." The group broke up, each turning to his own duties. Raffington checked the time. Everything seemed squared away. He needed to hurry onshore for a shower and uniform change.

*****

104

USS *Muskie* was moored at Pier 2 in the Navy Yard, next to *Constitution*. Her commander was sound asleep. Around him, the ship, really a small self-contained town of 330 souls, hummed with a life and vitality of its own, completely unlike that of her ancestress nearby.

Muskie was an Arleigh Burke Class DDG 51 guided missile destroyer designed to conduct rapid sustained combat missions in support of America's national interests. As navy literature explained, she could "provide multi-mission offensive and defensive capabilities . . . operate independently or as part of carrier strike groups, surface action groups, amphibious ready groups, and underway replenishment groups."

Muskie carried the world's most sophisticated weaponry. This consisted of the Aegis Weapons System (AWS), which contained the SPY-1D multi-function phased array radar, advanced anti-aircraft and anti-submarine warfare systems, and a vertical launch system for Mk-41 Tomahawk missiles.

To ensure optimum survivability, all-steel construction was used throughout the ship. Virtually impenetrable topside armor guarded vital combat systems and machinery. Crucial shipboard systems were hardened against electromagnetic pulse and over-pressure damage. Finally, her crew was insulated against nuclear, chemical, and biological agents.

In laymen's terms, she could go anywhere on the globe, anytime, and do practically anything, both offensively and defensively. If World War III broke out, *Muskie* was one of the best places in the world to be.

Smartwood received his wakeup call from the control room, just like in a first-class hotel. He rolled out of bed and ambled into the bathroom adjoining his three-room suite. He slept in long johns and kept his cabin perpetually at 75 degrees. He had spent too many cold winters in Maine. As a boy, he dreamed of tropical climes and joined the Navy just to get warm. He detested snow, the North Atlantic, and anything from Maine that reminded him of his deprived childhood. He found it terribly ironic that his last major command was aboard *Muskie*, named in honor of one of Maine's finest Senators.

By the time he had finished his shower, a mess boy had deposited a freshly cooked breakfast of scrambled eggs, whole-wheat toast, and fresh citrus fruits on the eating table in his stateroom. Two local papers and the *New York Times* accompanied his meal. A fresh uniform graced the bed, brass brightly polished. Glistening black shoes sat under his bunk.

After eating breakfast, he logged onto his computer to read the morning's situation reports and evaluate the readiness of his vessel. He answered various e-mail questions from his subordinate officers. After this brief stint of work, he settled back into an easy chair to read the papers and await the time to go on deck to greet his distinguished guests and the media. He tossed out everything in the *Globe* except for the Sports section, his favorite. As expected, the Sox were imploding. It was going to be a long summer.

His taciturn nature made him consider the day ahead as nothing special. He did not like Boston.

106

Never had, except for the shitass Red Sox, who were breaking his heart, as usual. Even in July, the city was too damn cold for his blood and too damn close to Maine.

The only thing he truly looked forward to was putting to sea. He wanted the Caribbean or the Pacific. Somewhere hot. A place where he could be useful. Even the damn Middle East. He hated being a glorified babysitter.

*****

At police headquarter, homicide division for the Central Precinct, Detective Lt. Murphy was aching to go off duty. He had been up nearly 48 hours straight. Two nights ago, the double homicide in the bear pit. Last night, two dead cops and a Russian woman half-dead from blood loss due to multiple knife cuts on her torso. He didn't know which one was worse.

It was nearly dawn and the paperwork he had to finish would push him well past his 7 A.M. shift change. He chugged some flat Coke from a can, hoping the caffeine would kick in, and ate his third Hershey bar of the night. The caffeine and sugar qualified as breakfast.

Technicians had photographed the crime scene and later the victim at Mass General. The digital photos were already downloaded into the department's computer system. Laser copies were printed and distributed to the homicide team. The color photos now sat on top of his desk. He was almost ready to shove them in an envelope and begin typing his preliminary report, when something caught his eye.

107

When he had examined the Russian woman's body at the scene, it had been night, and the cuts on her torso and breasts had been an unidentifiable, bloody mess. Now, in the brightly lit photos, enlarged for clarity, he could see what looked like patterns on her body. This was particularly true regarding the photos taken at the emergency room after her wounds were cleaned and before they were dressed.

He stared hard, trying to figure out what the patterns were. A magnifying glass helped a little. His eyes ached. Christ, he was tired. No one was around. He reached for his Camels. It was a dangerous move. Smoking in a public building in Boston was worse than committing treason. He sneaked two cigarettes in quick succession, hoping to unfog his brain. Before anyone came in and caught him, he opened the window and used an old manila folder to clear the air. As he was fanning, it hit him. He stopped moving.

Jesus, Mary, and Joseph.

He had remembered an old lecture by his BC High English teacher where the class had discussed great non-Western literature. He recalled the cover of the small, thin book he had read for the course. He pictured the writing on the book's cover: the intricate swirls, hash marks, lines, and dots. Odd script. Non-western. Not Asian.

Arabic.

The Russian woman had what looked like words from the *Thousand and One Nights* carved on her body.

He pawed through the papers on his desk and found the file concerning the bear pit homicides. The photos spilled out as he opened it. Again, he used the magnifying glass. They were there, he was sure of it. It was just a matter of looking harder. None of the photos came from the coroner's office. It was still too early for that. The shots were inartful, taken using a flash, the close-ups marred by the blood and dirt that encrusted the corpses. Imperfect photographs, hastily done by someone appalled by the gore yet duty bound to record its every detail. His photographs.

It took some time to find what he was looking for. There was nothing on the breasts. Their faces were unmarked. Thin arms and legs, the limbs of a junky, were untouched. After examining a dozen photos, he found them on their backs and buttocks. Lines and swirls. Dots and curlicues. Definitely. They were difficult to discern but there. Words. Like the ones carved into the Russian.

Murphy grabbed his phone and called the Chief of Detectives who, because of the two dead officers, had come into the station house earlier to monitor the pulse of the investigation.

"Chief? It's Murphy. Look, the MDC Locks murders . . . I think I got something. You might think this is a little crazy. Hear me out."

Detective Chief Wayne Rollins was generally a patient man. However, it had been a grueling night. Homicides in Boston were piling up. It was hard to stay on top of the caseload. He was frustrated and tired.

Rollins grew up in Mattapan, a black, working-class section of Boston. His father was a city employee and his family remained relatively well-off compared to many in his neighborhood. By the time he was a teenager, his block had fallen prey to crack and gangs. His parents did not earn enough to move the family to the suburbs. They hunkered down, a lonely outpost of decency and stability in a sea of filth.

The only ones he saw who tried to do anything about the neighborhood were the cops. The police kept a watchful eye. They worked hard and they cared. His family got on well with them. He kept his nose clean and even made friends with a few black cops at the community center. As a result, the BPD went out of its way to protect Rollins and his family from the encroaching madness.

Grateful, at an early age, he resolved to be a police officer. He did it for all the right reasons – the same reasons most good cops did – he wanted to help other people.

He took every case personally. It showed in the bags under his eyes and the intensity of his work effort.

"Cut the preamble, Murphy. Get to the meat. Nothing in this case can make it any crazier than it already is."

"Well Chief, you remember that seminar you sent me to last summer sponsored by the Feds and Interpol? The two-day gig, first day on serial killers, day two on international terrorism?" Murphy looked around, saw no one, and lit another smoke while waiting for the Chief's reply.

"Yes, I do. It cost me a significant portion of my training budget. I hope it was worth it. What's it got to do with this case?"

"Well, on day two one of the lecturers, an FBI guy, told us about an UNSUB that they'd been hunting for years. The perp was unique because he was both a serial killer and an international terrorist. Kinda like the Bo Jackson of evil."

"Huh," Rollins interjected. "I used to like Bo. Haven't heard his name for a while."

Murphy resumed his analysis. "Anyway, before five or six of the biggest bombings in Europe and Asia over the past decade, usually 10 to 12 hours before the attack – the terrorist attack – the body of a dead woman turns up. I mean, not that finding dead women is unusual – dead women turn up all the time – but after a while it became apparent that the timing couldn't just be a coincidence. Also, the cause of death was the same. They all died from stabs and blood loss produced by intricate knife wounds carved into their bodies. The cut patterns were identified as Arabic writing. It was mostly poetry of some type, sometimes anti-Israeli propaganda, sometimes radical Islamist shit. Very refined penmanship according to the forensics guys." Murphy paused briefly for more smoke. He coughed once, and then continued.

"Chief, that's what I'm looking at here. The photos of the two butchered girls from the bear pit. Last night's Russian blonde. The MO matches. The cuts on them are all in Arabic script. It's the guy. The same fucking guy. He's here, in Boston. And if he sticks to his pattern, something real bad is going to happen very soon."

Murphy heard a whoosh of breath on the other end of the phone. Rollins sounded intrigued. "You sure of this?"

"As I live and breathe," Murphy shot back.

"Okay. Let's think." Rollins took a moment before continuing. "What's going down this week?"

Before Murphy could respond, Rollins finished the thought. "Christ, what isn't? We've got the Parade of Sail this morning. The Sox game at Fenway in the afternoon. The Boston Pops outdoor concert and fireworks tonight on the Esplanade. Shit, that's quite a smorgasbord of targets. How do you see it?"

Again, before Murphy had a chance to answer, Rollins continued thinking aloud. "The Pops concert attracts 250,000 people. It has to be number one on the hit list. Fenway Park, 37,000 people, maybe more. That's number two. The Parade of Sail. I don't think so. This bastard can't be crazy enough to take on the U.S. Navy? What can he do? Sink a few tall ships, maybe? The logistics would be phenomenal. The return minimal. What's it gonna be, Murphy? Make the case."

The onslaught of nicotine had done wonders. Murphy's mind was now clear.

"Chief, I've read the file. This perp's always part of something very dramatic. Big stuff. High impact. Huge headlines. Unexpected. The Pops and Fenway Park are too predictable. I think he's going to hit the harbor. He's after the USS *Constitution*. Bush Senior is on board. So are the VP and the Secretary of the Navy. The ship's an important national symbol. Hitting us in the harbor would be a major in your face move. It doesn't get bigger than that."

Even as he said it, he knew it sounded absurd, but there it was. His gut told him it was the truth. A lot of people's lives depended on his gut. He was certain his hunch was right.

"Chief, trust me on this one."

There was another long-considered pause.

"Shit. You could be right. We can't take any chances. My ass is grass if we don't at least check it out."

Murphy heard a chair squeak at the other end of the line. "Feed this to Interpol immediately. Contact the FBI and the Secret Service. Get me a name and a face for this motherfucker. Get me a list of all this motherfucker's contacts and his known whereabouts for the last year. Put together a team to trace every lead on the case you have. If the operation is as big as we think is, he must be part of a larger cell. Contact all our friends in the Arab-American community. Lean on them if you have to. We need intelligence. I'll put a call into the squad that interfaces with Navy and Coast Guard security about the Operation Sail program. I'll alert harbor police, Special Operations, and the bomb squad and also feed this info up the chain of command."

Rollins glanced at his watch. "Christ, it's nearly six o'clock. What time does the *Constitution* sail?"

"I think around eight."

"Okay, not much time. No time really, if your guess is right. You have carte blanche on this one, Murphy. Let it rip. Pull out all the stops. Make every minute count. We need to find this motherfucker."

There was another pause, and then a final, somber, "Good work, Murph." The Chief hung up.

Murphy knew the Chief was excited. Rollins was a careful man who chose his words with deliberation. He had never heard the Chief string together four clichés in a row and say "motherfucker" so often. It was a new record.

113

He started making calls. A fresh cigarette dangled from his lips. He didn't give a rat's ass who saw him smoking now.

An hour later, a new idea struck him. Maybe the writing held a message? He signed onto his computer and accessed the name of a Muslim scholar at Boston University who often quietly assisted the BPD with sensitive issues involving the Arab-American community. The man, although a follower of Islam, was a patriot who knew that killing in the name of Allah was wrong. He despised Islamic radicals and did his best to squelch their pernicious influence, both at the university level and in the world at large.

Murphy called the number. At the tenth ring, someone answered.

"Professor Maloof? It's Detective Murphy with the BPD. Sorry to call so early. We need your help."

There was a short pause and then a quiet, "Yes. Go on. I assume this is important."

"It is. Very much so. Sir, I just emailed you some photographs from a recent crime scene. Could you look at them? It's writing, I think in Arabic. I need to know what it says."

"Yes. One moment please. Let me sign onto my computer. I'll put you on speakerphone."

Murphy heard some shuffling and clicks and then a groan.

"Detective, I wish you had warned me. These photos – they are difficult to look at. Poor woman."

"I'm sorry, Professor. I sometimes don't think like a civilian anymore. Please forgive me."

"Yes. No matter. I've read the words. They are Arabic."

Murphy was excited. "Please, what does it say?"

The professor cleared his throat. "It is somewhat hard to make out . . . the blood." His voice faltered. After a few seconds, he resumed speaking. "My best guess is this: 'Nail to the mast her holy flag. Set every threadbare sail. And give her to the god of storms, the lightning and the gale!'"

Murphy was speechless. Several seconds passed.

"Detective, are you there?"

"I am."

"Do the words mean anything to you, Detective? I do not recognize them."

"It's a poem, sir, by Oliver Wendell Holmes. It's called 'Old Ironsides.'"

"I see. Well, actually, I don't understand. Why would someone carve that onto another human being?"

"Revenge."

"For what?"

"For everything. For nothing."

"Detective, you've lost me."

"We may lose even more. Look professor, thank you. I gotta go. Oh, stay away from the harbor today, OK?" Murphy signed off and then dialed Rollins.

*****

Al-Buyid walked down the second story hallway of the safe house in East Boston, pausing to knock at each bedroom door and confirm his men were awake and prepared. He wore the typical American uniform of worn jeans and T-shirt, this one saying "Disney World" in faded colors. Bleary-eyed, he had been up half the night, making sure every detail was in place, repeatedly walking through the operation in his mind, searching for a weakness in the plan, some flaw that could later prove deadly.

So far, he had found none.

His neck hurt, his back was sore, and he knew he should have gotten more sleep. As he moved down the hall, he made sure his shoulders were square, his carriage erect. A professional military man, Al-Buyid had long ago learned the basics of command. Maintain good posture. Use a commanding voice. His men should never sense his fatigue or his worry. Tone and bearing were everything, ratty jeans and T-shirt be damned. At the end of the day, his strong will and discipline propelled his men and gave them the confidence and resolve to carry out their perilous plan.

Curses and coughing from the men awakening around him filled the air. A few bodies padded down the hallway to the modest house's single bathroom to expel the nervousness from their systems like men so often did readying for combat. From the first floor, he could smell breakfast being prepared and even hear some laughter.

Good. The men are in high spirits today. That will stand them well later.

At Mustafa's door, he lifted his fist to knock, but instead chose to push it open and peer inside. Mustafa was asleep on the bed. His face was beatific, expressing profound serenity. Al-Buyid watched Mustafa sleep. *If my wife had lived and borne me a son, would he have been so handsome?*

He thought about all his young men, all his would-be sons. Could he send one of his own flesh and blood to the slaughter? He considered his dead daughter.

Were she alive, could he send her to certain death in a mission like this? Even his formidable willpower could not control such odd musings.

Gazing at Mustafa, he felt a momentary tenderness. Instead of barking at Mustafa to wake up, he reached down to shake his arm. It was then he saw the maroon, crusted blood coating the hem of Mustafa's white shirt. This grisly discovery jolted him from his momentary weakness. He stepped back and roughly kicked Mustafa's bed.

"Wake up. Damn you, wake up!"

My son would never have been like Mustafa.

He knew Mustafa's dossier. The Libyan was a twisted and ruthless killer, a man without convictions or conscience, a man with no honor. He was not a soldier.

"Wake up! Where have you been, you dog? You have been absent two nights running? What have you done to jeopardize the mission?"

Mustafa's eyelids fluttered open. In one lithe move, he rose to a sitting position on his bed, crossed his ankles, and rested his hands on his knees.

"I have done nothing, Sea Snake. Your mission is safe." His tone was flat, showing neither respect nor disdain.

Al-Buyid fingered the bloody shirt. His fingertips came away rust-colored. He shook them under Mustafa's nose.

"Then what is this?" he demanded.

"You sent me to work as a waiter last night at the party. I dragged my shirt through some bloody remains on the meat-carving table. I am not a skillful waiter. Do not condemn me for being untidy."

Al-Buyid stared at Mustafa with amazement. In a flash, he extracted a Glock 19 9mm semi-automatic pistol from the shoulder holster strapped across his chest and put the muzzle against Mustafa's forehead. Mustafa heard the safety clicked off.

"Does this bring back any memories for you? You son of a whore, I know everything about you. I know who you are, what you are, and what you were."

Mustafa jerked his head away from the muzzle and glared at Al-Buyid.

"This morning I know you stink of death, Mustafa. On this, our day of victory, you already stink of the death of innocents. Remember, Mustafa, we must act like soldiers. Our actions must be justified. The world will not respect us if we act like beasts."

Mustafa struggled to remain calm. He looked coolly at Al-Buyid. He feared Al-Buyid more than any other man he had ever met. Al-Buyid had the certainty of a saint, inhuman discipline, fearful willpower and a clear moral code, all things Mustafa knew he lacked and would never have. Mustafa possessed only the false courage of a coward and the bravado of a bully. Choosing his words with care, he hid his fear and replied evenly.

"I thought we both worked for the mad mullahs in Tehran, don't we? As for the stink of death, you too have it, Sea Snake. I can smell it on your flesh. You walk hand in hand with death every day. And by tonight we will both visit death on many others, innocent or not." He looked defiant. "The mission is safe. I will do my part."

The two men locked eyes, neither wishing to be the first to blink or turn away.

Al-Buyid needed this man, however warped, for the mission. Afterwards was another story.

"A stalemate then, Mustafa?"

The younger man remained silent.

With his bloodstained hand, Al-Buyid reached out and grabbed Mustafa's upper arm, roughly pulling him from the bed to a standing position. Mustafa did not resist.

"Come, my comrade. Let us go and do what we both do best. Death requests our exalted company."

With that, the two men separated. Al-Buyid returned to his room to rehearse the mission and collect himself. Mustafa went to the kitchen for food. Within an hour, the group had finished dressing and eating and had packed their remaining gear in the two battered Ford Explorers parked in the driveway. They did not bother to strip the house.

The team drove in two groups through the sleepy streets of East Boston toward the docks. They arrived at separate locations and offloaded their supplies onto two nearly identical speedboats, elongated racing craft, which were practically all engine.

Of course, the Chosen One had a third boat all to himself, a very special boat. Mustafa drove the Chosen One to his craft, moored at a pier located several hundred yards away from the main assault force. The two waited together in the car for the phone call instructing them to begin, chatting amiably about the weather as if they were just two friends out for a morning fishing trip.

The phone rang. Mustafa answered. He hung up and nodded to his companion. Mustafa and the Chosen One got out of their car and walked to the boat.

Packed heavily with explosives, covered by a tarp, it rode low in the water. The two checked the craft's gasoline and engine and started it.

Before leaving the house, the Chosen One finished his martyrdom video, to be released online after his death. The team members had all stopped by to thank the Chosen One, sought his blessing, and prayed for his entry into paradise. Now it was Mustafa's time to say good-bye. Mustafa touched a hand to his heart and bowed.

"Allah be with you."

He could think of nothing else to utter to this religious zealot bound for death. What else was there to say? The fool was holding up well. This was no surprise, considering how high he was on hashish and heaven.

The Chosen One unexpectedly seized Mustafa's hand and solemnly shook it. Mustafa tolerated the gesture. The boy's hand felt like that of a corpse, soft, almost boneless, a feeling Mustafa knew well. His eyes were watery and mildly unfocused. The doomed lad nodded at Mustafa, clambered into the boat, cast off, and eased away from the pier. The small vessel idled a few minutes and then putted out toward the harbor. Mustafa returned to his car and drove to join his own boat crew.

At last, it had begun.

~ Chapter 7 ~

July 4, 2012

0800 hrs.

Eleni was late. She had to jostle her way through the crowd to the pier. Boat bag in one hand, security pass in the other, she skittered along in her new white Topsiders, flashing identification in every direction. The sailors and other onlookers parted for her. Dressed in a V-necked, red and white striped jersey and jeans, she was far too striking to detain and obviously accompanied someone important or was important herself.

At last, nearing the gangplank she spotted Zach, who stood on the quay, at ease, periodically scanning the crowd. He saw her at about the same time. She waved to him, trotted over, and gave him a big kiss on the cheek.

"You practically missed it." Zach's voice was tinged with annoyance.

"Well, I didn't, silly. I just missed the dumb speeches."

"And being introduced to President Bush, and to the Secretary of the Navy, and to my friend, Captain Raffington, not to mention that famous newscaster Peter Comstat who is a big-time sailor . . . and . . . ."

He knew she was a celebrity junkie, a secret devotee of *People* and other supermarket tabloids. It was one of her endearing flaws. He couldn't resist needling her about the missed opportunity to schmooze with the glitterati. Her face fell a little, and he realized he had gone too far. Gently taking her elbow, he steered her up the gangplank and onto the ship. A Navy Ensign piped them on board. This quaint ceremony lifted her spirits.

She brightened even more when Zach pointed. "Over there, love. Movie stars. They will be leaving soon. Let's go."

He navigated her along the starboard side of the deck toward the main hatch where most of the guests had assembled. She glanced down to avoid a line and saw his shoes.

"Nice shoes." She knew his weakness for proper dressing. Thrown off by the morning's events, Zach had accidentally put on brightly colored New Balance running shoes. They clashed with his khaki pants, white polo shirt, and navy blue blazer.

Zach ignored the taunt. He smiled and eased her ahead of him, giving her a sharp pat on the bottom as she passed, provoking chuckles from a few of the nearby sailors. Eleni took it good-naturedly and sallied forth to mingle with the celebs.

On the pier, the Navy band was working its way through the third from last piece in its program. As the "Navy Hymn" floated on the air, Captain Raffington, at the helm, prepared to give the command to ship the gangplank and cast off. Before he could speak, he heard the familiar voice of his Executive Officer,

Commander Allison Meyerson, shouting, "Permission to come aboard, Sir."

The cry of an infant followed. Raffington rushed to the gunwale. Meyerson was below, in civvies, holding her new baby in her arms. A bulging diaper bag hung over one shoulder. The Captain was startled, nearly speechless.

"Good God, what are you doing here? You're supposed to be home."

Allison Meyerson was short, broad at the beam and had flaming red hair. No great beauty, she nonetheless had an engaging smile and a keen wit. The smile hid her iron determination.

She grinned at him and once more asked, "Permission to come aboard, Sir."

Raffington glanced at his watch and saw that everything was still on schedule. The band had finished the "Navy Hymn" and was now into "Stars and Stripes Forever." Everyone had boarded. A handful of sailors herded the hangers-on gently off the ship and onto the quay. He had no time for this discussion. Meyerson was starting to piss him off.

"Permission denied, Commander. You are not on the list of approved passengers and you are on sick leave. I have a schedule to meet. We will talk about this in more detail when you rejoin the crew. Mr. Stehlin, secure the gangplank."

In a gentler tone he added, "Sorry, Allison." He gave her a brief wave and turned to leave.

"Goddamnit, Raff, permission to come on board!" Meyerson shouted.

Fortunately, the band broke into the first chords of "The Star-Spangled Banner," muffling her blast.

Raffington paused, stung by her tone, and then turned and ordered Mr. Stehlin to escort Meyerson onto the deck. She and the baby were there in a minute.

"Look, Allison, we don't want a scene here. This is too important a day."

"Gee, hi, Raff. Would you like to meet my daughter, Connie?" She held her baby out to him in her hands and he, the father of three daughters, cradled Connie, instantly smitten.

Just then, an Ensign reported to him, saluted, and handed Raffington a dispatch.

"This just came in from NAVCOM, Sir." Raffington, juggling the infant and confronting the defiant Meyerson, was momentarily distracted and stuffed the dispatch into his pocket. He glanced at the child and then at Meyerson.

"She's a real cutie. And she has one hell of a name. But, seriously, Meyerson, you are not supposed to be here and I have a job to do. I don't want any insubordination."

"I'm not being insubordinate. This is my day too, Sir. I've been the XO on this ship for two years and have worked as hard, if not harder, than anyone in this command to earn a spot in this exercise. How can you deny me my opportunity to earn a place in history?"

"Meyerson, I'm not trying to punish you and I'm not trying to hurt your feelings. Besides, how can I allow little Connie to sail with us? My God, she's been on this earth less than 24 hours. What if she gets seasick? What if you drop her? What the hell are we going to do when you need to breastfeed her?"

"Sir, this child was conceived at this station. I carried her through many months of duty on board this ship, including sail time. She probably has better sea legs than half the crew."

Meyerson barely paused for a breath before plunging ahead. "Sir, you know my grandfather fought with Admiral Nimitz in World War II. My father commanded a frigate at the tail end of 'Nam. I'm the third generation in my family to go through Annapolis. I will not be denied my place in this operation. I will not have taken from Connie the opportunity to sail on this ship, her namesake, on this special day. Sir, think of the thrill it will give her children and grandchildren. Think of the positive image it will give the Navy to have us on board."

Her arguments were passionate and persuasive. Raffington admired her spunk. She was a damn good officer. More important, she was a friend. He found himself relenting.

"All right, Commander. You and Connie can stay. I hope I'm not court-martialed and stripped of my command for this." He crooked a finger at the nearest officer. "Mr. Stehlin, please arrange a chair near the mainmast for Commander Meyerson and Connie. Fasten it to the deck. Create some shade and keep them out of harm's way."

"Aye, aye, Sir!"

He looked back at Meyerson, who was now smiling and composed. Connie gurgled.

"You know, Commander, if the Navy had wanted you to have a baby. . ."

". . . it would have issued me one," she completed the sentence. It was a new twist on an old joke and it made them both laugh. Raffington waved good-bye and headed to the quarterdeck.

"The Star-Spangled Banner" was beginning. Raffington drew himself up to his full height and saluted the colors. He always found it hard to feel truly dignified in a blue wool cutaway coat, doeskin britches and a cocked hat. He would have been surprised to know everyone on board found him a dashing figure, every inch a sea captain from old.

When the national anthem ended, he joined the guests. An á la carte brunch was planned, together with various speeches and awards. Those activities would chew up the next several hours. By 11:00 all the preliminary events had ended. *Constitution* was finally ready to depart. Relieved to be a Captain once again instead of a party host, Raffington took up station near the wheel.

"Prepare to cast away lines!" His command was relayed to the sailors standing by on deck by his temporary XO.

"Cast away lines!"

His new command echoed down the length of the ship.

"Lines away," came back, confirming that the ship was now free of her berth. The tugs eased *Constitution* into the harbor. The passengers lined the rail, eager to view the city as it slid past.

Five hundred yards out, a long string of intricate commands rang out. Sailors scrambled into the tops. The tugs disengaged. Sails were unfurled, hauled into place and secured. As the fabric caught wind and *Constitution* picked up speed, Zach glanced up. Each of the three masts carried a streaming blue pennant. The foremast pennant carried the word "Honor." The mainmast pennant said "Courage." The mizzenmast pennant had stitched on it "Commitment."

These were the three watchwords of the Navy. They were plain, solid words, laden with meaning. They were words Zach endeavored to live by. Important words he hoped his children would respect. He hugged Eleni to his side and drank in the day.

At the next pier over, *Muskie* also prepared to make way. Her giant GE engines were warming up and ready to go. At the bridge, Smartwood paused to light a cigar. He allowed himself one a day, and usually lit up after breakfast so he could savor its flavor and chew on the butt for hours. He clamped the cigar between his teeth and struck a match. It blew out in the freshening breeze before he could cup its flame. A young lieutenant stepped forward with a Zippo.

"Can I light your stogie, Sir?"

Smartwood bent to the proffered flame and slowly fired up the cigar.

"Thank you, Lieutenant. One thing, though. This is not a stogie. This is a hand-rolled Montecristo Blanco, made in Honduras of the finest tobacco in the world, and costs me $120 a box. Cheap politicians, riverboat gamblers, pimps, and frat boys smoke stogies. I smoke a cigar. Learn the distinction, son."

The Lieutenant didn't know whether Smartwood was teasing or scolding him. With Smartwood, one could never tell. Nevertheless, he instinctively chirped, "Yes, Sir," and quickly retreated to the company of his fellow officers, leaving Smartwood alone on the bridge to enjoy his smoke.

Smartwood watched *Constitution* depart. He gave Raffington a long, lazy wave as she edged past

Muskie's stern and out into the inner harbor. He looked down at his own deck and saw the cluster of reporters and other VIPs being welcomed on board by his staff. Spotting the retired news anchor Peter Comstat brought back fond memories of the times he had crewed on Comstat's sailboat in Boothbay Harbor. He decided it was time to be sociable, to do his duty as host, and began walking to the ladder leading from the bridge to the deck. As he descended the ladder and set foot on the deck, an ensign handed him a dispatch. At that moment, Comstat walked up and extended his hand.

"Theodore Smartwood? Captain Teddy Smartwood? The same pup who sailed with me years ago in Maine? By God, you've come up in the world, haven't you?" declared the legendary newscaster.

"Yes, indeed, Mr. Comstat." He grasped the older man's hand warmly. "I think the years have changed us both a bit. For the better, I hope."

Smartwood reached out and took the older man by the shoulder. "Let me show you my ship. It's a remarkable vessel. Come, be careful."

Smartwood guided the retired newscaster along the deck. Between the need to wield his cigar with one hand and navigate Comstat with the other, Smartwood had thrust the dispatch into his trouser pocket, forgotten.

Part II

Taking Her

~ Chapter 8 ~

July 4, 2012

1220 hrs.

Paul Murphy stood unsteadily in the bow of the Boston Police Department patrol boat, *Fitzgerald*. Reluctant to go off duty, he had volunteered to accompany Rollins on the harbor sweep. He had boarded *Fitzgerald* at Custom House Wharf at 0830, together with a contingent of Special Operations officers and Chief Rollins. The Special Ops team members, dressed in black jumpsuits, jump boots, flak vests and helmets, had deposited themselves in whatever comfortable spots were to be found on the cramped and utilitarian boat. Rollins, wearing his usual somber suit, striped red tie, and crisp white shirt, looked out of place inside the cockpit as he conferred with the Special Ops team leader. The roar of the engine obscured their voices as the boat tore up and down the inner harbor.

They had been plying the waters back and forth along the southern shoreline of Boston Harbor now for more than three hours, searching for signs of unusual activity among the spectators and hundreds of small pleasure craft that lined the harbor waiting to catch a glimpse of *Constitution* and the other tall ships. A similar boat inspected the opposite side.

Multiple craft from other local law enforcement agencies had also joined the hunt. Boston Harbor was packed with Harbor Police, MBTA Police, State Police, in addition to the other BPD launch. The heightened threat presented a bonanza of overtime pay for law enforcement and each agency gobbled its share of the bounty.

So far, they'd busted a couple of inebriated boaters. Nothing more significant.

Murphy was now crouched in the bow, field glasses to his eyes, carefully screening every boat for signs of menace, all the while monitoring the radio traffic and keeping tabs on his homicide squad's efforts to track down the suspected terrorists. He had not slept or eaten anything substantial for over 52 hours and the fatigue was obvious. The flak jacket he wore over his wilted suit and dress shirt caused sweat to pour down his back and trickle into his undershorts. It tickled. He couldn't find a way to stop this annoyance or even scratch it no matter how he repositioned himself at his perch. For at least the fiftieth time, he cursed his weight and age.

Every so often, he found himself drifting into a moment of microsleep, which annoyed him even more. He'd finally bummed a couple of go pills from the Special Ops commander to keep alert. He'd just taken the first pill and was waiting for it to kick in.

Earlier, just as Rollins had demanded, by 7:45 A.M. the detectives had succeeded in pinning a face and name to their quarry. Various law enforcement agencies around the world identified the killer as

Mustafa Almari, Mohamed Al-Mari, and similar variants. He was in his mid-twenties. Allegedly born in Libya and educated throughout Europe at the expense of the now-defunct Gaddafi regime, he was known as a ruthless and efficient killer. More than thirty bombings, executions, and acts of assorted violence against government and civilian targets from the Netherlands to South Africa were linked to him.

The one photo Interpol possessed showed a sleek, well-muscled, handsome man of medium height and build. He had black, dead eyes, olive skin, curly black hair and no distinguishing marks on his body. The Joint Terrorist Task Force was scrambled and all law enforcement agencies put on alert. The photo was distributed to all foot patrols, motor units, and watercraft. Naval Intelligence received it together with Murphy's report on Almari's most recent killing spree and the BPD's theories on the suspected terrorist plot aimed at the Parade of Sail.

The threat of a terrorist attack was relayed by the Navy to all the ships in its command as well as to the various tall ships. While the Department of Defense and the Chief of Naval Operations took the threat seriously, an attack was considered unlikely by the Office of Naval Intelligence, despite the BPD's evidence, and the event went forward as planned. However, readiness was moved to DEFCON 4. Marines were deployed to the Navy Yard. Coast Guard and Navy assets assigned to police the Parade of Sail were put on Force Protective Condition Bravo. Personnel received orders to stop and search any suspicious vessels and interdict any errant watercraft that broke the protective perimeter surrounding

Constitution's sailing route. The use of deadly force was specifically authorized.

Murphy, Rollins and the BPD had done all they could. On the water, it was now primarily a military operation. Between the destroyer, the Coast Guard cutters, and the BPD and other launches, there should be enough watercraft to detect and stop an attack. Murphy knew his role was largely over, but he still wanted a crack at catching Almari.

As he saw the various precautions come into place, Murphy gradually began to feel that a successful attack on *Constitution* was unlikely. The odds on getting by the Navy and Coast Guard were poor. Instead, he began to worry again about the possibility of an attack on the hundreds of thousands of tourists who had gathered in Boston from all over the country and the world for the Fourth of July festivities. A bomb or chemical weapon against the MBTA system or on one of the piers crowded with spectators lining the harbor would be devastating. The release of a biological hazard could be worse.

Murphy had called his wife to warn her not to take the kids into the city. She wasn't in. He left a voicemail and texted her to stay away from town. So far, she had not responded. This gave his churning stomach one more gnawing worry to deal with.

He rubbed his eyes and picked up the binoculars again. The speed was working and he felt more alert. It was after noon. By now, the Parade of Sail was well underway. *Constitution* was in the center of the channel proceeding east past India Wharf. It looked to him as if many of her sails had been set, but he still saw large numbers of sailors clinging to the yards and assumed a few sails had yet to be unfurled. Behind *Constitution* cruised *Muskie*, trailing by about a quarter nautical mile, just enough so that she would not accidently steal any of *Constitution*'s wind. Spread out in a V-pattern behind *Muskie*'s stern were *Eagle* and the other tall ships, perhaps a dozen in all, together with a sizable flotilla of official and unofficial small craft.

It was an awesome sight. Murphy relaxed a little. For a moment, he allowed himself to be entranced by the stately beauty of the spectacle.

*****

As Murphy peacefully watched the Tall Ships, Officer Victor Gonsalves of the East Boston Police Department was trying to calm a very agitated Miriam Zolly. Earlier, Mrs. Zolly had seen a report on the television about a possible terrorist threat. When she saw Mustafa's face pop up on the screen she practically lost her dentures. He was that nice boy who visited next door! She immediately dialed 911.

The dispatcher taking the call dutifully listened to the information, mostly incoherent, that she gave. HQ wanted every lead, no matter how remote, looked into. A patrol car was sent to investigate.

An hour later, standing on the street in front of Mrs. Zolly's house, Officer Gonsalves decided to give it one more try. In his most soothing voice he asked, "Now, Mrs. Zolly, calm down. Why do you think there are terrorists living next door?"

"I knew it. Oh, my God! I knew it all the time. See, there's a bunch of them. All dark-skinned, with curly hair. All night long, they come and go at odd hours! They have to be terrorists! Why else would they all be living together?" Her heavy jowls and the loose fat hanging from her bare upper arms quivered as she shouted and gestured towards the house across the street.

Gonsalves was swarthy and had curly hair. He knew that many immigrants, legal and illegal, routinely had large groups of males living together for extended periods in order to save money. His own Brazilian father had lived in such a house for five years before putting away enough money to bring his mother to the States. He found the elderly woman's arguments unconvincing.

"Mrs. Zolly, I'm sorry. I appreciate your concern, really. There's just not enough to go on here. I have other work to do, ma'am. If you can think of anything else, please give us another call."

He was tired of this overwrought septuagenarian and her overheated imagination. He got into his patrol car and drove away without bothering to look at the suspect house.

Mrs. Zolly watched the patrol car leave. Now she was angry.

Just because I'm old and fat, they won't even listen to me... Oh, my God! Oh, my God! I forgot to tell him about the man in the picture!

In an effort to catch the departing police cruiser, her muumuu billowing around her, she began running awkwardly down the street, arms flailing, rubber flip-flops flapping. In ten feet, she was completely out of breath and stopped. Gonsalves' car was long gone. The old woman stood gasping in the middle of the street, trying to regain her composure. Directly to her left was the house where she was certain the terrorists lived. She knew that no one was there because the two cars were gone and there was no radio playing – there was always a radio playing some awful music when someone was at home.

Well, if the police won't help, I'll do it myself!

Mrs. Zolly shuffled up the driveway and climbed the stairs to the side door. She peeked through the screen into the kitchen. No one was in sight. The remains of a large meal littered the kitchen table. Dirty dishes filled the sink. Whoever lived here had certainly left in a hurry. She tried the door. It was open. With a glance left and right, just in case any other neighbors were watching, she stepped inside.

Feeling titillated and brave, she tiptoed around the first floor of the house. She tried not to make noise. It was impossible. The old, uneven wooden floor creaked ominously with every step. Unfazed, she continued creeping about. Magazines in the living room had what looked like foreign writing on them. This excited her even more.

Mrs. Zolly entered a first floor bedroom and noticed a large map of Boston Harbor tacked to the wall. On another wall was a diagram of a ship. Earlier, she'd been so flustered that she'd forgotten her glasses. Without them, she could not see that well. She squinted and shuffled closer to read the ship's name.

On her third step, she felt something tug at her right leg and heard a soft click. She looked down. Near her knee was what looked like a piece of fishing line, which had snapped, and now lay slack against one wall.

That's strange.

She was now close enough to the diagram to begin spelling the ship's name. *C-O-N.* . . .

As she mouthed the letters, the entire house erupted in an enormous fireball. The blast leveled the homes on either side. It left a crater 10 feet deep. Mrs. Zolly simply disintegrated.

*****

Murphy heard a faint boom. He put down his binoculars to see where the sound had originated. A small smudge of smoke was visible across the harbor above East Boston. He picked up his radio and called headquarters. There was no report of anything unusual. He ordered the dispatcher to get back to him right away if there was any new information. When he hung up, he noticed the smoke had grown into a large, brown and gray plume drifting lazily into the clear, blue, cloudless summer sky. It gradually morphed into a blurry mushroom cloud. Whatever it was, it was a good-sized explosion.

Murphy stared without blinking. He found himself sweating even more heavily. As he waited for information, he had a sick feeling this was just the beginning of something he really did not understand and could not control.

~ Chapter 9 ~

July 4, 2012

1233 hrs.

On Al-Buyid's boat, they knew what the boom meant. Their discovery had come much earlier than expected. The premature explosion lent increased urgency to their mission.

The terrorists' speedboats floated in the middle of the flotilla of pleasure craft lined up to watch *Constitution* along the East Boston side of the harbor. It was a happy crowd. Radios blared rock and roll, country and rap. The music carried in every direction over the water. Boaters snacked, chatted, and used binoculars to watch the approaching ships.

Al-Buyid's men pretended to be a normal part of the merrymakers. They lounged around the back of the boat in swimsuits, read magazines, and drank Coca-Cola from an enormous cooler. Two men played cards. One had even gone for a short swim. When the blast went off, every man turned to look at Al-Buyid.

He glanced at his watch.

Attack now, or wait?

He wondered how the authorities had found the safe house so soon. Perhaps they now knew too much and some unpleasant surprise lay ahead for him.

They'd been very careful. It had to be Mustafa's fault. He was a pitiless killer, but a wild card. Al-Buyid regretted recruiting him.

A minute passed. No sirens sounded in the harbor. The Parade of Sail continued to glide past. Everything remained normal.

He casually lit a cigarette and went back to reviewing a map he had spread on the ice chest.

A fluke. They know nothing. We wait.

His men, taking their cues from him, kicked back once more. It was important to stick to the plan.

Surprise was everything.

*****

On *Constitution*, no one noticed the explosion on the far side of the harbor. They were enthralled watching the activity on deck and especially above deck, where the sailors swarmed, setting the sails. The precision and teamwork it took to raise, unfurl, and set the sails impressed Zach and Eleni.

They gazed up as the top men climbed the shrouds and ratlines to reach the yards. The sailors walked along the yards using footropes to their assigned stations. Zach pointed out that the heavier sailors typically stayed toward the center of the yards while smaller and lighter ones edged out along the yardarms to their outermost tips. A command rang out. In unison, the top men released the gaskets holding the furled sails in place. They pushed the sails off the yard, sending the canvas down in a rippling cascade. At the same time, the deck crew hoisted the yards into position by dint of sheer muscle power. They cleated and braced the lines, fixing the sails.

Throughout these activities, the top men clung to their stations using only footropes while balancing their midriffs against the yards as their hands did the necessary labor. This ballet occurred dozens of feet above the deck. Even in the relatively calm sea, Zach saw the sailors above him swing back and forth as the ship mildly pitched and rolled. The higher up they were, the more exaggerated was the motion. He could only imagine what it would be like to be up in the rigging in a heavy sea.

Once a sail was hanging in its gear, fully set, some of the top men retired to the deck. Small knots of sailors remained aloft, stationed on large platforms attached to the masts known as fighting tops. They were there in case of emergencies since it took time for the top men to scale the shrouds and rigging to their assigned positions, even under ideal conditions.

They had been underway for over thirty minutes and almost all three mainsails had been set. *Constitution* gradually accelerated as the acres of canvas captured the wind. Zach estimated her speed at around 3 knots and steadily rising.

Because working the sails required much of the spar deck to be covered with rigging, and necessitated room for the deck crew to move back and forth hauling, slacking, fastening or unfastening lines, the guests were confined mainly to the ship's waist, just forward of the mainmast. Of course, they were free to go below deck, but no one wanted to leave the open air for the confined space of one of the lower decks. The action was topside, and that is where they stayed.

The deck was packed. There were 120 guests and 30 members of the media along for the cruise. Because of the crowded conditions, the guests quickly had the opportunity to become acquainted. Eleni was delighted to rub shoulders with former President George H.W. Bush, who appeared spry despite his 88 years. The other government bigwigs were a lesser draw. Of course, Commander Meyerson and Connie were a huge hit. The press couldn't take enough pictures of them. Eleni, one of the few non-Navy women on board, volunteered to babysit when needed.

Zach didn't care about the celebrities and left the hobnobbing to Eleni. Given last night's fiasco, he made damn sure to avoid Eldridge and Mags. He found an unoccupied niche by the starboard rail near the bowsprit where he could concentrate on the workings of the crew and adjust to the ship's rhythms. There he stood, contented, casting an occasional glance at Eleni as she worked the crowd. Eventually she joined him. She took his hand, leaned against his shoulder, and shared his pleasure.

"What's next?" she quizzed.

"Next? Who cares what's next? It can't get any better than this. Isn't this incredible? It's so quiet. I had no idea an old frigate like this would be so quiet under sail."

"It is serene. Almost spiritual in its purity." Eleni paused and breathed deeply, turning her face upward into the warm light. She was happy to be basking in sunshine with her love.

From the east, she caught a glimpse of something shiny. It was a squadron of airplanes coming in at low altitude.

"What are those?" she asked, pointing skyward. By now, everyone was turning to look at the approaching aircraft.

"Those, honey, are the Blue Angels," Zach replied, "the Navy's precision flying team."

He riveted his eyes on the six speeding F-18 Hornets streaking toward them. They flew in a tight formation at 500 feet above the water. In the distance, the jets glinted silver and gold in the reflected sunlight. Their shadows chased below them like a ghostly escort. Wingtip to wingtip the aircraft hurtled toward the ships, a dense mass of power and perfection in the air.

"Gee, what's next? The Flying Elvi?" Eleni teased. He looked at her in mock consternation.

"Hey, show some respect. This is a Navy ship. Talk like that and you could find yourself walking the plank." As he spoke, the jets thundered over them. His voice was drowned out by their roar.

*****

For Al-Buyid and his cohorts, the Blue Angels' flyover was the signal they had been waiting for. The men stopped their swimming, card playing and other camouflaging activities. They clustered together in the cockpit of their black and gold Cigarette Racing speedboat, anxiously watching the sky, counting down the seconds until the planes swept overhead. The rest of the crowd, both on water and on land, became aware of the onrushing Blue Angels' salute, and eagerly anticipated their arrival. All eyes fixed on the incoming jets. No one watched what was going on at sea level.

As the aircraft drew near, Al-Buyid's driver revved the speedboat's engines. The two 1,350 horsepower Mercury twin-turbo V-8 motors sprung to life with a deafening snarl, loud enough to cause several of the nearby boaters to stare at the speedboat with curiosity and annoyance.

Al-Buyid did not care who paid attention to them. The assault was about to begin. He picked up his handheld radio and keyed the mike.

"Yankees suck!" he shouted.

He knew this particular transmission would draw no attention in Boston. The phrase's double entendre amused him.

The signal done, Al-Buyid steadied himself with one hand. He clapped his free hand on his driver's right shoulder and squeezed. "Now, Amal! Go, go, go!"

The engines thundered as the driver threw the boat into gear. Immediately, the craft sprang forward, clawing though the water at a rapid speed, dodging everything in its path. The second speedboat joined the chase.

Five hundred yards away, their target, *Constitution*, sailed lazily through the morning sunshine, its crew unaware of the radical Islamists moving in for the kill.

In addition to Al-Buyid's boats in East Boston, two other powerboats had been acquired. They were sheltered in Marina Point Bay, a luxury waterfront condominium complex in Quincy, south of Boston. The location was near to where the inner harbor broadened into the outer harbor and Harbor Islands.

The two white Baja 35 Outlaws and their five-man crews had departed Quincy earlier that morning and were idling near Spectacle Island, about a mile east of the mouth of the inner harbor. At Al-Buyid's bidding, they kicked their engines to life and began driving at breakneck speed directly for *Constitution* as it passed between Governor's Island and Fort Independence. There was nothing in their path other than a handful of pleasure craft and two small Coast Guard boats. Like everyone else in the vicinity, the Guardsman had their eyes cast heavenward, watching the Blue Angels.

Before the Coast Guard craft could react, the two Quincy-based attack boats had breached the protective perimeter.

It took mere seconds to reach *Constitution*.

~ Chapter 10 ~

July 4, 2012

1240 hrs.

Mustafa's bright red Cigarette had engine trouble. After a dramatic start in tandem with Al-Buyid, the boat's two engines unexpectedly cut out. Precious moments were lost reengaging the port engine. Despite every effort, the starboard engine would not turn over. Mustafa was furious. His eyes fixed on the approaching Hornets. The time to attack had come, and he was stuck.

More bad luck hit. A Coast Guard cutter slowed down and stopped 25 yards to port. The Guardsmen on board were now watching Mustafa's speedboat, aware of his vessel's apparent distress. He could see the Captain pick up a megaphone and turn in his direction.

"Coast Guard vessel to Cigarette boat. Do you need assistance?"

Mustafa stood and faced the cutter. The vessel carried a crew of twelve. On its bow was mounted a .50-caliber machine gun. The Guardsmen were outfitted in flak jackets and equipped with automatic weapons.

His crew had not yet armed itself. Their weaponry remained stored below or secreted in various gear bags on the deck. Mustafa's men faced the cutter with nothing more than their T-shirts and speedos.

Mustafa's mind searched for a response. He had to move fast. He must not draw any further attention to his craft from the cutter. With one engine dead, he could not easily break from the pack of pleasure boats surrounding him and outrun the cutter. If he stayed put and did nothing, he risked discovery and annihilation from devastating fire by the Coast Guard ship's weapons. He pointed downward and shouted back at the Captain.

"Tools! I just need to go below and get some tools!"

He waved to the cutter and smiled. The officer waved back and lowered the microphone to his side. He continued to watch, as did other members of the cutter's crew.

Mustafa's mechanic vainly tried to fix the starboard engine. Mustafa felt sweat trickling down his brow. The tension was unbearable. He knew he was out of time.

The moment had come, cutter or no cutter, stalled engine or not. With a subtle shake of his head, Mustafa keyed his men to move to their weapons.

Pretending to look for tools, he bent down and lifted a hatch, exposing a lazerette crammed with black nylon bags and army-green hard plastic containers the size of small suitcases. Mustafa lowered himself into the lazerette, which made the deck even with his waist. He bent and opened one of the green plastic containers.

Packed inside was a formidable FGM-148 Javelin hand-held missile launcher.

With his back to the cutter, he crouched and prepared the launching tube. The din of the jets drew closer and peaked as they passed overhead. He worked feverishly. His hands remembered the process by reflex, the result of many hours of grueling training in the Libyan desert. Time spent preparing him for a moment like this, when speed and precision meant the difference between life and death, success and failure.

The launcher readied, he kissed it for luck. From the corner of his eye, he saw with satisfaction the other members of his crew fiddling with gym bags, pretending to open the ice chest, and otherwise feigning routine activities while actually arming themselves with automatic weapons.

Mustafa slowly stood, his back to the cutter, blocking its view of the armed rocket launcher held low in his hands. In front of him, an elderly African-American woman on a nearby motorboat looked at him with a curious expression. He smiled at her and she smiled back, perplexed but friendly.

He then whipped around and sighted the missile launcher on the cutter. The Javelin normally required two men to operate it. It was heavy and cumbersome to hold, and it took all his strength to keep it steady. Several crewmembers on the cutter stared at him in amazement. Their faces gradually registered the horror to come.

One crewman, no older than 20, fumbled to release the safety on his rifle and raise it to firing position. It was too late. Mustafa centered the crosshairs where he estimated the boat's fuel tanks were located. His finger crooked across the trigger and slowly squeezed. The launcher belched smoke and flame rearward and the missile whisked the short distance between the speedboat and the cutter in an instant. It found its mark. The cutter exploded.

Glass, metal, plastic, wood, fiberglass, and body parts shot upward and outward. The Coast Guard vessel disappeared, leaving only a sucking hole on the water's surface, and then nothing at all.

The shockwave knocked Mustafa over. Pain filled his ears and he nearly blacked out. His speedboat practically swamped. A number of men on his team were grazed by flying debris and appeared mildly concussed. No matter – they had survived the first challenge. Mustafa rallied and shouted to his driver, *"Hojoom, hojoom, hojoom!"*

On one engine, the boat blasted forward, barely escaping the cascading debris from the cutter. The driver screamed at the top of his lungs like a man possessed as he zigzagged through the surrounding sailboats and power craft, frantically looking for open water, angling for *Constitution*'s tall masts visible in the distance. Mustafa's men loosed bursts of automatic weapon fire and lobbed hand grenades at nearby boats to daze and confuse the crowd and repel any would-be pursuers. A tall Somali threw smoke grenades left and right to add to the confusion. As they pelted toward *Constitution*, they left a trail of wounded and bleeding bodies and flaming hulks in their wake.

There were dozens of boats surrounding Mustafa's speeding Cigarette. Chaos was everywhere. Boats collided and capsized in their efforts to flee the moving fortress zooming toward *Constitution*. The congestion threatened to stifle their rush for freedom.

Mustafa's driver spotted a narrow opening ahead between two sailboats that were frantically trying to tack to avoid the onrushing speedboat. The gap was the only exit in sight. The driver shoved the throttle up a notch, reaching for every available RPM to give them the power to break through. The confused sailboats haplessly drifted toward one another, closing the escape route. Mustafa and his men leaned forward, willing their boat to go faster, shouting with fear and exhilaration. Ahead, the hole had narrowed to 20 feet, barely enough room for them to squeeze past.

The man working on the starboard engine of Mustafa's craft, oblivious to what lay ahead and fixated on his task, in a final frustrated attempt to beat the dead engine into submission, bashed it with his wrench. The motor sputtered pathetically before suddenly kicking to life. The driver noticed RPMs registering on the starboard engine's tachometer. He shouted with glee and shoved the second engine's throttle full forward, causing the speedboat to vault ahead. Its bow rose even higher skyward with the force of her sudden rush of speed.

In a flash, the speedboat split the gap between the two sailboats. Its sides scraped the two boats as it escaped into open water, leaving a hail of curses in its churning wake. Mustafa's crew looked backward toward the ravaged cutter and the trail of destruction they had left behind. They cheered and fired their weapons into the air.

"Silence!" Mustafa shouted. "We haven't won yet! Get ready for the real battle!"

He moved around the cockpit, exhorting the men to gather their gear in preparation for boarding. The gunmen settled down. They reloaded their weapons, checked their body armor and supplies, and steadied themselves for the final phase of the assault.

Constitution lay dead ahead.

~ Chapter 11 ~

July 4, 2012

1245 hrs.

While Mustafa plotted to destroy the cutter, Al-Buyid's glossy black powerboat streamed toward *Constitution*. In the cockpit, Ramee Bin Faroud stood, legs braced, a Stinger missile launcher resting confidently on his shoulder. Many years ago, almost another life to him now, Faroud had fought the Soviets as a young Mujahideen in Afghanistan. It was a brutal war, characterized by horrible atrocities on the Soviet side, and equally brutal reprisals by the Afghanis. Neither side gave quarter, nor asked for it. Faroud certainly never granted any.

In the early phases of the war, one of the Soviet's principal weapons against the Afghani irregulars was the low-level fighter assault. Russian MiGs, cruising at low altitude, would blast pockets of rebels with missiles, cannon, and raking machine gun fire. In a mountainous landscape such as Afghanistan, where there was often no place to find cover, such assaults had a devastating effect on the Mujahideen. Soviet air superiority severely curtailed the freedom of daylight movement, caused heavy casualties, and drove the Mujahideen from the desert and plains into the hidden recesses of the mountains and hills, leaving the Soviets the masters of open terrain.

That was until the Afghanis discovered and perfected the art of downing Soviet air assets using Stinger missiles supplied by the United States. Stingers were lightweight, portable, extremely easy to operate, and able to withstand the rigors of desert combat. Most important, they were incredibly accurate against low-flying aircraft. The missiles, shot from short distances away, were difficult to detect and practically impossible to evade. Soviet pilots flying at altitudes below 5,000 feet could not spot a lone Mujahideen hidden on the ground ready to launch a missile. Without warning, the infrared missile could swiftly hone in on its target and explode.

With Stinger missiles, despite having no air force of their own or significant ground-based artillery or anti-aircraft capability, the Afghanis recaptured the skies. Without air cover, Soviet ground forces began taking heavy casualties. Slowly, the Soviets ceded the open ground to the rebels and retreated to the cities and villages. With Soviet air and ground mobility destroyed, Mujahideen victory became a certainty, as Soviet morale and resolve crumbled and city after city fell to siege by the Mujahideen.

Faroud was one of the young Mujahideen responsible for the Soviet defeat. At the age of eight, he lost his left hand while picking up a toy that turned out to be a Soviet booby trap. Such tactics were commonly used by the Soviets, who utilized every method of treachery against the civilian population. When the hand healed, it left a declivity, which, to Faroud's delight, provided a perfect perch for the front end of a Stinger missile tube. While American boys played video war games, Afghani boys, Faroud among them, shot down genuine aircraft. By age twelve, Faroud had downed 14 fighters and several helicopters. By the end of the war, he no longer bothered to keep track of his kills.

Faroud's skills became legend. His devotion to Islam and the defeat of the West were unquestioned. Al-Buyid recruited him to play a delicate role in the mission. The time to fulfill that role had now arrived.

While Al-Buyid's speedboat streaked toward *Constitution*, the Blue Angels circled around and now closed for a second flyover from the opposite direction. Faroud sighted on the lead plane. Al-Buyid tapped on his shoulder, and Faroud released the first missile.

On the decks of *Constitution* and *Muskie*, few noticed the returning jets given the exploding cutter behind them. Fewer still detected the missile streaking toward the approaching squadron of aircraft above. Those who did notice could not comprehend what was happening, or dismissed what their senses told them as impossible.

For the Blue Angel team, the possibility of death was omnipresent. They flew supersonic aircraft wingtip to wingtip in dazzling, intricately choreographed maneuvers. The slightest hesitation, the smallest mistake, meant the likelihood of instant death, not only for the erring pilot, but for his squadron mates as well. At the speed they traveled, in the formations they fashioned, and at the low heights they chose, bailing out was not a viable option. While mistakes over the years were few, they invariably involved a fatality.

The squadron leader, Commander Mel Hunt, call sign "Hunter," had been running the squadron for two years. He was born to fly jets. He had attended Annapolis, commanded carrier-based aircraft in three oceans, and graduated with highest honors from the Navy's Top Gun fighter school in Miramar, California. He lived for night landings on aircraft carriers, dogfights, and speed. But he wasn't a fool or a cowboy. Those types didn't last long.

Like other commanders, he had received the last-minute warning from Naval Intelligence concerning a possible terrorist threat. He had evaluated the threat with his superiors and disclosed it to his team. The intelligence received was sketchy. There was no compelling evidence indicating a likely attack of any nature and the probability of such an attack was deemed low. The chance of an assault against aircraft was dismissed as practically nonexistent. Hunt and the brass made the decision to go forward with the flyover. His unit had backed the call 100 percent.

There was one caveat. Normally the squad flew with dummy missiles, no cannon rounds, and no machine gun ammunition on board. This was a routine precaution since many demonstrations occurred over populated areas and armaments would only increase casualties in the event of an unforeseen accident. In addition, the planes always flew in friendly airspace, so there was no need to be combat-ready. However, today the jets were fully armed in case of the need for offensive or defensive action.

Commander Hunt guided his birds in from the west for the second pass. The city and harbor spread out below were a beautiful sight. His machine hummed along perfectly. His wingmen were maintaining position and the rest of the delta-shaped formation was copacetic. All systems were go. The fighters were perfectly positioned to fly directly above *Constitution*, ready to execute a second salute by releasing trails of red-white-and blue-colored smoke to honor the ship.

As the squadron reached final position, Hunt saw a Coast Guard cutter explode ahead and to his right. Simultaneously, his radar signaled an incoming missile. In a micro-second, his radar screeched as the missile locked onto his aircraft. Heart thumping, he visually identified something streaking toward him.

"Incoming! Incoming! Begin evasive maneuvers now!" he yelled into his mic in an effort to save the other planes.

He jerked his joystick back and banked left, pouring on power to climb vertically. G-forces slammed him into his seat. The skin on his face tightened. He sucked oxygen to keep from blacking out. As his fighter arced skyward, the missile slammed into his tail section. The F-18 exploded. Armaments detonated. Jet fuel and metal fragments spewed in every direction.

The other five aircraft never had a chance. The missile was a bowling ball striking the first pin. When Hunt's jet blew apart, a spiraling fireball of debris engulfed the other F-18s.

From the ground and water, dumbfounded spectators watched the lead plane erupt into flames. In a second, flaming chunks of the other five demolished jets hit the water. Traces of the debris splattered the ocean near *Constitution*. The other ships in the formation were far less lucky.

*****

Smartwood stood on the bridge of *Muskie*, his binoculars fixed on the Blue Angel formation as it approached. As the commander of a destroyer, he hated planes. Much of his professional life had been devoted to figuring out ways to shoot them down. Nevertheless, he had to admit, the sight was impressive.

The Hornets drew near. He heard an explosion to his left. Before he could react, the lead Blue Angel aircraft disintegrated, tearing apart the remaining five jets. Instantaneously, tons of hot metal and burning jet fuel hurtled toward his ship. Smartwood spit out his cigar and screamed, "Hit the deck!" as he dove for cover.

One of the fragmenting jets struck his quarterdeck. The plane scythed a path of destruction and trailed burning aviation fuel the length of *Muskie* before plummeting over the fantail into the harbor. It skipped into a cluster of small sightseeing boats, ripped them to pieces, and killed men, women and children.

Smartwood jumped to his feet in time to look back and see hunks of flaming aircraft skim along the water surface toward the v-shaped armada of tall ships surrounding *Muskie*. Debris plowed into ship after ship. Some ignited. Others had their masts or steering gear severed, causing them to lose control and careen into adjacent ships in the tightly packed formation. Blazing fuel coated the ocean.

Three tall ships suffered gaping wounds in their hulls and began to sink. Scorched and burning crew members fell into water. Other sailors jumped into the flame-coated sea to escape shipboard fires. Everywhere Smartwood looked he saw hell and destruction.

Goddamn, it's Pearl Harbor all over again.

*****

Beside Murphy on the BPD launch Rollins was crying and repeating, "Motherfuck, motherfuck!" Murphy had never heard him lose control in the three and a half years they had worked together. For a second, Murphy was not sure what shocked him most: the terrorist attack or Rollins' lapse in composure. Still, Murphy reflected, it was an appropriate response.

Murphy was no less stupefied, but quickly rallied.

"Chief?" he shouted. "Chief, snap out of it. We've gotta help! What do you want us to do?"

Rollins remained too jarred to react. Murphy sat him down in the bow of the boat. Long ago, Murphy had done a tour in Iraq. He knew the look on Rollins' face. He understood the years of nightmares that would come after. Murphy turned and gestured for the helmsman to head toward the center of the harbor. He hoped the attack was over and nothing more was to come.

"Drive forward," he shouted. "We'll pick up survivors!"

The launch turned rapidly and accelerated into the holocaust of torched and gutted ships. Drawing close, they could hear the pathetic cries of the wounded and dying. The sweet, greasy stench of roasted human flesh filled the air.

~ Chapter 12 ~

July 4, 2012

1300 hrs.

Al-Buyid was not finished. He had not even really begun. The Chosen One lingered, waiting to add to the slaughter. As he rushed toward *Constitution*, Al-Buyid savored the imminent arrival of the attack's final surprise.

Ibrahim found he was enjoying his last day on earth. Few men have the luxury of contemplating the cessation of their mortality. He had lived with the knowledge of when his time would come for weeks now. In a way, his impending death had become an abstraction, a decision made, and once having been made, easily dismissed.

Reinvigorated in his resolve by Al-Buyid's lecture the night before, he had no regrets about his chosen course. Fate had driven him to it by devastating the life he had wanted to live. By choosing his own death, he rebelled against kismet and felt a defiant peace in controlling at least one aspect of his existence, even if it was the end.

The day had turned gloriously sunny despite a forecast to the contrary. The hashish in his system heightened the euphoria he was beginning to feel as he soaked up the sun's heat and waited for the signal. He was relaxed, hands on the wheel, engine idling. The drug produced soothing thoughts about what it would be like to see his mother and father again, to speak with his dead friends, to bathe in Allah's love for all eternity.

When the Blue Angels exploded, his reverie was violently disturbed. He focused his eyes on *Muskie*. His brain registered that the ship was on fire from jet fuel. *Fire. How beautiful.* He longed to become part of the fire so he could waft, like smoke, into heaven.

He put the boat in gear and began nosing toward *Muskie*. As he drove, his desire to merge with the fire grew. He began crying and had to wipe away tears streaming from his eyes. In the flames shooting from *Muskie*'s deck he imagined he saw angels, the faces of dead martyrs from the past, family and friends smiling at him and beckoning him forward into their embrace. Eager to join these figures, to be done with the now, he accelerated.

I am coming!

*****

Raffington stood stunned along with everyone else on board *Constitution*. For a moment, he thought the destruction of the Blue Angels was due to some terrible equipment malfunction. His first instinct was to slow *Constitution* down so he could reverse course and aid those behind him. Then he heard a shout from a port lookout.

"Sir, speedboats approaching from the aft port quarter!"

He ran to the side and glanced over the rail. Two speedboats, one red, the other black, were closing fast. At that moment, he heard another call from the foremast's fighting top.

"Sir, two speedboats approaching from dead ahead. There must be ten to fifteen men aboard. They look like they're armed!"

Raffington's mind raced. From his position on the quarterdeck, he took stock. Some passengers milled about, dumbstruck by the aircraft fiasco. Several of the civilian women were weeping. Baby Connie was wailing as loud as her tiny lungs could yell. Many people simply hung over the stern rail staring in disbelief. Others had slumped to a sitting position on the deck, in shock. His crew kept to their posts, but he could tell from their stricken faces that they were frightened and confused.

The only ones unaffected by the surrounding horror were the media. Like jackals, they flocked to the stern of the ship to record on video every available moment of pain and suffering, babbling aimlessly into their cameras and spreading the localized devastation to the world.

At the sound of the explosion, Zach had instinctively thrown Eleni to the ground and dropped on top of her. Now, the two were on their feet.

Eleni was dazed. "What was it? What happened?"

"I'm not sure. I think it was a missile." The two looked one another in the eyes and Eleni grabbed Zach's arm.

"My God, those poor people!" she cried.

Zach knew this was no accident. He had noticed the missile streaking toward the lead jet seconds before the plane vaporized. It must be terrorism.

Americans had died in U.S. waters. Shock and sorrow quickly gave way to anger. Bile rose in his throat. He could not remain helpless in the face of such aggression.

Someone will pay for this.

Zach heard the lookouts report incoming speedboats. He ran to the railing. Instantly, he surmised that taking out the Blue Angels was just the first phase of the attack. *Constitution* was the real target. He rushed to Raffington who was conferring with his officers.

"Captain, we are under attack!" Zach cried. Raffington acknowledged Zach with a curt wave of his hand. Although Zach and the Captain were friends, Raffington had no time for him now and no desire to take advice from a civilian.

"I am aware of the situation, Zach. Stay with the other guests. We're the professionals. We'll handle this." The rebuke caught Zach short. He was not used to being rebuffed.

"All right, Captain. Just let me know what I can do to help."

Raffington looked at him with bright eyes. "Rest assured, I will." He turned quickly back to his officers.

Zach returned to Eleni. "Eleni, it's bad. We're under attack! Whatever happens, stay close to me!" She nodded dumbly at him, barely able to comprehend what was happening. Her hand reached out and Zach grasped it. Together, they waited to encounter the new threat streaking their way.

161

*****

On *Muskie*, Smartwood remained on the bridge, giving rapid-fire commands to his subordinates. He received multiple reports and attempted to assess and contain the devastation visited on his ship. So far, the news was mildly encouraging. The damage was largely cosmetic. The ship's superstructure was slightly compromised and remained basically intact. Automatic fire suppression systems and the fire brigades had already put out most of the blaze. The crew shoved debris overboard to clear the decks. Casualties were minimal. *Muskie* had taken a sucker punch but she was still afloat.

Smartwood was beginning to feel that maybe he deserved a second cigar when his forward lookouts reported the four speedboats closing on *Constitution* at her stern and bow. He instantly grasped the situation. Although outwardly unemotional and unimpressive looking, he had a fine brain and could move fast when needed.

There was no way he could do anything about the boats approaching *Constitution*'s bow. He could not shoot through *Constitution* to reach them. The boats attacking from the stern were another story.

He turned to the closest officer. "Mr. Hathaway, open up on those two speedboats approaching *Constitution*'s port stern quarter. Fire at will, and on the double."

He pulled a fresh cigar from his uniform pocket and clamped it in his mouth. Chewing furiously he waited for his order to be relayed and the firing to begin. His XO approached.

"Sir, with all due respect, how do you know the speedboats are the enemy? Maybe they are just spectators coming to help."

Smartwood looked at him coolly. The man was a fool. He made a mental note to replace him as soon as possible.

"Mr. MacDonald, under the circumstances, I prefer to shoot first and ask questions later."

He turned his back on his XO and picked up his binoculars to watch the action. Within a few seconds, the ship's forward-mounted machine guns opened fire. Smartwood saw the rounds flying wildly past the two speedboats. *Muskie's* upper deck was simply too high above the water and too close to the speedboats to allow the angle of the machine guns to be depressed enough for accurate fire. Smartwood dispatched a Marine squad to the bow with orders to use its M249 Squad Automatic Weapon, grenade launchers, and their automatic rifles to sink the approaching vessels. Meanwhile, he increased engine speed to narrow the distance between *Muskie* and the attackers.

While the Marines ran forward, a starboard lookout reported another craft closing on *Muskie* amidships on the port side. Smartwood hurriedly trained his glasses on the new intruder. A 32-foot Boston Whaler headed directly for *Muskie* at full speed. It rode low in the water.

In a flash, he knew what it meant. *It's the goddamn* Cole *all over again.*

The harbor was narrow. He was surrounded by pleasure craft. Any fire he directed at the Boston

Whaler would likely hit multiple innocents on the northern edge of the harbor, and even possibly some of those on the shore. The motorboat was simply too close and moving too fast to stop. For the second time that day, he bit through his cigar. No choice was optimal. Whatever the downside, he had to do something.

He quickly ordered, "Have Marine Rifle Company B lay down fire over the port rail at that Whaler! Evacuate all personnel from below decks, except the engine room! Sound the alarms now, now, now! Engines, all ahead full! Move it, people, we've got a kamikaze aimed at our belly!"

Ibrahim, at the wheel of the Boston Whaler aptly named *Outrage*, was disappointed that the flames had died down on *Muskie*. Now only thick smoke drifted lazily skyward. To his surprise, Marines suddenly lined the taffrail. Bullets splashed around him.

For the first time, he felt afraid. The genuine prospect of imminent death became frightening, not a source of comfort or release.

Where are the welcoming arms of my parents and other the martyrs? Why do they not come for me?

More rounds punched through the fiberglass hull. The windscreen shattered.

Is this my time? Should I turn back? Maybe Allah has not really prepared me for this moment?

Determined to turn and flee, he tightened his grip on the wheel and reached out a hand to throttle back the twin 250 HP Mercury engines. In his drug-induced haze, he wanted to find Al-Buyid and speak with him about his doubts, to be reassured that his choice was the right one.

As his hand touched the throttle, rifle rounds from Company B shredded his chest. He slumped forward against the wheel. The boat accelerated. The Marines last glimpsed him as *Outrage* passed out of sight beneath *Muskie's* rail. Before the boat disappeared, more than one Marine thought he saw the young man at the wheel peer toward heaven, a terrible look of confusion suffusing his face.

The vessel slammed into *Muskie's* side. A gargantuan explosion rocked the destroyer. The ship shuddered and rose from the water. When it landed, it keeled over sharply to starboard. Then the vessel settled and rapidly began to list to port as water poured into the gaping wound in her hull.

The blast knocked the officers on the con to the deck. Smartwood struggled to his feet. Dazed from a blow to the head, he groped in his breast pocket for a third cigar. There was none left. He patted his trousers and stuffed a hand into his left trouser pocket. It emerged with a crumpled dispatch.

He unfolded the message and read the warning of a possible terrorist attack. His hand and arm began to shake.

Too late. Too goddamn late.

He let the paper drop from his grasp. It fluttered away, joining the other garbage littering the harbor.

He forced himself to stop shaking. All he could do now was try to save his dying command.

~ Chapter 13 ~

July 4, 2012

1304 hrs.

At Al-Buyid's command, a fifth speedboat, left lurking near the rear of the cavalcade below the Mystic Bridge, zoomed east through the harbor. The green Stingray 225SX passed through an inferno of wrecked and burning ships. Her crew of five, equipped with automatic weapons and rocket-propelled grenades, poured round after round into the bleeding victims floating in the harbor and the distressed carcasses of the ships they passed. They hunted down and shot what few unscathed survivors remained.

The gunners on *Muskie* spotted the speedboat and tried in vain to disable it. The speedboat's fierce speed and maneuverability, coupled with the possibility of hitting civilian craft, made accuracy impossible. After Ibrahim's boat exploded, all hands turned to saving the destroyer and there was no opportunity to continue shooting.

*****

On *Fitzgerald*, Rollins was distraught. He loved his country and his city with a passion. He hated thugs and criminals, and the men who had done this were the most despicable scum he'd ever seen. Worse than anything he could imagine.

The carnage around him was nearly overwhelming. Even his fellow police officers, all hardened veterans, were immobilized by the horror. Rollins fought for control. Somehow, he had to stop the terror and help save the survivors. Filled with purpose, Rollins snapped out of his funk.

The green Stingray was coming their way from the east. Rollins shouted to Doherty, Captain of the Special Operations Team. "We're gonna stop him. Whatever it takes."

Doherty was not so sure. His men had Mk-4s and hand grenades. They didn't have RPGs or missiles. To succeed, he had to get close enough to the speedboat to take it out with small arms fire. He was uncertain how to succeed.

"No way, Chief. We're slower. We're outgunned. They can dodge around and hit us from a distance and we can't hit back!"

The din from the launch's engines made communication difficult. Murphy saw the two men arguing and inched back to the cockpit. He butted in, shouting to be heard above the engines.

"We have to do something. We can't just float around out here pretending to be police."

Chief Rollins took another look at the speedboat and the crippled *Muskie*. He glanced at *Constitution*. She was now under attack.

Rollins grabbed Doherty's shirtfront. Inches away from Doherty's face he shouted, "I don't know what will work but we damn sure aren't going to sit on our asses while more people die."

Murphy stared at the two men expectantly. Doherty opened his mouth and shut it. Rollins was the highest-ranking officer. He decided to back off. "O.K., Chief. Tell me what you want to do."

Rollins released his grip and pointed at the green speedboat. He knew Doherty and his team would now obey him no matter the consequences.

"Captain Doherty, it's time to fight back. Get us close enough to that speedboat to blow it to pieces! I don't care what it takes. Ram it if you have to. Do not turn aside! Understood?"

"Yes, Sir! I do! And God help us!"

Doherty elbowed the boat's skipper, Lt. Frank Difinis, out of the way and took over the helm. Twisting the wheel, he aimed *Fitzgerald* directly for the oncoming speedboat. He powered the engines to maximum speed. The launch skipped through the waves.

Murphy felt good to be the hunter and not the hunted. He scrambled back to his position on the bow. He picked up an extra Mk-4, released the safety, crouched, and sighted over the rail. His fatigue evaporated. He was totally alert and fully engaged.

Behind him Rollins yelled, "We're coming to get you, you motherfuckers!"

The fifth speedboat was intent on trashing the helpless ships around her. She did not apprehend the new threat. The police launch closed from an oblique angle and was suddenly less than 500 yards away.

Fitzgerald raced on. Doherty used the wrecked hulks of watercraft for cover. One of the speedboat's crew fired a RPG at the launch. It smacked into the hull of a 15-foot sailboat behind them, leaving another burning wreck. In short time, the two boats were well within rifle range. The Special Ops Team and Murphy opened fire.

The jihadist driving the Stingray found lead plinking the water all around them. No true martyr, he knew his craft was essentially one big gasoline tank. Instead of engaging in a firefight, he decided to outrun the launch. If he could reach *Constitution*, his comrades would save him. The driver gunned the engines and sprinted for a patch of open water so that he could escape the launch, which was close on his starboard bow.

Doherty saw the target accelerate. He nosed *Fitzgerald* to the right. The best chance to catch the speedboat meant intersecting its path at a narrow angle. Doherty gambled the racer had little room to evade him due to the congestion. He picked his spot to cross paths with the speedboat and poured on the power.

In the bow of the launch, Murphy and the Special Ops Team emptied several clips at the fleeing prey. Both vessels skittered maddeningly on the waves. It was hard to aim and virtually impossible to hit anything.

At first, Murphy could not figure out why *Fitzgerald* abruptly switched direction and was heading due north. He soon realized both boats were on a collision course. As the two craft drew close, three men lined up on the speedboat's starboard with rocket launchers pointed at the police launch. The RPGs simultaneously discharged in a belch of smoke and flame. Doherty twitched to the right. Murphy nearly tumbled overboard. The rockets missed and landed harmlessly behind their boat.

Fifty yards separated them. Murphy saw the terrorists scrambling to reload the rocket launchers. They looked panicked. He smiled. One dropped a rocket while loading and had to fumble on the deck to find it.

Rollins appeared by Murphy's side, a .38 revolver in his hand. The launch made a beeline for the speedboat. No more hesitation, no evasive maneuvers. From the launch's bow, the Special Ops team poured round after round at the Stingray. Two men toppled over her side. The remaining attackers jettisoned their rocket launchers and grabbed automatic weapons. They stood braced in the speedboat, directing a wall of rifle fire back at the launch.

A cop grunted at Murphy's right and slumped to the deck. More bullets whizzed by. Some zipped directly over Murphy's head. Rounds splintered the bulwarks in front of him. He ignored everything but the dancing target ahead.

"The driver, get the driver!" Rollins cried.

Murphy looked over his shoulder. Rollins was standing nearby on the bouncing deck. The Chief had assumed a two-handed, crouched combat position, as if at the firing range. In the teeth of the incoming terrorist's fire, he emptied a fresh cylinder at the speedboat's driver.

Rollins' bullets hit home. The driver dropped, letting the wheel spin free. The speedboat arced violently to its left and flipped. It somersaulted a half-dozen times, ejecting the remaining combatants.

Its fuel tanks ruptured. Gasoline hit the hot engine. The speedboat became a tumbling bonfire. *Fitzgerald* veered madly to the left, toppling Rollins. Murphy also lost his balance and landed on top of him. The launch banked again abruptly and then slowed near the burning Stingray. A huge plume of water showered but did not douse the burning hulk.

Rollins and Murphy disentangled. They were amazed to be alive. Rollins smiled at Murphy.

"We did it, Murph. We got 'em!"

Murphy grinned back, breathless. The front of his pants was soaked. He felt the spot. The wet stain was cold. It was only seawater. He was relieved he had not pissed himself.

Murphy looked admiringly at Rollins. "I thought only a mad Irishman would be crazy enough to do what you just did. Are you sure you're not Celtic, Chief?"

Rollins clambered to his feet and used a speed loader to reload his weapon. He snapped the chamber back into place.

"Black Irish, Murphy. The craziest. Don't you ever forget it."

Rollins holstered his revolver and straightened his tie. Feeling more dignified, he slipped back to the cockpit to speak with Doherty. The Special Ops Captain was taking a breather. He had his canteen upended and was eagerly sucking down the last few sips. When Rollins approached, he wiped his mouth and screwed the cap back on.

"Man, I could go for a beer."

"Not yet Captain Doherty. First, let's go see what we can do for *Constitution*. If you do as good job, I'll buy the first round, and you know how cheap I am."

"Roger that, Chief. If it's on you, I'll make it a Harp's and a shot of Jameson's."

"You know, Doherty, you're a walking stereotype."

"And damn proud of it!"

Doherty circled to the right. Once more, he accelerated, this time angling for *Constitution* and the four speedboats that buzzed around her like angry hornets.

~ Chapter 14 ~

July 4, 2012

1308 hrs.

Raffington sent the ship's armorer racing below with a detail of sailors to empty the arms locker. *Constitution* was a commissioned warship in the U.S. Navy. As such, by regulation, she was required to carry weaponry. Since she functioned mainly as a tourist attraction, her arsenal was pitifully limited. The fearsome cannon that lined her decks were just for show.

She carried two Mk-4s, four Beretta 9 mm pistols, two Remington marine shotguns and a small amount of ammunition. Also a flare gun with half a dozen flares for use in emergencies. The armaments and munitions were stored in the orlop, the lowest deck of the ship. It would probably take the armorer at least 20 minutes to retrieve them.

Constitution had a small generator bolted to the spar deck. The power plant provided lighting to the lower decks and operated a speaker system. Raffington rushed to the mainmast and clanged the ship's brass bell to get everyone's attention. He seized a microphone and addressed the crew and passengers. "We are under attack. Four speedboats are coming our way. I want all passengers on the gun deck, immediately. Mr. Germano, get the men down from the rigging and assume a defensive perimeter around the deck. We will fight them off with whatever we have."

As an afterthought he added, "Do not panic. I am sure we'll be rescued momentarily." His voice did not reassure anyone.

Zajac and two sailors hurriedly herded the passengers down the stairways to the gun deck. Raffington ordered the remaining crewmembers to arm themselves with belaying pins, loose tackle and whatever else they could find that might serve as a weapon pending return of the armorer. Germano divided the command into groups, assigning a handful of sailors to each mast captain, and sent them to the railing to await the assault.

President Bush's Secret Service bodyguards approached. Agents Peter Gund and Oscar Choo had been with Bush since he was Vice President. They were loyal, so close to the old man that they had even parachuted with him in the summer of 1997 in commemoration of the day Bush had bailed out of his downed Grumman TBF Avenger as a young Navy pilot in World War II. They also joined him on his recent 90th birthday jump. The former President was like a father to them. They would not allow him to be captured without a fight.

"Captain Raffington," Gund said. "Agent Choo and I are armed. We both have .357 Sigs and five clips apiece. I have a backup .38 Smith & Wesson Chief's Special and some speed loaders. Choo has – what is it, Oscar – a Ruger or a Beretta?"

"A Beretta .32 Tomcat," Choo replied.

Gund continued. "The thing is, Captain, our primary mission is the protect President Bush. We think he is the main target. We will be looking for a way to save him. We will not be able to help protect your crew or your ship. Those are secondary goals to us. I'm sorry. I hope you understand."

It was a tough thing to say. Gund added, "We can let you have one Sig and our two backup weapons. They might help. But we are going to stay in the background and stick to our own agenda."

Raffington recognized these men were professionals. He appreciated their honesty. Their extra guns would certainly help.

"You do what you have to do. We'll find a way out of this."

Gund nodded grimly at Raffington. He turned over his Sig and spare revolver and ammunition. Choo handed the Captain his Beretta. Raffington shoved them into the pockets of his uniform coat. He quickly shook hands with the two Secret Service agents and President Bush. Gund and Choo paused to speak with the Vice President and Secretary's bodyguards. Against the advice of their minders, the VP and Secretary decided to take their chances with the ship. When the conversation finished, they disappeared aft.

"Mr. Germano, who's the best pistol shot in the crew?" he queried.

"With all due modesty, Sir, I am," Germano replied.

"Then this is yours." Raffington tossed him the Beretta and the magazines. "Make the most of it."

Where is the goddamn armorer?

"Aye, aye, Sir," Germano turned and went to his post.

A canister of tear gas suddenly landed on the deck, followed by more tear gas, smoke grenades and several stun grenades. Automatic weapon fire rattled along both sides of the ship. Several passengers and a handful of the crew went down, screaming. Raffington bounded to the starboard rail. Two speedboats, one red, one black, churned in circles around *Constitution* firing nonstop and lobbing ordinance. He couldn't find the other two.

Behind, he heard the occasional pop of Germano's pistol. It was a small and pitiful sound and did nothing to stop the attackers. He steadied Gund's .357 on the bulwarks, sighted on one of the boats, and fired off a few rounds. His bullets had no effect.

Zach had gone below with Eleni to the gun deck. When the fighting began, he hugged her and told her to stay. He ran up the ladder to the spar deck. Germano saw him.

"Go below, mister," he yelled.

"I'll be Goddamned if I'll skulk below deck," shouted Zach. "I can fight. When you were still in Navy ROTC, I was a cop."

Germano appraised Zach. He looked tough. Germano really didn't care if Zach went below or not. They would probably need all the help they could get.

"Welcome to the Navy, mister."

"The name's Zach. What can I do?"

"How are you at prayer?"

By now, the smoke and tear gas dissipated in the light breeze. Raffington noticed a few more of his men down, dazed from the stun grenades, clutching bleeding ears. When he looked over the side again, all four attacking boats had clustered near the bow. One boat on either side put down covering fire while men from the other boats tossed grappling hooks over the top of *Constitution*'s rail. His own men threw whatever they could at them: chairs, belaying pins, coils of rope. It had no effect. Several additional sailors fell with gunshot wounds.

"Everyone to the bow!" Raffington yelled as he charged forward. His remaining men ran pell-mell behind him.

Zach heard Raffington's order to move forward. He ran with the rest of Germano's contingent to the bow where Raffington stood. The Captain had by now emptied both his guns and drawn his sword. He waved it over his head in circles to encourage his men. In his full dress 1812 uniform, cocked hat on his head, he looked like a figure from *Constitution's* mythic past.

Raffington hacked at the grappling hooks. The ceremonial sword's blade was dull and useless. By now, the first intruders were climbing the ropes and at the railing. The Captain stabbed at a man, missed and brought an empty gun down on the assailant's head, knocking him over the side. Around him, his crew fought hand-to-hand, trying to prevent the invaders from jumping the rail and securing a foothold on the deck. From the speedboats below, the terrorists' covering fire remained relentless. The air filled with flying splinters as the bow rail and cathead shredded under repeated bursts of automatic weapons fire. The onslaught became so heavy the sailors could no longer get close enough to heave anything over the side or grapple with the attackers.

The defenders retreated to the waist and regrouped. Raffington advanced to the foremast, prepared to make a last stand. Four stun grenades flew over the side in rapid succession. Everyone, including Zach, hit the deck as the grenades exploded. When Zach lifted his head, a knot of gunmen swarmed over the bow rail, pistols and automatic rifles in hand.

Raffington braced his back against the mast. Deaf and nearly blind from the grenade blasts, he could barely make out the terrorists gathered on the foredeck. The ceremonial Marine Honor Guard who accompanied him at all times was dead, a useless antique musket near his body. Freyerhoff had been shot in the gut and sat on the deck, in shock. Raffington saw at least two other sailors down. They were losing the battle.

He lifted his sword above his head. It struck him as ludicrous when he shouted, "Prepare to repel boarders! Repel boarders! Charge!" Raffington leapt from behind the mast at a dimly seen figure, not knowing or caring what would happen next.

To his left, Zach saw Germano spin as a bullet tore off his right ear. The young officer grunted with pain, staggered and clapped his hand to the wound. A fresh round penetrated his forehead and he dropped in place. Zach seized the Beretta from Germano's hand and charged, screaming like a berserker. He fired at any hostile shape in front of him. When the pistol was empty, he threw it at the closest terrorist, and missing, quickly dodged to his right behind the single 18–pounder long gun mounted in the bow a second before the man ripped off a burst in his direction.

The attack wavered as more attackers thronged on deck. Zach noticed sailors falling back, singly and in groups. He heard a command in Arabic. The invaders switched from automatic fire to single fire. They stopped shooting indiscriminately at the crew. Rather, they took strategic aim and methodically picked off the few brave souls who continued to press the attack.

Zach emerged from behind the chase gun and lunged at a tall man wearing a gray sweat suit. The man easily clubbed Zach to the deck with the butt of his assault rifle and thrust the muzzle hard against Zach's chest. Zach tried to grab the barrel. The foreign fighter ground the muzzle into Zach's breastbone and grinned triumphantly. As if a child, he shouted "Bang! Bang!" at Zach. There was no point to further resistance. Zach reluctantly raised his hands in surrender.

Looking up, Zach saw Raffington fighting hand to hand with another attacker, and then Raffington was down. All firing stopped. The deck fell eerily quiet. The moans and cries of the wounded were the only sounds. The smell of cordite, blood, vomit, and sweat hung in the air.

His captor grabbed Zach by the shoulders and roughly dragged him to his feet. The invaders prodded and shoved Zach and the remaining members toward the main hatch cover. Other jihadists brought the passengers up from below. They separated the passengers and sailors, counting heads.

Zach surveyed the carnage. He ticked off at least seven servicemen dead, including all the junior officers. Captain Raffington made eight casualties. Behind him, the armorer lay sprawled on the deck near

179

the companion. The weapons and ammunition he had retrieved were scattered near his body, unused. Near the larboard cathead, the bodies of two terrorists were crumpled. Another gunman hung over a nearby carronade.

He was glad to see enemy dead.

Good. I hope you burn in hell.

*****

By the time the automatic weapon fire began in earnest and the first stun grenades landed, Gund and Choo were halfway to the rear stair hatchway leading down a deck. They hurled Bush to the ground and covered him with their bodies.

"Time to go, Sir," Choo shouted into the former President's ear.

Bush struggled to sit up. "Time to go? Heck, what do you mean time to go? Not goin' anywhere. C'mon. Let's fight."

Gund and Choo admired the old man's spunk but they could not risk having him captured. Gund spoke, "Sir, you know they are after you. Do you want to be taken hostage? Think how that would look to the country and the world. We cannot let them get you, Sir. You are too important. They can't have that victory."

Bush's face wrestled with emotion. He gritted his jaw.

"All right. Let's get on with it."

Gund and Choo lifted Bush up and hustled him down the ladder aft of the capstan leading to the gun deck. They ran along its length, one man on either side of the President, heading toward the captain's quarters in the ship's stern. Along the way, Bush tried to stop and console the passengers. He shouted words of encouragement to them as his bodyguards dragged him through the throng. At the portside door to the Captain's Great Cabin, he turned for one last moment and waved a sad good-bye. Words failed him. Gund gently pushed the old man into the cabin.

The sound of fighting was concentrated near the front of the ship. Gund and Choo skirted the long mess table and entered the Captain's State Room on the starboard side. The cabin was very narrow and sparsely furnished. They crossed it and ducked into the quarter gallery, containing the Captain's privy. The tiny space was cramped. Three arched windows gave them a fine view of the harbor. No terrorists were in sight. They saw a police launch gaining on them. Gund and Choo nodded at each other. Gund aimed his pistol at the center window and fired off a clip. They kicked out the remaining broken glass and splintered wood, making a large hole.

The launch drew closer. The fighting toward the bow reached a crescendo. Gund sensed the battle was near its inevitable climax in favor of the invaders. He turned to President Bush.

"Ready, Sir?"

Bush gave him the thumbs up sign. "If only Barbara could see me now." He held his nose and jumped out the window.

Gund and Choo were right behind him.

The driver in Mustafa's red speedboat, which bobbed at the bow, sensed movement near the stern. To his surprise, three bodies hit the water in quick succession. His compatriots had gone over the top. There was no need for him to remain in place. He pushed off the hull and gunned for the isolated figures bobbing in the chop. He accelerated, determined to run them down.

From the opposite direction, the Boston Police Department launch *Fitzgerald* barreled toward *Constitution* at full speed. The Special Ops team in its bow opened up on the red speedboat. Choo pushed Bush's head underwater for protection as the bullets flew overhead. The speedboat's driver quickly reconsidered and circled back to *Constitution's* bow. It was a mistake. The operator had miscalculated.

The two Coast Guard cutters the Quincy-based terrorist team had evaded earlier were closing in on *Constitution*'s bow. By now, the drivers of the other three speedboats had abandoned their craft and climbed on board *Constitution*. The Coast Guard gun crews let loose a withering barrage at the red speedboat, which was alone in the water. The rest of the enemy gunmen, engaged in mopping up operations on board *Constitution,* were unaware of the cutters, and failed to come to their comrade's aid. Trapped, the crimson speedboat sped north away from *Constitution*. It tried to outrun the hail of machine gun fire, but caught between the pincers of the two cutters, it failed. The speedboat exploded in a ball of flame.

Al-Buyid heard the explosion and charged to the rail. He had been one of the last attackers to board and was busy organizing the takeover. He saw the two cutters.

"Rockets, now!" he screamed and pointed. Two of his men took up positions and fired in the direction of the cutters. The Coasties, having successfully destroyed the red speedboat, broke off the attack.

A quarter mile behind *Constitution*, *Fitzgerald* came alongside the three swimmers. Murphy reached out, grasped one of the men by the arm, and hauled him into the launch. When the person, obviously an older gentleman, was safely inside, Murphy looked at him, astonished.

"Welcome aboard, Mr. President," he stammered.

Bush tilted his head to clear water from one ear. Straightening himself, with a wry smile, he replied, "Massachusetts sure is hard on Republicans, isn't it?"

~ Chapter 15 ~

July 4, 2012

1402 hrs.

Raffington landed on his hands and knees at Al-Buyid's feet. A few of Al-Buyid's men had beaten him and his face was bruised and puffy from the blows. He had lost his cocked hat. His fancy dress uniform was stained with blood and sweat. He hardly cut the same dashing figure he was when the battle started. Defiant, he struggled to rise. Once up, he glared at Al-Buyid.

The Navy crew and passengers stood sullenly behind Raffington. The terrorists surrounded them on all sides. They numbered sixteen. In high spirits because of their victory, the killers stood relaxed, weapons at the ready.

Germano and the other junior officers had perished in the struggle to save the ship. *Constitution*'s remaining non-commissioned officer, CPO Zajac, pushed through the captives and steadied the Captain. Al-Buyid glared at Zajac but did not try to stop him.

Mustafa made his report to Al-Buyid. "Sea Snake, we lost nine, including everyone in Hakim's boat and Mustafa's driver."

He did not include Ibrahim in the tally. The suicide bomber was considered dead before the mission had begun.

"Our provisions and munitions are on board. *Constitution*'s crew lost twenty-four, including its second in command and all the junior officers. Captain Raffington, as you see, is wounded. It is not fatal. There are seventeen other casualties in the crew. Most should survive."

"What about Bush?" Al-Buyid demanded.

Mustafa hesitated, unsure how to break the news. "The old dog got away. The coward jumped off the ship through a window."

Mustafa spat on the deck in contempt. "We captured the Vice President and the Secretary of the Navy. At least they tried to fight."

Al-Buyid wanted Bush. His loss was a disappointment, fortunately the only one, so far. The plan had worked well. He had anticipated at least 50 percent casualties on his end. They had done much better than expected.

Constitution was his. They had plenty of important hostages. Years of warfare had long ago taught him that all victories were relative, that no victory was ever truly complete or without a price. He was content. It was time to move ahead to the next phase.

"We have done heroic work here today, Mustafa." To his men he shouted in Arabic, "Good work, comrades. I am pleased."

The men fired several celebratory rounds in the air and whooped in triumph. Al-Buyid stepped forward to address the hostages.

"You are now prisoners of the Islamic Republic of Iran and its leader, Mahmoud Ahmadinejad." Curses and jeers greeted him.

"Silence! The next to speak will be killed." The threat had its intended effect. The hostages had no reason to doubt his word.

Al-Buyid turned to Raffington. Pointing to the United States flag, he ordered,

"Take down that rag."

Raffington bristled and drew himself to attention. His voice, filtered through teeth clenched with pain, was choked with emotion. "My name is John Raffington. I am a Captain in the United States Navy. My serial number is 237-14-7901. Under Article 6 of the Geneva Convention . . . ."

Al-Buyid cut him short. "Captain, I said take down that piece of filth." He stared at Raffington, hating him but admiring the man's courage. It was crucial to break him in front of his men.

"I'll burn in hell before I take down that flag or order any of my men to do so."

Raffington's voice was rock hard. Al-Buyid could feel a surge of excitement in the hostages. If given false hope, he feared they would be tempted to rush his men. He let a moment pass. While waiting, he closed his eyes and listened to the soft swoosh of the ship as it knifed through the waves and the occasional cry of a seagull in the distance.

Al-Buyid snapped his eyes open. "So be it."

He drew his pistol and shot Raffington through the right kneecap. Raffington collapsed to the deck, writhing in pain. Zajac bent to his side and pressed a hand to the Captain's wound to contain the bleeding.

Mustafa reached behind his back and extracted a whip from his waistband. It was an ancient cat-o-nine-tails usually kept in a display box in the Captain's Great Cabin. Mustafa had grabbed it while searching the ship for fugitives. In one lithe move, he stepped forward and brought the whip down on Zajac's back.

The nine knotted cotton cord thongs of the whip whistled as they descended on the helpless sailor. There was a sick slapping sound. Zajac cried out in pain and rolled away from Raffington. The back of his uniform blouse was torn and bloodstained where the knots from the whip tore through cloth and lacerated flesh. The hostages let out a collective gasp at the unexpected savagery of the attack. Mustafa landed several more blows before Al-Buyid called him off.

Pointing at Zajac, Al-Buyid ordered, "You! Stand up. You are the new Captain. Now take down that fucking piece of shit you call a flag. If you do not take it down, I will order my men to shoot you and execute anyone who refuses, starting with Captain Raffington."

Zajac, doubled over with pain, glared at Al-Buyid. His back felt like it was on fire. He bit his cheek in order to stifle the urge to shout. Never in his life had he wanted to kill another human being more. Before Zajac could speak, Zach stepped forward.

"I'll take it down."

Al-Buyid did not recognize Zach. *A year of surveillance and here was a new, unknown player. Always there are surprises, no matter how good the intelligence.*

The Iraqi considered the man in front of him. He looked strong and tough.

"Why do you volunteer?"

187

"It's simple. These are Navy men. You can't ask them to haul down their flag. They would rather die first. It's their duty. I'm a civilian. I'll handle it. You don't need to kill anyone."

Already I have a hostage willing to help. A spineless American. A weakling.

Although Al-Buyid despised Zach, the man might be useful.

Mustafa laughed. "I have met this one before." He twitched the whip in Zach's direction as if ready to strike. "Look at me! How is your pup? Did he live?"

Zach and Mustafa locked eyes. Zach did not reply. Mustafa was vermin. He wanted to exterminate him. His eyes said it all.

The exchange puzzled Al-Buyid. Some odd intimacy obviously bonded the two men. He asked in Arabic. "He does not seem like much, Mustafa. Who is he?"

"A rich American fool I met once at a party." He shook the cat in Zach's face. A few drops of Zajac's blood splattered Zach's shirt. Zach did not flinch, which angered Mustafa. "Later I will kill him and take his woman. Until then, Sea Snake, he is yours to use."

Al-Buyid chose to ignore Mustafa's blustering. He stepped forward and prodded Zach in the chest with the barrel of his pistol. "Proceed."

Zach walked slowly to where the flag hung in the stern. He unfastened the line and hauled it down, gathering it carefully in his arms. It was the saddest thing he had ever done. He could feel the eyes of the crew and hostages on him and hoped they understood he was trying to save lives, not betray them. He also wanted to buy time. Time, in every hostage situation, is the hostage's friend.

Zach walked back to Al-Buyid and held out the crumpled flag. As he did so, he stepped close to Al-Buyid and Mustafa and whispered, "I'll haul it back up after I kill you both."

The gunman nearest Zach overheard the threat and drove the butt of his Kalashnikov into Zach's stomach, dropping him to the deck. He then booted Zach in the head.

Al-Buyid bent and took the flag from Zach's hands. It was big and heavy. He bundled it into a ball and handed it to Mustafa, who strutted to the rail and flung the flag as far overboard as he could throw it.

The wind caught the fabric as it fell. For a brief moment, the flag unfurled and hung lazily in the air before it drifted into the water. Slowly, the red, white, and blue colors faded from sight as the ocean closed over it. Within seconds, the stars and stripes disappeared completely beneath the waves.

Mustafa returned and nudged a backpack near Al-Buyid's feet. A sliver of bright green fabric peeked from its partially fastened top.

"What about this, Sea Snake?"

"Yes, I almost forgot," he smiled. "Take care of it."

Mustafa opened the pack. He pulled out an oversized flag, green with a yellow star and crescent emblazoned in its center. Mustafa strode to the stern with one of his men and they ran up the banner. The wind tugged it open, causing it to snap in the growing breeze.

For the second time in American history, a captured United States fighting ship flew the flag of Islam.

~ Chapter 16 ~

July 4, 2012

1415 hrs.

While Smartwood concentrated on saving his ravaged ship, his subordinates provided him with a constant stream of intelligence. *Old Ironsides* was in hostile hands. She was headed out to sea. President Bush was rescued. American sailors were dead. Hostages were taken.

There had been no communication. It was odd. After rolling things over in his mind, he surmised the terrorists did not intend to blow up the ship. If that were their goal, she would have been destroyed by now.

The real intent was to hijack it. Although, for the love of God, he could not understand why. *What the hell can they do with it?* It was a puzzle he feared to solve.

He trained his binoculars on the old warship and thought. The damage to *Muskie* was contained. The destroyer could make headway despite the wound in her side. Headquarters dithered, apparently lacking a game plan for this scenario. Time slipped away.

Smartwood made a snap decision. It was essential to prevent *Constitution* from escaping Boston Harbor.

The farther out to sea she went, the harder it would be to rescue her and the hostages. And, although he hated to admit it to himself, if the old girl made it to deep water and sank, it would be nearly impossible to later salvage her. He shrugged off those terrible thoughts. *It must not come to that.* There was only one thing to do. Disable *Constitution* so she could not be sailed.

On *Constitution*, almost as if the terrorists had read his mind, armed men were flogging sailors up into the rigging, obviously with the intent to pack on more sail. Other hostages were bound to the masts and along the rail. More were manacled to boats or gratings at various locations on the deck with cheap plastic handcuffs. The array of captured civilians eliminated the option of shooting down *Constitution*'s masts and rigging. Too many unwanted casualties would result from such an attack.

Smartwood leaned against the superstructure, chewing on a pen. He wasn't going to risk another cigar. In fact, he was thinking about giving up smoking. He never wanted to be reminded about what had occurred this day. While pondering his choices, he quickly reached a conclusion.

"Mr. McDonald, radio shore command we are going to shoot off *Constitution*'s rudder gear. Get me your best gun crew." After the crew assembled, he descended to the main deck and moved to the forward-most gun emplacement. The gun crew was young, nervous, and untested. Smartwood looked at the chief gunner calmly.

"Son, they say you're the best gunner on this ship. Now's your chance to prove it. You see *Constitution* ahead? I want you to shoot off her rudder. I don't want you to shoot anyone on deck. Just hit the rudder. Do you think you can do that?"

By now, *Constitution* was nearly one-half mile ahead. It was well within range. The gunner peered intently at the old ship. He cocked the gun and pointed it.

"Aye, aye, Sir."

"Fire at will, Seaman," Smartwood commanded. The gunner set his sights and let loose.

At the sound of gunfire, Mustafa raced to the stern. Bullets plowed the ocean near the rudder. Other rounds thudded into the wood of *Constitution*'s oaken hull. He yelled to Al-Buyid, "The rudder! They're after the rudder!"

Al-Buyid rushed across the quarterdeck to where Myerson was roped to the mizzenmast. Since she had been out on extended medical leave for several months due to a difficult pregnancy, Mustafa and his team had failed to peg her as an officer. As a result, when the ship was captured, they treated her like a civilian.

The Sea Snake ordered her untied and seized her by the elbow. She was special. He'd had his eye on her since the beginning. A woman with a baby made a perfect hostage. With a gun to her temple, he dragged her and her screaming child to the stern.

"Rig me a bosun's chair," he ordered a nearby sailor. Zajac hesitated. He reached out a hand to stop his crewman. When a rifle was pointed his way, he reluctantly gave the order. Several sailors sprung to life. Meyerson, holding little Connie, was strapped into the seat.

"Lower away," Al-Buyid commanded. Amid the splatter of bullets, Meyerson and her child were lowered over the transom until they dangled inches above the water. Mother and child swung back and forth helplessly in front of the rudder.

Smartwood, field glasses to his eyes, was aghast.

"Cease fire!"

Enraged, he sputtered, "You sons o' bitches. You are not going to get away with it, you sons o' bitches!"

If he couldn't blow her up or shoot her out of commission, he sure as hell could ram her. Better she go down in Boston Harbor than in the deep Atlantic. At least the hostages had a fighting chance to survive close to land.

"Full ahead!"

On the deck of the *Constitution*, the remaining members of the press corps were unbound and shoved to the taffrail. The terrorists restored their cameras and sound equipment. Al-Buyid addressed the cameras.

"America, I have your ship, *Constitution*. I have its crew. I have your Vice President Baine and Secretary of the Navy Powers and other hostages. You will cease all efforts to take back this ship. If you do not, I will blow it up, with everyone on board." He then ordered the cameras to film the terrified Meyerson.

Al-Buyid looked behind and saw the crippled *Muskie* gaining ground. He became angrier and more alarmed. Even wounded, *Muskie* could easily catch *Constitution*. The menacing destroyer bore down. He once more addressed the television cameras.

"It is apparent that you do not believe me!"

He turned and ordered Mustafa to bring him the infant. Meyerson was hoisted up and the shrieking child was pulled loose from her arms. Meyerson was dropped back overboard. Mustafa handed the child to Al-Buyid who put a gun to Connie's head. The press corps kept their cameras trained on him.

"I will count to ten and if the *Muskie* does not stop, I will shoot the child!" He began counting.

Muskie was within 1,000 yards and gaining on *Constitution* with each passing second. She was soon close enough that her front bow wave began to lap *Constitution* and push her forward. From *Constitution*'s deck, the sight of the powerful destroyer plowing toward them was terrifying. Yet, Al-Buyid held his ground. He steadily counted, "Four, five, six, seven . . . ."

At the count of eight, *Muskie* suddenly slowed and veered sharply to port. A large wave buffeted *Constitution.* Meyerson was partially submerged and yanked under. The wave climbed *Constitution's* stern and threatened to poop her. It jolted everyone. Even the unflappable Al-Buyid grabbed a stay and hung on.

From the corner of his eye, Al-Buyid noticed a tall, bearded man on the bridge of *Muskie* give him the finger. Then *Muskie* faded from his immediate line of sight. *Constitution* steadied herself. The wind caught her sails and she plowed forward. She swiftly approached Fort Independence. The outer harbor and main channel to the open sea lay just beyond.

Zach came to, cradled by Eleni. She had been too far away to hear his conversation with the terrorist leaders or see him struck down. In the confusion surrounding *Muskie's* foray, she rushed to his side. Now, she stroked his brow as he revived.

"Zach, can you hear me? Zach, please talk to me!"

Zach's brain gradually unfogged and his eyes focused. He saw Eleni smiling at him. The polished deck under his backside told him they were still on the ship. Vaguely, he wondered what horror would come next.

Mustafa's face swam into his vision. It was the last thing he wanted to see. He started to say something to Eleni, to utter a warning, but before he could speak, he fell back unconscious.

Mustafa squatted next to Eleni. He offered a can of soda.

"Are you thirsty?" Eleni ignored him. He persisted. "Would you like something to drink?"

Reluctantly, Eleni looked at the new intruder. He seemed familiar. With a shock, she recognized him. The hair on the back of her neck stiffened. Mustafa regarded her quietly. He smiled, enjoying her discomfort.

"In my country, we understand thirst." He glanced at Zach, and then back at Eleni. With a smirk, he continued. "And pain, and loss, and sorrow. Things we will teach you spoiled Americans. Things I will personally teach this man and you."

Eleni's body began to tremble. She shrank from him as he reached out to stroke her golden hair.

Thirty feet away, Al-Buyid stood side by side with Faroud near the wheel, watching Boston shrink behind them off the starboard quarter of the ship. By now, *Constitution*'s crew had been separated into its usual mast teams and put to work. Under Zajac's direction, the ship hoisted a full complement of sail. Even her skysails and spankers had been set. It was the most canvas she had carried in more than a century.

Faroud carried his Stinger missile launcher strapped to his back. He did not go anywhere on the ship without it. *Constitution* was trailed now only by the two Coast Guard cutters, which maintained a respectful distance, wary of missiles, and hesitant to attack for fear of killing hostages. As the vessel passed the jumbo gas storage tank south of Boston, Al-Buyid pointed it out to Faroud.

"Do you think you could hit it?"

Faroud assessed the tank. Gaudy colors painted the ten-story structure like a rainbow. He assumed the artwork was yet another decadent symbol of support for homosexuality.

"Sea Snake, it is bigger than a tank or a helicopter. It does not move. It is like shooting a tethered goat." He covered one nostril and snorted, expelling a glob of mucus onto the deck near his feet. "There is no challenge to it."

"Do it, anyway," Al-Buyid commanded.

Faroud nodded and unencumbered his weapon. He located a missile among the munitions his comrades had hauled on deck. He fitted a rocket into the launcher and nonchalantly fired at the gas tank. A smoking arc sketched across the sky as the rocket tore toward its target. It struck the tank and punctured its side. For a moment, that was all that happened.

Disgusted, Faroud cleared his sinuses again.

"A dud."

Without warning, the sound hit and the shockwave from the explosion rocked the Afghan back on his heels, knocking him into Al-Buyid. The show was almost as good as the destruction of the Blue Angels. Spectacular flames shot skyward. A billowing mushroom cloud of smoke formed. Burning debris littered the ocean and nearby Marina Bay. Several boats in the marina caught fire. The blast blew out all of the windows at a high-rise across the small bay. Traffic on the adjacent I-93 highway ground to a halt as frightened drivers braked and gawked while speeding cars dodged pieces of falling metal.

Faroud pumped his fist into the air. It was a habit acquired from watching American television.

"Well done," Al-Buyid congratulated, caught in the euphoria.

Almost as good as killing the Blue Angels. However, without the death of any Americans, much less satisfying.

~ Chapter 17 ~

July 4, 2012

1250 hrs.

Four-Star Admiral John "Jolly" Rogers, the Commander of the North Atlantic Fleet, was ensconced at his desk at Fleet Headquarters in Norfolk, Virginia, contemplating a late lunch. The mess was cooking up burgers and dogs in honor of the Fourth of July. It was one of his favorite meals, and with the weather so fine, he would have the added pleasure of dining outdoors on the patio. America's birthday was shaping up to be a good day.

Rogers was a big man, a former Naval Academy lineman now going to fat, and faced with nagging heart trouble. He was scheduled to retire in six months. Most of his morning was spent on the computer hunting for real estate near Tampa. If his ticker did not give out on him, he would soon be spending the rest of his life walking the beach with his wife and Weimeraner dog Swabbie, surf casting, and sipping G&Ts on the patio. After 35 years in uniform, six blue water commands, and three wars, he was ready to wear shorts every day and feel sand between his toes on a regular basis.

With a finger on his wrist and an eye on his watch, he timed his heart rate. *Not bad.* His ticker was behaving and he was feeling A-OK. He was about to stand up and don his uniform jacket when a sharp rap sounded on his door.

"Enter."

The Admiral's Aide, Commander Spiros, opened the door and swiftly stepped into the room.

"Admiral, the *Constitution's* been hijacked!"

At first, Rogers thought it was a joke. He grinned at Spiros.

"Hell, the present administration hijacked the Constitution years ago, no surprises there." Then, seeing the stricken look on Spiros's face, comprehension slowly dawned.

"You mean the USS *Constitution*, don't' you?"

"Yes, Admiral. Just minutes ago. The first report came in from Captain Smartwood on the *Muskie*. *Muskie* was hit by a suicide bomber, like the *Cole*, but she's still afloat. *Constitution* is headed out to sea. It's all over CNN and the other networks."

Spiros flipped on the television as Rogers sat down heavily in his padded chair. In shock and disbelief, the old salt and his aide watched footage of Boston Harbor depicting the trail of charred and disabled watercraft and incinerated Navy jets left by the terrorist attack. Burning pools of jet fuel from the downed aircraft pockmarked the ocean surface. Here and there, a camera focused on a corpse or wounded victim floating amid the carnage.

An excited news bunny tried to make sense of it all. A camera cut to Al-Buyid's chilling speech on board *Constitution*. Rogers was outraged at the shot of

Al-Buyid holding a loaded pistol to the baby's head. When Al-Buyid finished, Rogers sprang to his feet and turned off the set.

He bolted into the hallway with Spiros trailing, barking non-stop orders.

"Convene the staff. Set up a situation room in 2B. I want direct communications established with *Muskie*. Get me all satellite Intel and the position of every ship and plane within 500 miles of Boston. I expect a preliminary status report and damage assessment in ten minutes. And get the Secretary on the horn."

"Admiral, the Secretary is on *Constitution*. He's one of the hostages."

Rogers pulled up short, and turned to face Spiros. "Hell's bells! Who else important?"

"Bush Senior," Spiros replied. "And the Vice President."

Rogers felt a jolt of pain shoot up his left arm into his chin.

Not now, Goddamnit! Not now!

Roger's father had flown with Bush's squadron in the South Pacific during WWII. George H.W. Bush was not just the former President of the United States, he was Navy. He was family. The news that Bush was on board was almost more troubling then the loss of the ship.

"Then get me the Assistant Secretary." He paused and added, "And call the mess and have two burgers, rare, and a hot dog sent up. Ketchup and pickles on the burgers. Mustard and relish on the dog."

He would be goddamned if a terrorist attack interfered with his Fourth of July lunch.

Ten minutes later Admiral Rogers sat at the head of an immense U-shaped table in Conference Room 2B. On the wall in front of him, a gigantic television monitor showed satellite images of *Constitution*, under full sail. Below *Constitution* were headshots of Al-Buyid, Mustafa and several other wanted killers, along with key information about their backgrounds.

Rogers had taken a nitroglycerin tablet and the ache in his arm and jaw was subsiding. He was on his last burger just as Chief of Intelligence Lt. Cmdr. Trevor Weymouth was completing his briefing.

"To sum things up, here's what we know. At least two dozen terrorists in five separate speedboats swarmed *Constitution* and boarded her after a brief firefight. We believe the enemy lost two boats and at least three men in the attack. Nearly 24 of *Constitution*'s crew were killed and at least 17 wounded, including Captain Raffington. *Muskie* was partially disabled by a suicide attack, similar to *Cole*. Zero casualties aboard *Muskie*."

It was a lot of information, all bad.

"The Blue Angels were shot down by one or more missiles during their second flyover. We're still sorting it out. Numerous small craft and several tall ships were damaged by gunfire or debris from the felled aircraft. A Coast Guard cutter was destroyed with all her crew. A gas storage facility located south of Boston was hit by a rocket and blown up."

Weymouth was perspiring heavily and paused to wipe his brow with a spotless white handkerchief. *God, I can't believe I'm sweating like this. Flop sweat.* He felt like he was in middle school, unprepared, and forced to give a book report to the class. Carefully tucking the handkerchief back into his rear trousers' pocket, he continued.

"The terrorists have *Constitution's* crew, the ceremonial Marine Honor Guard reenactors, and all the civilian hostages, including President George Bush the Elder, Secretary Powers, Vice President Baine, and a number of prominent Bostonians. A television camera crew from Channel 5 in Boston was allowed to transmit, but has now gone dark. Otherwise, we have had no communications with the ship." His voice wavered under the strain of relating the enormity of the tragedy.

"Most hostages are presumed below deck. A number of them are strategically arrayed on the weather deck, making it impossible to initiate combat operations without risking their lives. One was swung over the stern in a bosun's chair.

"We know a Mohammed Al-Buyid is in charge. He is a former Iraqi naval war hero who now works for the Iranians. We don't know who is captaining *Constitution*. She appears to be under full sail, heading north-northeast from Boston skirting the outer Harbor Islands, making for open water."

Rogers interrupted between bites of his food.

"Can *Constitution* hold up under sail?"

Weymouth had anticipated the question.

"We don't know, Sir. She's 215 years old. She was last put under canvas in 1997, on her 200th anniversary but only sailed as far as Castle Island, about two clicks from Constitution Wharf. Although she had substantial work done and refitting leading up to 1997, nobody's ever sailed her hard or further than Castle Island."

Rogers started in on the hotdog. Some dumbass had put brown mustard on it instead of yellow. It was that kind of day.

"What are their demands?"

The Intelligence Chief answered. "*Muskie* tried ramming *Constitution* before she made the outer harbor. The terrorists televised a threat to shoot a baby to force *Muskie* to disengage. You saw that on TV. Since then, there have been no demands. We don't know what they want or where they are headed. But we do know one thing – they tore down Old Glory and raised an Islamic flag."

A murmur of disbelief rippled through the room.

Rogers remained calm. He sipped some Coke.

"What assets do we have in the area?"

Weymouth cleared his throat and continued. "As you may recall, Admiral, as part of the War of 1812 Bicentennial, it's Navy Week in Boston. We sent up the *Muskie* for ship visits and public viewing. *Muskie* is no longer operational and not likely to be so for some time. She requires extensive repairs to her hull.

"The Blue Angels were conducting a flyover at the time of the capture. Regrettably, they are no longer a factor.

"The Leap Frogs are in Boston and remain on the ground. As you know, the parachute team is made up of SEALs and other special operations personnel. They are not combat ready but can be made so within hours."

Weymouth sniffed loudly and then took out his handkerchief and wiped his nose. The dog hair embedded in Roger's uniform always triggered his allergies. He neatly folded it before putting it away.

"Oh, there are two Coast Guard cutters trailing *Constitution*. That's it for Boston, Sir."

Weymouth reached nervously for a glass of water, lifted it, and downed the liquid in one long gulp. When Rogers made no comment, he resumed.

"Continuing on, Sir. Elsewhere, we have one Task Force deployed in the Mediterranean. It is currently off the coast of Syria, monitoring that country's civil war, also keeping an eye on Egypt, and poised to counter any threat or missile strike against Israel by Iran. A second Task Force is patrolling south of the Dominican Republic near Venezuela. We are showing the flag there in order to keep Chavez on his toes and discourage interference by Russia. Two submarines are in Groton and can put to sea immediately. The remainder of the North Atlantic fleet is docked in Norfolk."

Weymouth went for the water glass again, realized it was empty, and abruptly withdrew his hand. He remained awkwardly poised near the head of the table, unsure whether to sit or remain standing, awaiting further questions.

Rogers stared neutrally for a moment at his Intelligence Chief. A half-eaten frankfurter, leaking mustard, quivered in his right hand. He blinked rapidly several times before diverting his gaze.

Jesus fucking Christ. It's worse than I thought.

He tossed the dog on his plate in disgust. Settling deeper into the seat cushion, he tilted his chair back, laced his hands across his chest, and looked searchingly at the ceiling. In one of his first deployments, he'd resupplied an ice station near the South Pole. The white soundproof panels above his head reminded him of an Antarctic landscape. Bleak. Unforgiving.

In an even voice he declared, "So, we have the worst naval catastrophe in U.S. waters since Pearl Harbor and not one goddamn fully operational Navy surface ship north of the Mason Dixon line? Right?"

"Excepting the subs, yes." Weymouth's voice was now beginning to sound hoarse.

The earlier call Rogers had with the Assistant Secretary of the Navy had not gone well. The man was an artist with profanity. The Assistant Secretary was going to be forced to interrupt POTUS's golf game, always a dicey move. He took his ire out on the Admiral.

Rogers was still smarting from the dressing down he had received. It had been the most vicious verbal lashing he'd had since his days as a Middy. He briefly let his own temper flare.

"I said surface ship, didn't I Mr. Weymouth? Pay attention."

Weymouth dropped his gaze in embarrassment. He decided to sit. To redeem himself he added, "Please recall that there are the two Coast Guard cutters trailing *Constitution.* Oh, I neglected to mention this earlier. A Boston Police Department launch is bird-dogging the ship. Another cutter, the *David*, is assisting *Muskie.* Three other small cutters are converging, two from the north and one from the south. They should reach the area within hours." Weymouth looked around the room tentatively, searching for a friendly face or nod of approval. He found none. Rogers made no immediate reply.

The Admiral tilted his chair forward and crossed his arms on the table. He surveyed the array of starched uniforms and tense faces. Some of the brightest officers in the service were under his command, seated in the room. Many were combat veterans. Yet they all looked shell-shocked and confused. He smelled sweat and sensed their dread.

"*Constitution* is the oldest ship in the service. She is a national shrine. More than 500,000 Americans visit her every year. For them, and for most of the world, she is the living, breathing, symbol of United States naval power. We cannot and must not lose her.

"So, gentlemen. I have one question and only one question. How do we retake an 18th-century wooden warship from the Age of Sail using weapons and tactics from the 21st century?"

His eyes swept the room.

As he feared, there was no response.

Part III

Rescuing Her

~ Chapter 1 ~

July 4, 2012

1400 hrs.

Al-Buyid enjoyed the sight of the burning fuel tank. Feeling magnanimous, he ordered Captain Raffington removed to the captain's quarters. A tourniquet was applied to the Captain's leg. He was now jailed on the gun deck.

The only negative was the generator. It was badly shot up in the attack and no longer functioned. The ship was without lights, darkening the lower decks.

The bark held 150 invited guests, chosen by lottery, including the VIPs and the media. The enemy forced the VIPs and guests down onto the gun deck, except for several captives whom they kept on the spar deck. These unlucky hostages remained strapped to the masts, guns, and bulwarks as a deterrent to snipers or other would-be attackers. The press corps' usefulness at an end, it had been corralled, stripped of its equipment, and also imprisoned on the gun deck.

The Navy personnel, under threat of execution, were finally cooperating. Each sailor manned his or her station. Under the direction of CPO Zajac, the ship was now making headway north at a good clip. At this rate of speed, she would reach the rendezvous point by early morning.

The last time Al-Buyid looked back, the two Coast Guard cutters still trailed. There was another, smaller vessel behind the two cutters, but he could not tell its affiliation. Regardless, he was sure there was nothing to fear from his pursuers. He held many hostages and knew the reluctance of Americans to endanger innocent lives.

Al-Buyid stood near the helmsman on the quarterdeck, a hand draped casually over the butt of the pistol holstered on his belt. From time to time, he consulted a handheld GPS and barked course corrections at the sailor manning the helm. His men lounged idly around the deck, appearing to enjoy the cruise. Some cleaned their weapons. Others relaxed, appreciating the down time, knowing rest was needed for what lay ahead.

Zach had been jammed onto the gun deck with the other captives. He slowly regained consciousness to find himself sprawled on his back. His head ached. When he touched his crown, he felt a crust of dried blood. Pangs of failure ate at his heart. Fortunately, his mind was at last clear.

He took stock of the situation. The hostages were strewn randomly along the length of the gun deck. Their hands were bound in front with plastic handcuffs. A couple of gunmen armed with automatic weapons paced the deck.

Zach flexed his wrists to test the cuffs. They held tight. Trying not to draw any attention, he took inventory. His keys, money clip and wallet were gone.

He was pleased to find he still possessed a small Swiss Army knife tucked into his right pant pocket.

Next to him, Eleni lay curled into a fetal position on the hard and cold deck. She was quiet. Many of the other women were upset or nearly hysterical. So, too, were a few of the men. The sound of sobbing filled the chamber.

Several passengers stared morosely at their feet or blankly at the walls. Some crouched or sat on the deck with their heads cradled between their hands. There was no small talk, no brave chatter, no joking. What had started as a fun pleasure cruise had deteriorated into a hellish nightmare.

Zach noticed that a few of the passengers were wounded. One man in a plaid sport shirt had a ragged gash in his upper arm that was seeping blood. It had not been bandaged. The poor fellow was lying on the floor, groaning in pain. His wife held a compress to the wound to staunch the bleeding, to no avail. Several other passengers had visible cuts on their faces, hands, and arms. Their clothes were torn. They'd not eaten or been given water for several hours. A few licked their lips compulsively with thirst. Denied bathroom privileges, the captives had resorted to using an unoccupied portion of the deck near a forward gun as a latrine. A knot of injured sailors clustered near the capstan, tended by the ship's medic and two women volunteers.

Meyerson's status as a naval officer apparently remained unknown to the extremists. She was lumped in with the civilians. In a small gesture of civility, she was the only one not handcuffed, leaving her free to take care of her baby. Her haunch wedged against a cannon, she held Connie tightly to her chest and sang softly to the child.

The terrorists had closed many of the gun ports. Consequently, the light was dim, the air thick, and the temperature hot. Connie's diaper was full. The reek of baby poop mingled with the odor of blood, sweat, and despair permeating the air. It did not help that the ship had reached choppy water, making several of the passengers seasick.

Secretary Powers and Vice President Baine stood near Zach. The Secretary, a former Congressman from Connecticut, was dirty and disheveled. He glared fiercely at the two guards. Zach could see his teeth grinding with frustration.

Vice President Joseph Baine was holding up well, despite his age. Zach had not voted for the President and, like most Americans, considered the Vice President a clown. Now he had to hand it to the man. The VP maintained his composure. His spine was stiff and he, too, stared at the keepers in a venomous manner. His famous false teeth were unconsciously bared in a rare display of anger.

Near the VP were his two Secret Service escorts. They'd been overwhelmed and disarmed early in the struggle. Embarrassed and itching to redeem themselves, they carefully studied their surroundings.

Zach rolled over and whispered into Eleni's ear, "Stay calm. Don't worry, I'll be back." She squeezed his hand. He got up and inched his way cautiously through the crowd toward the VP and Secret Service agents.

When he was close enough to be heard, he whispered to the bigger of the two men, "Zach Colt here. I have a knife in my pocket. What can I do to help?"

He hoped the moans of the captives and the sound of the ancient ship creaking and groaning as it coursed through the waves would shield his conversation from the warders. If not, they would likely execute him.

The smaller agent nodded toward Zach. "Raul Hernandez. My partner's Delbert Grain." Hernandez was short and squat, with a face like a chiseled Aztec pyramid carving.

Grain, an older white man with a buzz cut, nodded to Zach as well, while keeping an eye on the gunmen. Both men searched the enemy for a weakness to exploit. It had been an error on their part to stay rather than to flee, as had Bush and his escort. Both of them were pretty banged up. Regardless, they needed to find a way out for their charge before things got hairier.

Without shifting his eyes away from the watchdogs, Grain spoke quietly. He had a mild western accent. "Right now, we can't do squat. They have the upper hand. I don't think they intend to kill us, at least not yet. Something else is up. I don't know what. We'll have to wait and see."

In a bitter tone Grain added, "Don't try to be a hero." He turned and grinned sourly at Zach. "That's our job."

Zach somberly nodded. Before he could speak, the sound of shouting, in Arabic, came from the spar deck. It was followed by several bursts of machine gun fire and the thud of bullets stitching *Constitution*'s hull.

At last, America was striking back.

*****

Just minutes before, the two Coast Guard cutters had received fresh orders. On board *Fitzgerald*, Rollins and Murphy watched in fascination as the cutters suddenly accelerated and closed in on either side of *Constitution*. As they did so, the foregunners let loose with the mounted .50 caliber machine gun, spraying both sides of the old ship with bullets.

Murphy cheered the decision to test *Constitution*'s defenses. He watched the two small vessels circle *Constitution* like angry bees, swooping in to gain a closer look and rake fire on the hull. Large splinters of wood flew off the ship's flanks. Excited screaming carried across the water from her decks.

Al-Buyid was perturbed, but not overly concerned. None of the fire was directed at the sails, rigging, masts, or spars for fear of hitting sailors or hostages. Nevertheless, he wanted the Americans to back off. This was obviously a feint. There was no time for distractions. He needed to stick to his schedule.

"Mustafa!" he shouted. "Mustafa!"

The young killer materialized at Al-Buyid's side.

"Mustafa. Go below and select 100 hostages. I think it is time for a swim."

"As you command," Mustafa shouted above the clatter of gunfire. He darted to the aft stair hatchway and ducked below.

The scene on the gun deck disgusted Mustafa. The Americans were huddled together, bleating like a pack of frightened camels. The smell was terrible. He seized a Kalashnikov from one of his henchmen and fired a burst into the overhead. The tumult stopped.

He handed the rifle back to his henchman and waded into the crowd. The cat-o-nine tails appeared in his right hand.

Mustafa avoided the VIPs. He pointed to a tall bearded man and screamed, "You, go to the stairway!" A flick of the whip sent the man scurrying. Strutting along the deck, he pointed to various men, women, and children. Others he tapped with the leather handle of his bloody whip. The gunmen hustled the selected victims to the ladder and goaded them topside. Most put up no resistance. The few that hesitated were savagely lashed by Mustafa. Some received a rifle butt in the gut or a sharp rap on the head from a guard, sufficient punishment to move them along without further protest.

When Mustafa neared Eleni, a wicked smile spread across his face. Sensing the worst, Zach slid between Eleni and Mustafa. Mustafa deftly sidestepped Zach, tripped him from behind, and whipped him across the face. With his hands still bound, Zach was helpless to resist.

In the chaos, Hernandez and Grain acted. Grain dropped behind Mustafa while Hernandez barreled into Mustafa's midsection. Mustafa crashed over Grain and sprawled on his back. Hernandez landed heavily on top of him and head-butted Mustafa. The terrorist went limp.

The jihadists had been busy herding the chosen captives up the ladder onto the spar deck. Their backs were to Mustafa. When they heard the commotion, they turned and pushed violently through the hostages to aid their brother.

Zach rolled to his side and plunged both hands into his side pocket, emerging with his knife. With a flick, the blade was open. He crawled to Grain, levered himself onto his knees, and sliced through Grain's cuffs. Grain seized the knife from Zach and cut Hernandez free, then Zach.

Hernandez scooped up Mustafa's weapon. There were too many Americans between Hernandez and the guards. He couldn't get off a clean shot.

"Everybody down!" he roared.

He fired a burst into the ceiling, which caused the hostages to crouch or fall to the deck in terror. The guards didn't duck. Hernandez sighted on a man and dropped him with a short burst. The other jihadists hesitated and backpedalled to the stairs. A terrorist fired wildly into the crowd as a comrade scooted up the ladder.

The man on the ladder paused before reaching the exit, swung around, and sprayed bullets indiscriminately in Hernandez's direction. He got lucky. A round caught Hernandez and the Secret Service agent dropped his weapon. As Hernandez fell, Zach dove for the automatic rifle, seized it, and leveled it in the direction of the guard. Before he could pull the trigger, the man had already disappeared. His cohorts scampered up the ladder behind him to save themselves as Zach let loose. The hatch slammed shut, leaving them once more in the gloom, but in possession of the gun deck.

Zach squinted through the haze of smoke filling the deck. Grain was sitting on top of an unconscious Mustafa. Hernandez was flat on the deck, plainly dead.

The agent saw Zach looking at his partner. "Hit him in the throat, right above the top of his Kevlar vest." Grain shook his head. "Crappy luck. He was a good man." Grain slapped Mustafa twice across the face, eliciting no response. "Seems like maybe this guy's a goner. Or he's real good at playing possum." He gave Mustafa another slap for good measure.

Most of the hostages were in shock. Surprisingly, none appeared dead or wounded by the gunfire.

Grain's eyes were sad. The price paid for their small victory had been the loss of his friend. They had the gun deck. A weapon was theirs. One terrorist was dead. Another belonged to them.

Grain stopped hitting Mustafa and raised one hand toward Zach in a silent high-five. "At last we won this round, cowboy."

Zach felt muted triumph.

It was only then Zach realized Eleni was gone. Frantically, his eyes swept the gun deck. He ran up and down its length looking for her. He knew she had not been herded above deck. During the mayhem, she had vanished. A sickening wave of despair swept over him.

My God! Where is she?

*****

On the spar deck, Al-Buyid watched a steady stream of captives emerge from below. When sudden gunfire erupted, he ordered his men to train their rifles on them. He rushed to the companion stairway and peered down. A hail of lead struck the housing

217

surrounding the exit. Several guards tumbled out of the opening onto the deck.

Al-Buyid sprang away to protect himself. At that moment, the last gunman flung himself through the opening to safety. Al-Buyid signaled for him to help. The two men feverishly wrestled the cover onto the hatch. Only then did Al-Buyid take a few deep breaths to take stock of what had happened.

He quickly calculated that the hostages on the gun deck posed little or no threat to his plan. They were trapped. The prisoners could not interfere with operation of the ship, excepting possibly the rudder mechanism housed in the Tiller Room on the berth deck. He doubted they would think of it. At worst, this revolt was a minor nuisance, which he could afford to ignore. He posted sentinels at the other stairways and one overlooking the rudder.

The Americans trapped below needed to be taught a lesson. The gunfire from the two cutters must be stopped.

"Faroud!" he howled. "Faroud!"

Faroud ran to his leader. Al-Buyid gestured angrily at the captives shuttled up from the gun deck.

"Throw them overboard! All of them! Now!"

Faroud's beetle nut stained teeth peeked out from under his beard. The diseased smile made him uglier. He and the other killers seized a woman hostage and dragged her to the netting spanning the open waist of the ship. The woman, overweight and in her fifties, put up little resistance. She turned limp as a rag. Laughing, they flung her over the side. Her huge splash made them laugh harder.

Their second pick, a young, well-dressed executive, kicked and punched. He was easily overpowered and tossed cursing into the ocean.

One by one, the hostages cowering on the spar deck were similarly dispatched. Those that failed to succumb were clubbed, kicked, and smacked into submission.

An Afro-American woman was shot in the arm for her insolence. Two teenaged boys eluded their pursuers and dove overboard on their own accord. A young girl of six was ripped screaming from her mother's embrace and catapulted end over end into the sea. Her bereft mother willingly plunged after her.

In just minutes, it was over. Some 80 hostages were gone. The machine gun firing had stopped.

The deck was quiet. Al-Buyid strode to the side rail. The sea behind *Constitution* was dotted with the pathetic figures of men, women, and children bobbing in the waves, fighting to stay afloat. Al-Buyid reached out and patted his imposing Afghan lieutenant on the shoulder.

"Good work, my loyal mujahid."

"Allah filled me with strength!" Faroud replied, thumping his chest.

"Inshallah," Al-Buyid answered. "Faroud, you are now my second in command."

"But what of Mustafa?" Faroud exclaimed.

"I did not see him escape. He must be in paradise."

Or Hell.

Probably the latter.

Rollins and Murphy were close enough to see the heartbreaking struggle. They were horrified as body after body hurtled over *Constitution*'s rail. Without distinction as to age and sex, the high and mighty of Boston were cast into the ocean like rubbish.

At the sight of the hostages propelled overboard, the captains of the two cutters had reduced speed and ceased fire. The Americans' probing attack quickly turned into a rescue operation. Joined by the *Fitzgerald*, the two cutters cruised back and forth, plucking drowning hostages from the waves. The heavy, thwack-thwack-thwack of helicopter blades descended. A Coast Guard Sikorsky MH-JA/T Jayhawk rescue helicopter hovered over a cluster of floundering passengers. The doors opened. Two Guardsmen deployed a basket, which they lowered to the people thrashing in the sea below. A rescue swimmer jumped into the water. The helicopter crew and swimmer worked together as a team and pulled half-drowned victims from the waves.

The wounded black woman was dragged limp from the water and given CPR. She sputtered back to life. The feisty executive survived, and was even able to help save some of his weaker fellows as they waited for rescue. The first hostage tossed overboard was never located. The little girl was saved. Her mother was not.

By the time the rescue operation ended, hours had passed. *Constitution* was a barely a dot on the horizon. She sailed east into the vast Atlantic, away from her home, toward an unknown fate.

~ Chapter 2 ~

July 4, 2012

1440 hrs.

At Coast Guard Pier in Boston Harbor, Commander Patrick Radkowski, in charge of Coast Guard District 1, closely monitored developments and coordinated his limited resources. He had deployed his two remaining cutters from Boston to pursue *Constitution*. It had been his idea to initiate a probe. Now with pursuit terminated, his ships were involved strictly in a search and rescue mission for the jettisoned passengers. Additional vessels had been requested from Coast Guard Stations located in Provincetown and Woods Hole to the south, as well as from Portsmouth to the north. Some of those units were out on extended patrol and were far away or needed to refuel before pursing *Constitution*. Others were docked for refitting. They were all in various stages of being en route.

One of his two rescue helicopters was assisting with the passengers. The other remained on alert at the Naval Air Station in Falmouth. A fixed wing aircraft from Cape Cod circled the area as a spotter plane, streaming real-time images of *Constitution* to HQ. A third cutter from Boston, *David*, assisted *Muskie*. He had yet to notify the families of the dead from the cutter Mustafa had destroyed. That, possibly the most difficult task, had to wait.

As he surveyed his map, an aide handed him the phone. It was the Director of Homeland Security.

"Commander, how are you?" a soft female voice asked.

"I'm well, Director, considering the tactical situation."

"Good. Good. I'm sorry for the loss of your personnel. A tragedy."

The Director sighed. "Well, we have quite a fiasco here. An extraordinary one. As a result, per 13 U.S.C. Sections 3 and 211, the President has directed that the Coast Guard now be placed under the command of the DOD and the Department of the Navy. You are to take orders from NAVCOM from now on. Admiral Rogers will soon contact you."

"I expected as much, Madame Director. After all, it was a Navy ship that's been hijacked."

"That's right. And not just any Navy ship. She is the oldest Navy ship – the very symbol of the service." The soft voice inhaled deeply.

"But beyond that, this operation requires bigger resources, which the Navy has. You've done a good job so far. Thank you. Keep up the good work." With that tepid praise, the Director hung up.

Radkowski was simultaneously angry and relieved.

It's been my men and women who've put their asses on the line. And now they want me to walk away. Homeland Security knows squat about Coast Guard operations. Transferring the branch to them in 2002 was a big mistake. Anyway, if things go to hell any further, I'm glad this operation isn't my baby. Maybe it's best the Navy is taking charge.

He'd done what he could with the resources at hand. The politics and the logic of the transfer were easy to understand.

Still . . . the Coast Guard has a score to settle.

In the midst of his musings, Radkowski's aide signaled a new call had come in, this time from NAVCOM. The aide thrust the phone toward him.

"Admiral Rogers, Sir. He sounds pissed off," the aide whispered.

Who wouldn't be?

Admiral Rogers' gravelly voice barked from the phone. "Commander, welcome to the Navy. I hate to step on your dick, but there's no way around it. Give me an update. I want to know the status of every Coast Guard ship and aircraft at our disposal."

In a precise and measured tone, Radkowski ran through his assets. When he finished, Admiral Rogers spoke.

"O.K. *Eagle* now belongs to us. I will deal directly with her Captain. *Muskie*'s scuppered for now. Place your cutter *David* under Captain Smartwood's command. You have a MSRT team on *David*, right? Smartwood will take over your MSRT team and merge it with his VBSS Team. It's Smartwood's show from there on. As for the rest, maintain your current rescue efforts and aerial surveillance. Keep your spare chopper and spotter aircraft at the ready. Try to have your other cutters rendezvous with *David* once they are in theater."

223

Radkowski heard a low chuckle on the line. "We have a few nasty surprises planned for our terrorist friends. I assure you, Commander, we will prevail."

"Yes, Sir!" Radkowski reflexively replied, with more assurance in his voice than he truly felt. Hc looked at his handset. By reputation, Rogers was a fighter and a wily devil. The full might of the United States military establishment was at his fingertips.

So far, the terrorists had the upper hand. No doubt temporarily. Things were about to change. Radkowski did not want to be in their shoes by this time tomorrow.

*****

Eagle was the pride and joy of the Coast Guard. She was a German-built, three-masted, 133-foot-long steel-hulled beauty. Formerly the *Horst Wessel*, the Nazi ship was captured by the Allies at the end of WWII. Given to the Coast Guard, she was the second oldest commissioned fighting ship in the world, second only to *Constitution*.

Eagle served as the Coast Guard's training ship. She held 123 officers and cadets, who referred to her as the "Dirty Bird" or the "Love Boat" depending on their mood. Besides training cadets, *Eagle* routinely participated in Tall Ship events and was a goodwill ambassador for the United States at ports of call all over the world.

When the attack commenced, *Eagle* was in the middle of the flotilla of tall ships, some one-half mile abaft *Constitution*. By a miracle, she missed being damaged by debris from the downed Blue Angels. She had not been close enough to any of the attacking terrorist speedboats to take any hits from machine guns or missiles. Her Captain, Billy Newtowne, cleverly sailed her through the carnage, dodging the burning hulks of other tall ships and watercraft. Too big to easily maneuver in the crowded harbor and thus unable to help with rescue efforts, she put out to sea. Now, she was passing Goat Island, one of the Harbor Islands. Since radioing in her status, Captain Newtowne had received no further orders.

Frustrated, Newtowne paced the deck with his hands clasped behind his back. A short, barrel-chested man with a weathered face, he was constantly in motion. His cadets respected him because of his deep knowledge of seafaring and because there was no job on the old ship he would not or could not do. Although decades younger, his charges could seldom keep up with his level of exertion or match his single-minded concentration. Behind his back, they called him "Wild Bill" for his fiery disposition.

After receiving the fourth consecutive "Stand by for further orders" from HQ, he knew what he had to do.

"Stand by my ass!" he muttered to himself. He had his XO pipe all hands on deck. When the cadets assembled, he addressed them.

"Cadets, the United States of America has been attacked. Your friends have been attacked. Your families have been attacked. This might not be Pearl Harbor or 9/11 but by God it's pretty damn close."

He raised his voice a notch. "Sometimes in war you need to take the initiative. That's what a good officer does. He assesses the situation and acts. If there are lives at stake, and the situation is dire, that can mean moving ahead without clearing channels.

"Today we choose to act. Today we sail to take back *Constitution*! All hands to their stations!"

The cadets, most under 21 years of age, fresh-faced and raw, gave their Captain a chorus of "huzzah!" before racing to their posts.

Newtowne stood by the imposing wheel, watching his crew with pride. He shouted orders to his officers, who in turn whipped the young Coasties into a frenzy of controlled chaos.

To shouts of "Lay aloft!" the topmen scampered up the ratlines and inched out onto the yards, unfurled additional sails and tightened lines. The deckhands turned the capstans as one, tightened the halyards, and raised the fore, mizzen and main sails. Gallants, topgallants, royals, and kites were added. The jib was lowered. Within minutes, a cloud of fresh white graced all three masts. As the wind filled the voluminous sails, they swelled and the ship began to pick up speed. Soon they were sailing large, racing past the Harbor Islands into the deep blue-green waters of the Atlantic.

Captain Newtowne did not know what lay ahead. He didn't have a plan. He wasn't sure what he would do if he caught up to *Constitution*.

What he did know was he had a good ship and an even better crew.

They may be green, but by God, they're game!

For now, that was enough

.

226

~ Chapter 3 ~

July 4, 2012

1736 hrs.

Smartwood watched from the con of his disabled ship as *David* drew alongside. She was one of the new Sentinel Class; 154 feet long, manned by a crew of 24, and armed with a remote-controlled .50 caliber chain-mounted stationary gun and four forward and aft crew-operated .50 caliber machine guns. Built to replace the aging Island Class Cutters, the new Fast Response Cutters were designed for long voyages. Lean and sleek, *David* could reach speeds of 32 mph.

On her deck, the Coast Guard Maritime Security Response Team stood geared up and good to go. *Muskie's* Visit, Board, Search, and Seizure Team was also ready. Both squads were keen for action.

Smartwood turned over command of *Muskie* to his XO, McDonald, who had redeemed himself in Smartwood's eyes during the clean-up operations. As he left the bridge, he tossed the newly minted skipper a cigar. "You've earned it, Captain McDonald." McDonald snapped a crisp salute.

Luckily, the damage to *Muskie* from the suicide bomber was not quite as severe as first envisioned. A stupendous hole was blown in her hull. Quick action by the crew had closed the bulkheads and sealed off the lower compartments, leaving only minor damage to the interior near the breach. She would be towed by tug back to Pier 2 for repairs. *Muskie* would survive.

Smartwood felt a rush of relief. *Thank God, she did not sink.*

As it was, *Muskie* would be out of commission for months. For now, he needed a new command, and that ship would be *David*. It was smaller, more nimble and equal to the task.

His men threw a ladder over the side as he perused *David* and her Captain.

"Permission to come aboard!" he hollered.

"Permission granted!" Captain Morris hailed back.

Smartwood threw a leg over the rail and found the first rung of the ladder. He hated ladders. He always worried he would slip and make a laughingstock out of himself. No Captain should land on his butt in front of his crew.

"Follow me," he directed to the VBSS Team as he descended. He scurried down the ladder as gracefully as he could and hopped onto *David's* deck, where he flicked a return salute to Captain Morris before reaching out to shake the younger man's hand.

"Sorry to divest you of your command, Captain." He didn't sound the least bit sorry. Morris could tell the Navy man was keyed up with excitement.

"No problem, Sir. What is your pleasure?"

The heavily armed VBSS squad came on board and secured the last of their gear. The Navy men mingled with the Coasties, shook hands, and compared equipment. Some had previously trained together.

Despite the tension and the gravity of their mission, they were able to joke and stay loose.

Smartwood reviewed the numbers in his head. Fifteen men made up his team. The Coastie team had another fifteen. *David* carried enough firepower to blow *Constitution* out of the water, if need be.

To be sure, destroying *Constitution* was not ideal. Capture, not conquer, was what he sought to accomplish. The plan cooked up by NAVCOM seemed feasible but incredibly risky. Certainly, all plans appeared doable from the safety of a wardroom. It would be a close run thing. If Smartwood were a betting man, he would at best have given the mission even odds.

"My pleasure, Captain, is to get underway immediately. We have some serious ass to kick."

Morris snapped to attention and again saluted. "Aye, aye, Sir." He lowered his arm and called out to his own XO "All engines full ahead."

The order was quickly relayed and executed. The sleek craft shot forward as the mighty GE engines unleashed their power.

The chase was on.

*****

Forty miles east of *David*, the rescue operation had wrapped up. *Fitzgerald* was choked with exhausted former hostages plucked from the sea, many on the verge of hypothermia. A few had broken bones in their plunge over the side. The small craft was full of weeping and moans of pain. The Special Ops team medic did his best to treat the injured, but there were too many for him to handle. In no time, almost all the men on the craft were assisting him.

Basically a harbor craft, *Fitzgerald* lacked large capacity fuel tanks. She was dangerously low on fuel. Her skipper, Lt. Difinis, was in a loud argument with Rollins about whether to turn back.

"Goddamnit!" Rollins erupted. "We cannot quit! Our people are on *Constitution*. Are you going to just let her sail away?"

"With all due respect Chief Rollins, this is my launch and my responsibility. We have sick and injured to tend to. I cannot risk their lives and I can't chance running dry this far out to sea. We're turning around, now."

Murphy thought Rollins was going to strike Difinis. He gently tugged at Rollins' sleeve. "C'mon Chief, we're done here."

Rollins shrugged off the touch and angrily turned his face in the direction of *Constitution*'s wake. Its faint outline was still discernible in the water. To the south, it was clear a storm was brewing.

The wind had picked up and the sky had clouded over. The air felt thick and heavy. Although daylight, the firmament had turned ominously gray.

Rollins felt despondent. The deteriorating weather suited his mood. *Dirty weather for dirty deeds.*

Over the ship's radio came word that the two cutters were ordered back to base. Rollins scowled at Murphy.

"That's it then? The terrorists have won?"

"I don't think so, boss. I'm betting there are still a few more innings to play in this ballgame. The Feds must have something up their sleeves. I don't see us giving up so easy."

Fitzgerald's nose turned. The small craft accelerated toward Boston. The cutters were already out of sight.

Two thirds of the way to Boston, *Fitzgerald* passed the streaking *David*. It was now quite dark. Lightning flashes crackled in the distance, silhouetting the cutter as she sped by. Although *David* was fully blacked out, Rollins and Murphy were close enough to discern the outline of the machine guns on her deck. She looked serious and deadly. A lone lookout perched in the bow waved at them.

Murphy waved back. "See, boss. I told you so. We'll get them. That boat means business."

Rollins was angry and disappointed. "Yeah. I sure hope so. Jesus, I wish I was on that ship. I want a piece of their ass."

A bright light briefly flared on *David's* bridge and dimly illuminated the face of a tall bearded man. The flash of light died into an orange dot that transferred to another hand and moved back and forth, leaving faint trails in the air like a sparkler on a summer night.

The glowing speck shrank and disappeared as the cutter dissolved into the gathering gloom.

Rollins and Murphy were subdued. Murphy considered finally taking a nap. Chief Rollins fumed, trying to work out in his head a way to get back into the fight. Without warning, the engines sputtered and fell silent. *Fitzgerald* drifted in the waves.

"Fuck," Difinis yelled. "I can't fucking believe it. What a fucking fucked up day!" He pounded the fuel gauge in a fruitless effort to squeeze a few more drops of diesel from the lines.

Difinis stopped swearing and picked up his radio's microphone. "Mayday, mayday. BPD launch *Fitzgerald* stranded 40 clicks outside Boston Harbor. Out of fuel. Require assistance. We have injured civilians on board."

"Roger that, *Fitzgerald*. This is *David*. We just passed you. We cannot render assistance. I repeat, we cannot render assistance. My apologies. Continue with your mayday call and stand by. Someone else will assist you. Over."

The radio went dead. Difinis quietly cussed out *David's* captain. He was about to repeat the distress call when ahead a bolt of lightning illuminated an enormous white object headed in *Fitzgerald's* direction.

"What the hell is that?" Rollins exclaimed.

"Chief, I know what it is!" Murphy responded.

Before he could say the name, Difinis spoke, "It's *Eagle*. She's a Coast Guard sailing ship. She was in the Parade of Sail. I guess she made it out OK. She'll help us. I think we're going to be alright." Difinis hopped back on the radio and soon established communications with *Eagle*.

*****

Earlier, *Eagle,* miles off the coast, had been overtaken by *David*. Smartwood was shocked to find the old dame this far out at sea.

"*Eagle*, this is Captain Smartwood on the Coast Guard vessel *David*. What are you doing out here?"

The radio soon crackled back. "*David*, this is Captain Newtowne on USCG training ship *Eagle*. We are pursuing *Constitution*."

Smartwood could not help smiling. He admired Newtowne's audacity.

"*Eagle*, this is *David*. You are ordered to stand down. Return to base immediately."

The radio squawked static, and then went silent. By then the *David* was well past *Eagle*. Smartwood keyed the mic a few times but received no response.

Morris glanced at Smartwood. "I hope he got the message."

Smartwood grinned. He sensed an affinity with Captain Newtowne. There was no doubt in his mind about what the other man planned.

"I think he did, Captain. I think he did." Captain Morris gave his new commanding officer a quizzical look. He was an odd bird, for sure.

"Anyway," Smartwood continued, "we have no time to trifle with *Eagle*. We have a ship to take."

*****

Newtowne grudgingly took up sail and steered *Eagle* alongside *Fitzgerald*. She slowed and *Fitzgerald* bumped along her side. A cadet tossed a line. Murphy caught it and tied off. Newtowne looked down at the smaller vessel and saw the Special Ops Team, the two cops in plain clothes, and every square inch of the small launch plastered with cold and shivering survivors. His first instinct had been to bypass *Eagle*, as had *David*, but he found he could not ignore a vessel in distress. Now, seeing all the rescued hostages, he was glad he'd stopped.

Maybe my Coast Guard training runs too deep.

Newtowne's men secured the craft and dragged the homicide detectives onto *Eagle*. His medic jumped into *Fitzgerald* to assist the injured, who were quickly transferred to the bigger vessel and taken below for treatment. The whole operation took less than thirty minutes. After the injured were evacuated, *Fitzgerald* was cast adrift. There was no time or spare manpower to save her.

Newtowne ignored his new guests and turned back to the more important task. "Let's get back under way, Mr. James!" he shouted. His cadets sprang to action and once more the big ship spread its sails and began to knife through the water. Newtowne left his post on the quarterdeck and walked through the forecastle until he stood in the bow.

The leading edge of the storm was almost upon them. The wind had started to howl through the rigging. They were well underway, running close hauled to the wind. He leaned forward, relishing the speed, urging his ship to go faster. Salt spray stung his eyes and he tasted the ocean in his mouth. Sailing fast at night like this made him feel wonderfully alive. He tried not to imagine the fight ahead. Like the storm, it would come soon enough, and then suddenly be over. For now, exhilarated by the chase, he grasped the head rails and leaned out, sniffing the air like a bloodhound on a scent.

I can smell you, you bastards. I can smell you!

~ Chapter 4 ~

July 4, 2012

1955 hrs.

Hours earlier, gunfire and the furious sounds of a struggle outside his quarters roused Raffington from his stupor. Incredible pain coursed through his knee and lower leg and he fought back a moan. The cabin was gray. He lay still, allowing his eyes to adjust to the weak light, unsure for a moment where he was. He stared at the skylight overhead and realized he'd been put on the sofa in the Captain's After Cabin. When a short-lived break in the clouds occurred, reddish light leaked into the room through the skylight and the cabin's three large stern windows.

He spied a man crouched near one of the two doors that led from the After Cabin to the Great Cabin. On the other side of the Great Cabin was the rest of the gun deck. The man was dressed in jeans and a T-shirt and held an automatic weapon to his chest. His back was to Raffington and his ear was wedged against the door. He was listening intently to the sounds of struggle just yards away.

Raffington guessed the noise meant some kind of rebellion was taking place. Eventually, the sounds outside the doors stopped. A short while later he heard bullets strike the stern of the ship. When he lifted his head to peer out the stern windows, several rounds shattered the glass. He fell back onto the couch and curled up for safety.

Then came screams from the spar deck. A body hurled past, darkening a window. Then another body fell, followed by dozens more, accompanied by more screams and thuds from the spar deck.

My God, they are throwing people overboard!

Raffington struggled to rise. The pain in his leg overwhelmed him and he passed out. When he awoke, hours later, it was close to sunset. He peered toward the door. His jailor had fallen asleep, propped against the wall.

As quietly as possible, he sat up on the sofa. He planted his good leg and swung the injured one onto the deck. The movement caused him to grimace. There were no readily available weapons in the cabin. He fought to clear his head and determine where he could find something useful with which to subdue the terrorist.

He couldn't stand well or walk far. It was impossible for him to swing a chair or use another piece of furniture to attack the man. A dresser to his left held a few nautical knickknacks. It was too far away to reach. Besides, as weapons, the trinkets were probably useless.

He reached below his shattered knee and felt along the inside of his right boot. There he found the small dirk he always carried. It was a replica of one in the Constitution Museum used by William Bainbridge, an early Captain of *Constitution*. Raffington's crew had presented it to him on his one-year anniversary of command.

He fished the dirk from his boot and clasped it tightly in his hand. Its four-inch razor sharp blade glowed dull red in the rays from the setting sun. Although the terrorist was mere feet away, the distance was too great to navigate successfully with his hobbled leg.

No matter, he had to try. Raffington braced himself against the seat of the sofa. He stepped forward with his sound leg and launched himself onto the back of the sleeping man. Both sprawled to the floor. The Captain tightened his left arm around the man's neck in a chokehold. His right arm flailed at the guard's body, stabbing anywhere he could.

The terrorist thrashed from side to side. The pain in Raffington's knee was excruciating. He made a noise deep in his throat halfway between a groan and a growl. Almost out of strength, he hung on, plunging the small dirk repeatedly into his opponent's chest and flank until the man relaxed and became flaccid.

Raffington released his chokehold and rolled away. He gasped for breath on the floor. With his left hand, he groped for the wall and, releasing the dirk, pulled himself to his feet. He reached out, swung the cabin door open, and stepped across the threshold into the Great Cabin. He limped to the giant oak chart table, steadied himself, and then lurched past it and fell against the door leading to the gun deck. He opened the door and prepared to step across the threshold.

A staccato burst of gunfire riddled his back. It sent him crashing face first onto the floor of the gun deck.

The wounded jihadist slumped to the deck behind Raffington, his last cruel act completed.

Grain and Zach, several feet away near the capstan, flinched at the gunfire. They snapped their heads around in time to see Raffington pitch forward. Zach ran to the Captain's side. He lifted Raffington's head. Raffington's slack face and glazed eyes told Zach the man was dead.

Grain swiftly stepped past Raffington and kicked the killer's rifle away. He examined the bleeding gunman.

"This one's still alive!" Grain growled.

Zach stared across Raffington corpse at the terrorist. The wounded man's breathing was labored. His lips moved.

Grain leaned over close to the man's mouth to catch what he said. The faint sounds of "Allah . . . Allah . . . Allah," escaped from the young man's lips.

Zach heard it, too. He rose and in one swift move snatched up the rifle Grain had kicked away. Making sure a round was chambered, he pointed it at the terrorist's head. Grain stepped aside, silent.

Zach wanted to shoot the murderer. He wanted payback for the loss of Eleni and the deaths of Raffington and of so many other good men and women. The wounded terrorist was his enemy, the enemy of all civilization, the sworn destroyer of everything he held sacred.

Still, he could not pull the trigger. He could not execute the man in cold blood.

Fortunately, the terrorist made the choice easy. The man's hand groped toward the holster at his side.

He tugged his pistol free and unsteadily raised it toward Zach.

That was enough. Zach smiled.

"Fuck you. Fuck every religious zealot who kills in God's name," Zach spat at the fanatic.

A single shot tore through the jihadist's brain.

The harsh sound reverberated in the sparsely furnished cabin.

Grain looked at Zach holding the smoking gun. "Now, that's what I call a mercy killing, partner." Chuckling at his own joke, he finished. "Yep. It's a mercy I didn't kill him myself."

"You know, Grain, I think we are going to work together just fine."

"Damn straight, cowpoke. So far, so good."

The two Americans lifted Raffington and placed him on the chart table.

Meyerson entered the cabin. All color left her face. Tears cascaded down her cheeks. Her lips parted, but she could not speak. She approached the dead Captain and touched him softly on the cheek. Then she whirled and rushed from the room.

Grain lugged the dead terrorist to one side of the doorway to unblock the rear entrance.

"Hey Zach, you ever notice how heavy dead people are?"

Grain's mordent sense of humor seemed fitting. Zach thought back to the time he had dragged his friend Fritz's lifeless corpse through the Panamanian jungle and buried it in the treasure pit under the banyan tree. He began to shake and feel sick to his stomach. His head ached. Doing his best to appear at ease, he replied, "Yeah. As a matter of fact, I have."

Grain looked at Zach with surprise.

Zach added, "It feels like it was a lifetime ago."

The big agent appraised Zach. "That's how it always feels, son. Always."

Grain and Zach reentered the gun deck to take stock of the situation. Grain went over to Secretary Powers and his boss, Vice President Baine. He spoke with them for a short time before rejoining Zach. The two officials kept to themselves, deep in conversation.

Meyerson had recovered from her shock and was nursing her baby. When finished, she handed Connie for safekeeping to a middle-aged woman in a red, white, and blue sundress, Eldridge's wife. Mags sniffed the babe's diaper and frowned. She found Meyerson's diaper bag and changed Connie. The child fell asleep peacefully in the woman's arms, belly full, unperturbed by the violence that had just taken place.

There were about fifty passengers left on the gun deck. In addition to those wounded during the initial capture of the ship, there were now several more who were in shock from the fight to rid the gun deck of the gunmen.

Before Raffington's death, Meyerson had organized a team to help the wounded. It consisted of women and the more elderly passengers. A second team comprised of four able-bodied men and women cleared debris and made the deck generally more shipshape. Hardened by the events of the past several hours, they did not even flinch when they lifted the dead guard shot by Hernandez and dragged him out of sight.

Zach approached Meyerson with Grain in tow. "Are you OK?"

Meyerson reached up to brush hair from her face. "Yeah. How about you? I saw what you and this big guy did back there." Zach heard a catch in her throat. "Captain Raffington was my mentor and friend . . . ."

"Well, he surely gave it his all, ma'am." Grain thrust out his hand and added, "It's about time we become formally introduced. I'm Grain. United States Secret Service."

"Grain, as in 'for amber waves of . . .'?"

"Yup. Mostly as in 'going against the . . . .'"

She clasped his hand. "I'm Commander Meyerson. As in U.S. Navy." She nodded toward Zach, "We've met before, right. You're Zach Colt, on the Board, aren't you?"

"Yes."

"I thought you were a lawyer? How'd you learn to fight?"

"I'm an ex-cop. I've been in a dust-up or two."

Meyerson raised an eyebrow. "I've never really liked cops," she said. "Until now, that is. Sorry."

Zach shot back, "I understand. No offense taken."

All three smiled, loosening the tension.

Meyerson grew serious. "Gentlemen, it's my ship now. I'm in command. I trust you don't resent taking orders from women?"

Grain shifted from one foot to the other. "I've served two First Ladies. One of them was Hillary. I got saddle broke a long time back."

Meyerson's face reddened. "I'll take that as a 'yes'."

Grain cocked a thumb over his shoulder. "As for those two honchos in the corner, I've had a little chat with them. Told them to behave. Let the experts handle the situation. I think they get it."

Zach had worked for many years in the law, a profession once totally dominated by men. Things had changed, and he had met his share of tough women lawyers and judges. Eleni was one of them. Gender didn't matter to him. Competence did.

"Not a problem, ma'am," Zach answered.

"Good." Then she added almost shyly, "That doesn't mean I'm not open to suggestions." She flicked her eyes around the gun deck. "This situation is pretty fucking unique."

Both Zach and Grain nodded in agreement. While they had been speaking, Zach surveyed the compartment. He now strode toward the bow, searching from side to side.

"There's one missing. One of the terrorists is gone. The one Grain tackled earlier. Mustafa. Where is he? Did you move him?"

"We just moved one body, the one Grain's partner shot," Meyerson answered.

"Christ," Zach cried out. "He must have escaped."

"I didn't notice," Grain protested. "My bad."

Zach ignored the apology.

First Eleni gone.

Now the psycho from Rowes Wharf.

Shit.

He had a very, very bad feeling in his gut.

~ Chapter 5 ~

July 4, 2012

2111 hrs.

The C-130 Hercules docked for fueling on the ground at Logan Airport was abuzz with activity. This normally quiet area of the airport, reserved for military operations, was now crammed with trucks and personnel. In the hanger, the 14-man Leap Frog precision parachute team had assembled.

Its members were probably the finest and most accomplished parachute artists in the world. The team was expert at precision drops and intricate multi-layered formations. Jumping from altitudes of 25,000 feet, they often reached speeds of 180 mph. Landings were so precise they could drop onto home plate in Fenway Park.

The Leap Frogs normally entertained crowds at airshows and Navy Week and other special events. In the past, they performed at NASCAR races and Major League baseball games. Earlier in the week, to the delight of thousands, the Leap Frogs landed on Fan Pier and later Boston Common.

What most civilians did not understand was that the Leap Frogs were composed of the nation's most elite warriors. Navy SEALs who volunteered for two-year tours of duty filled their ranks. Leap Frogs were not just entertainers – they were some of the best and most feared special ops warriors in the world.

Lt. Cmdr. Caesar Sconzotti had received his new orders two hours earlier. In a heartbeat, his mission had radically changed. The attack on Boston Harbor had converted a leisurely July Fourth drop into a soon to come life or death confrontation with Middle Eastern terrorists.

It was highly unusual for the Leap Frogs to be activated for an operation like this. Naval Special Warfare Command informed him that of the approximately 2,400 active duty Special Warfare Operators, his SEALs were the only outfit available. Even though his men had never fought together as a unit, he was confident they could pull it off. They had to.

Sconzotti was ready. He was 37 years old and had trained most of his life for moments like this. Brooklyn born, he was the third son of a baker and a schoolteacher. He had the olive skin and the soft brown eyes of his southern Italian ancestors and the toughness of their Roman forebears. When he was a boy, his father's conception of love was a hard slap to the back of the head for some infraction, real or imagined. His mother gave hugs and kisses but also made him memorize Shakespeare and learn to write with the precision and brevity of Hemingway.

He came from a devout Roman Catholic family. At an early age, he resolved to become a priest. After attending Fairfield University, he enrolled in a Jesuit seminary. He had successfully passed through his Novitiate and was in his Regency studying for an advanced degree in Political Science at Fordham when the tragedy of 9/11 occurred.

Suddenly, everything changed. Patriotism and the urge to protect lives made him join the Navy. Ambition and dedication made him try out for the SEALs. He passed BUDD/S and life was never the same. His education and personality, especially his high score in Conscientiousness, made him an ideal officer. He rapidly advanced through the ranks.

And he found a new calling – parachuting. Somehow, it jived with his spirituality. He found nothing makes a man trust in God more than willingly hurling his body from a speeding plane at high altitudes.

WARCOM had fed him his orders 20 minutes earlier. A few moments ago, he'd rounded up his men. He was just completing their briefing. The SEALs sat in a semi-circle around him. They were dressed in black from head to toe. Their faces were covered in black paint, their hands in black gloves. Not a glint of metal was visible. Deadly M4 SOPMOD rifles with muzzle suppressors, MP5 submachine guns, or short-barreled Remington M870 shotguns were strapped across their chests. A variety of grenades dangled from their webbing. Each man stared back at him with calm, determined eyes.

It was a quick briefing. Like the upcoming mission, it was short and to the point. He expected no questions. They would understand the plan and its risks. They would accept it without question and without fear.

Sconzotti felt pride as he perused them.

This is a suicide mission. They must know it. You sure can't tell it from their faces.

The task was daunting. The probability of victory next to zero. The United States did not throw away its citizen soldiers lightly. Here, however, there was little choice. His unit was closest. Its unique talents provided the best chance of success.

After briefing the men on the scope of the mission, Sconzotti closed with a pep talk. "Men, a long time ago the patriots of Boston came up with a motto, 'Don't Tread on Me.' Sound familiar? Well, the Navy later created its very first ensign with that motto on it. The ensign depicts a rattlesnake on a field of 14 red and white stripes with those four simple words.

'Don't Tread on Me.'

All eyes remained locked on him.

"Today, someone was stupid enough to stomp on that rattlesnake." He paused to look again at each man.

"It's time to strike back."

The team gave a shout of "Hooyah!"

As one, they sprang to their feet and filed behind Sconzotti up the ramp and into the waiting plane. Within minutes, they were airborne, flying east over the Atlantic.

*****

Admiral Rogers was not feeling jolly. The dull ache had returned to his left arm. He was sweating more than usual. It bothered him that his men might see his distress and think he was not up to the task.

Persevere. Or die trying.

Weymouth had just advised Rogers that the Leap Frogs were in the air. Rogers was aware the Leap Fogs had never seen combat as a team. With the war in Afghanistan, ongoing operations in Iraq, and a worldwide war on terror, special operations capabilities were stretched thin. The elite parachutists were all Rogers had. Even so, it had taken a long time, too long, to convince Naval Special Warfare Command of the need to deploy them. NSWC balked at the risk. It took intervention from the White House to OK the plan.

Weymouth was still briefing Rogers.

Yap, yap, yap. Weymouth sure likes the sound of his own voice. For Christ's sake, tell me something I don't already know.

Rogers clenched and unclenched his left hand to divert his mind from the pain. He dragged his attention back to Weymouth's dissertation.

"As you know, Admiral, *Constitution* is heading east, southeast. She is maintaining an average speed of about 10 knots. We do not know where she is headed or why she put to sea. Hypothetically, the terrorists may be sailing for Europe or perhaps Africa. We just do not know. We've had no contact with them and no demands have been made, which is extremely unusual for a hostage situation."

Rogers unconsciously cupped his left elbow with one hand and gently massaged it as he listened. Weymouth pretended not to notice.

"*Constitution* is old. While seaworthy for short trips, our marine engineers advise that she is not likely to last long in open water. In short, she could come apart at any time, especially if the weather continues to deteriorate and the seas roughen. Therefore, we are in a race against time.

"The Coast Guard cutter *David* is about two hours from the target. Unfortunately, there is a full moon. The weather is unsettled and rapidly worsening. Increasingly high winds are expected. Certainly not optimal conditions for covert operations."

He glanced at some papers on the table. "The meteorologists predict incoming cloud cover by 0200 hours. When the clouds descend, we hit them. *David* from the water, the Leap Frogs from the air.

"*David* will strike first. Her job is to create a diversion. Although we have two assault teams aboard *David*, we do not anticipate they will actually attempt to board *Constitution*, at least not initially.

"That task will fall to the Leap Frogs. While the hijackers engage *David*, they will parachute onto the ship. Once the Leap Frogs secure the spar deck, we believe *David* can close and assist with mopping up operations and evacuating the hostages. The attack should last under fifteen minutes."

"How many men on *David*?"

"Twenty-four plus Captain Newtowne."

And the Leap Frogs?"

"Fourteen."

"Tell me about the weather again."

Here Weymouth cleared his throat. "The weather, Sir, is always unpredictable."

Prevarication, the art of an intelligence officer.

"I know that, Weymouth. I'm not an idiot. I kissed King Neptune's ass and became a Shellback long before your father's testicles descended. What is the forecast?"

"A growing tropical storm is moving north from the Carolinas. It is has passed over Bermuda. It will likely blossom into a hurricane. Its outer edge may have already reached *Constitution,* but in any event certainly will by 0100 hours."

Parachute into a hurricane. My God, what's next? Rogers stifled his misgivings.

"Can the old girl survive the storm?" the Admiral continued.

Weymouth looked down and shuffled his papers. "Admiral, we do not believe so. She'll be nearly 150 miles out to sea. She will take it in the teeth."

Rogers bit his lip as the ache in his arm sharpened.

Goddamnit. More bad luck. We win back the ship and she still might founder.

"And if *David* and the Leap Frogs fail, what's the backup plan?"

"We are working on it, Admiral," Weymouth replied weakly. He stuttered again, "We're working on it."

"Work faster."

~ Chapter 6 ~

July 4, 2012

2240 hrs.

When the shooting on the gun deck began, Eleni screamed and went down. She did not know where Zach was. Her instinct was to flee. She crawled as fast as she could away from the melee, weaving in and out of the terrified hostages, who scattered like mercury dropped on concrete. When she found herself by the hatch near the capstan, she swung a leg over the edge of the opening, and groped with her foot for a ladder rung. She caught one, dropped fully through and climbed down.

There were no gun ports or skylights on the berth deck. The few tiny portholes were useless this time of day. Practically no light filtered down through the grating covering the main hatch. The long deck was approaching pitch black. Propelled by the mayhem above, she blindly ran for safety into the beckoning shadows.

Sightless, Eleni careened into something soft strung across the compartment. It brushed her face like a spider web. She recoiled from its touch and ran the opposite way, only to encounter a similar barrier. Frightened by the unfamiliar thing, she flailed at it and bolted off in a third direction. This time she tripped over a wooden chest on the deck and banged her head on an unseen post. Dazed, she stumbled back and fell onto her buttocks.

The stars in her brain gradually cleared. She rolled onto her knees and crawled like a baby, one hand outstretched. As she scuffled forward, her fingertips bumped into a hard ledge. She stood and encountered a chair. Beyond the chair was a table. Hand over hand she groped her way along the table until it ended. Unsure what to do next, she let go of the table and hazarded a step into the unknown.

More nothing. She bumped into a wall and then touched a door handle. Opening the door, she entered a chamber. Her right shin struck something hard. She determined it was another table. Exploring further, her fingers brushed something soft that swung when she pushed it. With both hands, she fumbled over the object. It was a hammock. Cautiously, she sat in its center. The hammock swayed and nearly spilled her. When it steadied, she slowly lay back and stretched out her body.

She strained to hear what was going on above her. The closed door of her small cabin and the varied sounds of the ship made it hard to make anything out.

Her nerves calmed. A profound sense of fatigue swept over her as the adrenalin induced by her escape washed out of her system. Her breathing slowed and she shut her eyes. Despite her desire to remain alert, the rhythmic sway of the hammock quickly rocked her to sleep.

She awoke to what sounded to her vaguely like a rifle being fired. After that, silence. Her head ached.

It was peaceful in her cotton cocoon. Groggy, she once more closed her eyes and drifted off.

*****

At the moment, Captain Raffington wrenched open his cabin door and was gunned down from behind, Mustafa seized the opportunity to escape. He had been feigning death, quietly composing himself for action. When Grain and Zach sprinted forward to assist Raffington, Mustafa rolled onto his hands and knees and scampered forward, past the mainmast, and dropped over the lip of the fore hatchway stairs. He missed the stairs and tumbled ten feet to the berthing deck, landing hard with a thud. His wind gone, he remained motionless until his diaphragm relaxed, and he could resume breathing. In that time, he looked around.

Blacker than Gaddafi's heart.

Using the pale rectangle of light above him from the hatchway, he oriented himself. He crawled at an angle toward the port hull. When he reached it, he continued to inch forward toward the bow. The inner hull was cold and smooth and felt slightly damp to the touch. He crept past the foremast, bumping over the huge knees protruding from the deck, until he could go no further. At that juncture, he wedged himself against the hull facing the stern.

He knew he'd taken a bullet in the side. It hurt but was not fatal. Falling down the stairs had not helped. Without making a sound, he first removed his belt and then the handkerchief in his back pants pocket. He folded the handkerchief into a compress, placed it on the wound, and cinched the belt hard around his abdomen to hold it in place. The makeshift bandage successfully staunched the flow of blood. Exhausted, he leaned back and plotted his next move.

The surrounding blackness did not bother him. He had spent enough time in stygian, airless hellholes around the world so that confinement, sensory deprivation, and silence were familiar. In fact, this was better than most prisons. At least there were no screams of pain from other prisoners being tortured. Or jailors to rape him.

Things were not going as planned. They had expected the Americans to act like sheep. Instead, they had fought, nearly killing him, and seized possession of the gun deck. The uprising would not prevent the successful execution of the remainder of the greater plan, but it was an affront to his manhood and an insult to his dignity.

He replayed how the Americans had accomplished their ambush. He knew Zach Colt and the shorthaired, older man were the ringleaders. He regretted not having killed Colt earlier when he'd had the chance. The man haunted him like an evil *jinn*.

And the other man. He would also die. They would all die.

My list grows long.

He flicked his eyes to his wristwatch. Its glowing face was barely discernible. Ten hours to go. Then it would be over. He had ten hours to kill, literally.

Mustafa struggled to his feet. His head suddenly felt light and dizziness seized him. He shot out a hand to steady himself.

By the Prophet's beard! I have lost more blood than I thought.

The tourniquet had come loose. He cinched it tighter, grunting with pain.

Before continuing, he patted his side to make sure his knife was there. Satisfied it was, he gingerly stepped forward. He gradually made his way to the stern, intending to use the ladder near the wardroom to sneak onto the gun deck. Near the wardroom, he heard the sound.

It was a soft, buzzing noise. Not part of the ship. Clearly human. Close by, hidden in the murk. He held his breath and listened more intently. The sound repeated itself. It rose and fell. The rhythm was familiar. He identified the sound as someone sleeping. Then he heard a voice. It was a woman's voice, soft, sultry, talking in her sleep.

He was not alone.

His spirits lifted. Wounded or not, female company was always welcome.

Zach could wait. He might as well enjoy himself.

Let the hunt begin.

As he began to stand, a wave of fatigue hit him. He slumped back down.

Damn blood loss!

First, he would rest. He sat cross-legged on the deck, back against the door, and quickly lost himself in vivid fantasies about the punishment he would inflict on the helpless woman hidden nearby.

~ Chapter 7 ~

July 4, 2012

2306 hrs.

Their group was small and weak. A single Kalashnikov and a few clips of ammunition were the only weapons liberated from the dead jihadist. Their depleted numbers made it next to impossible to take on skilled fighters, let alone do so without being better armed. More firepower was needed.

Zach, Grain, and Meyerson conferred. Too much time had passed in indecision. A plan was needed. They agreed it was critical to acquire more weapons.

"Meyerson," Zach quizzed, "this ship is commissioned, right? You must have some sort of arms on board?"

"We have an arms locker. We normally stock a few rifles and handguns. Captain Raffington ordered the armorer below to fetch our weapons when the attack started. The armorer was killed. We never got anything."

"Well, it's worth checking out," Grain suggested. "Maybe some are left. Where is it?"

"In the hold. It was built where the old forward magazine used to be. I have a key."

"Is there anything else?" Zach probed.

Meyerson hesitated, thinking. Then her face brightened. "Follow me!"

She led the way into the Captain's Great Cabin, past her dead captain. On either side of the room were glass display cases. One held several ancient cutlasses. The other had two braces of flintlock pistols.

"Ta da!" Meyerson joked, making a sweeping gesture with her hands as if she was a magician displaying a trick.

Grain laughed upon seeing the ancient weapons. "Hot damn! I always wanted one of these!"

He used the stock of the Kalashnikov to smash a glass display case and then extracted a cutlass. He twirled it in one hand. It looked surprisingly lethal.

"I asked for sword fighting lessons during Secret Service training. No dice, they said. Huh! It only goes to show, you never know!"

Zach took out a second cutlass and slid it into his belt. "Hardy har, har" he joked in his best pirate voice.

"Please," Meyerson pleaded, "stop acting like little boys. This is life or death."

Zach and Grain wiped the smiles from their faces.

Grain was abashed. "Sorry, ma'am."

"Me too," Zach added. He stepped across to the other display case and studied the flintlocks. They appeared well oiled and serviceable, not a bit like 200-year-old antiques.

Meyerson saw him looking at the pistols. "Yeah, they're pretty, aren't they? Believe it or not, they work. We use them for ceremonies and reenactments to entertain tourists."

"You're kidding? So you have powder?"

"Yes."

"Do you have balls?"

Meyerson chuckled, "What kind of balls?"

Zach realized what he had just said. "I mean pistol balls. Ones we can use."

"The only lead balls are the ones in the case," Meyerson answered.

Zach counted. "Four pistols, twelve balls. It's better than nothing."

"Not much," Grain opined. "You know how to use one of those bad boys?"

"I do," Meyerson responded.

"I've read about them," Zach added. "I think I can figure it out."

"Okey-dokey," Grain continued. "You two are the experts. I'll stick with cold steel." He twirled the sword once more for emphasis, then smashed the pommel into the glass, shattering the top of the case into splinters.

Meyerson reached inside, extracted two pistols and put them in the diaper bag. Zach stuffed the remaining pistols into his belt and loaded his pockets with the lead balls. He turned to Meyerson. "Let's get the powder. Where is it?"

"Where else? In the powder room."

"Uh-huh. And where might that be?"

"Below us, in the hold. In the original copper-lined aft magazine."

Zach and Meyerson exited the room. As Zach passed the bodies, he noticed the Captain's dirk embedded in the dead guard. He yanked it out, wiped the blood off on the sofa, and thrust it into the back of his waistband.

He glanced at Raffington. "My apologies, Captain. I think I need this more than you do."

Grain gathered the remaining cutlasses and cradled them beneath his left arm. He poked his sword into a pillow on a chair as if skewering a foe.

"Take that!" he exclaimed. Vastly amused by his own wit, he left the room to rejoin the other members of the band.

The three were greeted with backslaps and muted cheers when they emerged and displayed their prizes. Counting the swords, the old muzzle loaders and the Kalashnikov, at least nine hostages now had some kind of weapon.

Meyerson checked her watch. They'd been under way for hours and must be far from Boston. The sooner they struck back, the better.

"Time to get the powder," Meyerson ordered. "Grain, you're in charge. Stay here. I'll go with Colt."

Without waiting for an answer, Meyerson climbed into the aft stair hatch and disappeared into the darkness below. Before Zach could join her, Eldridge Horsley approached.

"I want to be of use."

Zach eyed the older man. He was thin, yet fit. One lens of his glasses had fallen out. A few bruises were evident on his face. His wife Mags stood fretting behind him, holding Connie.

Against his better judgment, Zach gave permission. "Alright, Eldridge. Maybe you can help."

The man lacked a weapon. Zach handed Eldridge Raffington's dirk. "Take this. Use it wisely. C'mon."

Zach turned away and began to descend after Meyerson. Horsley glanced quickly at his wife. Mags gave him an enigmatic smile. He mouthed a silent good-bye to her and vanished down the ladder behind Zach.

Part IV

Saving Her

~ Chapter 1 ~

July 4, 2012

2320 hrs.

Smartwood slowed *David* to a crawl about a mile behind where the radar indicated *Constitution* should be found. The old ship was somewhere ahead in the night, sailing at a good clip. Now it was time to ready *David* for the attack.

Unhappy within the confines of the pilothouse, he'd stepped onto the upper deck. The cutter rolled up and down in the growing swells. Weather reports confirmed a major storm heading their way. Whether a gale or a full-fledged hurricane was yet to be determined. He could smell trouble in the air, see it in the increased cloud cover, and feel it in the restless ocean buoying his ship. Braced on the bridge with a pair of binoculars, he scanned the horizon for any sign of *Constitution*.

Nothing and more nothing. He rotated through several compass points. She was out there, he knew. Radar and satellite imagery proved it. Despite this, he wanted to confirm her existence with his own senses. At last, aided by a pinch of moonlight, a phantom speck of white appeared. He watched long enough to be certain the object was moving and relayed its position to his navigator. Assured he was in the right spot, he put down the glasses and rubbed his tired eyes.

Now the waiting began.

He lit a cigar and puffed smoke rings. The delicate creations expelled from his lips immediately dissolved in the freshening night breeze.

"Ephemeral," he reflected.

About as solid as my career. With luck, about an hour from now it would all be over.

It would take a number of factors for a successful outcome. They had to wait for the C-130 to arrive. The cloud cover needed to thicken and obscure the moon. The wind had to be just right. Those were the easy variables. They had instruments to help figure them out.

The harder ones were predicting how effectively the enemy would react and how well his men and the Leap Frogs would execute the plan. He was sure of his crew. He was equally confident in the Leap Frogs.

The extremist fighters were the big unknown. How many were there? Were they well trained? What type of armaments did they possess? Above all else, would they fight?

He anticipated the jihadists would prove to be no match for the deadly commandos about to be unleashed upon them. Surprise was key. Also speed. More than anything, they needed luck. Lots of it. It was often far better to be lucky than good. Now was one of those times.

Smartwood had spent virtually his whole life in the service. The ribbons on his tunic attested to campaigns in Panama, Iraq, and Afghanistan. He learned hard lessons in leadership along the way. Even harder ones in loss and sorrow. It was a great privilege to lead fine Americans into battle. It was an even greater curse knowing that not all would come back.

Another puff of aromatic smoke drifted upward. He watched it, made aware by its progress that the wind had lessened and was now blowing fitfully from the south. The moon became blotted out by a prodigious bank of roiling clouds. Smartwood detected the faint buzz of engines overhead.

As he gazed up, a signal came in over his headset. "Execute!"

"Full speed ahead!" he ordered. The men on the weather deck and inside the pilothouse held on as the powerful boat accelerated through the swells, sending torrents of seawater gushing over the bow. Smartwood tossed his cigar aside and gripped a rail for balance. He wanted to yell, "Yahoo!" but knew it would be undignified. Instead, his face broke into a wide, open-mouthed grin as the salt wind and spray pounded his face.

It had been a long time since he'd cruised into battle on anything as small as *David*. He felt as if he were Captain Ahab on a mad Nantucket sleigh ride. The grin widened and his teeth gradually pulled back over his lips into a wolf-like snarl.

Why not?

He let out a yowl of animal pleasure, quickly swallowed by the wind. Caught up in the excitement, unbidden, the assault teams assembled on the deck below joined in. Soon the entire crew picked up the chorus, and the screaming engines of the cutter and the battle cries of its warriors combined as one as *David* charged into the fray.

Operation Recovered Honor had entered its next phase.

*****

In the night sky thousands of feet above *David*, the C-130 circled. Inside the cargo bay, Sconzotti and his men awaited the signal to jump. Some prayed. Others thought of wives, children, or girlfriends. A few meditated, clearing their minds of all extraneous thoughts in preparation for the coming fight. The more nervous ones rehearsed the operation in their heads, mentally walking through each element of the attack.

Sconzotti thought about baseball. He could not help it.

Shortly after the big plane took off, it had looped around Boston before heading east over the Atlantic. The pilot had called Sconzotti forward. Through the nose windows, he glimpsed Fenway Park, ablaze with light as the Yankees battled the Red Sox in the second game of their July Fourth doubleheader.

The old ballpark was celebrating its 100th year. Flags and banners festooned the stands. From above, she was a beautiful patch of green in a sea of scattered lights and gray concrete, an emerald in a dull iron crown. Despite the Boston Harbor holocaust, the game went on.

The Yankees were leading in the AL East race. The Sox weren't even in contention. However, the July Fourth contest was a tradition each side took quite seriously.

Even with all the trouble going down, Sconzotti had managed to listen to most of the first game on the radio between briefings and meetings. The Sox won game one. Jeter had done well in the afternoon game, as had A-Rod. The Sox pitching was better than last year and gave the Yankees trouble. Lester finally showed some mettle. Big Papi had earned every penny of his multi-million dollar free agent contract with homers in the 4th and 9th innings.

Damn Red Sox. Some clubs just do not know when they are beaten.

In the cockpit, the pilot had tuned into the color commentary. The game was running late. The Yankees were ahead by two runs in the bottom of the 8th. As the plane veered away from Fenway, the pilot shut down the feed. Sconzotti reluctantly rejoined his men.

Now all Sconzotti could do was imagine the final at bat of the 8th and the entire 9th inning as the big plane bounced and rattled toward the drop zone. He fantasized about a Yankee victory.

Suddenly, a voice came through his headset.

"Two minute warning."

Sconzotti rechecked his equipment. He closed his eyes.

Time for one last pitch.

The voice calmly said, "Ramp." Sconzotti opened his eyes.

The giant ramp in the back of the plane cranked down and the steady red light illuminating the cargo area turned to yellow. The plane banked sharply.

Time for a little DA.

Sconzotti lurched to his feet and clung to the fuselage as he walked toward the tail section. His men rose and lined up in pairs behind him. He moved partway onto the ramp. Deafening wind and air noise filled the fuselage.

Sconzotti stared out at nothingness.

Hello, God. I'm ready.

The transport flew into a thick cloudbank. Moonlight infused the vapor with an eerie white light. They became swaddled in a huge, glowing cotton ball.

With one hand, he adjusted his twin tube helmet-mounted night vision goggles and inched farther out onto the ramp until he reached the edge where he paused and looked back at his men. They stood side by side in the eerie green light caused by the goggles.

Together, they gave him the thumbs-up sign. He smiled.

What is this, maybe our 200th jump together? Just another day in the park.

The yellow overhead light turned to green. A loud buzzer sounded. He tapped the helmet of the man closest to him. Without hesitation, the man launched himself into the void, together with his partner.

Man after man jumped, until only Sconzotti remained.

He glanced one last time around the interior, making sure everyone was out.

"Adios, War Hawk," he spoke into the headset.

"God be with you, Avenger," the pilot replied.

He is.

Then Sconzotti backed up, took a running leap, and was gone.

*****

Al-Buyid felt on edge.

It had been too easy. He had not had contact with the enemy for hours. The Americans seemed to have backed down. He had seen enough of his foe in Iraq and Afghanistan to know this was not normal. Although a weak people at their core, the United States military, at least, had the steel to fight.

The question was, where and when?

Midnight was near. He had been permitted to proceed virtually unimpeded. Something was definitely not right.

He reviewed the day's events. The hostages on deck had been kept strapped in place since leaving the harbor. They were exhausted and near-frozen by exposure to the cold and wind in their pathetic summer clothes. Many were dreadfully seasick. Regardless of their condition, they provided him with a human shield around the perimeter of the ship.

Constitution's topmen had been forced to stay aloft. They too, were fatigued, hungry, and shivering, but held their stations. Al-Buyid had only let them down to use the head.

CPO Zajac remained by Al-Buyid's side, relaying orders to his sailors. The welfare of his crew was his only concern. He knew that if his sailors disobeyed or showed any signs of rebellion, more lives would be lost. He made sure they therefore obeyed.

Al-Buyid passed a minor course correction to Zajac who relayed it to the helmsman. The helmsman tugged gently at the wheel, forcing the elegant barkentine to turn slowly to the south. At Al-Buyid's direction, Zajac shouted more orders to trim the sails. The sailors jumped to their task, tightening the lines, taking up the slack in the canvas. The ship's speed increased.

In some respects, the most important part of the mission had not begun. Al-Buyid calculated that soon he would make contact with his confederates. He signaled for Faroud to approach. Zajac watched as the two men put their heads together and conversed quietly in Arabic. The terrorist duo was deep in conversation when the moon slipped behind the clouds and the sky faded from silver to gray and then to black. A greasy drizzle began to fall.

Bright flashes from the muzzle of *David*'s machine guns abruptly pierced the night. A red blur of tracers streaked toward *Constitution*'s starboard. A few rounds thudded into the hull. Several of the bound passengers cried out.

Seconds later the big cutter materialized behind *Constitution*. Al-Buyid saw its white hull churning toward them. He could dimly make out men massed along its rail in preparation for an assault. Searchlights from *David* suddenly danced over *Constitution's* hull and sails, blinding and confusing Al-Buyid and the other terrorists as they scrambled to react to the threat.

Al-Buyid shouted orders for his men to gather on the starboard quarterdeck. The gunmen swarmed to the side rail. They lined the bulwark between the tethered hostages. At al-Buyid's command, they opened fire on *David* as she tore alongside them. The hostages whimpered and ducked for safety.

David ripped past the starboard at a distance of 100 yards, every one of its guns firing. The enemy fighters ducked for cover, popping up haphazardly to return a fire.

Then *David* was gone. Moments later, she returned, this time along the port. Al-Buyid thundered for his men to change positions. The jihadists scurried across the deck to the opposite side where they once again lay down a withering fusillade as *David* roared past.

Faroud fired a Stinger missile. His aim was poor and *David* too fast. The missile passed harmlessly over the cutter's stern. *David* disappeared from sight.

Faroud stood and waved his hand at *David*, thumb up, cursing in Pashto. Many of the other terrorists joined him, displaying a cross-section of insulting Middle Eastern gestures, ranging from "ride the camel" to showing the soles of their shoes.

During the celebration, Al-Buyid took stock. None of his men were hit. No sailors had tumbled from the rigging. All the hostages were unharmed.

He felt brief elation before the emotionless, calculating part of his mind considered the ramifications of their good fortune. By then, *David* had come back into view. Again, his men took up firing positions. The cutter was upon them with lights blazing and the deafening sound of machinegun fire before Al-Buyid, in a burst of insight, realized what was occurring. As loud as possible, he howled, "Stop!"

It was far too noisy for his band to hear his command. Al-Buyid sensed motion out of the corner of his eye. A large, dark shape hurtled past *Constitution* to Al-Buyid's left and smacked into the water.

Alarmed, he looked up. Other black figures dropped from the sky. A few were silhouetted against *Constitution's* sails as they fell.

"*Khara!*" he shouted and pointed up. No one responded. He sprang toward the nearest fighter and batted away his weapon.

"Stop!" he yelled into the man's ear. "It's a ruse! Look up!"

At that moment, death came from above.

~ Chapter 2 ~

July 4, 2012

2348 hrs.

Admiral Rogers clutched the piece of paper in his hand.

Bullshit. This is total bullshit. Either that or I am the unluckiest son of a bitch on the planet.

He glared at Weymouth. It wasn't Weymouth's fault but he needed someone to blame. Junior officers were best.

"I don't believe this."

The look on the Admiral's face scared Weymouth.

"Sir, it's come from the top. I vetted it through OPNAV and Fleet Forces Command. I also confirmed it through a friend in the CIA. It is true. Regrettable, but true."

Rogers crumbled the dispatch and hurled it across the table.

On the screen in front of him, the battle for *Constitution* unfolded in real time. He could hear chatter from *David* and periodic squawks from Sconzotti's team. Occasionally, the screen would change as a different camera was accessed and fresh images from a new vantage point came into view.

First came *David*'s mad rush at *Constitution*. Next images of parachutists dropping from the sky. Gunfire and shouting. Jarring pictures of men tumbling into the sea. An upside down view of *Constitution*'s deck from a yardarm, showing frenzied, ant-like activity below and the muzzle fire from scads of weapons. Screams of pain. Curses in English and God knew what other languages.

As frightening and fascinating as all that was, Weymouth's news was even more unsettling. In the chaos of the engagement, Rogers concentrated on creating a small pocket of quiet in which to converse with Weymouth.

"The Iranians only have three Kilo Class subs. Three. We've known that for years," Rogers erupted. "Now you're telling me there's a fourth one? Not only that, you are reporting the cocksucker is 240 miles off the coast of New England?"

"Yes, Sir. I'm sorry to relay the news, Sir. The last we knew, all three subs were bottled up at the Iranian Navy's main base at Bandar-Abbas on the south coast. The facility is near the Persian Gulf adjacent to the Straits of Hormuz. The Fifth Fleet and Task Force 150 as part of CENTCOM cover that area. They still report all three subs in bay. No one knew of the existence of a fourth sub."

Rogers took off his bifocals and tossed them onto the table in disgust. He rubbed his forehead. *What a clusterfuck! A fourth sub . . . unbelievable!*

"Where did it come from? How did it manage to cross 6,000 miles of ocean undetected?"

"May I sit, Sir," Weymouth asked. Rogers bruskly waved a hand at him. He flicked an eye to the monitor in time to see the shadowy figure of a parachuting SEAL land upright on the deck of *Constitution*, only to be swarmed by three gunmen who leapt from behind a mast.

"We don't think it's part of the IRIN. We think it belongs to the Iranian Revolutionary Guard. As you know, they run a separate Islamic Revolutionary Guard Corps Navy, mostly small boats, short-range, fast attack craft and the like, as well as coastal-based missiles. They have a couple of mini-subs. Nothing capable of striking North America. The IRGC-N is equipped well enough to sink some of our bigger vessels in the Persian Gulf theater of operations, particularly if they attack en masse. To date, we were unaware of anything larger in its arsenal.

"Our hypothesis is that the IRGC-N got the sub from the North Koreans who got it from the Russians. We believe that the North Koreans built an entire supertanker around the sub to mask its existence. The supertanker sailed to Venezuela where it was dismantled in a specially constructed, covered dry dock facility near the obscure town of Porto Carabuno on Venezuela's northwest coast, releasing the sub. The sub subsequently headed east, then northwest skirting the Caribbean to where we think it is now."

Rogers shook his head in disbelief. "Tell me, Lt. Commander, doesn't this shit only happen in James Bond movies?"

"Not any more, Admiral," Weymouth replied with a tense smile. "If the mind of man can dream it, nowadays he can create it."

*****

273

Sconzotti rocketed through the clouds so fast for a while he could not breathe. Arms outstretched, the night air plastered his uniform against his body. When he popped out of the cloud cover at 10,000 feet, he pulled his ripcord. His black batwing parachute deployed and he became busy guiding his chute toward the tiny bright green pinprick of a ship illuminated by *David's* searchlights framed below in his night vision goggles. Past his feet, he could barely make out his men, stacked loosely one on top of the other for a tight landing.

It was an almost impossible drop. The target was fast moving and smaller than a baseball diamond. The ship, although caught in the glare of *David's* searchlights, was barely discernible in the waves. Even if he found it, landing would be hellish. The vessel bristled with masts, sails and rigging, all hazards to a safe landing. And there was the need to fight the hornet's nest of mujahideen in order to free the captives.

Dicey, at best.

But then again, these were the type of missions SEALs relished.

At 8,000 feet, Sconzotti realized he was coming in too rapidly and being blown off course. He spilled air from his chute to make a minor correction. It didn't completely work. The target was coming up fast, way too fast. Within seconds, he slammed face first into the billowed mainsail. It was like hitting a wall made out of pillows. The wall yielded, and he survived the impact, only to find himself sliding down the sail at breakneck speed.

He yanked out his Winkler WKII Utility Knife and plunged it into the sailcloth. The blade pierced the tough ripstock fabric and he clung to the hilt as he slid down. Foot after foot, the knife sheared through the strong reinforced nylon, slowing his fall. He struck a yardarm hard with his legs, bounced off and tumbled, only to be jolted to a halt when his parachute lines tangled in the rigging.

For a second, he hung upside down, looking at the deck. Bright yellow-green muzzle flashes came from below. When he realized men were firing at him, he scissored himself up, grabbed a ratline and slashed through his parachute lines. Upright and free, he flung the knife down at the shooters and unencumbered his HK MP5 Submachine Gun. The MP5 was set on fully automatic. Using his superior night vision, he focused on the figures below and retuned fire. His laser picked out a target. One down. Another target. Two down.

He swung his weapon aside, hooked a leg over a ratline, and slid 70 feet to the deck, where he landed hard, rolled, and sprang upright to find himself facing two new foes. A short burst of AK-47 fire tore up his left arm. Unable to grab his rifle, he unholstered his 9 mm Sig Sauer from his chest rig and popped four rounds into the closest terrorist. The second enemy, in the midst of inserting a fresh clip of ammo, hesitated, and Sconzotti bashed him in the head with the butt of the pistol and shot him through the chest as he toppled.

Over his headset, he heard multiple reports of "Boots on deck!"

Around him, his men fought like hellhounds. Some battled hand-to-hand. Two were concealed behind the foremast and galley stove pipe, engaged in gun battle with a clusters of terrorists near the starboard cathead. Above him, he could make out the twisted forms of three SEALs dangling lifelessly from the rigging. Over the battle sounds, a cry of "In the drink!" came across his headset. He guessed a few others had missed the ship entirely. They were beyond his help.

Poor bastards!

He did the math. Between missed landings and casualties, he had probably already lost more than half his command. *Unbelievable! Four, maybe five left.* Outnumbered, his men fought desperately for their lives.

A bullet pierced his right thigh and he crumbled to his knees. Another round slammed into the back of his helmet, dazing him. He rolled to one side, discharged his pistol at the shadow behind him, and heard a satisfying grunt of pain. The bullets whizzing in his direction momentarily stopped.

Is it over? He dragged himself to the bulwarks and propped his bleeding body next to a carronade. A woman hostage was slumped against the gun, her hands knotted to its carriage. She was young, no more than thirty. The right side of her jaw was blown away. Jagged red holes were stitched across her back. On the next carronade over, a portly man screamed for help as bullets pinged around him.

No such luck. Naptime is done.

Sconzotti ejected his spent pistol magazine, slammed another into place. The pain in his thigh was vicious. That was it for his right leg. He knew it was useless. His wounded left arm was dripping blood and going numb. Soon he would lose its use.

Slowly, he raised his head over the carronade and searched for a target. Toward the stern, he saw a gargantuan bearded man near the wheel holding a sailor to his chest as a human shield. In his free hand, the Goliath brandished a hand-held missile launcher of some sort. Next to the brute a smaller man crouched by the dully glowing polished brass binnacle. A *Constitution* sailor lay in front of him. The man by the binnacle carefully aimed an AK-47 at a SEAL partially protected by the capstan. Before Sconzotti could shoot, the SEAL was dropped. The marksman rushed forward past the capstan toward the main hatch cover, which had two boats strapped to it, shielding a second SEAL.

Sconzotti emptied his pistol at the runner, without effect. Using the cannon for balance, he levered himself to his feet and hopped across the deck on one leg to intercept the running figure. He flung himself in the man's path and tackled him to the deck. Sconzotti rolled to the side and brought his pistol up to bear, groping for a fresh magazine. He was too late.

Our Father, Who Art in Heaven . . . .

A rifle held inches from his face by Al-Buyid discharged in a dazzling flash.

All went black.

Standing over Sconzotti, Al-Buyid breathed in ragged gasps. Blood dripped from his left forearm where an errant round had opened his flesh. He looked around and saw his men had pinned down the last visible SEAL near the mizzenmast and were gradually closing in. Scattered about him, he counted the bodies of six of his mujahideen and four SEALs.

The blood from the man he had just killed flowed across the deck, wetting his shoes.

A stun grenade went off and Al-Buyid fell to the deck in agony, clutching his head. A hidden SEAL dashed out from the shadow of a carronade in a last ditch effort to mow down the small knot of enemy gunmen clustered near the foremast. The black-clad warrior was felled by a barrage of small arms fire.

Al-Buyid shook his head clear. The ringing in his ears gradually lessened. His eyes focused. From his spot on the deck, he grunted in satisfaction as he watched the American twitch, puppet-like, as multiple rounds ripped into his prone body.

The only surviving SEAL attempted to rush to his fallen comrade's aid, spraying shotgun blasts as he ran the length of the ship from the stern to the main mast. He was caught in a fusillade of bullets from the remaining jihadists who closed on him from all sides. When he fell, the firing ceased.

*****

On the television, the sounds of battle were dissipating. Most of the radio traffic had petered off. There was only sporadic gunfire. When the firing stopped, Rogers barked, "Status?"

A young Ensign turned in his chair to face Rogers. Tears welled in his eyes.

"It's over, Sir."

"And?"

The young man stiffened his back and faced his commander. He swiped at his eyes. In the strongest voice he could muster, he continued.

"We failed to take back *Constitution*, Sir."

*****

David and her crew circled *Constitution*, observing the battle unfold. Her sailors scanned the ocean for swimmers. Two SEALs were plucked from the water, half-drowned. One had a broken arm and leg. The other, once on board, had to be restrained by the Coasties from jumping over the side and swimming to the aid of his brothers. Three other SEALs were spotted and successfully rescued.

David's surprise attack was meant to distract the enemy long enough to at least give the SEALs a fighting chance to ambush the enemy from the skies. Smartwood wished his feint had worked better. Like most engagements, it came down to numbers. Too few SEALs had landed successfully.

He had stationed sharpshooters along the rail, but their efforts, given the high seas, were ineffectual. Through his glasses, Smartwood had watched in agony and growing despair as the NSW commandos were cut down.

Radkowski provided a running commentary of the battle to NAVCOM. When it was clear the tide had turned against the Americans, Smartwood pleaded for permission to attack.

Permission was denied. Command decreed that there were too many hostages on *Constitution* to risk a further assault. The anger and frustration on board *David* were palpable. No one was more distraught then Smartwood. In a strained and cracking voice, he gave orders for *David* to take up station behind *Constitution*.

As the cutter fell into position, a sailor shouted and pointed ahead. Smartwood raised his glasses anew and saw limp bodies tossed from *Constitution* into the sea.

Goddamnit, those are Navy men . . . .

He could not stomach this final infamy.

Ignoring his orders, he motored close to the bark and searched for the SEALs. Mercifully, the moon broke through the clouds and briefly illuminated the surface of the sea. He put out his launch and small boats. It took three hours to locate and recover five bodies bobbing limply in the swells, Sconzotti among them. The other dead heroes had been tugged below the surface, never to return.

When the recovery operation was exhausted, like a whipped puppy *David* fell once more behind *Constitution* and trailed her eastward. Soon, the tempest intensified. Mounting seas slowed her progress. Unexpected engine problems developed. Several of the surviving SEALs were so badly wounded that *David's* surgeon feared he could not save them and so begged Smartwood to return to base.

By dawn, *David* was in the teeth of a major storm and battling for her survival. *Constitution* was nowhere in sight. The accumulation of negatives was overwhelming. *David* was ordered to turn back. The other cutters closing from the north and south would take up the chase.

Smartwood kept to the bridge, smoking. He clutched the dog tags removed from the dead SEALs in his hand. Throughout his long career, he had served in many theaters. In every one of them, he had seen brave young sailors die.

This was the first time in U.S. waters. It added a new layer of sadness and rage. The force of his grip caused the dog tags to slice into the palm of his hand. A few droplets of blood carried to the deck and gleamed in the moonlight before the rain diluted them and washed them away.

Tears of blood.

He smeared the pink residue with the sole of his shoe, trying to wipe away his grief.

~ Chapter 3 ~

July 5, 2012

0316 hrs.

Zach followed Meyerson down the stairway with Eldridge close behind. They reached the berth deck easily enough. It was nearly pitch black. The thin, watery light filtering down the stairway from the gun deck penetrated a few feet fore and aft, almost enough to paint a few hammocks a ghostly white. Beyond the dim patch of light, complete darkness reigned. Next to him, Meyerson was bent over, busy hiking up her summer dress and tying it around her waist. Her no-nonsense white panties were clearly visible.

"Commander, I'm shocked!" Zach quipped.

Deadly serious, Meyerson shot back, "No time for modesty. We've got work to do." She glanced upward. *Please God, keep Connie safe.*

Meyerson then swung onto the ladder leading from the berth deck down to the orlop deck. When her head disappeared, Zach took her place. Wordlessly, Eldridge trailed Zach.

The berth deck had been dark. The orlop was even darker. Virtually no light from penetrated to this level and what little did created only a faint pool at the foot of the ladder. Once on the orlop, the three explorers paused. The old ship hit a big wave and Meyerson lost her balance and pitched into Zach. He steadied her until the ship settled. She smelled sweet from perspiration and mother's milk. Her scent was a welcome antidote to the rank aroma of old wooden ship that surrounded them.

"Thanks." Meyerson seemed embarrassed. "I guess I haven't got my sea legs fully back."

"Don't worry. You're entitled," Zach answered, smiling in the dark. "Where to?"

"One more deck to go." Trusting her memory, she felt her way to a hatch leading to the hold. With Zach's help, she moved the cover aside.

Meyerson briefly hesitated. "I've never been down here when it's been as black as this. But, I know the magazine is near the stern on the port. We'll need to feel our way to it. This deck has a long central passage with cubbies off each side. There are some unexpected drop-offs so the surface is not flat. Various kinds of equipment is stowed. We have to traverse a lot of space to get to the aft magazine. That's where the shells are."

"Oh my!" Eldridge commented. The older man sounded worried.

"Don't fret, Eldridge. We can do it," Zach countered. Addressing Meyerson, he added, "I think we should hold hands, so we don't get separated. You lead the way."

Zach felt Meyerson's hand touch and slide down his left arm until it found his hand. She grasped it tightly. Her hand was small, but strong.

He reached out for Eldridge and the two clasped hands. Eldridge's was fish-like, the fingers long and boney, his palm damp and uncalloused. It was the hand of a man who had never done a day of hard, physical labor.

Meyerson gave a tug and they were on their way. It was slow going. Zach could hear Meyerson's free hand slide along the walls of unseen compartments as she groped her way forward. When they reached an open door or other unusual transition point, she would stop and relay the news. The strangest part came when they were forced to cross an open stretch of deck with nothing to guide them. It felt like they were floating in space. Zach twice smacked his head on an overhead beam. There was no choice but to walk hunched over. Behind him he could hear Eldridge huffing and puffing, clearly out of shape and fearful.

After inching across a particularly long, empty stretch of deck, they halted.

"We should be close," Meyerson whispered.

"Why are we whispering?" Zach whispered back.

Meyerson let loose with a guffaw. "I don't know. It just seemed appropriate."

"I think we could scream our heads off and no one would notice."

Meyerson laughed again. "You're probably right!"

Eldridge was not laughing. "Excuse me, are we there yet? I'd very much like to be done with this and get back to my wife."

His dry, supercilious tone and Boston Brahmin accent annoyed Zach. "Hey Eldridge, cool it. Commander Meyerson's doing the best she can."

There was no response from Eldridge. Meyerson ended the awkwardness by speaking.

"The magazine should be about twenty feet further on. It's a small room to our right before the filling room and the bread room."

"Whatever," Zach responded. He was getting tired of being led around like a blind man.

Zach felt Meyerson tug his hand. "Let's go."

Once again, the three began their ungainly stop and go march. Within minutes, Meyerson halted and announced. "We're here! I think this is it."

She let go of Zach's hand. Zach heard keys jangling, the rasp of old hinges, and then scraping as a door opened.

Eldridge finally spoke. "It's remarkable that you have the keys, Commander. I commend you."

"Thank you, Mr. . . .?"

"The last name is Horsley. Given the circumstances, we need not be so formal. Please call me Eldridge."

"OK. Thank you, Eldridge. I may have been on maternity leave, but I am still an officer. I need to be prepared."

Zach and Eldridge stayed put, half-crouched, and listened while Meyerson entered the magazine. They heard her fumble around inside.

"Here! I found them!" Soon she was back at the doorway and Zach felt a heavy cardboard cylinder, about one foot long, shoved against his chest.

"Take this," Meyerson ordered.

Zach took the shell. It was a blank used to fire ceremonial salutes. "Eldridge, I'm handing a shell back to you, OK?"

"Yes," was the listless reply. Zach extended the shell to where he assumed Eldridge stood and felt it bump the man's chest. Eldridge grasped it. Zach turned back toward the magazine and Meyerson handed him another shell.

"That's it. Two should be enough. Let's head back."

Zach still hoped to find weapons. "How about the armory?"

"I'm certain Captain Raffington had already emptied it by the time the terrorists seized the ship. We're not going to find anything useful there. It's too far away and not worth the effort."

With a muffled swoosh and soft perfume of air, Meyerson swept past. Zach heard a yelp of pain. Meyerson apologized for accidentally stepping on Eldridge's foot.

Zach tucked his shell under one arm and reached out to find Eldridge with the other one. When he encountered the older man's hand, the trio began to retrace its steps to the hatch.

At the open stretch of deck, Meyerson announced, "Here's the hard part again. Be careful."

After several feet of travel, Eldridge sneezed and released Zach's hand.

"Gesundheit!" Zach reflexively said. Then he heard a soft, "Oof!" and a loud thump.

"Hello? Commander? Eldridge? What happened?"

No one answered.

"What the fuck is going on?"

Zach had barely finished uttering the words when a fist struck the side of his head. Something slashed across his belly, causing pain. He cursed and flailed at the invisible figure attacking him. The assailant did not utter a word.

Zach was losing and needed to regroup. He backed rapidly away. His head struck a low hanging crossbeam and he fell. Before he lost consciousness, he heard footsteps retreating in the dark.

~ Chapter 4 ~

July 5, 2012

0400 hrs.

Captain Shahin Jamshidi rested his head for a few extra seconds on the ancient prayer rug. It had been in his family for five generations, dating back to the Safavid Dynasty. The bald spot in the carpet, worn by years of devotions, caressed his forehead. Despite its age, it still smelled faintly of wool. Its lovely Buteh pattern of greens, blues, and pale ivory soothed his eyes and soul. His morning prayers were nearly over. This day, he had vastly more entreaties for his God than usual.

Head pressed to the carpet he chanted, "Oh Allah, the Precious, the Magnificent One, give our warriors strength this day to strike down the infidel. Make us your spear of justice. Guide our hand so that it inflicts grievous harm on our foe. Help us to humiliate the Great Satan and its Zionist lackeys. Welcome those who die today into Paradise!"

When he was finished praying, he sat back on his haunches. A German-made clock ticked on his small desk. It was one hour and nine minutes until sunrise. He rose to his feet and entered the small bathroom attached to his quarters. There he washed his face and

288

trimmed his short, black beard. Back in the cabin, he put on black pants and a black shirt, accented by blood-red shoulder boards piqued with the gold embroidery of his rank.

Last, he draped a small white silk scarf about his neck and tucked it into his uniform shirt. It had been a parting gift from his wife. She had fashioned it by hand and given it to him before his departure, knowing she was unlikely to see him again.

He remembered the moment well. He was granted shore leave to visit his family to celebrate Nouroz. All of his relatives had attended. His wife, Laleh, was radiant and the family's Haft Seen table was set with fruits, seafood, and other symbols celebrating the coming of spring. It was getting late. His guests had had their fill of sweets, forbidden wine and conversation and were ready to leave. He said his good-byes to them. Afterwards, he tucked his sons into bed and retreated to the bedroom with his wife.

They finished their lovemaking. Naked, Laleh walked to the bedroom's dresser and extracted the weaving from the top drawer where she kept her special treasures. She came to him while his back was turned and slipped the scarf around his head, blindfolding him, giggling in that soft girlish voice that had won him over when they first met in her father's garden twelve years earlier. He spun to face her, and she whisked away the scarf, still giggling, and stepped back. She held the pale cloth coyishly across her breasts.

"For you, my love," she whispered, and extended the cloth to him. "To remember me."

Her small reserve of bravery exhausted, she sank to the floor in a flood of tears. He lifted her and kissed her and they had returned once again to the bed. When they were sated, after she was asleep, he lovingly packed the scarf with his other gear and slipped from the room. He paused once to gaze upon his sleeping children, and then he was off to war.

The smell of her clung to the fabric. Oranges and cloves. He caressed the bandana and lifted a corner to inhale deeply her fragrance for perhaps the last time.

Love of Allah. Love of his country. Love for his Laleh and his two small children.

These were what drove him.

He tucked the scarf back into his tunic and knotted it loosely about his neck like a cravat. *Quite natty.* Grasping the door handle, he opened his cabin and entered the main walkway of the submarine.

Jamshidi liked to tour the sub before the crew's dawn *fajr*. His ship, *Astoh (Unconquered)* was brand new. He had received his degree in Maritime Engineering from Caltech long before joining the IRGC-N. Given his background, he had supervised every stage of her fitting out from her delivery in Venezuela to her launching. The Russians had designed her well. The North Koreans had added a few refinements. Iran had finished the task.

As he poked his head into every nook and cranny of the sub, his pride in their achievement grew. Kilo Class subs were originally designed by the Russians in the late 1970s and put into service in the 1980s. At least 33 had been sold by the Russians abroad, including the *Astoh*, which was first acquired by Vietnam, and later sold to North Korea. *Astoh* was

243 feet long and could dive to a depth of nearly 1,000 feet. She used diesel-electric propulsion and could achieve a surface speed of 14 mph and a submerged speed of 29 mph. By snorkeling at low speed, she had an effective cruising range of up to 7,500 miles.

Passive and active sonar protected the boat. She was coated with anechoic tiles to absorb sound waves from active sonar and mask her own engine noise to avoid detection by passive sonar.

Offensively, *Astoh* was equipped with six torpedo tubes and carried 18 torpedoes, as well as mines, surface-to-air missiles, and submarine-launched anti-submarine missiles. The torpedoes were a new, solid-fueled Hoot supercavitating, high-speed Iranian design, capable of reaching speeds of 225 mph with a range of 4 miles. They had been reverse-engineered from the Russian VA-111 Shkval design. The eight submarine-launched Saturn missiles were also new Iranian technology, previously unknown to the west, based on the Shaheb-3.

This mission had been *Astoh's* shakedown cruise. In the 3,000-mile journey east from Venezuela toward Africa and then north to this spot, Jamshidi had subjected his crew to innumerable drills. So far, his men and the ship had performed admirably. Stealth was absolute. Iranian-developed fuel cells had replaced the old electric batteries and the sub was quieter than ever. They snorkeled as little as possible. Strict radio silence was maintained.

The sub was immaculate. Everything was in its proper place. His submariners were happy and eager. He was confident in the boat's technology and the crew's training. They were ready.

Jamshidi returned to the Wardroom where his officers were completing their breakfast. His XO, Farshad Kourooshi, a short, hawk-faced man with absolutely no sense of humor, was just finishing the last of his feta cheese, lavash, and sour cherry jam. In contrast to his dour disposition, the man possessed a sweet tooth, and lavished heaps of the sugary confection onto the last bite of bread he popped into his mouth. Jamshidi sniffed the air and thought he detected the scent of fried plantain, a newly acquired taste from their stay in Venezuela.

Next to him, Ensign Faroukh Tehrani, tall, skinny, blue-eyed and of fair complexion, nervously nursed a cup of sweet tea. This was his first deployment and the strain of the voyage was proving difficult. Jamshidi made a mental note to keep a special eye on the young officer as the day unfolded.

His other officers idly chatted, read old newspapers, or scribbled notes to loved ones. Several read the Koran.

When Jamshidi entered the mess, they sprang to attention. He gestured for them to sit and assumed his own chair at the head of the table. Wordlessly, he made eye contact with each man. When the tension had reached its apex, he spoke.

"Inshallah, today will be the day." His men nodded.

"Our triumph will become legendary." Again, the men moved their heads indicating agreement.

Jamshidi raised his voice.

"We are the sword of the Prophet!" Now his men voiced their approval with small shouts and prayers.

He slammed his fist onto the table.

"We will prevail!"

As one, his officers sprang to their feet. Together, they pounded their fists against the tabletop and chanted, "We will prevail!" in ever louder refrains until the sailors in the torpedo room could hear the shouts.

Jamshidi threw his arms around the shoulders of his two nearest officers and hugged them to his chest. Righteous joy suffused him.

"Battle stations!" he commanded.

~ Chapter 5 ~

July 5, 2012

0520 hrs.

Eldridge poked his head through the stairway opening into the gloom of the gun deck. Almost immediately, he felt the cold tip of a rifle against his temple. He reached up to push it aside. The barrel held steady. His heart skipped a beat.

"Who is it?" Grain drawled.

"It's me, Eldridge Horsley," his thin voice quavered back.

"Glad to see you made it back, partner. You missed a lot of fireworks." Grain removed the rifle barrel. He reached out a hand and hoisted Eldridge onto the deck. "Where are the others?"

"I don't know. We made it down to a lower deck and then to the hold, I think. It was pitch black. When all the shooting started, we got separated." Eldridge was clearly chagrined. "I got scared and climbed back up. I'm, I'm sorry."

Eldridge could feel Grain's eyes boring into him.

"No problem, old buddy. I understand." The big agent continued his scrutiny. "I expect Colt and Commander Meyerson can take care of themselves."

"Yes, I believe so," Eldridge replied. His eyes blinked rapidly. Grain thought he detected a hitch in the man's voice. "They both seem very capable. Much more so than I."

By now, Eldridge's wife Mags had moved to his side and placed her free arm around his waist. She put her head against his chest and whispered. "I'm so glad you're back."

In the dim pre-dawn light, Eldridge could make out Secretary Powers and Vice President Baine sitting on the deck, their backs against a bulkhead. Both men appeared quiet and dejected. Baine's usual over-the-top grin was not in evidence. The other passengers were spread about the deck, some sitting, some stretched flat. A heavy air of despair permeated the chamber.

Eldridge was curious. "So what happened, may I ask?

"We're not entirely sure." Grain checked the safety on his rifle for the tenth time. He squinted along the barrel at an imagined target in the distance. "Our guys launched some sort of rescue operation. There was a whole lot of shooting. That was a couple of hours ago. Nothing has happened since then. The mission must have failed."

"Oh, no!" Eldridge blurted. "How unfortunate! What do we do, now?"

The Vice President struggled to his feet. He walked over and joined the discussion.

"I say it's time to take our best shot at the terrorists. They were probably weakened by the attack. If they were going to kill us, they'd have done so by now."

He looked hard at Grain. "Maybe some negotiations are going on. Maybe another rescue is in the works. I don't know." His voice deepened. He looked determined. "I do know this. I am tired of sitting around and being held hostage. I'm tired of doing nothing."

Grain smiled broadly. He was glad to see the Vice President had finally grown a pair.

"Well, Sir, we were waiting for Colt and Meyerson. They were getting the powder for the pistols, remember?"

"We can't wait," the Vice President answered. "It's close to dawn. Haven't you noticed? The ship has slowed down. In fact, I don't think we're moving anymore. Something's up."

With a start, Grain realized that the Vice President was right. The soft hiss along the hull had ceased. They were wallowing in the swells as if at a full stop.

"Goddamn! You're right! How'd I miss that?"

They heard excited shouting in Arabic above. That was followed by a dull thump against the hull. Then more hubbub. There were the sounds of footsteps running. Shouted commands in English then Arabic ensued.

Grain strained to make out the words. His mind struggled to figure out what was going on.

"I think they're abandoning ship," he concluded.

The Vice President looked skeptical.

"Here, in the middle of the ocean? How is that possible?"

The Secretary joined the huddle.

"If Grain is right, that means they don't need us anymore. In my opinion, that also means they're probably going to blow up the ship."

Grain pondered this. "Gentlemen, we're likely fucked no matter what we do. As for me, I'd rather go down fighting."

The other men did not respond for a long time. Finally the Secretary spoke, "In that case Agent Grain, we best get cracking."

Baine muttered his agreement.

Grain checked the magazine on his AK-47. There were not many rounds left. He had only the one partially used clip.

He counted heads. His little band mustered only a few antique edged weapons and the useless pistols salvaged from the display cases. They did not present much of a fighting force. Two of the men were reenactors from the ceremonial Marine contingent. They were middle-aged, overweight and looked very much out of place in their 1812 uniforms. Regardless, they were itching to fight. The rest were tourists chosen by lottery to do the turnaround cruise. A few of these men were younger and fitter. They too, voiced their desire to assist. No one from the media volunteered. The reporters and cameramen stayed to themselves, apart from the other hostages.

Grain was not particularly optimistic about their chances for success. *This is one hell of bunch for a last stand. Custer had better odds.*

He looked at his countrymen. They needed a leader. It was time to take charge.

"Men and boys, pick up whatever weapons you can lay your hands on and follow me!"

Grain led his rag-tag band into the Captain's Great Cabin. They gingerly removed Raffington's body from the chart table and placed it on the Captain's bunk. They dragged the table into the Captain's After Cabin at the very end of the ship. Above was a large skylight. Grain climbed on top of the table and reached overhead. He slowly pushed up a glass panel, stood fully erect, and peered out.

The first hint of daylight was peeking over the horizon. The sky was a heavy gunmetal gray. It was very windy. The rain had slowed to a drizzle.

The area immediately surrounding the skylight was devoid of men. Grain lifted the clear panel higher and slipped under its edge, levered himself through the opening and slithered onto the spar deck. One at a time, making as little noise as possible, his small outfit of volunteers came after him, until they formed a tight cluster of men crouched tensely behind the mizzenmast.

Past the foremast, in the forecastle, they spied a group gathered near the starboard rail. Grain recognized the terrorist leader and his scary Afghan lieutenant. He saw a short jihadist wearing a light blue tracksuit disappear over the side and then another. Keeping low, the agent crawled to the side rail and raised his head above the carriage of a nearby cannon to peer through the gun port.

Below, a rubber dinghy was tethered to *Constitution's* bow. A handful of terrorists were in the dinghy together with several men in unfamiliar black sailor's uniforms and berets. A tall, bearded man in a peaked cap stood near the back of the dinghy giving orders in what Grain guessed was Farsi. He shouted back and forth with the head jihadist. Beyond the dinghy, lolling in the waves was the menacing black hulk of a submarine, its con breaking the surface and water washing over its deck.

Sweet mother of God! The fucking Iranian navy!

A noise above distracted Grain. When he looked up, he saw American sailors perched in the rigging. They were attentively watching the submarine. There were not many left. A sailor stared at him and put his finger to his lips in a shushing gesture.

Grain crept back to his companions to convey the news. "There's a goddamn submarine and a dinghy offloading the terrorists. They appear to be Iranians. They look like they're in a big hurry to get out of Dodge."

"A submarine?" the Secretary blurted.

He added, "The only Middle Eastern country that could possibly pull this off is Iran. This is insanity."

It was a scenario long dreaded. While Iranian subs had penetrated as far as the Mediterranean, U.S. forces had yet to spot one in the North Atlantic, much less off the coast of New England.

"Mr. Secretary, we've known for years the mullahs aren't rational actors," the Vice President piped up. "But who in God's name would expect them to be this reckless?"

Grain had been thinking. "I don't care if they're Russkies or Chechnyans or Easter Islanders for that matter. We need to do something before the sub blows us out of the water. We need our own hostages. The terrorist leader would be best. We gotta grab him and hold out until the good guys arrive. That's our only chance for survival."

The Secretary had served in two wars. He was 65 years old, flabby, and suffered from emphysema brought on by years of chain smoking in airless government offices. Nevertheless, he was willing.

"I'm with you, Mr. Grain. I would rather give that a try than wait to be shot or torpedoed."

"Are the rest of you with me?" Grain demanded. He was met with a series of curt nods and tight-lipped smiles.

"OK. Here's how we do it. Most of the bad guys are already off the ship. There are only three or four left. They don't know we're here. So, we have surprise on our side."

He gave the men a confident grin. "I'll take half of you up the right side. Mr. Secretary, you take the other half up the left side. Make as much noise as possible. Make them think a fucking army is coming after them. Then fight like hell. We grab a terrorist or two, hopefully their chief, and drag him back here. Maybe we can even score an Iranian. Wouldn't that be dandy?"

The men seemed to understand. Only Eldridge looked reluctant to fight. He kept his mouth shut.

"Once we grab someone, we'll disappear down the rabbit hole and play hide and seek in the lower decks. That should buy us some time. Got it? "

Grain had little faith in the plan working but kept up a brave front. In his heart, he knew the enemy would sacrifice one of their own in a heartbeat.

"On three we go, alright?"

He didn't wait for an answer.

"One. Two. Three!"

Above them, the remnants of *Constitution*'s crew, perched in the rigging, watched helplessly as the drama unfolded below. Their numbers had been thinned by the recent firefight. Many had tried to help the SEALs and been killed. When the action died down, the surviving sailors were once more driven aloft. The terrorists threatened death if they moved.

Chief Zajac was knocked to the deck by a vicious blow from Faroud when the SEAL assault began. He'd been unable to join the fight. After the attack failed, he was revived and forced aloft with the rest of his command.

Peering from the bottom yardarm of the foremast, he recognized the pending attack. This was a fight he was not going to miss. As the small, desperate group of hostages threw themselves on the remaining enemy fighters, Zajac shouted to his crew, "Help them!"

Zajac seized a line and swung to the deck, knocking over one of the jihadists in the bow. Following Zajac's lead, the remaining crew members started swarming down from the yardarms and rigging, sliding down the ratlines and jumping from the stays to join the fray.

Faroud had tossed his weapon overboard to the waiting Pasdaran sailors. He was all the way down the rope ladder leading to the dinghy when the Americans struck.

Al-Buyid was isolated on the deck with just three men. A Chechnyan fighter standing near Al-Buyid raised his weapon to fire. Before he could shoot, he was struck by a belaying pin. Several tars quickly subdued him. A sailor seized his weapon and mowed down the other two radicals.

Al-Buyid tried to unholster his sidearm. As he did so, Grain tackled him on one side and Zajac on the other. The two big men carried him to the deck, where they pounded his face and head.

Al-Buyid yelled "Faroud!"

Faroud had reached the bottom of the ladder and stepped into the dinghy when he heard Al-Buyid shout his name. He turned to the Iranians. "Captain Jamshidi, you must help us!"

Jamshidi calmly looked at his watch. Time was up. If he did not leave now, he might lose his sub. Al-Buyid was expendable. "Go if you wish, Faroud. Our part is done."

The big Afghan cursed and for a moment looked as if he would backhand the Iranian Captain. Then, as the dinghy's engine revved to life, Faroud leapt for the rope ladder. One hand found a rung and he clung to it, feet trailing in the swells, as his other, maimed hand flailed for a handhold. With another curse, his crippled hand found the braided nylon and he pulled himself upward to safety.

Indifferent to Faroud's ordeal, Jamshidi ordered his men to cast off. Immediately, the dinghy was underway. He glanced backward and glimpsed the Afghan clambering upward like a crazed baboon. As a token effort, he ordered two of his crew to lay down covering fire at the deck rail and shoot into the sails and rigging as Faroud ascended. Before Faroud had reached the top, the dinghy was halfway back to *Astoh* and Jamshidi had turned his back on the fate of his confederates on *Constitution*.

*****

Zach awoke in darkness. At least he thought he was awake. To be sure, he brought a hand to his face and touched his cheek. The movement brought pain. Throbbing pain that began in the middle of his forehead and spread over the crown of his skull.

Now he was sure he was conscious.

Darkness. Everywhere. So dark he did not know whether his eyes were open or shut.

He had never experienced such darkness. It was darker than being beneath the forest canopy at night in the jungle of Panama. That was inky and creepy. When he was a boy, it had scared him beyond belief. In the jungle, at least there was a chance to occasionally glimpse a star through gaps in the foliage or see pinpoints of light reflected from a leaf or drop of moisture.

This was different. This was like being in a tomb. Or buried alive. Absolutely no light. Strain as he could, his eyes discerned nothing.

A brief spasm of panic passed through him. He lay motionless, waiting for the dream to come. Anticipating the fear, he tensed his muscles and clenched his fists. A few minutes passed. No dream. No night terrors. Instead, he remembered where he was and what he needed to do. His fists relaxed. He focused his mind and fought to calm himself. Soon, his heart and breathing slowed and the sweating stopped.

His other senses took on added significance. Not only did he feel pain in his skull, his side ached and he could smell blood. He reached down his abdomen and encountered a wet, sticky area. With a grunt, he levered himself to a sitting position. Probing his flesh, he found the hole, still seeping. He pressed his hand hard against his side and wiggled to a more comfortable position. For a while he sat without moving, feeling the ship around him, hearing it creak and strain, smelling its peculiar maritime odor of wet wood, paint, seawater and mold. He looked at his watch. The faint glow of the phosphorescent dial told him it was close to 5:16 A.M.

Fuck! Fuck! Fuck!

He banged his left fist against the hull in frustration. He had been out for hours. Exasperated, he closed his eyes and tried to piece together what had happened.

Who did this? Mustafa? It had to be Mustafa. The bastard carried a knife. He must be alive and hiding.

Anger flooded through his system, followed by a fresh determination to find Eleni and make Mustafa pay. He rolled onto his knees. The pain in his flank intensified. He could handle it. The pangs were far better than the potential psychological torment of his dreams. The physical anguish told him he was alive. It gave him resolve.

Zach struggled upright and using the gaps between the planking on the hull clawed his way to his feet. *Eleni. Mustafa.* He kept those two names at the forefront of his brain as he stepped off into the dark. He would find them. One to love. The other to kill.

Zach painstakingly inched through the darkness of the hold. With one arm outstretched before him and his head kept low, he crept along the inner hull, aiming for the aft hatchway, which he sensed might be nearby. He hoped he had not become turned around in the dark. It would waste precious moments if he inadvertently headed toward the bow.

He grunted and stumbled forward as a large wave slapped the hull and his foot struck an unexpected object. With both hands out, he landed hard, straddling a motionless form. It was warm.

Startled, he rolled onto his back and felt around. His hand first found hair, and when he slid his fingers down, he encountered the soft features of Meyerson's face. Scrambling closer, he cupped her head in his hands and put his cheek close to hers to see if he could find any evidence that she was breathing. Her inhalations were shallow and weak. She lived. He slid his hands down over her torso and felt the wet, sticky spot where her life seeped from her.

"Hold on Meyerson. I'm here. I'll help you. Hold on. You're going to make it."

He tugged off his shirt and then his undershirt, wadded the undershirt into a ball, and stuffed a makeshift compress inside Meyerson's dress to staunch the bleeding. He quickly slipped his shirt back on. Then he cradled her in his arms and lurched to his feet, more determined than ever to find his way out. As he staggered toward the hatch, Meyerson began to moan.

"Connie, Connie, mommy's here. Connie . . ."

Zach felt his heart breaking. Meyerson's whispered entreaties were far worse than the wound in his belly, his thirst, or even the despair in his heart over Eleni's disappearance.

The ship's motion altered and he surmised that for some reason *Constitution* had stopped. He pushed ahead even harder. So subtle that he was not even sure it was real, his eyes discerned a shade of gray ahead that stood apart from the tenebrous surroundings. It was the stairway. At the base of the ladder, he slung Meyerson over his shoulder and climbed. He did not pause on the orlop or the berth deck. Two rungs at a time, he surged upward towards the light.

When he emerged onto the gun deck, two of the women hostages saw him and gasped. He slid Meyerson's limp body onto the deck, and they rushed forward to assist. One was a petite blonde woman, no older than twenty-five. She gently pried Meyerson's hands apart. A cannon shell slid to the deck. The other woman stroked Meyerson's hair and did her best to soothe the bleeding woman as Zach sat feet away, trying to regain his strength.

Most of the men were gone. So was Grain.

Zach was confused. "What's happening?"

The blonde looked up. "The Secret Service guy, he talked them into attacking the terrorists." Before she finished speaking, the rattle of automatic weapons came from above.

Zach seized the shell near Meyerson. He put one hand on the blonde woman's shoulder. "Take good care of her."

Meyerson stirred. Her eyes fluttered open.

"Save her. Save my . . . Connie. Save my . . . ship." Her head fell back.

Zach's eyes filled. He picked up Meyerson's shell, turned and jogged toward the stern. When he reached the chart table in the Captain's After Cabin, he saw the open skylight. He yanked both antique pistols from his belt and laid them on the tabletop. Using his teeth, he ripped open the shell, spilling black powder all over his torso and the flat surface. Holding a pistol upright in one hand, he scooped up powder and poured it into the barrel. He pulled his handkerchief from his back pocket and used his teeth to rip off a small piece of the cotton fabric. Fumbling for a lead ball, he cradled it in the cotton and jammed the patch and ball into the tip of the muzzle. He tore off another bit of cloth and put it top of the ball, removed the pistol's ramrod, and tamped the ball and makeshift wadding into place.

Then he pointed the pistol and half-cocked it. He dribbled some powder into the pan. When he was done, he pulled the frisson plate back and fully cocked the gun. Finished, he set the loaded weapon on the table. Then he began to repeat the process with the second pistol.

All the while, the sounds of fighting above intensified. Zach's hands shook. *C'mon, c'mon. Faster! Faster!* He almost dropped the unfamiliar weapon. He'd read about such pistols in books. They were primitive but deadly. This was the first time he had actually loaded one. It was maddeningly slow work.

After the second pistol was loaded and cocked, he slid the brace into his belt and climbed onto the table. Swiftly, he climbed through the skylight onto the quarterdeck.

The scene was chaotic.

Tracers from the Iranians in the dinghy tore into the sails and rigging, cutting jagged streams through the leaden dawn light. Occasionally, a bullet would find its mark and a sailor would fall from the rigging onto the deck. Those seamen who had not been able to join the hostage's desperate attack had retreated for shelter into the fighting tops of each mast.

A brawl was under way in the forecastle. A ball of snarling, kicking men fought fiercely hand to hand, some upright, others tangled on the deck. He raced toward the action.

When he reached the base of the mainmast, Faroud's head appeared above the bulwarks. The mammoth terrorist levered his body on the top plank, a polished 16-inch Khyber knife in hand, ready to leap onto the backs of Grain and Zajac.

Zach pulled a pistol from his belt. On the run, he aimed and fired. A dull pop sounded, heavier and lower pitched than the machine gun fire crackling overhead. He peered through the small cloud of smoke caused by the discharge. A ragged red hole blossomed in the middle of Faroud's forehead. The lifeless body tottered for a moment before the ship rolled, and Faroud fell backwards into the sea.

On the move, Zach reached Grain and Zajac as they exchanged blows with the terrorist chief. He extracted the second pistol from his belt and thrust the muzzle near the extremist's face.

"Stop!" he screamed. "Stop or I'll blow your fucking head off!"

Arm raised for a blow at Zajac's head, Al-Buyid froze. He glared at Zach.

"Fuck you, you American pig!" he shouted. His right fist started toward Zajac's face.

Zach pulled the trigger. There was a boom and a bright flash as fire blazed from the muzzle of the old pistol. Al-Buyid screamed and clutched his right eye as he staggered back, tripped, and sprawled onto the deck. Grain flopped on top of him, rolled him over, put him in a chokehold, and dragged Al-Buyid to his feet.

Somewhere in Zach's mad charge, the pistol's top wadding had jolted loose and its ball fallen from the barrel. Most of the powder had leaked out as well. What little that remained had ignited, spitting out the leftover wadding. Fine bits of gunpowder pocked Al-Buyid's nose, cheek, and forehead, some smoldering, creating a hideous tattoo. The hair on the top of his head was smoking. So was his fierce mustache. His right eyebrow and eyelashes were burned away. Where his right eye had been was a pulpy mess, leaking jell and blood from the remnants of an eyeball.

The badly scorched Sea Snake fixed his good eye on Zach. The man's jaw was clenched shut to stifle any cries of pain. The muscles on his neck bulged from the effort. Zach thought he could hear teeth breaking. His visage was crazed with hatred.

Baine and Powers came up. The VP dazzled Zach with a smile. "Great job!"

"Can it, Baine," the Secretary lashed out. "This isn't a campaign stop. Take one of this guy's arms and let's find some rope." The two officials dragged Al-Buyid aside and clumsily attempted to bind him.

Behind Zach, above the cries of the wounded and dying, came strange yowling. He turned and saw Eldridge hanging over the rail, staring at the blank space in the ocean where the sub had been.

"You promised!" Eldridge wailed between sobs. "You promised to take me!"

Zach stepped past Al-Buyid, grabbed Eldridge's shoulder, and yanked him around.

The spindly older man was blubbering like a child. "They promised!" he sobbed. "They promised to take us. And now they are gone!"

Zach backhanded Eldridge across the face twice. That stopped the caterwauling. He shook Eldridge and yelled into his face, "It was you, wasn't it! Down in the hold! You stabbed me, there, in the dark! You butchered Meyerson!" Zach had seldom felt such murderous rage.

"You're one of them, aren't you, you bastard!" He raised his hand to slap Eldridge again. Zajac caught it. He held it firmly and spoke softly to Zach.

"Easy, Mister. We don't need him dead. We need information."

Zach relaxed. The rage drained from him. "You're right. My blood was up."

Zajac released Zach's hand. Zach reached out and grabbed Horsley's chin. He lifted it, put his face close to Eldridge, and asked, "How did it go down, old man?"

Horsley was shattered. Too undone to care who knew the truth. He started jabbering. Once he started, he could not stop.

"You know what I do, don't you, Mr. Colt?"

"I know you run V-Oil, that company that provides free oil to poor people."

"Yes, that's right. Every time you and the other plebes visit Fenway Park, that orange neon sign you all see and worship, that belongs to me. Many things in Boston belong to me. My family has been here a long time, Mr. Colt. Long enough to become wealthy. Long enough to become powerful."

Zach did not know if the old man had lost his train of thought or if he was crazy.

"So what, Eldridge. You run V-Oil. You cozy up to one of the worst dictators in the world to buy oil and suck out millions of dollars in salaries for you and your wife under the pretense of charity. So what? What's that got to do with," Zach gestured at the carnage surrounding them, "this?"

Eldridge slid his body down the wooden bulwarks until he sat on the deck. He crossed his legs, Indian style, and looked up at Zach. The older man's eyes were bright with tears.

"Why everything, Mr. Colt. You see, some time ago one of my Venezuelan friends asked me to do a favor." The word "favor" came out "fayvah" as Eldridge dropped the "r." It only made Zach despise the man more for his ridiculous upper class accent.

"I was asked to host some Middle Eastern gentlemen in our fair city. They were quite unusual tourists, you see. Unique, I might add." Eldridge almost seemed amused by what he was saying.

"Get on with it, Eldridge," Zach spat out.

"At first, they asked me to go shopping for them. Acquire a few odds and ends, such trifles as speedboats, AK-47s, grenades, rocket launchers. The usual." He searched Zach's countenance. "Do you know how easy it is to buy those types of things in our country? Our gun laws are so pathetically lax."

Zach gently poked Eldridge with the barrel of his pistol. "Go on. I don't need your bullshit social commentary."

"So I did. In return, they deposited a great deal of money in my offshore banking accounts. I didn't ask questions, and they told me little. Life went on. My good work on behalf of the poor and downtrodden continued apace."

He stared off into space for a moment. "Then this fella turned up." He pointed wearily at Al-Buyid. "He is a very serious man, Mr. Colt. He told me things I'd rather not have heard. He asked me to do things I'd rather not have done. And I did them. I had to. I was already in too deep. There was no way out."

Eldridge chuckled dryly to himself. "You know, Mr. Colt, Moliere once said, 'behind every great fortune is a great crime.'"

"Balzac, asshole."

"Excuse me, what did you say?"

"It was Balzac, asshole. Didn't they teach you anything at Harvard?"

"You attended Dartmouth, did you not, Mr. Colt?"

"Yes."

"A school for savages, drunks, and louts."

Zach punched Eldridge twice before Zajac had a chance to stop him. It pleased him to watch the blood dribble from Eldridge's patrician nose.

"There are those of us who love it, you pathetic, weak, effete fool."

Eldridge rubbed his jaw. "Apparently so."

"Finish the goddamn story, Eldridge."

"Well, so I kept helping them. In return, they promised to save my dear wife and me. They promised to take us with them. And now, here we are." He waved a hand limply at nothing. "And here I am."

Grain was disgusted. "If I just kill the son of bitch here and now, nobody'd rat me out, right?"

"Don't ruin your career, Grain. He's not worth it," Zach answered.

Grain turned his attention to Al-Buyid. "Hey, you. What do you have to say for yourself? It's come to Jesus time, Mohammed."

Before Al-Buyid could answer, the sky unexpectedly brightened. A lovely pink haze suffused the horizon.

Al-Buyid saw it and his face softened. He unclenched his jaw. Looking to the horizon, he spoke a phrase no one recognized.

Grain was perplexed. "I know that's not Arabic or Farsi. What is it?"

Zach looked at his friend. "It was Greek."

"Greek?" Zajac sputtered. "Why the hell is he speaking Greek? We're not fighting Greece, are we?"

"Not lately. Maybe we ought to, considering what they are doing to the world economy," Grain answered. Turning to Zach, the agent asked, "What does it mean?"

Zach and Eldridge exchanged a look. Zach spoke first. "It means, 'and when the rosy-fingered dawn appeared, back to the camp they took their homeward way.'"

"It's from *The Iliad*, Mr. Grain. By Homer. Perhaps you've heard of it?" mocked Eldridge.

"Was it on HBO?" Grain responded, grinning.

~ Chapter 6 ~

July 5, 2012

0529 hrs.

The atmosphere inside the situation room at Fleet Command was exceptionally tense. Weymouth had just stammered another vague answer to one of Jolly's precise questions. The Admiral was incensed.

"What do you mean we can't find the goddamn sub?"

"Just that, Sir. Neither our satellite surveillance or aircraft reconnaissance has been able to detect it."

"Then reposition the satellite! Get more planes in the air! Do something!" The Admiral was livid.

"We can't, Admiral. There are too many other targets being watched and too few satellite resources. Army, Air Force, CIA, FBI, NASA, NSA, everyone is competing for their share. It may take a while for a lens to free up."

Weymouth hated being dressed down by Rogers. The man reminded him of his awful stepfather. Always angry, questioning his every movement.

How ironic. But he's right. I only have excuses.

Weymouth did not quit. "As for aviation assets, since NAS Brunswick closed in 2011, we have nothing nearby. NS Jacksonville committed all its Orion P-3C

314

sub-hunters from Patrol Squadron Eight, the Fighting Tigers. We convinced NAVAIR a short while ago to deploy its new P-8A Poseidon equipped with hydrocarbon sensors from NS Jacksonville, but even at its top speed of 490 knots, it will take another 45 minutes to cover the 1600 miles to the target area. Patrol Squadron 5 remains in reserve.

"There's more bad news, Sir. The hurricane has moved rapidly up the coast. It has reached New England. The eye will pass east of Cape Cod at 0800. It should be a Category 3 by that time."

Jolly scowled. "It's July. Awfully early for a big storm."

Weymouth jumped on the point, happy to discuss the weather as opposed to Iranian subs. "You're right, Sir. Global warming, Sir. Two Thousand and Twelve has been a peculiar year for weather. This hurricane is just another example. It built early southeast of Cuba. It has been gathering strength moving through the Caribbean and up the eastern seaboard. No one could have predicted this."

"Maybe we'll have famines and locusts next," Jolly exclaimed. He struggled to remain calm. "OK. Let me summarize. Tell me if I've missed anything. Since *David* broke contact, we do not know exactly where *Constitution* is, who is on her, or who is alive or dead. We don't know where the IRGC-N sub is, or even if the sub is Iranian for that matter. Our eyes in the sky have come up dry. Our birds haven't yet arrived. The two subs from NS Norfolk are in the area and hunting but so far have been unsuccessful. And to top it off, we have a major hurricane bearing down on a 200-

plus-year-old wooden battleship packed with civilian hostages and captured American sailors."

The more Admiral Jolly spoke, the quieter the room became. He let the silence hang. When the tension reached the breaking point, he continued.

"Get me on a plane, Commander. I am not going to sit here on my ass any longer. It's time to ride the tiger."

Weymouth gulped loudly. The Admiral pointed a finger at him. "You're joining me!"

*****

Eleni's dreams were filled with the sound of gunfire. Even now, as she came to consciousness, she thought she heard the report of a weapon from somewhere above her on the ship. But that was not the most annoying thing. The buzzing and tapping from below were incessant. It seemed as if it had been going on for hours. She could not ignore the irritating sounds, much closer than the noise from above, and they eventually caused her to become fully awake.

She sat up and concentrated. The whirling was muffled, diffuse, and impossible to pinpoint. In an effort to hear better, she pressed her ear against the hull. That helped. Now she was sure that someone was drilling and pounding on the outside of *Constitution*. The vibrations seemed to be almost below her.

Determined to solve the mystery, she cautiously opened the door to her small cabin and crawled out into the larger gloom beyond. She wormed her way along on her hands and knees to the next cabin, where she groped for the door, found it and entered. Once inside, she listened again with her ear to the planking. The noises were louder. She was closer but she was not yet on top of it.

Deciding to start over, she repeated her journey from cabin to cabin until she was certain she was above where the most intense vibrations and hammering were taking place. Sightless, she felt along the inner hull until her hand hovered over the spot where her fingertips detected the fiercest vibrations. Someone was definitely doing something to the exterior hull. It was suspicious. She had to get out, find Zach, and let him know.

The door to her cabin squeaked open. She felt a strange presence intrude into her confined space. It was human. She smelled man-smell and blood. She sensed evil.

Hardly daring to move, Eleni made herself small and shrank against the painted wood of the cabin wall. She forced her breathing to slow down and quiet in the hope the intruder would not notice her. Maybe whoever it was had heard the noise and was exploring just as she had been. Maybe she would not be found out.

An almost imperceptible current of air brushed her cheek, followed by dragging and scraping noises. She thought she heard the sound of someone's hand sliding across wood.

A guffaw erupted, built to a hearty chortle, and ended in rolling peels of mirth as the unseen person laughed out of control. The lunatic sounds of joy almost drowned out the drilling noises. It reverberated through the small, dark chamber.

Eleni remembered a haunted house she had visited at Hebert's Candy Mansion one Halloween as a child. It was located in a small town outside of Boston. She was with her mother and older brother. Visitors could pick from three levels of fright: green for not scary; yellow for somewhat scary; and red for very scary. Her brother picked red. At every twist and turn, she was terrified by unseen spooks and goblins that jumped out at her, laughing and screaming demonically. When a witch popped out near her face, she clutched her brother's hand for dear life and wet herself. He teased her and dragged her ahead to the next horror. Defenseless, she was forced to acquiesce. When they finally exited, she threw herself into her mother's arms and cried uncontrollably.

The same deep feelings of fear and helplessness swept over her now. Only this time the frightening laughter was for real. And her mother was not nearby to comfort her.

She launched herself toward where she assumed the door would be. A hand brushed her bosom. Another hand grabbed her hair. The door was open and she blundered through it, lashing out wildly at her attacker. Free of the cabin, she dropped to her knees and rolled. She stopped rolling when she found herself under a nearby table. Footsteps padded by near her head.

An angry voice hissed, "Come out, come out, wherever you are!"

Eleni held her breathe and waited.

If the bastard wants to play hide and seek, so be it. Let's see who's smarter.

In the freezing ocean, against the exterior hull, two Iranian SCUBA divers struggled to complete their complicated task. They were identical twins, Adel and Ahmad, now in their early thirties. The two were swarthy, gray-eyed, and black haired. Both were lean, hard and possessed fierce devotion to country and faith.

Their father and mother had been part of the gang of students that had invaded and occupied the United States Embassy in Tehran in 1979. Leaders in that seminal event, both parents quickly rose to prominence in the new Revolutionary Guard. Now the patriarch and matriarch occupied key political posts in Tehran while their offspring were set loose on the world to wreak havoc on the enemies of Islam and the Iranian Republic.

The boys were raised as fanatic Islamists, steeped in every aspect of radical Shiite doctrine, and ingrained with a fierce hatred of the Great Satan. First came Madrassa, with its endless hours of memorizing the Koran. Then specialized Revolutionary Guard schools where more practical skills were learned. Last, Tehran University, capped by military training in the Revolutionary Guard Corps.

They were apt students and favored spawn of the ruling Iranian political establishment. As such, when their education was finished, they had their pick of careers.

Their parents originally came from a small seaside village where the family often vacationed when the twins were young. The brothers grew up loving the sea. It was only natural for both to gravitate to the burgeoning IRGC-N. They distinguished themselves by developing and implementing the swarming tactics used by IRGC-N against American warships. Soon, they were officers.

This mission was the apotheosis of their lives. Secret training lasted for months. Days were devoted to practice in the warm waters of the Sea of Arabia. Their expertise was honed and tested. And then tested again. Despite this preparation, things were not going well.

Before *Astoh* surfaced near *Constitution* to fetch back the terrorist cell, the twin divers departed the sub via a special detachable underwater sled affixed to a platform on the sub's superstructure. They traversed the distance to *Constitution* in no time. The sled stopped beneath the shadow of the ship.

Their cargo was a large object. Its code name was "the package." It looked strangely like a dolphin. Long and narrow, it was painted black to blend in with the hull.

They were below the ship's waterline. Using a tool similar to a nail-gun, the divers drove eyebolts through the hulls copper sheathing into the planking. Each diver tied off to a bolt so as not to be swept away. Then they started the real work.

The skin of the package was heavy-duty plastic surrounded by a specially constructed floatation housing that made it neutrally buoyant while they worked to attach it to the hull. First, they pressed it firmly against the exterior hull. A unique form of water-activated glue held it temporarily in place while the ship bounced heavily in the roiling seas. Using custom-made drilling equipment and long, sturdy threaded bolts, they drilled through the copper and into the side planking in order to fix the package to the exterior hull.

At least that was the plan. However, the device was not cooperating.

Simply positioning the object was difficult. More than half their air supply was exhausted by the effort. Once it was glued, they feverishly worked to fasten it permanently in place using the self-threading bolts.

A bolt in the upper left corner broke in two. They tried to bash it home with handheld hammers. Underwater, the process was slow and inefficient. The next two bolts slotted properly through their flanges and penetrated the planking quite nicely. After that, the drill stopped functioning. The backup drill worked briefly until it, too, failed.

Only two bolts held the package securely in place, at opposite corners. The heavy casing clung tenuously against the hull. They tugged at it to see whether it would hold. There was no movement. Whether their efforts would suffice was unknown. It was all they could do.

Their mission was over. They had labored too long. *Astoh* was gone. There would be no rescue. In minutes, their oxygen would run dry.

Surrender was not an option.

They had anticipated this possibility. The twins unclipped themselves from the eyebolts. They swam toward one another. Tenderly, they touched facemasks and mouthed silent good-byes. Like synchronized swimmers, they simultaneously unsheathed their diving knives.

Clinging face-to-face, they plunged the blades into one another's backs. A brief eruption of blood and air bubbles ensued. Their dry suits filled with icy Atlantic saltwater. Blood loss and extreme cold rapidly led to unconsciousness.

The brothers drifted lazily downward into the depths of the freezing, gray-green water, locked together in death as they had once been in their mother's womb.

~ Chapter 7 ~

July 5, 2012

0608 hrs.

The huge rogue wave caught them by surprise. It slapped *Constitution* hard amidships and caused the mighty boat to keel over to starboard. Water poured over the bulwarks, flooding the deck. Vast quantities of seawater shipped through the gun ports on the gun deck, turning the interior into a wading pool.

Constitution's masts dipped terrifyingly close to the ocean's surface. The tips of the main yards almost kissed the sea as the titanic wave reached for her sails and rigging. For a brief moment, the ship teetered on the verge of capsizing. Then, with a prolonged shudder and hair-raising moan, she righted herself in a slow arc until the masts once more pointed toward heaven.

When the frigate began its dizzying acrobatics, Zach and the other men clustered on the fore deck were caught unawares. They scrambled to find secure handholds.

Zajac clung to a cathead as torrents of water washed over his body. It took all his strength to withstand being swept overboard.

Grain was tossed backward and wedged against a cannon's carriage. Unhurt, he struggled to his feet only to be showered by a mass of rigging torn free by the force of the assault. A shackle struck him on the shoulder and head and he fell to the deck, dazed, tangled in the debris.

Zach skittered thirty feet across the deck as if on a waterslide. He bounced into the starboard bulwark. With both hands, he held on to a carronade's carriage. He found himself staring almost straight down into the sea as the whopping wall of seawater spilled over the deck and threatened to suck him overboard. Unable to keep his grip, he sloshed in the other direction as the ship righted herself. Jolted yet unhurt, he came to rest lodged against the larboard bulwark, retching seawater.

As the ship struggled to remain afloat, Zach spied Eldridge sitting astride a foredeck cannon, riding it like a mechanical bull. The old man was laughing hysterically. The gun's carriage broke free. The loose cannon careened across the deck, Eldridge on top. It did a three hundred and sixty-degree turn before striking the port side of the vessel. With a loud thud and crunch of splintered wood, the weight of the cannon punched a hole through the bulwark, catapulting the gun and its mad rider through the air into the whirling green maelstrom beyond.

Zach blinked away brine and struggled to his feet. The sky darkened dramatically and began to cough rain. Scattered droplets rapidly turned into wind-whipped sheets of water, accompanied by riotous lightning and booming thunderclaps. He could hear the cries of the trapped passengers below. All around him, broken spars and detached rigging littered the deck. Fallen yards and torn sail partially covered the main hatch and trailed over the starboard side rail. Shredded sailcloth flapped violently in the howling wind. Loose tackle, sprung halyards, and detached lines whipped crazily overhead.

Grain groaned. Zach was simply too depleted to help him. Zajac struggled to the downed agent and used his tattered uniform blouse to staunch the flow of blood from a head wound. Grain's collarbone appeared broken. When Zajac hauled him to his feet, he cried out in agony. Zajac quickly sat the big man back down and held him steady, providing what comfort he could.

Somewhat muddled and gasping for breath, Zach surveyed the rest of the deck, searching for other survivors. Here and there, a sailor clung to some bit of secure material, be it a grating, a cannon carriage, a sheet bit or fife rail. He counted fewer than a dozen. Al-Buyid was nowhere in sight. Zach assumed he'd, probably been swept overboard.

Dear God, where is Eleni?

To his right, a female hand protruded from the wooden grating covering the main hatch. Meyerson's voice shouted, "Get me out of here! Is anyone alive up there? Help!"

Zach crawled over to the spot and peeked down. "Commander I thought you were almost dead!"

"Not yet. I lost some blood, that's all. Nothing fatal."

Zach was relieved. "Good! Have you seen Eleni?"

"No. I don't know where she is."

Meyerson saw Zach's face spasm with anguish. She sympathized with him but needed him to be fully engaged to help.

"Don't worry. We'll find her. Get me out of here first."

Zach did not respond.

"Zach, wake up. All the ladders are broken. There is debris blocking the other hatches and stairways. Get me out of here! I've got to try to save the ship!"

Zach came around and lazily saluted her. "Aye, aye, Ma'am." There was no way to free her except to break the grating. Zach scanned the deck and spotted a loose cannonball wedged under a pile of fallen hawsers. He freed it and lugged it to Meyerson's location.

"Watch out below!" Zach hoisted the 24-pound iron ball overhead and smashed it onto the grating. The ball bounced harmlessly to one side.

"You can do better than that!" Meyerson shouted up at him.

Zach retrieved the ball. He lofted it and attacked the grating again. Still no result. He kept at it. On the sixth try, he heard wood crack and the latticework begin to splinter. On the ninth attempt the wood gave way and the metal sphere punched through. A small hole had opened up. Zach dropped to his knees and tore at the wood. Soon he could reach down and pull Meyerson through. The wounded officer and Zach sat facing one another on the deck. Her pretty summer dress was a wet, torn, bloody mess.

"Excellent job, Zach. Thank you."

"Anytime," Zach panted. "What's it like below?

"Hellish. That last wave threw the passengers all over the place. Water poured through the gun ports and hatches and swirled us around like we were in a blender. We have a number of head injuries and broken bones to contend with. My medic's alive. He's helping the wounded."

"And Connie?"

Meyerson smiled. "I managed to hang onto her. She's fine. She'll make a good sailor one day. Now Mrs. Horsley is taking good care of her."

Inwardly, Zach blanched. He held his tongue. Meyerson had enough on her plate. There was no need to disclose Eldridge's treachery and death. As for Mags Horsley, he doubted she was a part of any plot. Eldridge no doubt kept his treason a secret.

He smiled at Meyerson. "I'm glad to hear that. What next?"

Meyerson eyed the sky and surveyed the shambles. Her face turned paler. The deck was choked with storm damage. Swinging tackle threatened to decapitate the unwary. The thick stay holding the mizzenmast had come loose and the towering mast wobbled visibly and swayed with every movement of the ship. Some of the downed canvas trailed in the water, creating a sea anchor that threatened to drag the ship onto its side again.

"Let's get to work!" Meyerson shouted. A rapid string of orders spat from her lips.

"Zach, free up Zajac, I need him. Take Grain below for medical treatment."

Turning to the remnants of her crew, she ordered, "You men over there, form a party and cut loose that trailing sail." Pointing aft she yelled, "You others, start clearing the deck." She singled out two nearby men, "You and you, tighten the slack on that preventer stay. Hurry!"

The shell-shocked swabs shed their weariness. They jumped to complete their tasks, eager to save their ship and their own lives. Months of hard training took hold and soon the weather deck started to become shipshape.

Cutting free the loose sail and rigging trailing in the ocean was the most formidable task. Zajac rounded up the few ancient cutlasses the captives had earlier used to subdue the Mujahideen. He distributed them to his crewmates. They hacked viciously at the wreckage. The old blades did the job. As the sailors worked, they prayed another rogue wave would not strike and finish off the old girl.

A jagged bolt of lightning struck the water not 200 yards from *Constitution's* stern. Its electric blaze illuminated a beautiful and surprising sight. In the distance, the snow-white hull of *Eagle*, under a full spread of sail, plowed through the monstrous waves heading in *Constitution's* direction. She was a pale angel coming to their rescue.

The haggard band of sailors on board *Constitution* broke out into a spontaneous, if ragged, cheer. Zach, although not part of the brotherhood, joined with them.

A second bolt struck the water. Zach and the others made out topmen and deckhands on *Eagle*. As the vessel closed, she took in sail and slowed, maintaining a safe distance in the growing vortex.

There was a flash and an orange projectile flew in their direction. It fell short of the hull. A second shot followed. It too splashed at a distance.

Zach was perplexed. "What's that?"

Meyerson recognized the tactic. "It's called a donkey dick. They're trying to send over a line so the two ships can tie up. We're too far apart. The sea's too rough. It's not going to work."

Seconds later, Meyerson pointed, "Look! Boats in the water!"

Eagle had maneuvered parallel to *Constitution.* Two longboats splashed down into the sea, manned by brawny and determined Coast Guard cadets. The fragile looking craft made their way across the rough seas toward *Constitution.* Every yard of progress was achingly slow. The launches zoomed up and down the heavy swells like cars on a roller coaster. A boat would appear, and then disappear, swallowed by a wave, only to have it pop up and plunge over the crest before beginning another long downhill slide into the trough, once more vanishing from sight.

Although making way was perilous, the gap between the two ships slowly closed. Twenty feet out, they saw through the lightning and pounding rain a figure in the closest boat stand, plant his feet, and fling a line toward *Constitution* even as the tiny launch and bucking frigate threatened to collide. A female sailor on *Constitution* pounced onto the line, grappled with it, and with the assistance of two other seamen firmly secured it to a cleat.

The *Constitution's* crew members steadily hauled the Coast Guard boat closer, until the two craft were barely six feet apart. Meyerson ordered two seamen to throw rope ladders over the side. The two wind-whipped ladders dangled above the sea, swinging back and forth along the hull like broken pendulums.

Pulling closer, the lead boat came within grappling distance of a ladder. The seaman standing upright in the bow, *Eagle's* Captain Newtowne, leaned over and used a long grappling hook to sweep for one of the ladders. After several tries, the hook caught and he pulled the shaft hand over hand to draw the ladder close enough for him to finally reach out and grasp it.

Four feet away from *Constitution*, Captain Newtowne timed his leap for the ladder to coincide with a rising wave. He tossed aside the grappling hook and jumped. One hand secured a rung. Clinging one-handed to the rungs, he hit *Constitution's* hull hard, bounced off, and barely managed to grasp another stringer with his free hand. For several excruciating seconds, he swung back and forth, his feet grazing the waves, before a heavy gust of wind plastered his body against the hull, pinning him in place. It was just the break he needed. He thrust up a hand, grabbed a higher rung, and pulled his body up. Then his feet found the lower rungs and he held tight, resting before looking upward at the anxious faces above. With a triumphant smile, he at last began climbing skyward toward the railing.

Below, his craft crashed repeatedly into the hull. A cadet managed to grasp the base of the second ladder. Using his body as a human anchor, he held fast to the ladder and urged his comrades onward. The boat emptied as a string of cadets mounted the swaying ladder and made the perilous trip toward *Constitution's* deck.

The top of Captain Newtowne's head cleared the rail. Eager hands reached out and pulled him to safety. Once on deck, Newtowne straightened his shoulders, wiped the water from his eyes, and found he was staring directly into the face of a small, disheveled woman. To his surprise, the woman saluted.

"Commander Meyerson, Sir. Welcome to my ship."

Newtowne grinned at the absurdity of the situation. He saluted back. "Captain Newtowne. United States Coast Guard." He looked hard at the woman.

She stood proud and erect. Around her, the members of *Constitution's* thin crew were either gathered near the ladders or hard at work repairing her. Newtowne turned his gaze back to Meyerson. This was a Navy ship. Meyerson was a Navy officer. It was her command. Things looked under control, or at least as under control as they could be given the circumstances. Commander Meyerson no doubt knew *Constitution* better than he did, and after what had gone down, by God she deserved the right to save her.

Rank be damned.

"At your service, Commander. How can we help?" Newtowne dropped his salute and reached out to shake Meyerson's hand. Meyerson took it, letting out a long sigh of relief. Before she could speak, two new bodies popped over the side rail.

Chief Rollins came first, drenched and spitting seawater. He looked completely out of place in his sodden suit and regimental striped tie, which had been shredded by the rope rungs as he climbed the ladder. Once on deck, he straightened his jacket and tie and strode purposely toward the two officers, only to have his street shoes slip out from under him on the slick deck and send him sprawling.

Behind him, Detective Murphy's bulky frame had also flopped over the rail. Murphy landed with a thud. He found himself eye to eye with his Chief. As usual, Rollins looked moderately pissed-off. Finding himself on his posterior, Rollins's usual poise and dignity had completely evaporated. A smile tugged at Murphy's lips, then spread to a grin and ended up a full-fledged bray of mirth. Against his will, Rollins found himself joining in. The two laughing cops edged closer and helped one another stand. Arms linked for mutual support, they swayed their way to Newtowne and Meyerson.

"Detective Chief Wayne Rollins and Detective Lieutenant Paul Murphy!" Rollins yelled over the din of wind, cascading rain, and flapping sailcloth. "Boston PD!"

"Christ, I forgot about you two! How the hell did you get here?" Newtowne frowned at the duo.

Murphy yelled back. "One of your cadets, Patrick Murphy. The Boat Captain of the second boat. He's my oldest sister's youngest boy. Did his favorite uncle a favor."

Newtowne understood it was the Boston way. Nevertheless, he yelled back, "That boy's in for a boatload of demerits. We don't need any more civilians on board."

Rollins interjected, "Wait a minute, Captain. This is an ongoing police investigation. We have every right to be here."

"Not on my watch. You are way out of your jurisdiction. You'll just be in the way."

The two men glared at one another. Before another word was exchanged, Meyerson intervened. "This is my ship. Stop bickering! I'll say who stays and goes. For now, we need every hand we can get. So, stand down!"

Chastened, both men fell silent. Zach, who had been listening, shouted a question. "Do either of you two have a gun?"

The two cops looked at him. Zach was a beat up, filthy bloodstained mess.

Rollins did not care for the intrusion.

"Who the hell are you?"

"Zach Colt."

"So what?"

"Listen to him," Meyerson interrupted. "He knows his stuff. He helped save this boat and killed at least one of the terrorists."

The two cops gave Zach a fresh look. Murphy patted his chest and nodded, "I'm armed. So is the Chief." Rollins grunted.

"OK," Zach plunged on. "Just hear me out. The terrorists' leader – he was either swept overboard or is still here. If he is here, we need to find the bastard. My girlfriend's also missing. I know she is still on board. Since you can't sail, and neither can I, I suggest we form a team and scour the lower decks while Commander Meyerson and Captain Newtowne try to keep us from sinking. OK?"

A few heartbeats passed. It was a plan. No one had a better one. Newtowne nodded his assent. Rollins again grunted affirmatively. Murphy loosened the buttons on his sodden sports coat and reached inside. He undid the thumbreak snap on his shoulder holster and loosened the pistol inside. "Game on."

Rollins eyed Zach. "You know this ship?"

"Yes. I've learned it the hard way."

"Alright. For now." Rollins reached behind his back and drew his service revolver, a stainless steel snub-nosed S&W .38, flicked off the safety and tucked it into the front of his waistband. He saw Zach eye the revolver. "I'm old school, baby. Lead the way."

"Let's do it." Zach headed for the companion stairs leading down to the gun deck. Rollins and Murphy hurried to join him. Zach scampered down the broken ladder onto the gun deck. When he landed, a blood-curdling scream erupted from the berth deck and filtered up through the aft hatchway. Loud and shrill, it carried above the wind. Zach froze. His heart beat faster. There was a catch in his throat as he throttled the strong emotions flooding his heart.

He knew that voice. It was Eleni.

"Come on!" he shouted and scrambled down the second ladder into the gloom of the berth deck. The two cops scurried after him. A new scream erupted. This time, from a man.

~ Chapter 8 ~

July 5, 2012

0620 hrs.

Miles away, traveling silently below the tempest raging on the ocean's surface, *Astoh* made her way south at full power. Jamshidi had been pacing the con with excitement since departing *Constitution's* side. His part of the mission was over. As far as he knew, it was a resounding success. All they needed was to escape. A mad dash down the Atlantic coast, through the Caribbean, and back to the security of his secret base in Venezuela.

He could do it. How could he not succeed? Was not the storm a blessing, a means to baffle his foe and hide his presence? Allah smiled upon him and his crew. The certainty of the true believer comforted him.

While *Astoh* fled, the Navy was hard at work locating the intruder. The United States had at its disposal a vast array of anti-submarine warfare tools. They were all in use.

A large system of underwater listening posts, built during the Cold War, stretched throughout the North Atlantic. Known as SOSUS, after the fall of the U.S.S.R., most of these installations had reverted to civilian control. The Navy continued to operate some. All the posts were constantly monitored by both the military and its much more numerous civilian counterparts. Now they were on full alert.

The Pentagon adjusted its satellite orbits to survey the area of *Constitution's* likely passage. Their powerful infrared sensors penetrated the storm and searched the surface of the sea.

Fixed wing P-3 Orion aircraft flown north from Florida combed the ocean, braving the elements. They used active and passive sonobuoys, dipping sonar, radar, magnetic anomaly detection sensors, infrared detectors and other hi-tech tools. The planes also seeded a wide area with aerial torpedoes designed to pick up evidence of submarines.

Navy SH-60 Seahawk helicopters and their Coast Guard peers likewise skirted the edges of the storm. The choppers used similar advanced technology to detect the enemy.

The Air Force Reserve Command, headquartered in Georgia, was activated. Giant-sized C-130J and WC-130J "Hurricane Hunters" combed the airspace over the ocean's surface where *Constitution* was thought to be.

Admiral Rogers was in the air. He sat strapped into a seat on a Boeing E-6B Mercury Command and Control Aircraft plunging into the eye of the storm. The plane dipped and jolted violently. Every gyration sent a wave of pain up Jolly's spine. He chewed nitroglycerine tablets as if they were candy.

Goddamn my fat ass! Can hardly fit into one of these seats anymore.

A computer was secured to the desk in front of him. He clutched its mouse like a vice to prevent it from flying across the cabin. The Admiral was riveted on the continuous live feed of data on his screen. Occasionally, an aide would pass him a slip of paper containing some piece of intelligence that had not found its way into the torrent of electronic information before him.

His head hurt and his eyes were dry from intense concentration. Amid all the facts and figures, the hunches and predictions, he searched for an iota of data that could turn the useless mass of information into the possibility of victory. So far, he'd found none.

Weymouth, strapped into an adjacent seat, looked green. A puddle of vomit surrounded his shoes. Try as he might, he found it nearly impossible to focus on his computer. It didn't help that more vomit splattered the screen and keyboard. He hated airplanes. He'd joined the Navy to avoid having to muck around in the dirt, and because in his heart, he knew man was never meant to fly. For him, the mission was sheer hell. Like his boss, he hoped and prayed for a ray of sunshine, both literally and figuratively.

At 0655 a piece of intelligence caught his eye. It came from an improbable source. He picked up a phone and called a special number in Virginia.

In 2010, the Defense Advanced Research Projects Agency (DARPA) had launched a top-secret anti-submarine warfare project, ACTUV. The initials stood for the Anti-Submarine Warfare Continuous Trail Unmanned Vessel program. Under the program, unmanned surface vessels were constructed. Designed to track submarines, they were operated by land-based personnel. The Navy intended to deploy the ocean-based drones in numerous settings to free up manned craft.

These small, robotic ships were a little over 62 feet long and slightly less than 20 feet wide, roughly one and one-half the size of a school bus. The submersed main body resembled a sled with twin electric propellers and cruised 30 feet below water. Attached to the rear was an arched superstructure that rose a little over 12 feet above the water and contained the communications center and various sensors. Weighing in at 157 tons, the drone could stay at sea for 30 days and travel almost 2,000 miles without refueling. It was small, had a top speed as fast as or faster than the average diesel sub, was easily maneuverable and hard to track.

The vessels were equipped with sensors capable of detecting the quietest diesel-operated submarines. They also possessed advanced autonomous navigation and anti-collision features. These enhancements allowed the drones to remain on continuous patrol without disrupting international shipping.

In the aftermath of 9/11, the program accelerated. Given the demands of the ongoing War on Terror, ACTUV went fully operational years before schedule. Small squadrons of drone vessels patrolled the waters off major cities on the Atlantic and Pacific coasts of North America, unknown to the public.

ACTUV Operators were located in secret facilities at Norfolk Naval Base. The first wave of these new fighters was handpicked and clandestinely trained. High schools, colleges, video parlors and online gaming forums across America were combed for the best computer gaming talent, young men and women capable of spending long hours before a screen, hooked on the thrill of simulated combat, quick-reacting, intelligent, and gifted with nimble fingers.

Star players of *Dangerous Waters*, a simulated submarine hunt game, were especially valued, particularly those who scored well on *ACTUV Tactics*, a program designed by DARPA and made available free to the public in order to improve ACTUV performance. Young gamers jumped at the chance of using their skills in a real-world environment. After all, controlling state-of-the-art technology to blow up stuff with powerful, sophisticated weapons was much cooler than playing games. The Navy created a new unit for these savants, the SHARKS. The acronym stood for "Subsurface Harassment, Attack, Reconnaissance, and Kill Squad."

However, the Navy found the gamers hard to keep. Such unique recruits did not do well in a disciplined environment. Many had ADHD and could not bear the dull routine of searching empty waters with no payoff. So, the swabbies got creative. A loose command structure was implemented, similar to hi-tech companies in Silicon Valley. Uniforms became optional. Offices resembled large playrooms equipped with pool tables, big screen TVs, sofas, ping-pong tables, vending machines, and random gym equipment. Duty hours were short so concentration did not flag. Innovation and creativity were encouraged.

In the early hours of July 5, Seaman Wesley Carpenter, one of the first SHARKS, was on his sixth Coke of the night. Several ratty comic books and crumpled candy bar wrappers were scattered on his desk. He was close to coming off duty and bored out of his mind. The endless grid pattern he navigated for his drone vessel, nicknamed *Bathman* by him, was dull and so far, unproductive.

To make things more interesting, he had started to toggle his little vessel into an unusual search pattern. He tried to spell "screw the Navy" in cursive script. The battering from the hurricane his little craft experienced made it challenging. While working on the "N", one of his sensors detected something unusual. He ran a few tests. The signature did not match that of a school of fish, whale, or a known surface vessel. It resembled that of a diesel submarine. Seaman Carpenter straightened from his habitual slouch. Now, he was fully engaged.

"Hey, Ron, check this out!" he called to his friend, Seaman Ron Tanzi, located at the adjacent console. Tanzi got up and walked over to take a gander.

"Holy shit! I've never seen that before! I think you've hooked a submarine!"

"Awesome, man! Bro, get the LT."

His Lieutenant walked over, took one look at the screen, reviewed the data, let out a low whistle, and picked up a phone. He laid a hand on Carpenter's shoulder. "Outstanding job, Carpy." Then he dialed his superior.

From hundreds of miles away, Seaman Carpenter used a trackball to guide tiny *Bathman* on the trail of the fugitive Iranian sub. The sub was detected near the outermost part of his drone's 250-mile operational radius. He had to work fast to keep it in range. He popped open another can of Coke, unwrapped a Snickers bar, and settled in for the chase. Nearby, the other operators were busy guiding their craft to the new search zone.

Seaman Carpenter was more excited than his mates were. Not only had he been first to find the sub, he was also one of a handful of operators with a weapons system incorporated into his drone. Little *Bathman* came equipped with two state-of-the-art Mk-48 ADCAP torpedoes.

Not only could Carpy chase. He could kill.

The IRGC-N was about to find out that in the modern era of naval warfare, few things were deadlier than a highly trained 23-year-old American gamer, jacked on caffeine and sugar, determined to win . . . and with a menu of high explosive devices at his fingertips.

~ Chapter 9 ~

July 5, 2012

0642 hrs.

Zach nearly collided with a woman at the base of the ladder. She was holding on tightly against the violent motion caused by another towering wave slapping the side of the helpless ship. Rollins and Murphy stumbled gracelessly down the ladder after him. When the three steadied themselves, the scene appalled them. The surviving passengers and a handful of wounded crew were, for the most part, dazed or in shock.

Zach grabbed the shoulder of the woman near him. "Did you hear screams? Where did they come from?"

The passenger shook her head from side to side. Zach pushed past her to descend to the next level. He had to find Eleni. Nearly frantic, he shouted over his shoulder to Rollins, who was close behind. "Down! We need to go down a deck."

Rollins vaguely understood what this meant and nodded affirmatively. The men rapidly descended to the next level.

The berth deck was even more confusing than the gun deck. They had moved from gloomy to stygian blackness. The trio clustered together at the foot of the ladder, breathing hard, struggling to stay upright, listening for voices as the ship shifted around them, hoping their eyes would adjust to the absence of light. After a few moments Zach spoke.

"OK. This is the berth deck. It used to be strung with hammocks from bow to stern. Now there are a few hung for the tourists to see. Mostly, it's open space. Except at the stern. There's a big wardroom in the back of the ship with several cabins. They were sleeping quarters for officers. I don't recall how many there are. First, we'll search the bow. Then the deck outside the wardroom. Then we'll go inside and search every one of the cabins."

"Jesus, this place is creepy. Feels like I'm in a crypt," Murphy quipped. "Smells like one, too."

Zach ignored the banter.

Rollins did not like the absence of light or the confined feeling of the berth deck. "I think we should stay together," he suggested. "We stand a better chance as a team than going it alone. Agreed?"

"Affirmative, Chief," Murphy responded.

"Fine with me," Zach added. "I'll go first. Hold on to my shoulder."

Zach let go of the ladder. The ship lurched and he shot his hand up to the ceiling to balance himself. When the vessel steadied, he moved ahead. Together, they shuffled along the perimeter of the deck, starting for the bow.

The overhead deck was low, and they walked hunched over, which added to their strain. Occasionally they encountered a hammock or post and needed to work their way around it. They skirted the cable bitt before passing the sickbay, scuttle, and storage in the bow. They didn't find Eleni or hear anything beyond the sounds of wind, waves and protests of the old ship as she fought to stay afloat.

At the bow, with Zach in the lead, they turned around and felt their way back toward the stern. They passed by the main hatchway. Beyond it they encountered the mainmast and near it, the chain-pump casings, which protruded upwards from the deck.

Nothing.

Zach halted beside the chain pumps. In his head, he visualized the configuration of the stern. He turned to his companions, even though he could not make out their features in the blackness.

"We're near the bulkhead separating the crew's quarters from the wardroom. There are cabins on this side of the bulkhead. There's a door to the wardroom on the left and right. Inside the wardroom there are more small cabins and at the very back, a hatch to the bread room and storage space for the officers. We need to search every square inch."

Rollins laid a hand on his shoulder. "I'd search Hades to find the bastards that attacked us."

Murphy, a big man, was gasping for breath behind Rollins. The amphetamines he swallowed earlier were wearing off. His back was in spasms. He'd already thrown up three times from seasickness. Most of it was on his pants legs. He stunk.

"You can count on me, Chief."

Zach led them to the starboard cabins located outside of the wardroom. With Rollins on one side and Murphy on the other, he yanked open a door. Silence. He crept in and searched the small space with his hands. No one was inside.

They repeated the process in the three remaining cabins. Then they crept across the front of the wardroom bulkhead and started to search the four larboard cabins.

By the door to the first cabin, Murphy paused and muttered, "Damn, I could use a cigarette!"

Rollins was about to hiss, "Shut up!" when he had an idea. "Hey Murphy, you smoke. Do you have a lighter on you?"

Murphy stopped. His lighter was usually kept in one of his jacket pockets. He thrust his hands in. No dice. Just to be on the safe side, he patted his shirt and pants pockets. As his hand glided over his right hip, he felt a lump. He poked inside and discovered the treasure.

"I'll be damned! I found the lighter!"

Zach whispered, "Keep it down! Any light will help speed things up. Murphy, stay on my left. Rollins, on my right. When I open a cabin, use the lighter."

They took up their positions. Zach flung open a door. Rollins leveled his revolver. Murphy thrust his hand inside and flicked on the lighter.

Mags Horsley sat on the deck, wedged tightly into the far right corner of the little room. She clutched a sleeping infant to her breast. Tears glistened on her cheeks. Her body rhythmically rocked back and forth. She was whispering to herself, "We're all going to die. We're all going to die."

The old woman's distress moved Rollins. He gently approached her. "Nobody's going to die, ma'am. We're with the Boston Police Department. We're here to help you." He reached his hand out to her. She shrank away from him.

"No, stop!" she screamed. "You don't understand. The ship. Horsley told me all about it. It's not what you think. It's a death ship! It's a Trojan horse!"

"A what?" Murphy barked.

"A Trojan horse," Zach repeated. His mind flashed back to the conversation on deck with the lead terrorist before the monster wave struck.

The Iliad. "The rosy-fingered dawn . . . ." Now I get it.

At last it made sense. He knelt next to Mags and looked her in the eyes. "I think I understand, Mags. The terrorists never cared about *Constitution*. They have bigger things in mind, don't they? This hijacking, all of it, it's a trick, isn't it?"

She did not respond. He roughly grabbed the woman's chin.

"What are they planning? Tell us."

A thin, veined hand reached up and wiped an errant strand of gray hair from her eyes. Her body sagged. She would have dropped Connie but for Zach quickly sweeping the bundled infant into his arms.

"It's a bomb," she quavered, her voice barely audible. "This ship. It's one big bomb."

Her eyelids twitched. "They want the ship to be recaptured. No one will expect a bomb on the ship. They want the Navy to sail it home."

She wept into her hands. "When we reach Boston, they are going to detonate a dirty bomb in the middle of the harbor."

She rocked back and forth, racked by sobs. "The Iranians were supposed to save us. We can't go home. It's not safe. We'll die."

She suddenly leaned forward and reached for the baby. "Poor Connie. Poor, poor little girl."

Zach batted her aside. Her reaction was fierce. A finely manicured hand slashed at his face, leaving four parallel cuts on one cheek. He leapt back.

"Stay away from me! Don't touch me again! My husband will kill you for that!"

Zach, stunned by the vehemence of her attack, wiped blood from his cheek. His sympathy withered. She was a traitor. She and her husband had sided with their country's worst enemies and plotted to kill Americans. He looked down at the screeching harpy with contempt.

"I don't think so. You're husband's dead, Mags. He's in hell, where he belongs."

All the fight left her. She slumped against the hull.

Murphy exclaimed "Ouch," and the flame went out.

"We're done here," Zach announced. The three men left the cabin. Zach offered the baby to Murphy.

"Find Commander Meyerson. We'll finish here."

Murphy took the child and held her tight against his shoulder, lightly patting her back.

Zach locked the door from the outside, leaving Mags alone in the dark.

"What a pissah," Murphy opined. "A wicked pissah."

~ Chapter 10 ~

July 5, 2012

0707 hrs.

On the spar deck, order was taking shape. With the fresh manpower from *Eagle*, Meyerson had formed several new squads. The cadets tasked with clearing the deck had finished. All the fallen lines, tackle, broken spars and splintered pieces of yardarms were heaved over the side.

Another squad braced and secured the damaged standing rigging and repaired the running rigging as best as possible. A third one put up storm sails. *Constitution* now ran with the wind, and though severely buffeted, was no longer in immediate danger of capsizing. If she could ride out the storm, she might survive.

Meyerson and Newtowne agreed it made no sense to risk the lives of all the passengers and crew. *Eagle* was the safer of the two vessels and more likely to survive the blow. They decided to evacuate *Constitution* and run her with a skeleton crew. Once *Constitution* was tidied, Meyerson prepared to offload the passengers, cadets, and her crew. She would remain to captain *Old Ironsides*. Newtowne likewise decided to stay. If there was the slightest chance *Constitution* could make it, he needed to help.

Six cadets went below and rounded up the fit and wounded from the gun deck. The guardsmen formed a human chain and passed them up to the spar deck. Vice President Baine and Secretary Powers were instrumental in maintaining order and morale. The VP could still work a crowd, even one as downtrodden as this. His backslapping manner and well-honed Irish bonhomie lifted everyone's spirits.

Like most of the passengers, Baine and Powers had numerous abrasions and cuts from the ordeal. To their credit, both insisted on being the last two cared for and transferred topside.

Eagle's small boats, left tethered to *Constitution's* hull, had swamped. A group of cadets and some remaining *Constitution* crew readied three of *Constitution's* five small boats. Lack of manpower and crippled equipment made it impossible to unfasten and lower the Commodore's Barge, so they left it strapped on the grating covering the main hatch. The fifth boat, stored next to the barge, was a small cutter. It was too damaged to be seaworthy.

Connie was nowhere to be found. Nor was Mags. Zach and his search party had not returned. Meyerson needed to look for them. It was not a task she could delegate. The storm's intensity was building. Time was running out.

Meyerson hurriedly said good-bye to Zajac. Battered but still able to function, he did his best to stand at attention.

"Chief, you're in charge of the crew. Make sure they make it home."

"I will Ma'am. God bless you!" He moved to a boat and supervised its loading.

She spoke briefly with Grain, who could barely walk, and who had been ordered off the ship with the others. A makeshift bandage circled his brow.

"I guess my rodeo's over, right Missy?"

"Yes it is, you old outlaw. Stay safe."

Grain shouted "Adios," and gave a jaunty salute as he shuffled his way to the nearest boat.

Meyerson moved to the quarterdeck to supervise more of the evacuation and direct the helmsman. She helped distribute the passengers, crew and Coasties among the two remaining boats. The small craft were all going to be heavily packed. Several more seamen volunteered to stay behind. Meyerson ordered them to go.

The Captain's Gig rigged to the stern was set to be lowered away. The larboard cutter, commanded by Zajac, and starboard whaleboat were nearly filled. Baine and Powers started to make a scene as Newtowne assisted with loading the gig.

"Give my seat to one of your men," Baine demanded.

"And mine, too," Powers added.

Newtowne had no time for posturing. The weather continued to deteriorate. He could feel the mercury dropping. It was becoming a major blow. The transmissions coming over his walkie-talkie confirmed his hunch.

"Gentlemen, get in the boat. I have no time for bullcrap. We've had enough heroism for one day."

The determined face of Newtowne told the two politicians it was pointless to argue.

Baine was chastened. "Of course, we'll follow orders." He reached out and gave Newtowne a two-handed shake before climbing into the Captain's Gig.

Powers was the last one over the side. "Good luck!"

The three boats were lowered and immediately away. It was a perilous crossing. The small vessels wallowed in the swells as their crews rowed furiously for *Eagle*, which had hove to 200 yards off *Constitution's* stern in order to take on the fragile human freight. Huge waves slapped the crafts and threatened to swamp them. The wind blew hard, throwing them off course. For every five pulls on the oars, they made only a foot of progress. Were it not for the youthful strength of the crew manning the sweeps, they would not have done it. Madly buffeted about, it was a long, tense crossing.

The Captain's Gig made it first and was secured to *Eagle*. The two whaleboats succeeded as well. All three were lashed together to make a floating platform. Brawny teenagers dragged the injured and traumatized men and women onto *Eagle's* spar deck. By the time the transfer was complete, the two sailing ships had blown a mile apart.

Meyerson and Newtowne were left with a handful of sailors to man *Constitution*. The volunteers were ordered aloft to trim more sail. Meyerson intended to weather the hurricane with the absolute minimum amount of canvas necessary to allow the ship to run with the wind.

After the sails were set, Newtowne and Meyerson conferred near the wheel. The howling wind and rain masked their words. They shouted at one another to be heard.

Red-faced, Newtowne was nose-to-nose with Meyerson. He was angry. "Commander, the ship is secure. You've done enough. I am relieving you from command. For God's sake, go! Find your child!"

Meyerson, faithful to her duty, had so far resisted his entreaties. Knowing now the ship might survive, for once in her career, she capitulated without protest. Meyerson raised her hand to salute. Arm halfway up, she suddenly leaned forward and hugged Newtowne. Stunned and speechless, he gently pushed her away. "Go, Commander. That's an order!"

Meyerson disappeared from Newtowne's sight down the hatchway nearest to the wardroom. He watched her go and mouthed a silent prayer for her.

Newtowne steadied himself against the helm, almost knocking over the helmsman, as the ship crested and slipped down a mountainous swell. Rain pounded his back. The howling wind made the rigging sing. Lightning strikes dappled the water with fire. The thunder was deafening. The wild beauty of it was awe-inspiring. He felt transported, beyond fear.

"Set a course, south by southeast! Steady, Mr. Anthony! Keep her nose downwind!"

"Aye, aye, Sir!"

Newtowne stepped to one side and sought a more secure stance near the binnacle. Although the sun was up, it was hard to tell it was daylight. The sky was greasy, gray, and ominous, shot through with sickly panes of green-yellow and rent by jagged flashes of lightning. He knew, bad as it was, it would get worse. It was going to be a quite a ride.

In his wildest dreams, he never imagined he'd be sailing the USS *Constitution* into the teeth of a hurricane. It was a stirring and romantic notion. The realty of it would be a living hell.

I've done all I can. I hope the old girl can hold together.

Now we are all in God's hands.

*****

Meyerson reached the gun deck. The long expanse was empty, littered with scraps of clothing and other filth. It stank of excrement, vomit, and blood.

This is what a ghost ship is like.

A clumping sound came from behind her and she was startled when Murphy's head popped into view. She was even more startled to see a tiny bundle held like a football in the crook of the big cop's arm. Small hiccups escaping the folds of the blanket confirmed it was Connie. Unbidden, her milk began to flow. She rushed to Murphy.

"Does this little angel belong to you, ma'am?"

He held the baby out. Meyerson tenderly took the child and held her close. She loosened a corner of the blanket surrounding the baby and saw two big brown eyes staring up at her. Connie began to squawk.

She's hungry. Meyerson undid the buttons on her dress.

"How did you find her?"

"She was with Mrs. Horsley. We thought she'd be better off with you." He did not elaborate.

Meyerson sniffed. "You stink. Worse than Connie."

353

"I get seasick"

"It happens." Connie started to whimper.

"Look, there's no easy way to say this, but there's a dirty bomb on board. We don't know how it got here, where it is, or when it might go off. Our guess is it's timed to explode when the ship gets back to Boston. We've got to keep away from the city."

Meyerson's moment of happiness shattered. "A dirty bomb? Impossible."

"I'm sorry, it's true. One of the terrorists told us," he lied.

Before Myerson had a chance to respond, he diverted her attention. "Say, who's sailing this thing, anyway?"

"Captain Newtowne from *Eagle*." She reached out her free hand to swing onto the ladder to go up to the spar deck. "He's got to be told."

"Do not move!" a voice shouted from the gloom. Footsteps approached from the stern. In an instant, Al-Buyid was next to them. He had a gun.

His burned and mangled eye wept blood and oozed yellow pus. Murphy imagined the pain must be ferocious. He wanted to belt the bastard in the eye and watch him shriek.

"I thought you were dead," Meyerson cried out.

"Not yet. Not yet. I was just playing, what do you call it here? Hide and seek? Yes, hide and seek. Now you are 'it', correct?" He smiled mirthlessly and signaled with the gun. "The game is not yet over. I am still enjoying it. So, up we go."

He poked the barrel into Murphy's ribs. With his other hand he bruskly frisked the cop. Not finding anything, he shoved Murphy.

"Move!"

Murphy grasped the ladder and climbed.

Al-Buyid made a mocking bow for Meyerson's benefit.

"Ladies first."

With a wince, Meyerson felt Connie latch on. She couldn't help but look down. Then she slowly raised her eyes to meet the gaze of the cyclops next to her.

"Isn't she beautiful?"

Al-Buyid hesitated. Embarrassed, he diverted his gaze from her breast.

How absurd – it is not the time for sentiment. I am a military officer. The mission is not complete.

He drove the gun into her belly.

"Move, woman!"

The blow opened the stab wound in Meyerson's side. She bit her lip with pain. Warm blood leaked down her abdomen. She complied without further comment.

Murphy was the first one on the weather deck. The ferocity of the storm nearly bowled him over. He spied Captain Newtowne, the helmsman and a handful of sailors near the wheel. Before he could shout, Meyerson pitched up behind and accidentally bumped him. He stumbled on the roiling deck and fell.

The motion caught Captain Newtowne's attention. He left his men and started toward Murphy and Meyerson. Unseen, Al-Buyid crouched in the fore stairway exit, aimed, and dropped Newtowne with one shot.

The sailors leapt forward to aide Newtowne. Al-Buyid bounded onto the deck and pressed his pistol against Meyerson's temple. He ignored the prostate cop.

"Don't move or I will kill the woman!"

Using Meyerson and her baby as a shield, he approached the cluster of sailors. They balked, unsure how to react to the threat, fearful of causing harm to their superior. Al-Buyid took advantage. He pushed Meyerson in the back and shot the four men in quick succession, each in the chest. The helmsman backed away, hands up in surrender. Al-Buyid laughed and waved his gun toward the frightened mariner.

"Fight, you coward!" he jeered.

Meyerson stopped. Distracted by his focus on the remaining tar, Al-Buyid banged into her back. She stomped viciously on his instep and drove her left elbow back into his ribs. He grunted and doubled over.

"Run!" Meyerson shouted to her crewman. She turned and faced Al-Buyid, blocking his vision of the fleeing sailor. The swabbie bolted for the aft companion leading to the gun deck.

Al-Buyid straightened and tried to aim. Meyerson stepped into his line of fire. He switched direction. She moved with him.

"Damn you!" he cried and struck her across the temple with the barrel of his pistol. He fired off a round just as the sailor jumped into the open hatchway, eliciting a cry of pain from the fleeing man.

Meyerson lay on the deck. She set Connie aside, crawled to Al-Buyid and grasped his ankle, trying to throw him off balance.

Even their women fight like demons!

He kicked at her head. She rolled away to evade the blow. Frustrated, Al-Buyid stared down at the helpless mother.

A gold medallion had emerged from under Meyerson's dress collar. It was a small Star of David.

"You are a Jew?"

Meyerson clutched the medallion tight to her chest. It was a Bat Mitzvah gift from her father and mother.

"I am." Her voice quavered with rage and defiance. "And a woman, a mother, a Navy officer and a citizen of the freest nation on earth. I and others like me are your and your masters' worst nightmare."

He was momentarily surprised but quickly recovered. Her boast explained much. Exterminating her would be even more satisfying.

"Then die, Jew." A bullet tore through Myerson's hand, bisected the gold keepsake and pierced her heart.

Hidden a short distance away, Murphy had not moved. At the sound of Meyerson's voice followed by the new pistol shot, he raised his head and looked.

"No! No!"

Murphy got up and charged straight at Al-Buyid.

Al-Buyid heard footsteps and cocked his head. Somehow, he'd forgotten the cop. He swiveled and brought up his pistol.

At the sight of the pistol, Murphy hesitated. Unbidden, only one thing came into his mind. Run and hide. Before Al-Buyid could bear down on him and fire, Murphy bolted past the mainmast and wheel and jumped into the shrouds securing the mizzenmast. He grabbed the ratlines and climbed. The higher he got, the freer he felt. A pistol cracked and a bullet passed close to his head. He climbed faster. When he reached the fighting top he levered himself onto the platform and stopped. The great ship swayed beneath him. Turbulent sky surrounded him. He peered over the lip. The lunatic below with the gun looked like an ant.

Al-Buyid could not touch him.

No one could touch him.

He was safe.

*****

Zach crouched near one of the two bulkhead doors separating the wardroom from the rest of the berth deck. He held Murphy's pistol. He had swapped Connie for the weapon when Rollins had ordered the Sergeant to take Connie topside. His other fingers lingered on the door handle. Rollins was poised behind him, his .38 in one hand, the Bic lighter in the other. Zach whispered, "1 . . . 2 . . . 3!" and wrenched open the door.

They rushed into the wardroom. Rollins pointed his revolver and flicked on the lighter. Eight feet away, Eleni was pinned against the mess table by Mustafa. Her top was ripped open. A hand clamped across her mouth pulled her head back against his left shoulder. Zach saw the long, delicate, white arch of her neck. A vein throbbed near its base. Her eyes were wide with fear. Across her windpipe lay the winking blade of a knife grasped in Mustafa's right hand. Sweat glistened on Mustafa's forehead. His perfect white teeth curled in a thin-lipped, mocking smile.

Everyone froze. Eleni locked eyes with Zach.

Her eyes pleaded, "Kill him."

Fury seized Zach. He lifted his weapon and chanced a round. It was a poor shot. The bullet struck Mustafa's right elbow, which exploded in a puff of shattered bone and sprayed blood. The knife clattered to the deck. Mustafa released Eleni and staggered back. He screamed hideously. With each backward step, Zach pumped another bullet into him until his pistol was empty. Rollins joined in.

The Libyan danced backward, jerking with each round, illuminated off and on by the strobe-like flashes of the discharging weapons. The heavy slugs tore through his lungs, his gut, his bladder, his liver, and finally his heart.

When the dying terrorist crashed to the floor, Rollins walked over to him. He bent and held the lighter close to illuminate the man's face.

Mustafa mustered an evil grin. "You cannot hurt me. I am already free," he gasped.

Rollins digested the taunt. "Really? Free? You know jackshit about freedom. The way I see it, the only freedom you have left is the freedom to die." He straightened and pointed his revolver.

"Never forget. It's my – POW – city – POW – you tried to destroy, – POW – motherfucker!"

When Rollins finished, he let his spent revolver slip from his grasp and drop to the floor.

The lighter died out. All the oxygen had left the room. Zach sucked cordite and burnt powder into his chest. There was so much adrenalin flowing through his system he felt like retching.

Mustafa was the fourth man he'd shot in twenty-four hours. It was getting easier to do. He wondered what new kinds of flashbacks he was likely to have in the future.

Rollins reignited the lighter, lifted his arm, and swept the cabin. Zach tore his eyes away from Mustafa's corpse and refocused on Eleni. She had rolled from the table onto the deck as the hail of gunfire unfolded. He tossed away his empty pistol and rushed to her side. She was unconscious. He kneeled to embrace her. When he lifted her, her head lolled back. A thin red line across her neck trickled blood. The cut was not deep. It would not prove fatal. When he felt her arms curl around his back, he knew she was alright.

He eased her to her feet.

"Rollins, can I borrow your jacket?"

"My pleasure."

Zach took the suit coat and used it to cover Eleni.

"You're OK, babe. It's over," he assured her as he helped her into it.

Eleni found herself quaking.

"Am I Zach? Am I really? I thought I was going to die. He trapped me in a cabin. I fought hard, Zach. I hurt him and ran away." She started to cry.

"He caught me here, Zach. He cut me. He was going to rape me. My God, he was going to kill me." Zach held her. She sobbed into his shoulder.

Rollins cried "Shit!" and the light went out. "Sorry! Too hot."

After a decent interval, Rollins spoke again. "Zach, we have a job to do. We've got to find the bomb."

Eleni pulled away. "Bomb? What bomb?"

"There's a bomb on board, Eleni. The terrorists are going to try to blow up a dirty bomb in the harbor once the ship made it back to Boston. We need to find it."

The new threat focused Eleni's mind. The strange noises. It made sense.

"I know where it is, Zach. I fell asleep earlier. When I woke up, the ship had stopped moving. I heard noises. Pounding. Whirling noises, like a drill. I couldn't figure it out. Now I understand. I know where the bomb is, Zach! It was under me!"

"Exactly where?" Rollins asked.

Eleni felt stronger. Finally, she was able to be of use. "A deck lower. Near the back of the ship."

'Right," Zach added. "There's a deck under us, Rollins. The orlop. It's below water level. We've got to find the bomb and get it off the ship."

"Shit. How big is this tub, anyway?"

"Big."

"You know how to get there?"

"Yeah."

"Screw it." Rollins' voice was weary. He released a long sigh.

"Might as well give it a try. We can die now, or we can die later. It makes no difference to me anymore."

Zach thought about Eleni and the bomb.

"If it's OK with you Chief, I'd rather not die at all."

~ Chapter 11 ~

July 5, 2012

0738 hrs.

Sixty miles south of *Constitution, Astoh* surfaced. Jamshidi put up the antennae and sent a report to headquarters in Iran. Updates from HQ advised the ongoing storm grazing the coast of Massachusetts had reached hurricane strength. *Constitution* would be swept out to sea southeast of Boston Harbor. IRGC-N Naval Intelligence predicted the old ship would not survive.

The news was crushing. Jamshidi's elation evaporated. The plan had gone awry. He was shaken.

The package attached to *Constitution*'s hull was a radiological disposal device, otherwise known as a dirty bomb. It contained hundreds of pounds of radioactive material packed around high explosives. The Russians had pioneered the concept in the late 1970s. At least one Cold War-era dirty bomb had been stopped at the U.S.-Canada border. Other RDDs were rumored to be floating around Europe and the Middle East.

After the Stuxnet virus in 2010 disrupted Iran's plans for producing nuclear weapon-grade plutonium, the mullahs were furious. They wanted revenge.

Deprived of the means to create a nuclear missile, they turned to a simpler solution.

Tehran regarded a dirty bomb as the perfect weapon in their campaign of asymmetrical warfare against the Great Satan. While not capable of leveling a city, it could disperse radioactive material over a wide expanse, contaminating any urban area for years to come. Hundreds, if not thousands, would sicken. Many would die from exposure to radiation. The city would become a wasteland. Mass hysteria and fear would ensue. Political instability would follow.

The Mullahs relished this prospect. Nuclear missiles could wait. The dirty bomb would suffice as temporary payback for the U.S.A.'s disruption of Tehran's even more murderous long-range plans. Better to strike first with the weapon at hand then wait for the inevitable attack by Israel, America's lackey.

They anticipated Al-Qaeda would be blamed. Iran would suffer no consequences.

Al-Buyid concocted the plan. Hijack *Constitution*. Plant the bomb on her. Allow her to be recaptured. Count on the Americans to be so relieved to reclaim their treasure that they would never search for the hidden threat. Wait until the ship was back in Boston Harbor to detonate the device. Poetic justice achieved for the sins of the past and the present.

Jamshidi now realized the grand design would fail. *Constitution* would perish at sea in the tempest. Boston would be spared. The vagaries of wind and water had accomplished what the U.S. Navy could not – preserve the Athens of America from further devastation.

Worse news arrived. *Astoh's* Sonar detected something tracking her. The Iranians could not identify it. Its signature was not in the data bank. It was not large enough to be a submarine or conventional surface warship. It was an odd size for a whale. It was surely not a small craft, since none could likely survive the hurricane-force winds and pounding seas. Yet there it was, maintaining a distance west of *Astoh,* apparently able to keep pace with the rapidly moving sub.

Unsure what he was facing, Jamshidi began evasive maneuvers. *Astoh* decreased speed, changed course, dove deeper, and released several noisemakers to throw off the hunter. All non-essential tasks within the sub ground to a halt in order to reduce noise. In near silence, practically at a standstill, she sank deeper in the frigid North Atlantic.

Thirty minutes later, things were no better. The unknown vessel clearly was tracing their every movement. In fact, it had closed to within 20 miles. Whatever it was, it was accurate and fast, even faster than his boat. Incredibly, it was able to withstand the severe weather.

With every fresh report, his apprehension grew. Not only had the mission failed, he and his crew now faced possible annihilation at the hands of an unseen nemesis. Jamshidi gave the order for full rudder right and to dive deeper.

Sweat formed on Jamshidi's brow. It trickled down his neck into Laleh's scarf. When he touched the fabric for luck, it was almost sopping wet.

He was accustomed to shallow water operations in the Persian Gulf and Arabian Sea off the southern tip

364

of Iran, where a sub could hover quietly near the bottom for hours to avoid detection. In the bottomless Atlantic, there was no place to hide. It was imperative to find a useful thermal layer to mask his location and movements. And quickly. The unknown vessel had closed to within 10 miles. Glancing at his Crew Chief, he did his best to wipe a sleeve across his brow casually. Unaware, he bit his upper lip hard, almost drawing blood. Despite his best efforts, the strain in his face was obvious to all.

Jamshidi could sense the 52 men under his command begging him to save them. Images of their wives, sons, daughters, and of his own beloved family flashed through his head, clouding his decision-making process. Although already beyond *Astoh's* routine operational depth of 800 feet, he gave the order to keep diving.

Down, farther down into the seemingly limitless ocean was their only possible salvation. With a crush depth of 1,000 feet, the sub now had a thin margin of safety to play with before self-destructing.

His navigator called out depth readings in an increasingly agitated voice. The incessant pinging of the sonar merged with ominous metallic groans as the submarine's hull reacted to the enormous pressure of the water above. Jamshidi felt the weight of 30 atmospheres inside his skull. Behind him, his Crew Chief began to pray.

Unbidden, the rest of the crew took up the chorus. Whether they made noise no longer mattered. They were snared in the sonar tentacles of their pursuer. Swept up in the drama, hovering in the shadow of death, Jamshidi abandoned any pretense of command. He joined the prayers.

*****

Admiral Rogers was finally beginning to feel close to normal again. His heart no longer pounded as if ready to jump through his ribcage. His stomach was less volcanic. Cruising at 23,000 feet, although violently jostled by the remnants of the passing hurricane, he was strangely at peace.

The intelligence verified *Astoh's* location. Satellite imagery confirmed the target as did infrared detection. *Bathman* was in position. The drone was ready to blow the Iranian sub to hell.

Checkmate.

Time for the kill.

Jolly no longer believed in God. Sure, he pretended to. No one advanced in the service by openly declaring atheism. However, he'd seen too much random death and ruin to put any faith in a benign divinity. Instead, he trusted science, his own senses, and reason. Radar, sonar, infrared imagery, photographs. Touch, sound, sight, and smell. Objective evidence. It all assured him the Iranian sub was living on borrowed time. Although godless, he was not completely merciless. On some level, he pitied the poor bastards who were about to die. That quantum of pity was infinitesimally small.

He was even happier when advised *Constitution* had been located. Reports from *Eagle* confirmed the old ship remained afloat, had been evacuated, and was now under the control of Commander Meyerson. With luck, she would hold together long enough to outlast the storm.

The ship is as tough as they came.

If history is any guide, she will prevail.

Weymouth tapped the Admiral on the shoulder, jolting him from his reverie.

"Sir, we have the green light."

Jolly cracked his knuckles and arched his back. "Execute," he grunted. Weymouth relayed the order.

*****

In Virginia, a staccato voice crackled in Lt. Brent Dane's headset. He placed a hand on Seaman Carpenter's right shoulder and squeezed. In a deep baritone, devoid of emotion, he ordered, "Smoke 'em, Carpy."

Seaman Carpenter had enjoyed the chase. Now it was time for the payoff. He started the arming and launching sequence for the two 650-pound Mk-48 torpedoes cradled in *Bathman's* belly. With mounting excitement, he completed the sequences and waited for the green firing light to blink. When it did, without hesitation, he punched the firing button home. On his screen, a thin white line began to creep from the green rectangle of *Bathman* toward the red circle of the Iranian sub.

More than 1,300 pounds of lethal high explosives guided by the world's most advanced navigation and tracking system swam effortlessly toward *Astoh*.

Soundlessly, it was over. Where there had been a blinking red circle on Seaman Carpenter's screen, now there was nothing.

367

Carpy sat motionless in his contoured chair. At the twitch of his index finger, a submarine filled with men had just died.

This was not a game. Although not very introspective, he paused to consider what had occurred. Something real had just happened and he needed to process it.

How should I feel? Elated? Sad? Maybe a little of both?

His act was justified. He had served his country honorably against a ruthless foe. There was comfort in that. The rest he'd sort out some other time. Perplexed but not overly perturbed, he reached for a fresh candy bar from the stash kept in his drawer.

"Hey Lt. Dane, guess what? I just wasted six million dollars of taxpayer's money."

"Not wasted. It was money well spent, sailor."

The joke fell flat. There was a long silence.

Lt. Dane was an Annapolis graduate and amateur military scholar with a contemplative bent. The moment moved him.

Spear, sword, bow and arrow, battering ram, catapult, crossbow, cannon, torpedo, missile. The long march of technology in naval warfare continues.

When Lt. Dane spoke again, his voice was somber, his mood subdued.

"Y'know Carpy, you just maybe changed the history of naval warfare."

Seaman Carpenter gave his superior a quizzical look.

"Huh?"

"Carpy, have you ever heard of John Paul Jones, John Barry, Oliver Hazard Perry, Stephen Decatur,

David G. Farragut, George Dewey, Arleigh A. Burke, or Bull Halsey?"

"Nah."

"They are Navy heroes. Relics of a lost age when men and ships fought on lakes, rivers and seas, with flesh, steel, powder, fire and lead, driven by passion, spirit and physical courage almost beyond description. They are your progenitors, Carpy."

"Cool."

Lt. Dane did not reply. The mindless remark chilled him. He wished he'd been born in another era.

Those giants are forever gone.

Replaced by Carpy.

And Bathman.

~ Chapter 12 ~

July 5, 2012

0816 hrs.

Searching the orlop deck was in some respects less daunting than combing the upper deck. There was greater open space and fewer cubbyholes. Since they were deeper in the sea, the violent pitch and roll felt diminished, certainly more so than the upper decks, but still significant.

Yet it took time.

Hot, dark, airless time.

Time spent bent over at the waist to avoid hitting wooden deck beams.

Time spent feeling up and down the inside walls of the hull.

Time listening for any odd sound that might clue them into the whereabouts of the bomb.

Time wondering if soon time would run out.

About 40 feet from the stern, they became aware of an unusual pooling of water on the deck. Zach reached down to feel it. It was cold. He tasted it. Salty.

"This is not rain. It's seawater. There's a leak somewhere close by. It could mean something."

Rollins was skeptical. "It probably doesn't mean anything. This whole boat is awash in seawater, Colt.

We're on a wild goose chase. You're just indulging in wishful thinking."

Eleni spoke for the first time since they had left the berth deck. "Turn on the lighter, Mr. Rollins, please. We've come this far. It's worth a look. We have to at least try."

Rollins briefly flashed the lighter. The illumination lasted only a second before Rollins snuffed it out. It was enough. A short distance ahead, they saw water trickling down the inside of the hull.

Zach rushed forward. He touched the hull where it bulged inward. Sweeping his hands across the wood, he found two protrusions marked by splintered planking, all leaking.

"Rollins, take a look at this."

The Chief of Detectives felt his way forward to Zach's side. Zach guided Rollins' hand to the vicinity of one of the bulges. Rollins flicked on the lighter. Its feeble light bathed the hull.

He brought the flame closer to examine the wood. "Whatever it is, it looks like they stuck something to the outside of the hull." Rollins let the lighter go out. "So, what do we do?"

Stumped, Zach had no answer.

Eleni joined them. She had heard their comments.

"It's not in the ship? They attached it on the outside?"

"Yes. It must have happened when the sub came. They anticipated the ship would be recaptured. They counted on no one looking for a bomb after *Constitution* was rescued, certainly not one below the waterline."

"So, what do we do?" Rollins repeated.

"At least we found it. I can't think of a way to dislodge the thing. I suppose it could go off at any moment. We need to get topside and warn Newtowne and Meyerson and get off the ship. *Constitution* can't be allowed to sail home. If another ship is close by, we might be rescued. Or maybe some Coast Guard choppers are in the air despite the storm. If we are picked up, we can get someone to defuse the bomb, assuming *Constitution* survives the hurricane."

He tried to keep his voice optimistic. Eleni did not reply. He wished he could see her face. It wasn't much of a plan.

"I'd rather die in the water than get blown the hell up," Rollins announced. Then he added, "Motherfuckers," to no one in particular.

"OK, Zach," Eleni finally said. Her voice ached with sadness and resignation. A second later, Zach felt her hand slide into his. She gave a quick squeeze. "I'm up for a swim."

"That's my girl." He squeezed back.

Zach reached out and nudged Rollins. "C'mon, Chief. Up we go."

"I'm with you. I just hope we don't run into any sharks! Never liked damn sharks. Especially great whites. Too pale looking."

As they ascended, savage gyrations of the old ship made movement difficult. It took twenty minutes to find the nearest stairway. It took thirty minutes to climb to the berth deck, then to the gun deck, before finally clambering up the last fore stairway into the faint light of day. In the process, they were tossed and shaken until they felt their teeth would fall out.

When Zach's head popped out onto the spar deck, he lustily inhaled the clean, cool, ocean air, trying his best to flush out the stale funk from the lower decks and clear from his mind the foul memories of violence and death he'd encountered.

Before mounting the deck, he carefully looked around. The ship was seemingly deserted. The storm sails were puffed out and the ship headed downwind. The force of the hurricane had somewhat slackened. Heavy cloud cover and rain persisted. Lightning strikes flared in the distance. Strong gusts of wind continued to pummel *Constitution*.

No one was visible.

Who is steering. There must be someone doing it.

The deck rolled under his feet. He struggled to keep his balance. It was filthy weather but he guessed the worst of the storm had passed.

Or they were in the eye.

Wary, he reached down and helped Eleni up. When she stepped free, the wind pressed Rollins' borrowed suit jacket against her body and whipped back her hair. She closed her eyes tight for a moment, adjusting to the brighter light, and then opened them wide, expectant.

"We're alone!"

Rollins pulled himself up and joined Zach and Eleni. Clearly happy to be outside once more, a broad smile of relief graced his face. He opened his mouth to say something. Before he could speak, a bullet tore through his shoulder and he fell at Eleni's feet.

Zach jerked Eleni down and put a finger to her lips to silence her. He crawled to one side of the fore stairway and peered toward the stern, trying to spot the shooter. A second round sent splinters into the air near his face and he ducked for cover.

A strange laugh erupted nearby. It started as a disjointed series of staccato barks before sputtering out in a fit of prolonged hacking coughs. When the coughing quieted, Al-Buyid's voice rang out.

"Your comrades, they are all dead. You should give up. I've won."

The terrorist's voice was unsteady. Zach could tell he was suffering.

Good.

"Go to hell!" Zach taunted. "How's that eye doing, you son of a bitch?"

A third bullet zinged over Zach's scalp and struck the fireplace funnel behind him. Eleni shrieked.

"It is fine. I only need one eye to kill you and your whore," Al-Buyid yelled back.

Zach lifted his head and spotted the Iraqi standing near the wheel, pointing the barrel of his pistol in the air. He clutched the wheel with his other hand, bracing himself against the ship's random tossing.

Al-Buyid gestured with the gun. "I am the Sea Snake! Look around you. There is no one left to help you. Is it not clear I have prevailed?"

The blood from Rollins' wound spread across the deck and soaked Zach's shoes and pants legs. The Chief stared up at the sky. His eyes blinked. He turned his head in Zach's direction. A hand groped for, found and tightened around Zach's ankle.

"Don't you give up. It was a lucky shot that got me, that's all. You can take the mofo, Colt."

Zach glanced back at Al-Buyid, who struggled to stay upright as *Constitution* bounced and wallowed in

374

the storm's residue. Eighty feet separated the two men. The Commodore's Barge and damaged cutter strapped to the main hatch cover gave Zach some shelter.

"Eleni, stay here. Don't move."

Zach crawled to his left, rose to a crouch, and darted up the port side, using the small boats as a shield. An errant shot flew past. By then, he was beyond the aft stairway and behind the mainmast. He pressed his body into the wood, trying to make himself invisible. Al-Buyid was a stone's throw away. Another bullet whizzed by. Zach crouched low and peered around the mast.

Captain Newtowne's body lay stretched on the deck near the capstan, a bullet wound in his forehead. He was surrounded by dead sailors. Meyerson lay past him, a small, still, bundle at her side. A trickle of blood leaked from her mouth. Murphy's body was no doubt somewhere near as well, likely beyond Zach's sight.

Rage exploded inside Zach.

It has to end.

A deep, guttural growl escaped him. He charged from behind the mainmast and zigzagged toward Al-Buyid. A round ripped through his left forearm. Zach blitzed past the capstan, tackled Al-Buyid's legs and knocked the man backwards. Al-Buyid landed on his back and together they slid along the deck until the terrorist bumped up against the mizzenmast.

Al-Buyid sat up. His wind had been knocked out and he was gasping for air. He gathered himself and raised his pistol toward Zach for the kill shot.

In the fighting top, Murphy watched the drama on deck play out, 60 feet below. He was physically and mentally spent. His brain moved like molasses.

So many deaths. What have I done to stop them?

Guilt and embarrassment overwhelmed him.

He'd spent his whole life fighting evil. The one-eyed man below was evil incarnate.

He could not let evil win.

Jesus, Mary, Joseph. Sweet Jesus, Blessed Mary, and Holy Saint Joseph.

Timing the roll of the ship, he jumped.

Murphy's body slammed into Al-Buyid and drove him hard into the deck. The pistol slithered from Al-Buyid's grasp.

Zach started for the pistol on his hands and knees, ignoring the pain in his forearm.

Al-Buyid's hand emerged from under Murphy and groped for the gun. When he could not reach the pistol, he shoved the cop's body aside and crawled for it. His pelvis and collarbone were broken. A shaft of bone protruded through the skin of his right bicep. He groaned in pain with every movement.

Neck and neck, the two wounded combatants clawed across the heaving deck for possession of the weapon.

Al-Buyid was closest. He reached it first. With a cry of triumph, he grabbed the pistol and rolled onto his back. Zach was four feet away, near Al-Buyid's feet.

It was an easy shot.

Now feel the bite of the Sea Snake!

At that moment, Connie bawled. The sound of the infant took both men unawares.

Al-Buyid hesitated. Pistol in hand, he dragged himself next to Meyerson's corpse and found the baby by her mother's side. He parted the thin blanket concealing Connie from sight, revealing her angry, squalling face.

Even more so than earlier, Al-Buyid found himself strangely confused and touched by the child. His eye lifted from her bleating face and swept the carnage on the deck, taking in the dead bodies and destruction he had wrought. He looked up at the sky, then down at the weapon in his hand. He stared for a few seconds at Zach, who had not moved, before shifting his gaze once more to the infant girl. She quieted and gurgled at him.

All babies are the same.

Al-Buyid remembered his wife. He pictured her with his own infant daughter at her breast. The American bombs had killed them. Vaporized them. Left him alone in the world. Made him a ghost. Turned his heart to stone harder and blacker than the *Kaaba*.

That is what had started all this.

That was why he was here.

Yet, at the end of his jihad, what had he accomplished? Many of his enemies had perished. He had killed a woman, a mother, and soon this small child would die.

A flood of emotions cascaded over Al-Buyid's features. His intact eye blinked rapidly and his body stiffened. He looked one last time at Zach before raising his pistol. Zach locked eyes with Al-Buyid, and braced for the bullet.

377

"I won," Al-Buyid said to Zach in an ambivalent voice.

The Sea Snake placed the gun's muzzle in his mouth and pulled the trigger.

*****

Eleni ran to Connie and scooped her away from her mother's bloody corpse. She crossed to Zach and helped him to his feet. He was weak from fatigue and blood loss. When he tried to walk, he nearly stumbled and fell.

The green flag of Islam flapped wildly above the poop deck. Zach pointed to it. "Help me there."

Eleni and Zach lurched to the flag line. Zach uncleated it and pulled the banner down. He unclipped the cursed rag, wadded it into a ball, and flung it overboard.

"Now take me to the wheel."

Eleni eased Zach to the wheel. He clung to it and turned the drifting ship so she ran with the wind. The sails puffed and *Constitution* plowed a steadier, less fitful course. After a few minutes, the strain was too much on Zach.

"Eleni, help me. I can't do it alone."

Holding Connie with one arm, Eleni curled her body tightly against his back. She locked her left hand over his on the spokes of the wheel.

She didn't say a word. Nor did Zach. Together, they steered the ship.

Two hours later, overhead, muffled by distance, came the heavy *thwump-thwump-thwump* of helicopters. The clouds broke. The wind held steady and the rain slackened to a drizzle. The waves subsided.

Zach made out a long ribbon of beach in the distance.

They steered for it, intent on grounding *Constitution* in the clean, white sand.

Intent on going home.

THE END

~ EPILOGUE ~

Zach and Eleni succeeded in beaching *Constitution* on First Encounter Beach near Provincetown.

A demolition team removed the dirty bomb. It was defused and shipped to Virginia for analysis. Word later leaked out that Saddam Hussein's minions had originally designed it in Iraq in the early 1990s.

In the ensuing months, a small village on a deep river in Venezuela mysteriously disappeared from the face of the earth. Venezuela claimed an oil refinery exploded.

Seaman Carpenter and his superiors knew better.

Carpy received the first newly-created Distinguished Warfare Medal and a big promotion.

The mullahs did not escape unpunished. In mid-August 2013, precision airstrikes obliterated large sections of Tehran. So, too, were the four principal IRGC-N naval bases.

Russia and China did not intervene. North Korea made threats but later backed down, as usual. Iran had no other useful friends.

The world breathed a sigh of relief. So did most Iranians, who seized the opportunity, toppled the despotic regime, and implemented a secular democracy. The long-hoped for "Persian spring" had arrived.

Rollins recovered. He was back to work within a month. He never set foot on a boat for the rest of his life.

Murphy didn't make it. His was the biggest police funeral in Boston's history.

Grain returned to active duty in Washington, chasing counterfeiters.

Captain Raffington, Lt. Cmdr. Sconzotti, and Commander Meyerson were posthumously awarded the Navy Cross. Lt. Commander Peter Germano received a Silver Star. They rest in Arlington National Cemetery.

The Coast Guard named its next cutter USCGC *William Newtowne*.

Captain Smartwood faced a court of inquiry for the loss of *Muskie*. He was exonerated. Afterward, he resigned his commission and moved to the hottest, driest town he could find in Arizona, where he later opened a cigar shop.

Admiral Rogers retired to Tampa. Six months after he left service, he suffered a fatal heart attack while walking Swabbie on the beach. His wife, unable to care for Swabbie due to her own ill health, gifted the dog to Weymouth.

It took several months for Zach's body to mend. While he recuperated, he worked on his foundation and courted Eleni. On July 4, 2014, Eleni accepted his proposal, made on bended knee on the Esplanade, right before the 1812 Overture kicked off the fireworks. It was a bit dramatic, but fitting.

In her many lustrous years of service, *Constitution* had never hosted a wedding. Zach and Eleni's nuptials were the first. They wed on a fine October morning, standing before *Constitution's* newest commander, Captain Prospero Zajac, elevated from the ranks due to his distinguished service during the recent unpleasantness.

Eleni was stunning. A pearl necklace, a wedding present from Zach, covered the thin scar on her neck.

Zach wore the Presidential Medal of Freedom and the Congressional Gold Medal. He was only the fifth such person awarded both honors.

Their newly adopted daughter, Connie, was the sweetest flower girl ever seen.

Boston shone in the crisp fall sunlight, unblemished, unbowed, every bit the shining city on the hill.

~ ACKNOWLEDGEMENTS ~

Many thanks to my friends and fans who spurred me on.

A special thank you to the Captain and crew of USS *Constitution* for their hospitality, courtesy, and access to the ship. She truly is a marvel and the U.S. Navy does a fine job keeping her shipshape and open to the public.

Thanks to "Cousin Steve", the "Doctor", the "Professor", the "Navigator", "Maggie's Family", the "Teacher", the "Georgian", and other friends from the Dog Park for reading the text and offering sound advice.

Merci beaucoup Nana, my staunchest supporter.

As always, thanks to Liz, who will be forever H.O.T. to me (figure it out), for firmly believing I will not become the next Herman Melville, i.e., dead before I am a famous and successful writer.

~ ABOUT THE AUTHOR ~

Michael D. Urban was born outside of Pittsburgh, Pennsylvania. He lives near Boston.

Ironsides' Peril is the second installment in a series of thrilling adventures featuring Zach Colt which began with *Drake's Coffin*.

Mike has lived and traveled in Central America. He has worked in federal law enforcement and most recently was a trial lawyer in private practice.

Mike on USS Constitution *during the October 2012 turnaround cruise commemorating the 215th anniversary of her launching*

www.michaeldurban.com
@Michael_D_Urban

CPSIA information can be obtained at www.ICGtesting.com
Printed in the USA
BVOW02s2223091213

338594BV00001B/1/P